NET IMPACT

Dick Thornby Thriller #1

Donald J. Bingle

Cover Design by Juan Villar Padron
D.I.A. Image by Arina P. Habich, Licensed via Shutterstock

This book is published by
54°40' Orphyte, Inc.
St. Charles, Illinois

**54°40'
ORPHYTE,
INC.**

ISBN 13: 978-1-7323434-1-2

For Jean Rabe: the best friend any writer could have.

PROLOGUE

The squad moved through the unfamiliar terrain with practiced ease. Hawk was on point, scanning the all-too-near horizon methodically. Peregrine and Shrike trailed at an oblique angle to either side at least a grenade-blast's diameter behind, side points in a classic diamond pattern combat formation. Completing the geometry, Pigeon trailed the same distance yet again behind them, swiveling his head back at uneven intervals to watch their six.

The landscape sloped sharply, but unevenly, upward toward the cloudless, frozen blue sky. Huge slabs of rock, graffiti-free this far from respectable civilization, were strewn about their path like a young girl's jacks across the floor.

Hawk flicked his vision involuntarily heavenward as if a giant, red rubber ball might be descending to crush the squad while the enormous, granite jacks were swept up by a gargantuan eight-year old. He chuckled softly at his own paranoia. He'd seen plenty of bizarre things in his time, to be sure, especially in this strange land. This mission, in particular, presented dangers both from the terrain and from the authorities, should the squad be detected and an assassination

1

team scrambled. But big, rubber balls wielded by colossal eight-year olds were not among them.

He slowed for a moment to verify the coordinates for the rendezvous against their tortuous progress through the wilderness, checked the time on the bulky, multi-functional chronograph on his left wrist, and then pressed the sub-vocal microphone hanging down from his headset against his neck with his beefy left hand.

He spoke without opening his mouth, in essence silent to everyone not hooked into the squad's encrypted digital frequency with a properly-tuned, algorithmic descrambler. The sub-vocal mike took a bit of getting used to, but with some practice it was so effective it sometimes seemed as if the squad members could read each other's minds. "We're close." Hawk gestured with his right arm at the arc of boulders blocking their vision up-slope. "In there, no doubt."

He stopped in his tracks and made a circular motion with his right hand while sending another sub-vocal command. "I want a three-sixty scan of the perimeter, around and above, before we go in."

Peregrine, Shrike, and Pigeon all stopped and began their scans, each starting with their individual sector priorities. Hawk trusted the group, trusted his men—this wasn't their first stroll in the wilderness—but he obeyed his own orders, doing a full sweep in all directions. Starting at twelve o'clock and then shifting in uniform increments through a complete arc in all dimensions, he systematically studied the view with a focused, penetrating gaze. After he completed the process using his own keen eyesight, he repeated the routine with the magnification turned up full on his precision optical scanner, a device that was a damn sight better than military grade and for which he had paid a pretty penny of his own hard-earned cash to possess.

The place was desolate and almost Spartan in its lack of significant landmarks. They never would have found the location for the meeting without a GPS device. The terrain was trackless, featureless, and empty beyond imagining. There were no buildings in line-of-sight. Not even a simple yurt could be found tucked into one of the numerous draws and valleys. No mine entrances could be spied perched on the sides of the steep slopes. The broad expanse of sky above was vacant, as if from a time primordial. Not a single plane or jet trail marred the uniform cobalt; no birds wheeled and screed in the thin air at this altitude. The silence of the area was palpable—they hadn't seen any wildlife on the ground since Peregrine had flushed a deer hours and hours ago.

When everyone had confirmed what Hawk's own observations had told him, he motioned for the group to continue forward in combat formation. Even though he hadn't signaled for it, a quick glance back told him they had all, like him, instinctively crouched lower as they moved into the circle of boulders for the anticipated rendezvous.

Hawk had to scramble hand-over-hand to make his way through the arc of boulders that ringed the meeting place like jagged teeth. Despite his attempts to be stealthy, he dislodged a few loose stones, which skittered down as he sought purchase in the crannies between slabs of lightly-veined, gray granite. He cursed at himself for the clumsy noisiness of his approach. When he finally reached a vantage point, however, perching like a bit of meat caught between teeth badly in need of flossing, he could see there was no one in the circle of stones to have heard his less-than-professional approach. He did a full scan of the surprisingly grassy, level area forming an oval in the midst of the protective rocks. The giant chunks of granite appeared from this vantage almost as if they had been placed with Stonehenge precision to fortify the simple field. When he found no sign of the squad's rendezvous counterparts or anyone else, he motioned the team forward and secured a protected covering position with a broad field of fire on the inner slope of the rocks.

Net Impact

One by one, the rest of the squad entered the circle and set up secure positions along the eastern arc of rocks and crevices to await their contacts. Hawk checked his chronograph and snarled softly. The other side was late.

Never a good sign.

The waiting was merely tedious; the second-guessing he was doing while he waited was torture. His mind raced, now unoccupied by the mundane mechanics of a stealth march through unfamiliar territory in a land more foreign than he had ever encountered before. It was a civilization that played by its own rules and was ruled by a largely faceless coterie of zealous bureaucrats who had immense power and their own hidden agendas. Things could happen here you could never believe, even though the powers-that-be proffered their citizens a façade of freedom and a semblance of self-determination.

In a place like this, things could go suddenly and terribly wrong.

So the worries raced through Hawk's mind. Was the squad being set up? Were the rebels they were to meet really rebels and not government goons on their own clandestine mission, a mission targeting his team's destruction? Had their long, lonely trek to this place been detected? Worse yet, had the squad members been identified and massive retaliation already been put into action, not just here for him and his squad, but back home where everyone he loved worked and breathed and played, unaware of his role in this world, never assuming he could be this person and do the things he had done?

A chirp from Shrike broke his reverie. A force was moving into the teeth opposite their positions. The clatter of stones cascading down the far side of the fortress rocks gave the approaching group away even before they could reach the jagged openings allowing entry to the field spread out below. The noisy approach didn't say much for their capacity for stealth, but then again, his own earlier approach had been

4

considerably less than ninja-like. He started to smile at the thought, then caught himself. This was no place for self-deprecating distraction—not here, not on a mission. The noise could be a ruse. He signaled for the squad to do another quick scan in all directions just in case the noise was a deliberate distraction for a move on them from the rear.

Professional paranoia. That was his job. He'd learned from the best.

A quick series of chirps and calls from the squad revealed his paranoia was misplaced, this time. He didn't care. One day it wouldn't be and he would live to talk about it. Except, of course, he couldn't talk about it with anyone outside the organization. And inside the organization you just didn't do that kind of thing—it ruined the whole macho bullshit mystique of being a big balls covert op.

Oh well. There was a lot he couldn't talk about. That, too, he knew too well, was part of the job.

Finally, what he prayed were his squad's true counterparts in this rendezvous came into view. The first to appear in the v-shaped opening between two boulders stood up straight in full view and gave a hearty wave to the seemingly empty field. Silhouetted by the bright light of the western sky, he presented a target that was a sniper's wet dream. "Anybody here yet?" the shadowy figure yelled, then looked around the interior of the circle of stones. "What an awesome place for a party!"

Rebels. It had to be real rebels. It was hard to fake that kind of oblivious stupidity.

Hawk used a small metal mirror from his pocket to flash light in his counterpart's face to attract his attention. Once Party Dude noticed the signal, Hawk stood and motioned toward the middle of the field. Party Dude gave an excited wave and motioned back to the rest of his people to follow him over the rocks and down to the field itself, then leaped and skittered his way to the grass with agile grace. Hawk signaled for Shrike and Peregrine to move to the field, too. Pigeon stayed in his roost, crouched in a crevice with a view both inside and outside the granite perimeter. There was no reason to show their full hand yet. Hawk could call Pigeon in when he needed the contents of his backpack. Besides, someone needed to keep an eye out for threats, whether internal or external to their little gathering place.

Hawk moved down toward the field. It was an awkward climb down, so he didn't rush. Instead, he moved with the deliberate, methodical style of a trained professional. Not only would it be embarrassing to tumble down the slope in front of their counterparts, but he also wanted to convey to these rebels that he and the members of his team were competent and responsible—not some fly-by-night goons for hire. The stakes were, after all, enormous, most especially for the rebels. If this exchange was traced, they didn't have the kinds of resources Hawk and his team had to protect themselves or just to disappear, if it came to that.

As he made his way down-slope, Hawk took in more details about the rebels and the situation, comparing and contrasting the two groups' approaches to the mission. Hawk's team was coordinated, disciplined, and alert. Party Dude's team was disorganized and casual. Hawk's team had arrived on time. Party Dude's crew was late. Hawk's team dressed in simple, loose clothing in a variety of dark, natural shades—the kind of thing that allowed easy movement and provided passable camouflage in most outdoor settings without looking like military or hunting camo gear. On the other hand, Party Dude's casual, fashionable clothing featured more logos than the average NASCAR jumpsuit.

The various swooshes and crests and polo ponies on Party Dude's gear each would have been understated and tasteful in a class-conscious preppy kind of way if worn in isolation. In combination with all the other understated and tasteful logos, along with a few more garish pieces of affinity-wear touting energy drinks, software, and special-effects laden movies, the ensemble was quite dizzying and, frankly, exhausting to behold.

Party Dude's five-member (that Hawk could see) team followed their leader down, each exhibiting the same fluid movement and the same tacky fondness for logoed fashion-wear. It was like they all shopped for overstocked and irregular clothing at the same Stop and Swap flea-market in rural Tennessee. The group members were all Caucasian in terms of their facial features, but their movements had an Oriental feel to them. Hawk didn't really care—whatever they looked like and whoever they were, he knew who they were doing this for and that made all the difference in the world.

The other group took the field and started pitching tents before Hawk's squad finished descending. Hawk arched an eyebrow as he strode to the center of the field, proffering his beefy hand to Party Dude for a shake. Party Dude gave him a fist bump, instead, which Hawk did his best to adjust to.

"Welcome to our shindig, bro," exclaimed Party Dude.

"Bitchin' to be here, man," responded Hawk with faux gusto. He didn't know whose benefit all this jovial camaraderie was for, but it was best to play along. "Staying the night?" he asked, gesturing at the hodge-podge of mismatched tents quickly being assembled.

Party Dude gave a wide grin. "Absolutely, bro, absolutely. Nobody comes this far for a meet and greet. They come to party. Relax. We'll chat. We'll eat. *We'll discuss areas of mutual interest.* We can have sex, if you're into that kind of thing."

Hawk stiffened and not in a sexual kind of way. "Er, no." He waved his right hand dismissively and tried his best to give a hearty, casual laugh, although it came off a bit ragged. "Uh, I gave it up for

Lent." Lent had ended months ago, but Hawk was pretty sure this guy wouldn't know that.

Party Dude took the rejection in stride. "That's cool. Lots of grunting and groaning and what does it get you? Better than that, I've got a bootleg of the latest *Transformers* sequel coming out next month. We could watch, or maybe I could swap you a copy for something cool. Got anything?"

And there it was—the code phrase he had been told to expect: "a bootleg of the latest *Transformers* sequel." Even though it sometimes felt completely ridiculous to do all this clandestine spycraft crap, especially when you were standing in a field in the middle of nowhere with nobody else watching, it paid to have ingrained good habits over the long run.

Hawk smiled. "Nothing that good, I'm afraid. Just the never-released pilot for *Buffy: The Vampire Slayer*."

Party Dude frowned.

Hawk knew why. He hadn't offered the appropriate item in trade. He never gave the response to a code-phrase right away. Someone who knew the right phrase to offer, but not the expected response, would always eagerly accept whatever they were given. Someone expecting something else would hesitate. Or come back around for another try.

Or shoot you. It wasn't a game without risks.

Party Dude considered for a moment, then wrinkled his nose. "I could get that on eBay. Besides, Alyson Hannigan makes a much better Willow. What else you got?"

Hawk smiled. "I've got a listing of hidden features in the new *Grand Theft Auto* sequel coming out next week. Interested?"

Party Dude gave him another fist bump. "Interested? There isn't a guy in the world that doesn't like cars, tits, and explosions." His head tilted to one side. "Except maybe the Pope. . ."

Hawk laughed out loud. "Don't know about the tits and explosions—but he's got a Popemobile. Anyone else you know got one?"

Now it was Party Dude's turn to laugh. "They oughta let you boost one of those in the game. Now that would be rad."

"Sounds like we have a swap, then," said Hawk, eager to get the business end of the transaction done, not that what they were really swapping had anything to do with robots, cars, or whores.

"Sure, bro, after the party."

Hawk was disappointed not to finish up the business quickly, but he understood Party Dude's concerns. Maybe he didn't trust someone on his team. Maybe he thought his group had been detected traveling to this remote place. Maybe he was worried about what a recon satellite would show over a short time lapse photo spread. He had said it all on their first exchange: "Nobody comes this far for a meet and greet." He and his squad had to hang and chat about topics relevant to Party Dude's cover so his presence here could be explained credibly to whoever might inquire. So, it was pop culture for males 18 to 30 years old for a few hours.

He could do that. But Hawk did wonder if this meant his subscription to *Entertainment Weekly* could be written off as a legitimate business expense ... as if his simple, pedestrian tax returns reflected anything at all to do with this facet of his life.

Hawk chatted with Party Dude a bit more, then wandered over to tell Shrike and Peregrine to settle in for the night. Meanwhile, Party Dude's team started a campfire. Hawk had no idea where they got the fuel—trees were sparse this high up—but he understood the choice for their rendezvous spot better now that he knew this shindig was part of the cover. It had to be a spot where the fire and the gathering wouldn't attract others. Although a simple campfire can be seen from miles away, the circle of protective rocks prevented that here. Of course, the light of a campfire could always be seen from above, from a higher elevation or aerial reconnaissance. But this site was already well-elevated and an aerial view via high-altitude spy plane or even passing satellite surveillance tasked to take a look would show nothing more than what appeared to be an overnight campout/party.

Party Dude was cleverer than he looked.

But apparently not clever enough.

Without warning, there was a flash and the camp erupted in chaos as an invisible shockwave of pressurized air radiated out from where one of the rebel's tents had once stood. Hawk's combat sense screamed at him that there had been an explosion, but there was no smoke, no fire, and no charred debris. Instead of the sharp boom of an explosion, there had been a deep rumble. Hawk scanned the area, flicking his eyes from point to point in rapid succession, desperate to acquire more data. The data, when it came, made no sense at all. He watched as some sort of strange orange death-ray bolted down from an unseen location far above, vaporizing everything it touched in an instant. In the immediate aftermath of the momentary pulse, people and objects in the surrounding area were knocked asunder.

Rebels were shouting, fleeing, searching for cover, and firing small arms randomly into the sky. Untrained civilians often react badly to danger, but panic comes in a heartbeat when people are simply being vaporized by an invisible enemy with an impossible weapon.

There was no reason to be subtle anymore. "Abort! Abort! Abort!" screamed Hawk, as he dashed toward Party Dude's tent, calling for Pigeon to do the same, in the hope of making the exchange before it was too late. The tent disappeared in a bright flash of orange light, however, as Hawk approached. He skidded to a stop, just barely avoiding being touched by the bizarre orange glow. He looked helplessly at the weapon in his hands. He would use it, if he had a target, but this situation, this bizarre death from above made fighting useless. He raised the gun as he scanned the field looking for an enemy, looking for some way to retaliate or simply defend, but he did not fire.

In the few seconds it took for Hawk to assess the situation, it deteriorated even further. The orange light fell upon the field again and again. Each time a tent or a rebel or a gigantic, granite boulder simply *disappeared*. No debris, no crater, no wounded left behind. Chaotic cries of confusion rang out from the rebels, but there were fewer voices with each passing moment and it wasn't because the panic was subsiding.

"Take flight," Hawk yelled to his squad over the tumult of the remaining rebels' shouts and the soft bass whoomph that accompanied each appearance of the orange energy beam wreaking destruction on the remote meeting place. The secretiveness of the sub-vocal microphone was not needed for the urgent and obvious orders Hawk needed to convey, both to his men and to their rebel counterparts. "Scatter now!" He slung his weapon and obeyed his own order.

Someone was going to pay for this screw-up, Hawk vowed. He glanced back at the obliterated camp as he gained height in his effort to escape the strange fortress of stones. A lot of people were already paying for this screw-up. He hoped he wouldn't be one of them.

Hawk doubled his speed. Survival was his only goal. He didn't care what it looked like.

CHAPTER 1

Dick Thornby didn't look like anybody's idea of a spy. He didn't have the steely stare and the long, lithe body of the spies of popular fiction. He wasn't wearing a designer evening jacket. Nor did he have the non-descript, average height, average weight, bland, gray, middle-management look of the men favored by the CIA, FBI, and other acronym agencies of America.

At 5' 10", with the stockiness of a former offensive lineman, it was easiest for Dick to buy his clothes at the big and tall men's shops proliferating in the increasingly portly suburban communities back home. Dressed in a cheap suit and tie he'd picked up in just such a place, he was perfectly disguised as yet another small-time American businessman deplaning from the long haul to Auckland, New Zealand—in coach. He was well aware his employer could afford to send him first class, but such extravagance did not match his cover, so he passed on the luxury, despite the discomfort.

Instead, he trudged down the gangway to the terminal with the rest of the unwashed masses, everyone groggy from sleeping fitfully for too long in seats too small for comfort. It was easy to stay in character with the crowd—grouchy and bone-tired from the trek. He waited in weary resignation for his bags, then dutifully got in the immigration control line. With a well-worn passport and his traveler information form in his left hand and a rumpled trench coat draped over his right, he performed the familiar traveler shuffle—wait, push your bag ahead with a foot, shuffle forward, and wait again. Finally, it was his turn.

The courteous immigration officer gave him a cursory glance, then flipped open his passport and stamped a page. A moment later the Kiwi official waved him through. No strip search today.

Once in the airport concourse, Dick maintained cover by exchanging U.S. dollars for New Zealand dollars at the crappy airport rate, just like other unprepared tourists. Turning toward the exit, he squinted at the brightness of the morning sun as he took in the rest of the terminal. He reached into his carry-on bag and donned cheap, dark, aviator sunglasses and a rumpled, fabric fedora matched to his trench coat, then surveyed the scene again.

He looked like a dork, he knew, but the tacky accessories completed the middle-class traveler ensemble. Sometimes it was good cover to look like a dork.

Besides, the sunglasses were actually anything but cheap. In reality they were highly sophisticated micro-enhanced lenses issued by his employers at the Subsidiary. Along with allowing communications from headquarters and providing heads-up video/Internet display, the sunglasses had a variety of other handy features.

Most Subsidiary operatives used a sleek, modern, wrap-around style for their special shades, but Dick was not nearly cool enough to pull that off without looking conspicuous. Aviators matched his look much better. Of course, just like the fancy wrap-arounds, or even everyday sunglasses from a discount superstore, the aviators let his eyes roam at will without raising suspicion. Along with the hat, the glasses also foiled most facial recognition software. The cheap, loose-fitting jacket and baggy suit pants he wore concealed his muscular physique, as well as the scars he had picked up along the trail from college football grunt to team leader with U.S. Army Special Forces to Chicago cop to Subsidiary operative.

Dick didn't know who had dropped this latest hot potato into the Subsidiary's lap. He didn't need to know and he didn't care. All he knew was that bad guys were dealing arms. Not just chicken-shit automatic weapons (though those killed enough civilians on their own), but major hardware and top-secret design specifications. In this case, someone had stolen high-grade security-clearance plans for a state-of-the-art item that could help turn the tide in a major conflict and absolutely blow away the enemy in a minor one.

Net Impact

Dick's job was to get the plans back—surreptitiously if possible—but at any cost necessary, if it came to it.

Looking around the terminal again, Dick spied his immediate goal. No, not a buxom bimbo ready to brief (and debrief) him or a local contact masquerading as a limo driver. Those things didn't happen, not in the real world. Instead, his first goal was to drag himself to the discount car rental counter and book a car using the same fake name he had used on arrival. Then he drove around Auckland a while pretending to look at potential sites for expanding his phony franchise-sandwich-shop cover business.

Misdirection accomplished, he dumped the rental car at a downtown parking garage, grabbed his luggage, and headed for the garage's dingy restroom. There he donned a muted tan and green flower print tropical shirt and casual khaki pants, along with a brown, kangaroo-leather and nylon mesh Australian style hat, one with neither side tacked up. He splashed a bit of cold water in his face, rubbing it vigorously to create a bit of a blush, as if he had already been on vacation a few days and gotten just a bit too much sun. Then he walked out of the washroom and into a nearby tour agency, a different man.

At the vacation counter, he booked a bus tour under a new alias, this time adopting the persona of a Canadian school teacher on holiday. The all-inclusive ground tour featured a bevy of retirees spending their children's inheritance on a once-over of the big North Island highlights: hot springs, geysers, scenic vistas, and sheep. Lots and lots of sheep. Dick ogled the sights with his elderly companions as the bus headed south. He finished the three-day tour at Wellington, on the southern tip of the North Island. That same day, he ferried across the Cook Strait and into Queen Charlotte Sound, disembarking at Picton, on the South Island. There he changed IDs again, becoming an American tourist and bird-watcher.

He wasn't a chameleon, wasn't "the Shapeshifter," the legendary Subsidiary operative he heard had the ability to blend in anywhere, be anyone. And the changes in ID weren't because anyone was following him. He had checked in all the usual ways. Nothing. Just a middle-aged, overweight English lady, who made moon-eyes at him from a distance during the North Island bus trip. It was clear to him she wasn't a spy—she was too out of shape and too obvious about watching him. She was just a spinster who was hoping for a fling on holiday, but who never worked up the gumption to actually speak to him.

No, he was clean along his whole route as far as tails of any kind were concerned. Still, changing clothes, accent, and identity was routine. If you cover your trail, no one can track you, whether forward to mission destination or backward to source, no matter when you get noticed.

Espionage is all about making the other side work for their information.

In Picton, Dick boarded a train for the long trip southeast to Dunedin, where the mission proper was supposed to take place. He settled in for the ride, getting off at the longer stops just long enough to watch birds and make notes about them in his copy of *Birds of New Zealand*. Bird-watching was one of his favorite tourist disguises. It gave you an excuse to look wherever you wanted to and to wander off from the chitchatting crowds alone.

Chitchatting carries risks.

The easiest way to lie is not to have to talk in the first place. Dick wasn't a skilled linguist, so he mostly got sent on missions to English-speaking countries. But even when you speak the same language as those surrounding you, a false accent can be spotted easily. A faker's greatest fear is always running into some tourist from wherever he is

15

claiming is home. No matter how good, your accent and your knowledge of home will never match up to that of the true residents.

Sure, you can take classes and learn to speak any language with any accent you want, local or foreign—the Defense Language Institute is particularly good at that sort of thing—but going to class to learn to speak twenty different kinds of English didn't appeal to Dick. Especially, not when he could accomplish what he needed to by simply hanging a pair of birding binoculars around his neck.

Besides, he got a charge out of the fact Ian Fleming had lifted the name "James Bond" from the cover of a bird-watching book left in the Caribbean hotel room he was using to pen the first 007 adventure. Masquerading as a bird-watcher brought the whole fact/fiction spy thing full circle.

Finally, the train arrived in Dunedin and Dick joined the tourist throngs in all the standard visitor activities at the station, oohing and ahhing at the incredibly long, covered platform, snapping pictures of the Victorian-style clock tower, and shuffling into the station to gawk at its thousands of tiles laid in geometric designs. At the station shop, Dick picked up a few postcards and a local paper. He also asked the clerk to get him one of the souvenir pins in the display case, which caused a bit of confusion. He kept asking for a "pin" and the clerk kept handing him various souvenir "pens." Even when you spoke the language, the local idioms could screw you up. Who knew they called pins "badges" here?

As the arrivals cleared, Dick sat on one of the platform's benches to read the paper, paying particular attention to the classified ads. After circling one or two, he made his way to a pay phone and dialed a local number. He had a brief conversation, writing down an address in the margin of the paper as the chat concluded. He hung up and immediately went to the main entrance of the station and hailed a cab.

Forty-five minutes and one short test drive later, Dick was the proud owner of a used 2005 Yamaha TDM900, dickering the owner down to $12,000 NZD. The sporty bike featured a smooth-running engine with a throaty purr and enough thrust to provide a jolting burst of acceleration when needed and to sustain high-end cruising speeds without straining. The front shocks were also sufficient to permit off-road capability, which could come in handy. On the other hand, the bike wasn't new enough or flashy enough, even in red, to draw too much attention from thieves or passersby.

Dick paid cash and tucked the motorcycle's pink slip into a pocket of his knapsack. (The vehicle title wasn't actually pink here in Kiwi-land, but then titles weren't really pink anywhere as far as he knew.) He'd dump the bike (with the keys in it) after the mission and never record the purchase. Odds were high the ride would get lifted and either stripped for parts or passed from one low-life hood to another in poker games over the next five years. If, instead, the bike was returned to the ex-owner by the local constabulary, the perplexed fellow would likely just grin, apply for a replacement title for the one he had "lost," and re-sell the bike again, doubling his profit.

Purchasing a used bike like this made Dick's movements much more secure than a stolen vehicle or a rental car with a GPS device. He was on a legal ride that wouldn't be tracked. To be sure he wouldn't be stopped for existing wants and warrants on the license tag, Dick simply stepped away from the seller and made a quick call on his secure cell-phone before consummating the sale. The call was routed locally through the Kiwi cell network, then scrambled and uploaded by the agency's in-country infrastructure—most likely a branch office of Catalyst Crisis Consulting, the management consulting company that acted as a cover organization for the Subsidiary—to an untraceable satellite communications interface two generations beyond the United States' Echelon System, and beamed down to the Subsidiary's HQ back in the States. A few keystrokes by a computer whiz on the other end and Dick had confirmed the owner and the tag number for the vehicle were on the right side of the local authorities.

All this was, of course, routine. Dick didn't know exactly how the Subsidiary was funded, but in his experience it wasn't exactly cash conscious. Still, mundane craft like this was both a normal and cost-effective way to do business in a tourist-friendly country like New Zealand. It was unnecessary and would be mind-blowingly expensive to scramble a jet to insert him into hobbit-land via a HALO (High Altitude/Low Opening) drop or some nonsense like that. He didn't put that kind of thing past the Subsidiary's capabilities; there was just no reason to do it when you had fake identification, plenty of time, and solid, dependable, clandestine workhorses like him.

Dick studied a local street map and familiarized himself with the roadways. Then he took a quick spin to do more of the same and to get a feel for the quirks of the bike. Once he was comfortable with his ride and his environs, he drove thirty minutes outside of town on the north side of Otago Harbor to Port Chalmers, where the deep-water docks hosting cruise ships and cargo containers were located. He parked the bike a few blocks away, grabbed his binoculars and bird book, and headed toward the waterfront.

He triggered the communications prompt on his micro-enhanced sunglasses. "Asset in place," he reported. "Surveillance commencing."

He was surprised when Glenn Swynton, the Subsidiary's overseer of operations, answered his call, instead of some low-level communications tech.

"Anything of note to report?" queried Glenn, all British and efficient, as always. "I was just updating Director Tammany on the status of all missions *in situ*. I'll put you on the box and you can brief us both."

Great. Now he was reporting in to both his boss and his boss's boss—everybody's boss—Dee Tammany, Director of the Subsidiary. True, she wasn't usually the prick that Glenn was, but Dick had expected a two second conversation with some mope in the ops center, not a quiz by the powers that be. What time was it in Philadelphia anyway? Didn't these guys ever sleep?

He cast his complaints away and mustered up his best official reporting tone: "Arrived on schedule without incident. Local transportation secured. Target area in sight. No activity to report. Everything quiet."

He heard Dee give a brief laugh. "It's always quiet before the bad guys show up."

"Roger that, Director."

"Don't let us keep you then. Good hunting," replied the Director in a tone which was both friendly and dismissive at the same time.

"Keep us informed," added Swynton in a tone which was both dismissive and demanding at the same time. The Brit had a knack for that.

"Roger and out." replied Dick. He could be a good little soldier. But he was an even better operative.

CHAPTER 2

Dick's mission in Dunedin was to find a Kestrel. Not the feather and bones variety—those weren't indigenous to New Zealand. No, the Kestrel he was looking for was made of polycarbonate filament, Mylar sheathing, and high-tech optics and electronics.

The Kestrel 84 was the latest state-of-the-art workhorse in the ever-burgeoning field of UAVs—unmanned air vehicles—the miniature spy planes used for reconnaissance, targeting, and, in some cases, delivery of precision, ground-directed explosives.

Although first conceived in Dick's great granddaddy's day with the Kettering Bug (basically a torpedo with biplane wings) during World War I, UAVs really got underway in the 1960s. Back then, camera-laden, radar-jamming Firebees flew thousands of largely unheralded missions in Vietnam. The Americans (and others) began developing UAVs in a major way in the 1980s. By the 1990s, Pioneers were helping to target artillery during the first Gulf War and being used in place of in-country human intelligence in Bosnia.

The road wasn't always easy or smooth along the way. Billions were spent on R&D for UAVs prototypes that just never worked the way they were supposed to. That's the nature of military contracting, in general, and aviation development, in particular. But the development of cheap and sophisticated GPS devices and lighter, stronger components eventually turned the tide.

Of course, bigger was usually the way of U.S. government weapons. Strapping modified Hellfire missiles onto the largest of the drones, the Predator, turned UAVs into an unseen terror from above during the second Gulf War. They also were critical in locating and destroying targets in Afghanistan and Pakistan in the War on Terror. Air Force "combatants" sitting in air-conditioned warehouses in California piloted the big boys. (They might bitch about traffic like everyone else, but not many people get to alleviate their road rage by vaporizing a terrorist cell and three goats after a long commute.)

But better wasn't ignored for the sake of bigger. Other, smaller UAVs, like Shadows, Ravens, and Dragon Eyes were developed that could be flown from nearby command centers, or even from the field by the grunts who deployed them. The Maveric, used by Navy Seals, was designed to look like a lazily circling turkey vulture from the ground. Ultra-light materials and inflatable wings allowed small UAVs like the Wasp, or TiGER flying hand grenades, to be carried by the average soldier.

The Kestrel 84 was of the smaller variety. Marrying cheap GPS, even cheaper laser pointer illumination, and digital photo and communications technology with amazingly sturdy, but light, frame construction, the Kestrel could be carried in an inconspicuous, protective tube during deployment. On the front lines of a confrontation, an infantryman could then quickly assemble and launch the device. Once aloft, the UAV could reconnoiter the battle scene, paint targets for laser-guided weapons, and jam field communications.

The Kestrel 84 had a large wing-size to weight ratio, which meant it could stay aloft a day or more. It was also easily guided by a simple digital controller with a high-resolution flat-screen video which automatically broadcast GPS coordinates. The real beauty of the video array was that linkage between the camera's auto-focus chip and the GPS software meant that the coordinates broadcast were not those of the drone, itself, but the coordinates of what the camera was viewing at the cross-hairs in the middle of the vid-screen.

Best launched from a roof-top or minor elevation (the top of a panel truck was good), the Kestrel 84 could be flown right from the front lines. Anyone who played a lot of Ultimate Frisbee could even get the Kestrel airborne from ground level with a good, strong wrist flick. Small and high-flying, the Kestrel presented such an insignificant visual and radar profile and was so quiet as to be practically undetectable from the ground. At the same time, it had a feature that could make its presence known if desired. The so-called "buzz-kill" option broadcast the whiny buzz most closely associated with model aircraft fields in order to let enemy personnel know they were being surveilled. In early operational deployments, that clever piece of counter-intelligence intimidation was responsible for more than one clandestine gathering of drug lords or jihadists breaking up and bolting for cover.

Yep, the Kestrel 84 was a nice asset to have on your side. Yet, despite their forward deployment by U.S. forces in various hot-spots around the world, one had never been captured. A small charge hooked into a coded ultra-low frequency carrier array (the same type of thing used by nuclear subs to verify launch codes without surfacing) created a nice self-destruct mechanism which had the functional equivalent of a dead-man's switch.

That no-capture record was still intact, but some yahoo defense contractor too busy back-dating options and not busy enough securing his top secret military files had been hacked and the materials, construction, and coding specs of the Kestrel 84 pilfered.

If the hack had been accomplished by a terrorist organization, the harm would have been irreparable. Plans would have been traded by Al-Qa'eda cells, Iranian nationals, and IRA splinter groups at light speed. The technical specifications of the top secret device would have filtered down to Basque separatists, Honduran rebels, and Cupertino, California computer game designers not long after.

The Subsidiary had determined, however, some geeky kid here in the land of the Kiwis had performed the hack. The kid was apparently stupid enough to fail to understand the consequences of what he was doing (to himself and the world), but smart enough to mastermind the hack and understand what he had stumbled into. Of course, the kid was also greedy enough to want to profit from his endeavors.

The powers that be in the Subsidiary—probably Glenn Swynton— had alerted a few contacts in local law enforcement who had worked with the agency in the past, but the kid had disappeared by the time the local constabulary arrived on scene. Their investigation suggested the kid genius had connected up with a local gang—no doubt through some bully who had regularly beat on the kid during his early teen years at school. The bully or bullies apparently had sufficient contacts in the underworld of drugs and guns that they understood what the kid had found and knew how to auction it to the highest bidder. While the hacker probably had been paid off with a few tens of thousands of dollars (New Zealand) and a couple of hookers for the weekend, the gang, an offshoot of the Pan-Pacific Indigenous People's Front, was looking for a seven, maybe eight, digit payout. The prospect of a payday like that meant there would be plenty of muscle, plenty of weaponry, and plenty of technical expertise associated with the sale, verification, and exchange, probably from both sides of the transaction.

Dick didn't know anything more about the exchange, except that a communication intercept suggested Pao Fen Smythe, a Hong Kong based trafficker in arms and information, had been in touch with the local Maori gang affiliated with the PPIPF to set up the time and place for their "transaction."

Once Pao Fen's organization had the Kestrel 84 plans, it was just a matter of time before very bad things started happening. Soon the Taliban would be deploying counterfeit Kestrels to spy on infidels in Afghanistan. Not long after, Al-Qa'eda cells in the U.S. would be using them to scope out security measures at nuclear power plants upwind from jam-packed football stadiums.

The sale of the top secret plans was supposedly going to be at Port Chalmers harbor tomorrow. That's why Dick was here today, away

23

from his family yet again, scoping out the waterfront, checking for unusual activity and learning the ins and outs of the port environs.

Port Chalmers' main docking facilities were on the north shore of Otago Harbor, about thirty minutes east of the city center. A gleaming white cruise ship was docked in the midst of the "secure area," a chain-link fenced open space with a small visitor's center. The quarantined area had a security gate for verifying passports and cruise ship IDs for those coming in and for checking packages for contraband fruits and other foodstuffs for those coming ashore. It also contained a series of adjacent docks for small boats offering sightseeing cruises and fishing outings. Farther east, past several warehouses, two huge cranes for loading cargo ships towered above a concrete field of cargo containers and an adjacent dirt yard filled with piles of wood chips and row after row of huge logs.

For a place that touted its eco-tours and green-friendly conservation practices, New Zealand exported a shitload of forestry products. Every few minutes another tractor pulling a long trailer stacked with six or eight huge tree trunks would barrel down the narrow shoreline road, slow briefly at the gate for the lumber and container yard, then lurch into the yard. There the rigs would halt while a huge, pincer-armed loader removed the logs from the trailer one-by-one and added them to the end of one of the long rows of tree trunks, until the stack was as high as the arm of the loader could reach.

Like all guys, Dick got distracted for a few moments watching the big machines work. When his son, Seth, was still in elementary school, Dick had often taken him to the high-rise construction sites downtown to watch the equipment. Seth would make roaring sounds as the engines strained and Dick would "beep" along with the warning device whenever something backed up, giving Seth a playful, ticklish poke in the ribs in time with each "beep," "What's that?" Seth would ask between giggles, pointing at one of the giant yellow machines.

24

Instead of answering with "truck" or "bulldozer," like most dads, Dick was always very precise in his response. "That's a John Deere Excavator," he would reply. "That there's a Caterpillar Backhoe Loader." Seth would repeat the name in a whisper after each identification, furrowing his brow as if it would help him remember. If the kid ever needed to know the difference between a high-speed dozer and motor grader, Dick was a great father.

From his experience with Seth watching construction workers handle their rigs, Dick could easily tell that the driver manipulating the loader was good. The pincers of the loader were worked with finesse. Even though there was no barrier at the end of the row he was working on, the guy laid the timber down with enough precision and subtlety that the huge logs didn't slip down or roll off, fraying the end of the stack.

After a few moments of big machines time, however, Dick got back to the task at hand. The trade wouldn't be in the open near the cruise ship—too many witnesses for the protective firepower sure to be associated with the exchange to go unnoticed. The cargo container and wood-stacking areas had similar issues—too busy, too open, and too visible during the day, and too suspicious after dark. That meant the most likely location for the trade was one of the nearby warehouses.

Dick took up a position on a small rise in the shore road. The spot had a fair view of most of the warehouses to the east and was in the shade near a shelter for the local bus service—a place where he could see, but not draw a lot of attention, even in the Aloha shirt and floppy hat he was wearing.

He flipped open his bird book to the chapter on gulls and shore birds, raised his German-made Leica binoculars, and started the long, laborious work of studying the warehouses one-by-one, noting doors and windows, obvious security features, lighting, and traffic patterns. He used the information to draw conclusions as to which warehouses were abandoned and which ones were too busy to be the likely location of an exchange. It was tedious, mind-numbing work; not nearly as interesting as what the spies in the movies were always doing. It was more like police stakeout—hours of waiting around, the boredom punctuated only by an occasional doughnut and the awkward fumbling associated with having to pee into a cup.

Eventually, however, Dick narrowed in on a warehouse—Pellman's Secure Storage—just off the edge of the secure area for the cruise ships, between there and the wood and cargo storage fields. The place was well-maintained and reasonably secure. There was even a security presence.

For starters, a guard stood on either side of the main entrance opposite from the side facing the visitor's center. Two more guards were patrolling the perimeter (one moving clockwise, the other counterclockwise, around the building at all times—a security routine only a thug would think clever or effective). That made four guards surrounding this single warehouse. One more guard, maybe a sniper, looked only in the direction of Pellman's as he paced on the roof of a taller warehouse nearby. Dick concentrated on the rooftop guard's position, but was unable to locate any sign of a sniper rifle or shooting nest. Still, that made five guards—a bigger security force for this one warehouse than the sovereign nation of New Zealand had allotted to guard the entire port facility.

The large security presence made Dick twitchy. The information he had received said the exchange wasn't occurring today, but there was a lot of manpower on site already. The exchange could be happening this very moment, while he stood loitering outside.

Suddenly, a firm hand grabbed Dick's right shoulder. "Excuse me. What are you looking at?"

Dick's combat senses took over and he wheeled quickly around, dropping his binoculars to thump lightly on his chest as they reached the end of the strap. He grabbed the hand on his right shoulder with his own left hand, dipping that shoulder and shifting his weight at he prepared to fling his opponent over his shoulder. He stifled his movement and the expletives that flew to the tip of his tongue as his "assailant" came into view. A middle-aged haus-frau wearing a loose t-shirt and culottes, along with a sun hat and a pair of Swarovski binoculars, cringed back from his touch with a light yelp and a confused expression.

"Oh, s-sorry, you startled me," Dick stammered, dropping her hand and taking a half-step back. He nodded in brief apology and then gestured broadly toward the warehouses along the waterfront. "I think there's a Lesser Black-Backed Gull in with the Kelp Gulls over on the east side of the roof of the Visitor's Center, just this side of those big warehouses near the cargo containers."

The woman eyed him with obvious suspicion, then lifted her binoculars and peered at the roof of the Visitor's Center. "You mean those Dominican Gulls?"

Dick smiled. Birdwatchers loved to show off their superior knowledge. "Kelp Gulls are also known as Dominican Gulls. I'm talking about the Lesser Black-Backed Gull I thought I saw walking about near the middle of the flock."

The woman looked doubtful, but peered at the rooftop again. "I don't see it. You must be mistaken," she said with a sniff. "The Lesser Black-Backed isn't found here anyways."

"A few have been spotted in Australia, so it's possible one has made its way here, too. That's why it would be such a find." Birdwatching was an easy cover to fake when talking to those not knowledgeable about such things, but when you ran into somebody who knew the birds and the lingo, you still had to have a cover story that stood up. No birdwatcher would look at a flock of gulls for hours on end without a damn good excuse.

27

Net Impact

The woman took another long peer through her expensive binoculars. "I don't see anything but Dominicans."

Dick feigned disappointment by slumping his shoulders exaggeratedly. "You're probably right."

"You know," said the woman, a hint of triumph in her voice. "If you travel round the bay to the Otago Peninsula on the south side, there's a Royal Albatross Center, as well as an Eco-Tour which features both Blue Penguins and Yellow-Eyed Penguins. I'm told it's quite spectacular." She sniffed again. "Much more interesting than gulls. Blue Penguins are 'lifers' for most birders."

Dick noted her cruise ship ID hooked to the strap holding her binoculars. Cruise ships rarely stayed in port for more than a day. "Thanks," he said enthusiastically, "I'll try those spots later in the week." He gestured toward the small boat docks. "Just waiting on a harbor tour boat right now. Thought maybe I'd gotten lucky during the wait." He deliberately left it ambiguous as to whether he was waiting to go out on a tour or waiting for someone to get back from a tour. Ambiguity is your friend when you lie for a living. "In the meantime, maybe I'll take another look." He swung his binoculars back up and began to stare again at the flock of Kelp Gulls.

The woman obviously had no more tolerance for his gull fetish. "Well, I hope you get lucky. But I don't think it's likely." He heard her stroll off to the bus shelter and start up a conversation with a young woman who had been waiting patiently for the next bus.

Dick maintained his concentration on the roof of the Visitor's Center for a few minutes, then slowly slid his gaze back over to Pellman's Secure Storage and took up his monitoring task yet again. After a while, he sauntered over toward the security gate and pretended to watch some sparrows for a few moments as he observed the security procedures for a busload of tourists returning to the ship after an early morning excursion. Satisfied with what he learned, he headed back into the center of the city, checked out information at a tourist kiosk that told him what cruise ship would be docking tomorrow and what the dockside to downtown shuttle bus schedule was. Then it was back to the docks for another quick check of his target site. He parked the motorcycle nearby and took a shuttle bus back into town to his hotel, checked in with the powers that be, and made an early evening of it.

He had a long, dangerous day ahead of him. His stint as a soldier, back in his younger days, had taught him both decision-making and reaction times were improved by getting a good night's sleep before a mission. Besides, if he was going to die, he preferred not to die tired.

CHAPTER 3

Dick slept in. The scheduled meet wasn't until the end of the afternoon and things could go quite late afterwards. If all went well, he would be riding his motorcycle all night to get to Picton, then hopping a ferry to Wellington for an early-morning flight out of the country. If things didn't go well, he might need all his wits and strength just to deal with the situation. Besides, he wasn't fully acclimatized to the time differential. Finally, he got up, dressed in a pair of jeans and a loose bowling shirt and went downstairs for a filling brunch, heavy on protein and fats, but light on carbs. He also had three cups of the bitter swill that passed for coffee on this island—it never hurt to caffeine-load when you were about to start an op.

At midday Dick went back to the Dunedin train station and mingled with a group of tourists from the cruise ship docked for the day. He found a perch near one of the spectacular stained glass windows on the landing for the second floor—correct that, first floor (ground level was known as ground floor, not first floor, here)—and took a few shots with his camera. It didn't take long before someone else came by to do the same thing, an English couple by the sound of their accents.

"Excuse me, sir," Dick said with a slight Tennessee twang. "I'd be most appreciative, if'n you might take my picture in front of this here window. You can get a post card of the place, but nuthin' says you been there like a picture of you in the shot your own self."

"Certainly, certainly," replied the gent. "I had the same thing in mind."

"Well, then," he said with a wink as he walked over. "You do me and I'll do you and the missus. Take a picture, I mean." He smiled at the woman while he handed over his digital camera to the husband, then turned his attention back to the man and the camera. "You'll need to press this here button first, 'cause it's all backlit from the window and I want everyone to see my smile, not just some dark shadow blockin' the light." His eyes flitted around the man's person and possessions as the gentleman looked intently at the camera. "Then just press here when I say 'sex.'"

The woman twittered. "I thought you Americans always said 'cheese.'"

He turned toward the woman, taking a half step back, and bobbed his head once. "Meanin' no disrespect, ma'am. Cheese is good, 'specially if'n you're from Wisconsin, but sex is better. It always makes me smile ... and it never gives me gas later."

The couple chuckled amiably as he moved into position in front of the bright window and the man squinted into the colorful light to frame the photo.

"Sex," drawled Dick and the man clicked the button.

Dick moved quickly to the man's side, nodded approvingly at the picture on the digital screen of his camera, then took the man's camera to return the favor. The couple obligingly shouted "sex" when he signaled them, drawing a few curious looks from those milling about on the floor below. It didn't take much persuading to get the couple to smooch in silhouette in front of the window for a second shot. Then the tour bus driver strode through the station, gathering his gaggle of sightseers, and Dick returned the photographer's stuff—well, almost all of it—as the now giggly English couple darted for their motor coach.

Dick fingered the credit card sized piece of plastic in his hand for a moment, then thrust it in his right front pocket and started walking away from the train station, back toward his hotel, where he made his preparations for the rest of the day.

An hour later, he hung his binoculars around his neck and a large camera bag over one shoulder, heading for the downtown stop of the cruise shuttle bus operations. The day was sunny and warm—from what he understood, it had been unseasonably warm for several days—but he wore dark clothing nonetheless. He had changed into dark gray trousers, a black t-shirt covered by a dark, gray and blue patterned Aloha shirt in muted tones, along with a black baseball cap festooned with the silver fern that was one of New Zealand's national symbols, and his dark, cheap-looking, aviator sunglasses.

He waited with a growing crowd for the two o'clock shuttle bus back to the cruise docks. The bus was twenty minutes late. As soon as it arrived, it was mobbed by cranky travelers loaded down with cameras, video recorders, light jackets, and shopping bags full of souvenir purchases. While the front rows quickly filled, Dick made his way to the back, dropped into the middle of a seat for two, and pulled his cap down over his eyes, as if resting from a rigorous day of looking at unfamiliar things.

It took more than a half hour before the bus groaned to a halt at the security gate to the cruise dock area and the door swished open to admit a security guard. The guard—an eighteen or nineteen year old girl with a deep tan and crisply pressed khaki pants and a shirt festooned with security authority patches—asked to see the passengers' cruise cards and some sort of photo identification, like a driver's license (passports, Dick knew, were held by the cruise line during a voyage). The type A personalities in the front row already had their cards out and ready to go. Everyone else grumbled and fumbled until their groping hands tumbled upon the necessary identification.

The girl's verification of identification for purposes of entering the secure embarkation area became more and more cursory as she moved back. Dick wearily held up the cruise card he had swiped from the English gentleman earlier in the day, fanned toward the clerk with one of his many U.S. licenses peeking out from behind. He hadn't even bothered to alter either card to match the other in name; he had noted the quality of the security the day before when he was birdwatching.

Sure enough, when the security gal got within three rows of Dick, she spied the ship's logo on the cruise card and gave a short wave of compliance, then quickly made her way back to the front of the bus. She disembarked and headed into the security office, where a soap opera was playing on a portable television set.

He didn't blame the crisply-uniformed gal or the nation of New Zealand for the crappy security. This was just the preliminary process. The ship had its own, better, security procedures, involving checking digital photos imbedded in the magnetic strip of the cruise cards, and airport quality metal detectors and x-ray screening of carry-on items as you got onboard.

Dick, however, wasn't going onboard, so dock-side security was all he needed to deal with. And, face it, there was nothing that interesting or valuable in the cruise ship security area itself to warrant more scrutiny or muscle than security gal possessed, just some overpriced shops selling last minute souvenirs, a bank of pay phones for cruise ship personnel to call back home to Romania or the Philippines or whatever, and a bar where you could drink cheaper than onboard a cruise ship.

Dick browsed the shops and picked up a local Tui brand beer at the bar, swigging it casually as he pretended to be interested in postcards, pins (badges), and genuine New Zealand wool products. Eventually, he sauntered through a back exit from the mini-mall of touristy shops, into an alleyway full of loading docks and rubbish cans, to the one valuable thing the cruise ship security area did have—a chain-link fence bordering the adjacent commercial security area.

He needed a back way into the commercial space filled with warehouses, cargo containers, and timber. The security gate up on the shore road for the cargo facility was manned by several beefy security personnel armed with automatic weapons. Truckers pulling the long loads of local timber were waved through quickly—they were undoubtedly all recognized by sight and the open nature of the cargo (basically wheels strapped on either end of a pile of freshly cut logs) left no room for stowaways. But others seeking entrance to the secure commercial area were checked thoroughly by the guards. Maybe that was because there were rail containers full of valuable stuff to steal and maybe it was because local thugs used the nearby warehouses for their own purposes. It didn't matter to Dick.

What did matter was that Pellman's Secure Storage was where the meet involving his targets was going to be at sunset. The best way to get into the secure commercial area in which the warehouse was located was from the unguarded border fence between the two allegedly secure areas. Dick hid behind a rubbish bin until the two guards he had seen the day before made their pass through the alleyway behind Pellman's Secure Storage, criss-crossing one another without even a guttural grunt of greeting. Both turned east to continue their circuit as they reached either end of the alley. The rooftop guard several buildings away was out of sight—his viewpoint offering no angle on Dick's chosen position in any event.

Without further hesitation, Dick darted to the fence, feeling the familiar surge of adrenaline and narrowed concentration that always kicked in during an op. He used a small wire-cutter to make a slit near one of the metal posts standing at six foot intervals in the chain-link fencing between the two areas. There, the slit would be harder to see on casual observation. He slipped through the gap and then used a small twist-tie to tack the opening shut so it would not show after he left. Dashing across the small alleyway on the other side of the fence from the Visitor's Center, he ducked behind a roll-on, roll-off waste container and jumped up to a loading platform for Pellman's Secure Storage.

Two minutes rewiring the box for the security system nearby and less than thirty seconds picking the lock on the personnel door next to the big-overhead door for loading cargo made a liar out of Pellman, whoever he was. Pellman's Storage was by no means secure.

Dick entered the building with quiet, deliberate speed. There were guards in front of the warehouse and, he assumed, in it, too. At first chance, he moved up from ground level, the default line of sight for anyone patrolling inside, clambering to the top of one of the taller wooden crates and jumping lithely up to the lowest level of the steel shelving filling most of the warehouse. It was darker here, the shelves blocking the lights at ground level, as well as obscuring the sunlight filtering in the frosted glass ventilation windows high above. Dick pressed the temple of his aviator sunglasses twice, activating the low-light vision feature. He climbed higher and higher into the shelving as opportunities arose, creeping without sound ever upward and forward toward the main entrance to the warehouse.

As he had expected, the area near the main entrance was devoid of shelving. Aside from a few empty pallets and a propane powered fork-lift parked haphazardly on the south side of the main doors, the floorspace was clear. Frosted glass skylights and a sixty foot drop from the ceiling to the concrete below provided great visibility, even when he switched off the low-light feature on his glasses. Of course, the openness would also allow anyone down below to see him lurking on the edges of the shelving.

To prevent that, he reached into a pocket on his camera bag and ferreted out a small electronic device. Accessing another pouch on the bag, he pinched off a piece of clay—okay C-4 explosives, but the stuff wasn't dangerous without a detonator—from a larger bloc. Shimmying up a support post at the edge of the shelving, he stuck the explosive on the corner of one of the glass skylights. It would grip better there than on the corrugated steel of the ceiling and it would be less obvious there than on one of the shelving struts. Once the putty-like substance was in place, Dick pushed a small electronic device into

35

his makeshift adhesive. He pointed the narrow end of the device down, angling its small aperture toward the center of the empty space on the floor below. Then he slid down to the top shelf and retreated behind a skid of green and yellow farm equipment parts.

Once concealed, he pulled out what would look to a casual observer to be a simple cell phone and pressed buttons until a picture appeared on screen showing the open area in the warehouse, as viewed from the camera he had attached to the C-4 stuck on the skylight. He fiddled with the brightness and contrast for a few minutes until he was satisfied not only with the resolution currently on screen, but with his ability to adjust it quickly to increasing light, should the meet occur with the main bay doors open. Then he uncoiled the ear buds from a small pocket on the side of the leather case for his phone and plugged the jack in, twisting one bud into his left ear. He hunkered down to wait.

Soon one of the patrolling security guards approached. Dick poised with his fingers over the controls on his phone. As he watched the guard cross the open area, he adjusted the gain on the device's microphone until he could hear the man's plodding footfalls at an acceptable level through the earbud. That way he knew he would be able to immediately hear any conversation taking place below without chancing blowing his ear-drum because the volume was set too high. Volume worries were also why he only ever inserted one ear bud when listening in electronically—you never want to risk your hearing in both ears at the same time. Besides, he wanted to keep one ear open for ambient sound about him, just in case anyone approached his surveillance nest.

It was a long, stiflingly hot wait. Dick took note of the routines of the guards as they made their rounds, but there was not much else to do for several hours, except sweat and watch the shadows on the wall lengthen as the time for sunset drew near. He twisted his wedding ring idly and thought of Melanie while he waited. Sure, a lot of years had gone by—their boy, Seth, was practically grown-up now. And there wasn't the same heat as on their honeymoon in Jamaica—all room service and lovemaking and no sun, surf, or sand. But they still held hands at the movies and would always sneak a kiss while they watched the credits after everyone else left the theater. Besides, they had plenty of happy memories to keep them warm.

When Seth was little, he went through a Magpie phase. If he saw something shiny, he would just reach and grab for it: dangly necklaces; discarded gum wrappers on the sidewalk; knick-knacks on low-lying tables; cans in the recycling bin; whatever. Still, Melanie kept Seth under control. She held his hand, she steered the cart down the center of the grocery aisles, and she always carried single-use wipes to clean-off Seth's hands when he picked up something less than sanitary.

Dick was not quite so attentive, which might not have been that much of a problem, except it was Christmastime and all around lights flashed, decorations sparkled, and tinsel glittered. He let his guard down as Seth played in the living room and Melanie finished preparations for their annual holiday party. Before he knew it, he heard a commotion and turned to see Seth pulling on a branch of the Christmas tree in an attempt to reach a shiny, silver ornament.

Even with all his training and reflexes, he couldn't move fast enough to stop what was coming. The tilting tree reached the tipping point just as he lunged for it. While he protected Seth with an instinctive forearm thrust to the tree, he succeeded only by deflecting the ungainly evergreen into Melanie as she entered with a bowl of party punch. In the flash of a moment, the tree was a jumble of broken decorations, the punch was a puddle of fruit juicy red on the beige carpeting, and Melanie was a soaking human backsplash.

Instead of getting angry, though, Melanie simply looked down at the mess and then back up at Dick and Seth, her unmistakable lopsided, one-dimple smile flashing beneath her sparkling green eyes. "I think I'm a bit punchy," she pronounced. Dick scurried for towels and volunteered to mop up the mess while Melanie changed into something drier, but she insisted on helping: "We're a team," she said. "You never have to do things solo, when you're part of a team. You never even need to ask for help."

Dick never did ask for help; he was a self-reliant guy. Most spies are. Still, he almost always wore his wedding ring on missions. It was a simple gold band without engraving or other identifying characteristics, so it didn't put his cover or his family at risk. It reminded him who he really was, why he was doing this for a living, and who, ultimately, he was protecting. It also provided a handy excuse for breaking off conversations he didn't want to have. "Gotta go meet the missus," he would mumble, then wave and wander off to attend to more important, secret business.

It was up to him to protect Melanie (and Seth), to protect the world, from anything and everything evil and dangerous. He knew it was corny, but he loved his spouse. Recently, though, he wasn't sure she could say the same thing.

Suddenly, a barked command drew him out of waiting mode. The two inside guards he had tracked during the afternoon, now joined by the crisscrossing outside guards and yesterday's rooftop lurker, made a quick, full sweep of the warehouse and took up positions at the perimeter of the open area. The main bay opened and the two door guards he noted the day before stepped in. They turned and motioned in a black Range Rover with tinted windows. It pulled well into the warehouse and parked.

A large, well-dressed, dark-skinned man got out of the driver's side (the right side here in New Zealand). After scanning the area, he opened the rear passenger door and a much shorter, wiry man alighted from the vehicle. The man in charge was wearing upscale casual-wear in light colors and a Panama-style hat, which, at first, obscured his visage from Dick's camera's viewpoint. But then the man's head tilted up to say something to the driver and the lens got a good freeze-frame: Pao Fen Smythe.

CHAPTER 4

Dick fine-tuned the gain on the microphone in the device he had stuck to the corner of the window, high above the scene of the meeting. Pao Fen snarled terse commands at his lackeys. The muscle snapped to without hesitation or complaint, producing a folding table and two chairs, which were set up in the middle of the open area. Then the guards and the driver took up positions around the perimeter of the area, two on each side, one facing out, and one facing in toward the table.

Pao Fen sat in one of the chairs, pushed well back from the table, his legs crossed at the knees, feigning nonchalance as he waited. But Dick wasn't fooled. The arms dealer was tense. Pao Fen's right leg bounced slightly and he looked at his Rolex with ever-increasing frequency.

Finally, there was a muffled shout from outside and Dick heard the murmur of a vehicle pulling up in front of the open bay. The guards tensed as showtime approached. Pao Fen took a final look at his precision chronometer and stood up languidly in place, his head swiveling slowly toward the bay door.

A man Dick did not recognize walked into the frame. A good foot taller than Pao Fen, he wore dark slacks and a loose short-sleeved shirt. His short-cropped hair was dark and he sported geometric tattoos of the style favored by the Maori tribesmen on the North Island. Apparently the two sides had chosen a mutually inconvenient location.

The Maori leader extended his right hand to Pao Fen.

Pao Fen ignored the proffered handshake. "You're late," he said, his aggravation evident even in the flat monotone of the clipped statement.

"Yes, I am," replied the stranger, his tone even, refusing to take the bait. "But now I'm here." The accent had an English cast to it, like all New Zealand variants.

Pao Fen sneered. "I don't like to be kept waiting, especially for a meeting that was quite unnecessary in the first place."

The taller man shrugged. "I like to know who I'm dealing with. Besides, there's the whole exchange part of our business. Goods must be exchanged."

Pao Fen took off his hat and turned to his left for a moment, away from his companion, as he laid the hat on the table. His left eye twitched and he reached up to smooth down his slick, black hair. "A stupid and unnecessary complication which distracts from the main transaction. Any fool can see it increases risks for trivial gain."

The eyebrows of the second man turned downward and his brow furrowed. "So does insulting one's host in his own land, especially when one has hopes of doing business." He turned as if to go. "We have other interested buyers."

Pao Fen's left eye twitched again. He ran his tongue over the front of his teeth before replying with obvious forced politeness. "I meant no offence. I wished merely to make clear no future meetings should be anticipated. All future transactions will be conducted ... at a distance ... in the manner of ... the funds transfer here."

The local turned back. "Very well. Let's get on with it."

Pao Fen snapped his fingers and one of the guards on the south end of the perimeter, the guard facing the meeting, slung his weapon and hopped into the forklift nearby. It quickly disappeared off-camera, but Dick could hear the whine as hydraulics extended the forks high above the head of the driver to retrieve a crate on one of the platforms in the upper reaches of the shelves. He thanked his lucky stars he had not set up his surveillance nest in the row where items were being retrieved.

Soon the forklift returned, a pallet holding a large crate cradled in its tines. The load was lowered to the floor between the table and the open bay door. With a curt nod from Pao Fen, another guard, this one from the west side, grabbed a crowbar and stepped forward. Pao Fen tapped his right foot and plastered a forced smile on his face as the guard opened the crate. The local man walked over and peered into the crate as packing straw was tossed out onto the floor, reaching in to shift things about to look deeper into the crate.

"It's all there," growled Pao Fen. "A Stinger surface to air launcher and enough rockets to take down six tourist-laden 757s, if you aim well and you actually believe that's going to help your cause. Mind that you pay attention to the battery maintenance for the ejection motor. It can be a problem if you don't follow procedures." He motioned at the layer of material lower in the crate. "Underneath, you have a dozen AK-47s, two cases of grenades, and a Barrett 50 caliber, the M82A1 version, with Optical Range Scope and armor-piercing and incendiary rounds. It's all fine merchandise, but why you needed us for this manner of low-level inventory, I have no idea. There's a half-dozen dealers at gun shows in the U.S. who will ship you small items like this with no questions asked. Give me a fortnight and I'll wager I could find a drug gang in Auckland or Wellington willing and able to supply such rubbish."

The man at the crate stopped poking about and looked over at Pao Fen. "Let's just say it helped establish your legitimacy. Besides, what's wrong with one-stop shopping?"

"As you wish," responded Pao Fen with a dismissive wave of his hand. "Enough of the party favors, let's get down to the raison d'être for tonight's gathering."

Finally. The Subsidiary sure as hell didn't send him almost ten thousand miles to deal with this low level static, although he suspected the threat posed by militant Maoris to jumbo passenger jets would be a surprise to the intel community when he reported it. Hell, half of the computer jockeys in intel probably thought there was nothing more dangerous than hobbits down in Kiwi-land. But, enough of that. Where were the plans for the damn Kestrel?

When Dick returned his attention to the screen, the Maori leader was looking over his new weapons. A younger Maori, carrying a laptop computer, was walking into view from outside, where the visiting vehicle had parked. Finally. Dick tensed for action as he assessed his tactical situation.

The Maori tech set the laptop computer on the table. He sat down, opening up the laptop and powering it on. The tech's fingers flowed efficiently over keyboard, but Dick couldn't make out the screen. He swore silently. Even the keyboard itself was blocked from the camera's view from this angle, so he doubted the tech guys could get much from the digital memory of his spy device.

After a few moments, the Maori computer geek swiveled the laptop screen yet farther away to face Pao Fen.

"As you can see," he said, "we are ready for the exchange."

Pao Fen gave the tech a steely stare. "You understand, we are paying for the sole copy of the plans. We are buying an exclusive. No copies, no other buyers." He turned to the Maori leader. "If we find out otherwise, there will be consequences."

The tall Maori stopped gawking at his purchases and looked up. "You have brought what we wished to acquire. We don't double deal."

Pao Fen's mouth twisted into a tight smile as his eyes returned to the laptop and scanned the screen. He nodded. "Very well. As soon as we have the plans, we shall give you the Ma . . ."

Everyone jumped as the deafening blast of a cruise ship horn drowned out all speech, all hearing, all thought. Dick grabbed the wires and flung the earbud from his left ear in an instinctive reaction. With the gain up on the camera microphone, his left ear was still ringing even after the horn blast ended; he just hoped it wasn't bleeding. His instincts were good. Another shrill blast cut through the warehouse, so forceful as to cause dust motes in the air to shimmer and throb in time to the frequency.

He forced himself to ignore the sound and concentrate on what was happening on his video screen. The guards were obviously tense. While two had their hands over the ears, letting their automatic weapons dangle on their slings, the rest were keyed up, looking for targets, their trigger fingers twitching. The Maori tech had his fingers in either ear, cartoon style. Pao Fen grimaced at the overwhelming clamor. The Maori leader's face bore an angry scowl.

The horn blasts triggered Dick's combat reflexes. The tension on the warehouse floor was rising and he instinctively knew something bad was about to happen. His mind went into tactical overdrive, preparing for the worst. Eight guards, including Pao Fen's driver, stationed in pairs on each side of the open area, plus the tall local, the young Maori tech, and Pao Fen Smythe. Eleven opponents. And him with no back-up.

Without even thinking, he assigned all of his adversaries names. Eight reindeer: Dasher (Pao Fen's driver) and Dancer to the north near the haphazardly parked Range Rover. Prancer and Vixen, the two criss-crossing guards he had seen before, by the door to the east. Scanning southeast, past the forklift and crate to the south were Comet and Cupid. Almost straight beneath him were Donder and Blitzen on the west. Even though he knew Pao Fen Smythe's name, the man in charge with all the toys automatically became Santa in his mind. The tall local was the Abominable Snowman. The Maori tech he dubbed Rudolph.

It wasn't Christmas, not for months, but the names popped unbidden into Dick's mind. All those Christmases watching *Rudolph: The Red-Nosed Reindeer* when Seth was still young, no doubt. How bizarre was that?

He cast the disturbing thoughts juxtaposing family and work aside. *Stop reminiscing and pay attention!*

"Damn tourists!" The Abominable Maori leader pounded a fist on the table just as the second blast ended, causing the laptop to bounce and turn slightly. Dick got the briefest glimpse of bright blue in the corner of the screen that bumped into view. Then a third blast buffeted the warehouse again.

The camera-view vibrated with the horn-blast, then suddenly began to zoom in rapidly on the scene below. For the briefest second, Dick stared at the remote control for the tiny spy device—the camera didn't have that kind of telephoto zoom capability. Then he realized what was happening. He dropped the remote at the same moment the camera hit the concrete floor of the warehouse. The horn blast had shaken it loose from the C4 holding it to the window.

Dick was moving to the shelf at the edge of the opening when he faintly heard someone say: "What the hell is that?" He couldn't tell who had spoken, but it didn't matter. All that mattered now was the laptop. The plans for the Kestrel 84 were on that laptop and it was up to him to retrieve it, if he could survive the coming fire fight.

Just another bad day at the office.

Time to take care of business.

He pulled a Micro Uzi submachine pistol and a couple of spare 32 round magazines he had tucked under the waistband at the small of his back, beneath the loose fitting, open Aloha shirt. He quickly edged toward the end of the shelving unit. Without bothering to look or aim, he held the machine pistol angled downward and away from his body and let off a burst of random fire down below to seed as much panic as possible. He hoped most of the combatants would comply with the implied request of his barrage and seek cover. Those who didn't protect themselves would undoubtedly stand slack-jawed in the open, looking for an adversary to shoot at. The ultimate decision on which path to take, Dick was convinced, depended on the ratio between their respective IQs and their testosterone-fueled macho bullshit aggressiveness.

Dick loved testosterone-fueled macho bullshit aggressiveness in an adversary. He snicked a new clip into position to replace the one emptied in his two-second burst, then used a shelving support to swing into full view of the space below. Most of his foes were proving their intelligence by dashing for cover, but three of the reindeer had bigger egos than brains. Prancer and Vixen, to the east, and Comet to the south, were all standing in the open, guns angled upward, scanning for something to shoot at. When they glimpsed him, they started firing, even before they had swung their automatic weapons around to target their adversary. He didn't mind. They were wasting their ammunition. Besides, the cacophony of gunshots, impact thuds, and ricochets was creating an unholy din of thunder, which would help confuse the bad guys. He knew how many opponents he faced; they had no clue. For all Santa and Rudolph knew, the entire New Zealand army was assaulting them—if New Zealand had an army. Dick wasn't sure, but he thought they had sent like three guys to Iraq.

Whatever. Despite the already deafening noise inside the warehouse, Dick was about to make things louder. Creeping forward, he sighted the forklift through a spot between a machinery crate and another shelving support and aimed for the propane tank fueling the device, then squeezed off a single round. The sound of his shot was lost in the echoes of the tumult below.

The shot pierced the tank cleanly. Pressurized gas spewed out, enveloping the forklift and its surroundings in a choking, blue haze. Prancer actually laughed when he saw the propane gas was merely escaping and that the tank had not blown up, like it would have in the movies. Vixen and Cupid were merely wrinkling their noses from the ethanethiol added to make the odorless gas smell.

46

Dick smiled. Time to find out how stupid these mugs really were.

He poked his weapon out into the open for a second, then pulled it back and threw his arms up to shield his face and head. His defensive position meant he never knew whether it was Vixen or Cupid who commenced the spray of automatic weapons fire toward his little hidey-hole. Whoever it was, flame burst from the end of his weapon as he did so, igniting the cloud of expanding propane gas, guaranteeing at least part of the herd wouldn't be joining in any more reindeer games.

The resulting explosion rocked the warehouse, sending crates and merchandise crashing down from the swaying shelving units and shattering every skylight on the east side of the building. Slivers of glass sliced down through the black smoke coursing up from the fireball. Dick could hear curses and cries of pain as the greasy black smoke began to pour through the now broken skylights into the twilight sky above.

He snatched up his camera bag and scrambled down to the concrete floor of the warehouse. Donder and Blitzen both crouched behind a pallet of dog kibble in the next row over, peering over the lumpy top toward the center of the open area. Blitzen frantically shouted for someone to tell him what to do.

Dick delivered a response via high-velocity rounds ticked off with efficiency from his machine pistol. Donder and Blitzen died like the good little foot soldiers they were: scared and clueless and stinking of blood and shit.

Ignoring the smell, Dick moved forward into his adversary's former position, a good place to hole up for a moment while he assessed the scene. Anyone who knew where Donder and Blitzen had taken cover wouldn't be firing indiscriminately toward them. At least that was the theory. Still, he had to hurry; firefighters were no doubt scrambling to put on their boots and rush here even now—and they were used to driving on the wrong side of the road.

Net Impact

A quick scan of the area revealed Prancer, Vixen, and Comet were all, as he had expected, down from the explosion. Dead or unconscious, he didn't care. He would be gone before they woke up in any event. That left Cupid to his right, Dasher and Dancer somewhere behind the black Range Rover to his left, and Santa, the Abominable Snowman, and Rudolph someplace straight ahead, probably crawling toward the cars in an effort to escape. He couldn't see them. Smoke billowed from the forklift and from packing material and cargo set ablaze on the south side of the warehouse door, where an inrushing breeze ferried oxygen to the flames.

He didn't have time to search and destroy—he only had to confuse his enemy. He ran forward into the smoke, heading east, where he hoped to find Rudolph with the laptop. As he bolted, he shouted "Don't shoot!" as loudly as possible. His ruse had the desired effect. After a brief hesitation, guns blazed into the opening toward where Dick had shouted. Dasher and Dancer blasted away on the north and Cupid followed suit on the south. It had taken a moment for the remaining reindeer to process that the voice crying out was not one of the herd, so Dick was well east of the spot they fired at by the time the team reacted. With any luck, the young bucks would shoot each other, or at least pin each other down while they traded fire. He didn't wait around to test his theory or his luck.

The air cleared as Dick sprinted toward the open bay door on the east. He saw Santa—Pao Fen Smythe—running down the alleyway to escape. He started to raise his weapon to fire, but lowered it a heartbeat later. Offing Santa would make any day a good day, based on what he knew of the scumbag, but Santa was not his primary objective. *Stay on mission.*

The engine in the dark Lexus outside purred to life, and Dick saw the Abominable Snowman jink the gearshift into drive. Again, not his objective. No passenger was visible, so he let the Abominable Snowman thunder back to his cave on the North Island.

Rudolph possessed the laptop. The laptop held the plans for the Kestrel 84. Rudolph was the one he needed to find. Too bad his freakin' nose didn't glow.

Fortunately for them both, though, Dick knew Rudolph's IQ was probably higher than the IQs of all of the remaining reindeer combined. The kid was a tech, he was smart enough to take cover in a firefight, and he was smart enough to hide. He would probably be smart enough to deal.

Dick scuttled a few yards away from the door and quickly rifled through his camera bag, pulling out the remainder of the C4 he had brought, along with a detonator. He armed the C4 with precise, rapid movements, then ran to the corner of the bay door and slid the deadly device along the concrete into the middle of the open area, where he could still see it in the clearer air near the floor. He fired two shots into the floor a few feet on either side of the block, just to focus attention on it.

"Hey, tech boy," he yelled. "That's four pounds of C4, under my control. Enough to take down this warehouse and you in it. You're smart; you know what it can do. If you're lucky, the concussion will kill you so you don't slowly burn to death when you're trapped by the falling debris."

Dick waited a few moments for a response. None came, although the shots from the north and south finally subsided.

"Smart enough not to give away your position by responding, I see. Or maybe unconscious. I'd bet on smart." He paused again, before continuing. "Slide the laptop out the door and in ten minutes I'll be too far away to detonate the explosives. Or I can destroy the laptop and you, too. Your choice. It's no nevermind to me."

Net Impact

He saw a shape moving through the smoke from the north toward the bloc of C4. He fired. His first shot was sufficient to take down the shape—Dancer, he thought—but he held down the trigger for a burst, just for effect.

"Now you've gone and made me impatient," Dick yelled. "Ten seconds." He smiled to himself, "Counting down by primes, asshole. Seven, five, three, two ..."

The laptop came skittering out of the warehouse into the alleyway with surprising force. It looked a little beat up, but he didn't care. He loosed another burst of automatic weapons fire into the doorway with his right hand while he scooped up the laptop with his left hand.

"I'll be waiting a bit to see if anyone comes after me, so just settle in. In ten minutes, I'll be out of range." He waited ten seconds and fired off another burst. "Still here."

With that, he took off at a lope, the opposite way down the alley from the direction Santa and the Abominable Snowman had gone—no need looking for more encounters. He could sneak through the wood products yard and circle back around to his bike while the authorities were sifting through the rubble, trying to figure out what happened. Speaking of which, as soon as he reached the end of the alleyway and turned the corner where he would have some cover, he reached for the detonator. He pressed the button and the C4 ignited in a white flash that lit up the sleepy twilight and reflected back from the white hull of the cruise ship, now well on her way to the mouth of the bay.

Even though he was at a relatively safe distance, he flinched and instinctively ducked down for a second at the flash of the explosion. He always scoffed when super-cool movie spies walked away from an explosion without reacting. Dick did nothing to suppress his survival instincts; he didn't care if he looked cool. Not only did ducking present a lower surface area to the blast wave propagating outward, making it less likely to knock you over, bending down also meant that any errant shrapnel flung unusually far was more likely to hit you in the ass than in the back of your head.

He'd rather put his ass on the line any day.

The secondary explosion from the Range Rover followed about thirty seconds later, occasioning another flinch. The armaments and ammo would pop off over time, holding firefighters at bay for a considerable period, no doubt. About forty-five seconds had passed since he had recovered the laptop, which, he thought, made him a liar.

A liar, but a survivor. One who left no witnesses and no clues, not if he could help it.

CHAPTER 5

Dick breathed in the smoky air with a sigh of relief as he jogged past the warehouses, along the waterfront toward the stacks of native timber in the nearby storage yard.

The heavy equipment for handling logs was parked and motionless in the timber facility. No doubt there was a guard, but he knew the guy would be preoccupied with the explosion and fire two warehouses away, either watching the timber nearest the conflagration with hose in hand, lest the fire spread, or heading for the road to direct emergency equipment when it arrived; Dick could finally hear the sing-song wail of fire engines in the distance. In either event, Dick was not worried about confrontation.

Instead, his thoughts focused forward, to his mandatory break between missions. Melanie and Seth used to rush to greet him when he got home from "business" trips. Seth would ask what he had brought him and Melanie would smile and squeeze his (hopefully shrapnel-free) ass while she gave him an enthusiastic kiss. But not anymore. Now he was met by sullen scowls and it wasn't because of his lame, touristy gifts or a sudden decline in the quality of his kisses or the firmness of his ass. Things had not been going well at home; Melanie had wearied of his chaotic schedule and frequent absences and he was increasingly a stranger to his son. Seth was more interested in computer games, action movies, and chatting with friends, than he was in construction equipment or fatherly advice on school and sports. Dick hoped to make up for lost time with both Melanie and Seth during the break—maybe a family road trip. He'd give it some thought on the long flight back.

With a sudden jolt, his reverie and the laptop he was carrying were both shattered by a high velocity round fired from somewhere in the backlit gloom behind him. He ducked into the nearest row for cover. Crap. One of the damn reindeer must have escaped. He peered back, looking through a "v" formed by two huge pieces of New Zealand Radiata Pine.

It was Dasher, Pao Fen's driver. No doubt he had taken off running through the warehouse the second Dick had hefted the C4 through the door. If Dasher was true to his name, he could have exited out a back door and circled back along the waterfront after the explosion. Dick should have been watching his six and not daydreaming about playing catch with Seth while Melanie made lemonade in her fetching yellow sun dress.

His family would be the death of him yet.

Dick pulled his Micro Uzi again, ready and willing to shoot it out with Dasher, but then caught the sound of sirens again, now much closer. Even with ammo popping off in the blaze, the police might investigate gunfire, especially if there was an extended battle. He would have, back when he was a cop. Cops had little to do during a fire, he knew, except keep the crowds at bay. Truth be told, cops mostly sat around at a fire with their thumbs up their asses while the firemen did the dangerous stuff.

He had a better idea than a running gunfight in the dark, surrounded by cops. He ran part-way down the row between stacks of logs, then scrambled up the left-hand stack. The jutting ends of the cleanly sawed-off logs made it an easy climb. In just a few seconds he reached the high edge, then used his upper body strength to slide atop as he let go of his toe-holds. He kept as low a profile as possible and surveyed his position.

This would do.

He shoved the remains of the shattered laptop into his camera bag and fished out a small, cylindrical shaped device, then waited and watched.

Dasher lurked at the corner of a line of logs one row over. In a burst of speed, the wisest, or perhaps just the swiftest, of the reindeer darted across the open space between the rows of stacked logs, then pulled up. Dick's assailant snuck along the end of the pile on which Dick laid in wait. Dick pulled the pin on the M84 stun grenade he was holding, then shoved the flashbang as deep as he could down a crevice between two ancient logs, without regard for the scrapes to his knuckles in the effort. He pulled his hand out from between the two massive trunks, then skittered away with reckless abandon along the top, away from the end where Dasher was creeping.

Counting to himself, Dick closed his eyes tight and threw his hands over his ears just before a brilliant flash of light and powerful, booming shockwave thundered from the midst of the stacked logs. The grenade produced no fragmentation, but the blast pulsed the logs up and out, eliminating the contact friction holding them in place, sending the short end of the stack rolling, unencumbered at the open end, toward the dark water of Otago Harbor. Blinded by the powerful light of the flashbang, Dasher probably never saw the rolling avalanche of native wood that tumbled toward him. All Dick heard was a muffled cry of surprise as the logs rolled down and over Dasher, trampling the last of the herd.

Dick jumped quickly off the row of logs, just in case it unraveled completely. He ran for the main road at the far end of the storage area. The thoroughfare was clogged with emergency vehicles, some still arriving, some parked haphazardly across the right-of-way. Fortunately, all eyes were on the fiery conflagration engulfing the warehouse and he was able to exit the cargo yards without difficulty or interrogation.

In ten minutes, he was at his bike. He recovered the bullet-ridden laptop from his camera bag, dumping the armaments and most of the other gear the bag had been carrying into the bike's storage bin. Snagging a large Zip-Loc from the miscellaneous gear, he dropped the computer in, zipped it closed, and tucked the Zip-Loc in his camera bag. He shouldered the camera bag and mounted the bike, starting up the motor and twisting the throttle. The vibrations confirmed the motorcycle was running in good order, even though revving the powerful engine created little sound above the explosion-punctuated roar of the nearby fire.

Dick headed off, cutting around side streets to avoid the thick of equipment in the immediate vicinity, then threading his way through stopped and blocked traffic. In just a few minutes he was screaming down the main road as additional emergency equipment screamed back at him as it rushed toward the scene of what had by now become a massive conflagration at the cargo and timber port. This was the easy part. In two hours he would be on the road headed toward Christchurch. In fifteen hours, he would be just another tourist winging his way back to the states from a vacation in New Zealand with a few souvenirs.

Of course, life wasn't easy. Not at work. Not at home. Certainly not when fleeing full-out on the wrong side of the fucking road from what was sure to be reported as a major terrorist incident with stolen goods and enough explosives and ammo to topple Grenada or Nevis or one of those other bullshit island nations that didn't count for squat except during the opening ceremonies at the summer Olympics.

The line of stopped vehicles tipped him off more than a klick before the actual blockade. He rumbled the bike onto the shoulder, as if to move up the line, then halted to survey the situation. Kiwi cops were interviewing drivers and searching vehicles up ahead and they seemed to be taking their time and doing it carefully. Worse yet, a squad car was moving down the lane of stopped vehicles at a slow, but even, pace. No doubt one function of the approaching policemen was to inform drivers what was going on and solicit their cooperation. The other function, though—the real function Dick knew from his years on the force—was to keep an eye out for someone, someone like him, who would rabbit rather than face the scrutiny of a security point.

Dick hated to be predictable, but he really had no choice. He was hemmed in on this stretch of road, with no real alternate route. The more he dithered, the more the distance between him and the cop shrank. He turned the bike back into the roadway, making an effort to avoid being spotted by cutting between a panel truck and an empty van used for hauling tourists to sheep shearing demonstrations. He got into the unclogged lane heading the other direction and kicked the bike up a gear, moving away from the blockade and the police car at a deliberate, but unpanicked pace, his eyes glued to his rear view as he started to slowly add on speed.

Then he saw the mars lights of the police cruiser flick on—it was K-Mart blue light special time in Kiwi-land—and he geared up again, twisting the throttle savagely to redline the engine and gear up yet again. The police cruiser lurched forward to follow.

He didn't have much time. Things were congested back at the port and every moment was another moment the police could be on the radio calling in back-up, broadcasting his position, his description. For all he knew, they could be calling in choppers. And there was no way he was going to get into a firefight with the cops. Sure, he'd killed innocent people before and he would do it again. It was one of the prices paid for keeping the world safe from the really bad guys. But he had been a cop. Once a cop, always a cop. He wouldn't engage the police, not if there was any other way.

He slammed down the road—he was actually catching up to a fire engine racing ahead in the distance, but he paid that scant attention. Every moment was spent looking right, toward the bay. Finally, he saw what he needed.

A bevy of watercraft had congregated not far off shore, the passengers ogling the explosions in the warehouse district to the east like fireworks on Venetian night back when Dick lived in Chicago. A long, unobstructed pier poked out from the shore, ending about twenty meters from a guy who was resting on the handlebars of his idling SkiDoo as he watched the fiery show. Dick gunned the motor of the Yamaha, straining it yet further and jinked the bike to the right, onto the entrance for a parking area near the pier. The rear end of the performance bike slid out from under him as he took the sharp turn without losing speed, but Dick muscled the powerful ride back into position. He aimed for the pier, popping a wheelie and standing up as the motorcycle came to a short curb separating the parking area from the sidewalk leading to the pier.

The police vehicle in pursuit was surprisingly muscular for such an eco-friendly little country. Its tires squealed in protest as the cop driving braked for the turn-in, but Dick was rapidly losing interest in the police pursuit. His entire attention, his entire focus was riveted on the rapidly approaching end of the pier and the idling SkiDoo. He cranked the throttle tight to the maximum and rocketed off the end of the pier.

Before the bike even began its arcing descent toward the salty water of the bay, he made his move. He launched himself off the bike, causing it to veer awkwardly to the left in recoil as he jumped to the right, aiming for the SkiDoo and doing a half-somersault to bring his legs forward. The well-muscled Kiwi hunk who had been enjoying the pyrotechnics was still reacting, his eyes following the flashiness of the revving, shiny bike as it leapt for the water, when both of Dick's feet caught him square in the chest. The hunk was propelled off the side of the surfrider, his arms flinging themselves across his six-pack in instinctual reaction to the blow, when Dick slammed into the seat of the already running vehicle. Dick reached for the controls with one hand, maxing out the throttle, causing the rocking SkiDoo to surge forward away from the flummoxed, soaking rider and into the spray caused as the bike splashed down into the bay.

As he grappled for control of his escape craft with his right hand, Dick reached into his left pocket and fingered a small electronic gewgaw, triggering the self-destruct device contained in his bag of tricks, still in the back compartment of the now submerged and rapidly sinking bike. The charge did its work, exploding with a white hot whoomph. The special mixture of phosphorous and explosive compounds of the self-destruct not only destroyed the gear, but ignited the remaining explosives. An expanding white ball of annihilation rose from the depths of the bay and burst forth, showering Dick, the bewildered boating onlookers, and the hood of the police cruiser screeching to a halt at the end of the pier.

Glancing back, he could see the local cop calling for back-up, but Dick didn't worry. Most of the local constabulary was undoubtedly on scene at the warehouse fire. They would be hard-pressed to bring any resources to bear where Dick was headed: the southern coast of Otago Harbor.

Unlike the bigger coastal towns in Australia and New Zealand, Dunedin didn't have a pricey, spectacular bridge connecting the headlands of the bay at a height sufficient to allow seagoing vessels to cruise unhindered beneath. To get from one side of the bay to the other, it was either take a boat, or drive pell-mell for forty-five minutes down one side of the bay, through the center city, and back up the other side of the massive body of water.

The police in the cruiser could commandeer a boat to follow him, but by the time that happened, he would be more than half-way across the bay. A concerned boating citizen could initiate his own pursuit, but Dick smiled at the possibility. Would you go after someone who had just launched their motorcycle into the bay to steal a surfrider, then blew up the evidence by remote control? Sure the authorities had radios and manpower, but he bet both were currently focused on the conflagration still brightly blazing to the northeast. Besides, those limited resources would only be effective if he was hemmed in someplace back on the northern coast; here the cops had no idea where Dick was going to land on the long and desolate southern coast.

He never even knew if they tried to catch him. In a surprisingly short time he was back on dry land and making good speed in a boosted BMW away from the Otago Peninsula, away from Port Chalmers, away from his mission—moving toward his real life. A change of clothes, vehicle, and cover ID, and Dick was soon winging his way across the empty Pacific Ocean, alone with his thoughts. He didn't even have the vital laptop within reach anymore.

He'd been forced to put the trashed laptop in his checked luggage; there was no way to get a laptop with an obvious bullet hole past security without raising suspicion. He knew HQ would be pissed if it got lost, but lost luggage is generally held for at least a year before being auctioned off—it would be as good a storage place as any in the meantime. He could go back and find it if he had to. Besides, he had upgraded to first class for the long flight home. First class baggage might be pilfered, but it was rarely lost. The airlines knew better than to screw over people who could afford to hire lawyers.

Dick had picked up a few cuts, scrapes, and bruises from his encounters at the warehouse and the log storage yard. He spent part of his long trip home figuring out what lies to tell his family about how he had gotten them. It was a damn crappy job that made you lie to your family, even crappier than his cover job at Catalyst Crisis Consulting as a technical specialist for wastewater treatment facilities.

He leaned back and closed his eyes. With the international dateline, he would actually arrive back in the states about the same time he had left New Zealand. Good thing he wasn't paid by the hour.

Net Impact

As always on long flights, he turned his thoughts to Melanie and to better, happier times: Melanie in her bridal-shower-gift lingerie; Melanie giggling as they made up silly songs one time in the middle of the night; Melanie cradling Seth after seventeen hours in labor. Melanie.

Maybe his happy memories were clichés, but that didn't make them any less real to him. That didn't lessen how they made him feel, how they got him through the bad days. He was just a regular guy; he wasn't a poet. He was a spy.

And even though he was a spy, Dick loved his wife. Imagine that. Dick smiled as he imagined just that.

Then sleep caught up with him and the scene faded to black.

CHAPTER 6

Dee Tammany bounced on the balls of her feet, then jumped lightly back and to the right, then left, fists up, the soft waves of her brunette hair flouncing in time to her footwork. She looked for an opening, but found none. Her opponent, six foot four if he was an inch, grinned as he looked down at her. Like her, he was moving on the balls of his feet, but without bouncing—just slow easy steps to keep his torso square to her shifting position. His fists were also up, but in a relaxed, easy way. He clearly knew he had the upper hand. Dee shifted again, as she took in his chiseled body, the incredibly broad shoulders and heavily muscled arms forming the wide section of a triangle that narrowed down, moving past a heart-shaped tattoo reading "Mother" above his left breast, to a narrow waist beneath six-pack abs.

God, she loved the look of younger men.

He used her distraction to his advantage, choosing the moment her eyes had flicked down to his waist to rush in to her right side, her weak side as a southpaw. He attempted to grab her right arm at the elbow, no doubt to pull it forward and twist her around so he could get a choke-hold on her from behind with his massive left arm. She dropped her right shoulder as he moved in and spun, throwing out her left leg to try and catch him behind the knee as she escaped, but he sidestepped the move without even looking at her leg. His dead, brown eyes fixed always on her center of mass.

Damn it, she thought, as she bounced back again, squaring up their now-reversed positions, if I hadn't chosen a sports bra this morning, I might be distracting him instead of vice versa—even though I'm old enough to be ... his older sister. Too much work and not enough play was having an effect on her—and she knew better than to play at work.

"You're not focusing, Dee," he said as he began to circle slowly, always to her weak side, with silent, ballet-like moves. "Is your mind

61

on something else?" His dark eyes remained steady on her, giving nothing away.

Admitting she'd been admiring his physique was not an option, not even with Marco, her live-in security guard/driver/sparring partner. It wasn't professional. More important, it wasn't smart. So, she lied. It came easily. Even before she became a spy, long before she became Director of the Subsidiary, the most secret of all the secret espionage agencies in the world, she had gotten a double major in communications and psychology. She not only knew how to lie with easy assurance, she knew how to make it convincing to the recipient of the lie at a deep psychological level. "It's the 'Mother' tattoo," she taunted. "You don't seem like a mama's boy. It's so incongruous, it's distracting. Is that why you got it?"

Despite his Mediterranean complexion, Marco flushed red from the scalp beneath his close-cropped black hair, past the gunslinger moustache, and across his chest, accentuating the heart-shaped frame of his tattooed tribute to motherhood. His dancer's steps faltered for just a half-second. "I told you before, I was drunk ..."

Dee flicked her right wrist to the side as a feint as she leapt toward him, feet first, low and to the left, attempting to get both her legs in the narrow gap between his as she dropped. She succeeded and swept left with her left leg, trying once again to catch him behind the knee as she simultaneously crooked her right leg, purposefully over-balancing her fall to force her knee up into his groin. She knew he would countermove, but he had a Hobson's choice: keep his footing and endure the knee to the crotch or fling his left leg back to avoid the assault on his manhood and spin to the floor as his pivot leg collapsed mid-spin.

Instead he surprised her by throwing both legs straight back and springing ever so slightly forward, so her left leg caught his rock-hard calf and her right knee sailed cleanly under his now-levitated body.

For an instant, her opponent seemed to hang in mid-air above her, parallel to the floor, before gravity's relentless attraction pulled them both crashing to Earth. The training mat cushioned the assault to her backside as she hit, but Marco's body whoomphed down on the top half of her body a split second later. "Mother" descended straight into her at eye level and Marco's abs and hips crushed down on her torso, forcing the air from her lungs, even as he attempted to catch and cushion his fall by forcing his arms into the mat.

As Marco rolled lithely off her to her left, Dee curled her knees up and rolled to her right side, her ribs heaving. She winced and tried desperately to catch her breath. As her vision cleared from the pain, she saw her live-in assistant, Mitzi, standing in the doorway to the exercise room. Mitzi had some papers tucked under her left arm, and was holding the usual morning breakfast tray: a pot of coffee, a small glass of orange juice, a bowl of hot Kashi, and assorted fruit.

"If you were Angelina Jolie, or even Katherine Heigl, I could have sold a picture of that to the Enquirer for one, maybe two, million. How come no one ever invites me to the play room for fun?" Mitzi was young, mischievous, and Dee's only connection to the "real" world in which people who weren't professional spies lived.

Marco remained silent, standing quickly and striding to the far wall of the room. He draped a towel across his shoulders as Dee uncurled and elbowed her way to a sitting position.

"Katherine who?" asked Dee, still sitting on the floor.

Mitzi rolled her eyes and set the tray down on the table on the windowed side of the exercise room. *"Grey's Anatomy?"*

Dee shook her head as she got up and headed to the table for breakfast. "Psychology major, not psychiatry. Never had to take those med-school courses."

Mitzi rolled her eyes again and shook her head. "You need to get out more."

Net Impact

Marco sauntered over, his eyes flicking over the tray, his right hand reaching out to snag a piece of fruit. Mitzi slapped it away, with a wink. "And you need to get out. Boss lady's got work to do." She took the sheaf of papers from under her left arm, unfolded them and dropped them onto the table next to Dee's Kashi. "Stuff's happening in the world."

Dee furrowed her brow, snapping into business-mode. She sat down and ate mechanically as she concentrated on the papers. "Anything big?" she asked, flipping through the captions on the various sheets.

Mitzi shrugged her shoulders as she started to leave the room, close behind Marco. "I didn't see anything about the upcoming fall television shows, so I didn't bother to look."

Dee didn't smile and didn't look up. Time to go to work.

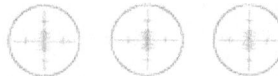

Less than an hour later, Dee had finished both her morning briefing paper and her breakfast, had showered and dressed, and had been driven by Marco to her office at Catalyst Crisis Consulting, LLC—the management consulting company which provided an extensive menu of analytical and security services to companies, governments, and wealthy individuals around the world, but also provided cover for the activities and facilities of the Subsidiary. Glenn Swynton, the Subsidiary's operations liaison, was already at HQ when Dee arrived.

Glenn was always at HQ from what Dee could tell and he always was impeccably groomed. Today Glenn wore a tailored charcoal suit which looked like it might have sprung out of the display window of one of the fashionable bespoke boutiques on Savile Row in London. Dee had no idea how Glenn did it—she would bet the contingency budget he couldn't get a suit like that made in Philadelphia. Maybe he had measurements on file and a kick-ass professional shopper on retainer across the pond. Dee might have asked, but Glenn also always had an aristocratic edge to his cool, English accent that did not encourage banter or friendship. Dee had long-ago accepted that their relationship would always be professional and practical, much like Glenn, himself. Cordial enough to prevent friction, but never warm and, God-forbid, never casual.

"Have you seen the Dunedin footage?" said Glenn by way of greeting.

"I read the briefing synopsis on the way in," replied Dee as she made her way past Glenn to her desk. "I haven't seen pictures."

Glenn thumbed a remote and a flat-screen panel flared to life across from Dee's desk. The high-definition, plasma screen displayed with vivid clarity the red and yellow and orange and black of a huge conflagration engulfing the warehouse district and adjoining lumber and cargo container yards of the harbor at Port Chalmers, near Dunedin. Although the sound was turned off, the picture jiggled visibly as a series of burning tractor-trailers in the cargo container yard exploded, sending metal flying in all directions.

Glenn folded his arms without mussing his double-knotted, one-of-a-kind silk tie. "Damn American operatives. Once, just once, I'd like to see one of them handle a warehouse surveillance without blowing the bloody thing up."

Dee ignored the dig. Glenn Swynton could be a haughty bastard and a tough son-of-a-bitch, all at the same time. That's why he was responsible for interfacing with operatives and, on occasion, extricating them from whatever trouble they got into with the various agencies and governments of the mundane world. The agents needed someone to run interference for them with the authorities, whether legitimate or clandestine. They also often needed a fierce chewing-out and a firm hand. Glenn provided whatever was needed without flinching. But, when he wanted, Glenn could also be the most diplomatic liason Dee had ever met. That's why he also had the task of coordinating meetings, both with other espionage and law enforcement agencies and with the various national representatives who had established the Subsidiary after 9/11.

If Glenn was being this blunt, he was obviously trying to goad Dee into some kind of response. No sale.

"When was this taken?" asked Dee, inclining her head to indicate the screen.

Glenn sniffed. "The feed is real time, of course. The initial explosion and resulting fire began almost thirty-six hours ago. The local fire brigade had insufficient resources to bring the blaze under control before it spread to the entire port facility. Beside the immediate losses to merchandise, goods in transit, and lumber exports, the damages to the port facilities themselves—cargo cranes, warehousing facilities, refueling stations, and the like—will take years and millions of dollars to rectify. The New Zealand government is absolutely bonkers over it and for good reason. Truth told, every contact we have in the South Pacific is asking questions and not waiting for a response before they draw their own conclusions."

While Dee was not indifferent to the collateral damage the Subsidiary's missions sometimes produced, she also knew more than anyone the loss of life, property, and stability the Subsidiary had prevented during her tenure. Even with this setback, the agency was well into the plus column. She refused to take Glenn's bait.

"What did Thornby say when he got back?"

Glenn's eyes narrowed. "He said 'Mission accomplished, I think,' then dropped a bullet-riddled, non-functional laptop on the table for the computer techs to try to put back together again. Then he headed home for his mandatory rest period between assignments."

Dee frowned. "That's it?"

Glenn's mouth pursed, giving him the kind of severe look male models had when they strutted down the runway showcasing the types of haute culture clothing he wore everyday. "He said everything else was in his remote report after the warehouse meet. Apparently some Maori terrorists, if you can imagine such a thing, were trading the plans for the Kestrel 84 for cash, small arms, and weaponry which would allow them to shoot down wide-bodied passenger jets. No new detail as to how they got the plans in the first place. The hope is that the only copy is on the recovered laptop." Glenn tilted his head toward the tech bullpen, arching an eyebrow. "Luke Calloway, that tall, Aussie tech in the computer department, has the laptop now. Luke said it may take awhile to reconstruct the laptop's databases, if it can even be done. If the plans are not there or if the Maoris were smart enough to back up the files elsewhere, we will have destroyed the economy of Dunedin for the foreseeable future for no benefit whatsoever."

Dee sat in her ergonomic chair, then looked up to fix Glenn with a dismissive stare. "I doubt passengers jetting into New Zealand would see no benefit to our agent's activities, if they ever knew what the armed faction of militant Maoris intended."

"These nativist cabals are all talk, no action, I'm sure," replied Glenn coolly as he flicked off the video display and turned to exit, his perfectly coiffed brown hair remaining somehow motionless both during the spin and as he finished the abrupt turn.

Dee said nothing, but she hummed *Hail, Britannia* to herself with a wry smile as she set about her morning tasks.

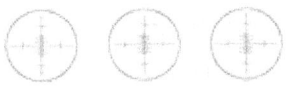

Net Impact

Pao Fen Smythe paced back and forth in front of the huge, mahogany desk in his Hong Kong offices, his teeth clenched, his eyes twitching as they darted from side to side. Even in his own high level of agitation, he was self-perceptive enough to know his body showed—and all of his subordinates knew—he was seething in irritation.

Why? Only a select few in his organization knew what had transpired in New Zealand. Fewer still actually understood exactly what is was about his Kiwi misadventures that had put him in such a foul state. His irritation was not fueled by the personal danger he had faced, nor by the minor scrapes and bruises he had suffered in making his escape from the botched exchange with the Maori PPIPF thugs who were playing IRA wannabes. His anger was not focused on the minor loss of inventory destroyed in the warehouse fire. Nor could his aggravation be blamed on the loss of any significant sum of money; the exchange of funds had never occurred. No, Pao Fen was only truly upset because of the lost opportunity to get his hands on the Kestrel 84 specs.

When the exchange had been interrupted—no doubt because of shoddy communications security on the part of the Maoris—Pao Fen had missed a chance to snag a piece of information that would set him apart from his competition. The Kestrel 84 specs could be sold for a tidy sum, more than the Maori realized. Moreover, the specs could be sold again and again and again, to governments and insurgents across the globe.

No doubt the buyers would use the device to gather information that would allow them to do terrible, unspeakable things: bombings, kidnappings, terrorism. No doubt some of their targets would be innocents: religious adherents, civilians, children. Pao Fen couldn't care less. The deal was his only concern. How could it be resurrected?

His Maori contacts were all either dead or laying low, so there was no progress to be made there in re-initiating the buy. But, Pao Fen knew, New Zealand was not the only place he could look. In fact, his best cyber-technicians had been on the case since the night of the warehouse debacle. No one had reported any progress, however. In fact, no one had reported in on the electronic search at all. He knew it was probably because no one liked to give him unpleasant information. It's not that he ever shot the messenger—well, not since he was a low level thug for one of the Nine Families of the Triad. But he did have a tendency to swear like a sailor in Mandarin.

He'd have to work on that. Even executives in criminal organizations needed to hone their management skills. And management skills for an arms merchant were largely people management skills. His organization sold everything from AK-47s to purloined plans to black market Exocet MM40 missiles purchased from third world generals who wanted to buy retirement chalets in the Swiss lake country. Procurement, illicit transportation, inventory, security, and sales were all people-intensive activities.

He'd try to be pleasant to the cyber-tracking supervisor, no matter how unpleasant the news. After all, the tech workers were some of the most difficult to recruit into an old-style organized crime organization like the Triad. Mundane hackers were easy, but the more sophisticated and proficient the skill set, the more likely the individual could make more money at considerably less physical and monetary risk working for Baidu or HiPiHi or some tech start-up offering stock options that could quintuple or more in an initial public offering—a financial liquidity event most criminal organizations could not duplicate.

He strode to his desk and picked up the phone from the opposite side, punching in a number with fierce stabs of his index finger. There was no need to be pleasant until the underling actually arrived.

"Please come by my office as soon as convenient," he cooed with distaste. "I would like to get an update on your search." He paused for a short reply. "That would be most appreciated."

He walked around his desk and forced himself to sit down, leaning back and interlacing his fingers behind his head in an effort to relax. He still remembered his martial arts training as a child and called upon it to calm himself, slowing his breathing and relaxing his muscles one-by-one as he waited for the underling to arrive.

The supervisor, a wiry, middle-aged man who was very precise in his movements, entered his office about ten minutes later. The underling bowed and then approached Pao Fen's desk, waiting until Pao Fen motioned to sit in one of the stuffed-leather and lacquered-wood chairs on the opposite side of the desk.

Pao Fen wanted to bark "Report!" but he stifled the urge. "It is pleasant to talk with you again, Ki Wan Shen. Have you had any success in locating the plans for the Kestrel 84 or the individual holding them?"

Ki Wan Shen's cheek twitched, but the man did not flinch as Pao Fen had thought he might. The wiry supervisor hesitated a moment, however, before shaking his head. "We have been unable to locate the item sought in our searches thus far. We may need to employ resources elsewhere."

"Please do whatever is needful," replied Pao Fen, doing his best to keep any edge out of the command. "What about the individual who last held the plans?"

"It is most perplexing." Ki Wan Shen leaned forward in the chair. "We have searched the area in which he was last known to be located most thoroughly and have been unable to track him."

"Given the ... unraveling ... of his support structure, shouldn't he be somewhere nearby?" One trick Pao Fen had learned long ago for dealing with computer techs was to always use euphemisms. Words like "elimination," "demise," and "destruction" tended to make them uncomfortable. And an uncomfortable employee is an employee with an up-to-date résumé circulating both here in Hong Kong and possibly even in Silicon Valley, if they had hopes of an H-1B visa.

Ki Wan Shen frowned. "Certainly, individuals do not disappear or travel large distances without ... support. Perhaps he had unknown allies or ... others ... who may have spirited him away." The supervisor stopped, then bit his lower lip.

Pao Fen could tell the man wanted to say more. "Please continue, supervisor." If the man refused, Pao Fen was unsure he would be able to stop himself from pistol-whipping the information out of him. Instead, he gave a broad smile, doing his utmost to ooze sincerity.

"If you or our ... associates in the field ... could identify the party who disrupted the physical exchange in Dunedin, that information might aid our search. As it is, we have cast a very wide net attempting to locate those involved in suspicious trading activities."

Pao Fen's eyebrows shot up. "That is a wide net, indeed. Does it not strain our searching resources?"

The supervisor relaxed back into the chair. "We have managed to attach ourselves unseen to certain government searches of a similar nature."

"Then I'm sure you will be successful. Soon." replied Pao Fen with a head nod of dismissal. He hadn't really meant the last word to come out as a separate sentence, with the threat implicit in such narrative structure, but the old ways died hard.

When Ki Wan Shen had left, Pao Fen no longer felt compelled to look pleasant. His face once again felt tight, his furrowed brow rigid. He knew that when alone or dealing with functionaries who required intimidation instead of coddling, a stern scowl was his countenance of default. He picked up the phone again, stabbing as before with his finger, this time dialing a different number.

"Come here, Mr. Lee" he commanded without bothering to exchange pleasantries. "I need you to find someone and something for me." He hung up without waiting for a response.

Hawk pinged the squad members individually, each on their own separate, pre-arranged emergency frequencies. For good measure, he mixed in identical calls to another dozen or so random frequencies, just in case anyone was listening. Despite the relatively low value of the information that could be gleaned from his call, he didn't want to take any chances. After all, something had already gone wrong and in a big way. That meant infiltration of either his organization or the rebels' organization, a leak, or damnably sophisticated electronic surveillance of the entire realm of operations.

None of that could be good.

Accordingly, despite his other precautions, he was also careful and quick with his message: "Do not respond. Do not respond. Rendezvous Theta Six."

As soon as Hawk finished sending the messages, he turned off his com unit, then destroyed it. He dumped the remains and took off again at top speed, implementing a string of evasive maneuvers just to be sure.

The thing was, he couldn't be sure, not anymore.

He headed for a remote destination where he had stashed a spare com unit and some other gear against future need. That future had come and it didn't look good.

Hawk wished there was someone outside the squad he could talk to, but he was alone. Even when surrounded by others, he'd always felt alone.

Bad times foster self-reliance and build character—that's what a counselor had once said. Given how much his life sucked lately, he must have one hell of a lot of character.

He continued on. He didn't know what else to do.

CHAPTER 7

Even though he had slept most of the way on his return from half-way across the world, Dick was weary as he sped along the New Jersey Turnpike toward home. It hadn't always been this way. Back when he played football in college, he was charged up and, let's face it, horny after a tough game on Saturday. He would party hard, go parking down at the quarry with Melanie (before they got married—before they had to get married), and still show up for his shift at Chicken Unlimited on Sunday mid-morning with energy to spare. Same thing in the Army—not that he saw much real action in his eight years there. Storming the beaches on Caribbean islands to evacuate some med students or take some petty dictator into custody didn't really get the adrenaline pumping that much. He missed out on the first Gulf War though no fault of his own, except unfortunate timing of a career change, so he actually saw more action as a Chicago cop than he had in his Army days. But even after chasing gangbangers down alleyways and skulking through the dangerous hallways of public housing complexes, late into third shift, he had always felt pumped up and raring to go for more.

Now it seemed like he was weary even before the mission started. It wasn't the work. He'd made a good career choice when the Subsidiary recruited him. The benefits and pay were better, much better, than he had gotten in the Army or the C.P.D. and he didn't need to deal with all the extraneous crap that determined whether a government worker would ever see a raise or a bonus, no matter how much it was merited. He didn't have to worry about departmental budgets and politics and tax levies. Better yet, he never had to answer loaded questions from naive "investigative" reporters looking for a ratings boost, no matter who it hurt. Dick also liked to work on important stuff and nobody did more of that from what he had a need to know than the Subsidiary, and he was sure he couldn't even see the

74

half of it. The freedom of action to do what he felt best, whatever the consequences, the relative lack of bureaucracy, and the nifty tech gizmos were just extra toppings on the pizza.

Maybe it was just that he was getting older. He had a kid in college—okay, junior college—himself for Chrissake. Cell phone batteries weren't the only things that wore down both from time and overuse. But, deep in his heart, he knew his weariness was inversely proportional to his distance from home, increasing or decreasing depending on which direction he was heading.

Nothing dramatic had happened to hurt his home life. Neither he nor Melanie had been unfaithful, he was sure. Her one-dimple smile was for him alone. But time and his increasing and increasingly lengthy absences had taken their toll. Dick was less and less a part of the team.

None of his jobs had been especially family friendly. None were conducive to attending the long line of Kodak moments fathers were supposed to have with their sons—the soccer games, the family camping trips, the vacations to sunny amusement parks, the photo sessions before the prom. He'd missed most of those moments. And, as Seth had become older and more rebellious in his teen years, Dick had been busy. Protecting a Canadian oil pipeline from eco-terrorists, thwarting the assassination of the German Chancellor during a diplomatic visit, and preventing neurotoxins from being dumped into the Glasgow water supply, those were important moments, too—not that he could tell any of that to Seth or Melanie.

The Subsidiary was very specific about what he could and couldn't say about his job to anyone, including his family. At his pay grade—at all pay grades for all he knew—that meant he couldn't say a thing. Melanie and Seth believed Dick was a consultant at Catalyst Crisis Consulting, LLC, providing technical advice regarding the operations of large-scale wastewater treatment projects. The cover was very useful in explaining sudden international travel, a modicum of discretion in discussing business in polite company, an intermittent work schedule that was far from nine-to-five, and a healthy pay-check. On the other hand, missing Seth's science fair awards because he was trying to prevent leaking sewerage at an aging cow-shit processing facility in north Texas didn't carry the same weight as the truth, that he was part of a black ops team sabotaging centrifuge facilities in Iran so its nuclear weapons capability would be delayed.

Of course, his family could never know that. It wasn't their fault. And it made his life harder—lying to his family.

As Dick finished the drive, exiting the turnpike and making his way past the driveways and shade trees of their upper middle class subdivision in New Jersey, he decided it was up to him to buck up, to try harder, to make things work, despite the challenges. He needed to reconnect with Seth and he longed to put a smile back on Melanie's lovely face and make her worry-lines disappear. It was mid-morning when he arrived back home. The day was warm and sunny and wonderful in every way.

He would start today.

Dick parked in the driveway, popped the trunk to grab his travel bags, and walked with a deliberately jaunty step toward the front door. The porch light was on despite the time the day. Although Melanie always left it on at night when he was out of town or Seth was out with friends, to make sure they wouldn't stumble if they came home in the dark, she was too eco-conscious to let it burn in the daytime—he had never gotten around to putting it on a light sensor like he had promised. She would have undoubtedly put in the sensor herself, if Dick hadn't stripped the screws on the cover when he had installed the compact fluorescent bulbs last year with his power screwdriver. He could picture the bemused expression on her face as he had grumbled about the chore.

"The new bulbs use sixty percent less energy," she had chided, her green eyes twinkling beneath her stylish, yet practical, brunette hair. "We're saving the planet in our own little way. You shouldn't be grouchy about saving the world, even if it is a little inconvenient at times."

If she only knew.

Still, it was odd that the lights were still on. Maybe she'd slept in or just forgot. Maybe it was a reminder to him to put in the damn sensor so it would turn itself off during the daytime.

He went inside. The house was still, the curtains closed against the late summer heat. "Dad's home," he called out, but got no response. He dropped his bags and wandered to the kitchen, opening the side door to the garage. Melanie's Subaru was gone, as was Seth's scooter.

Dick had surprised Seth with the scooter on his seventeenth birthday—one of Dick's few parenting highlights since he had joined the Subsidiary. Seth loved that scooter and genuinely had loved Dick for giving it to him. Dick knew it gave the kid a range, a feeling of freedom, and a level of both coolness and responsibility that a bike no longer could at his age. Melanie, he knew from her squint-eyed expression, had not really approved, but she supported his decision.

They were a team; at least they had been then. He was going to rekindle that old team spirit. He wondered for a few wistful moments if she still had her old outfit from the Pompom Squad.

But then his training kicked in and the mood was lost as more observations trickled into his conscious mind unbidden. Dick took in the staleness of the air and the silence of the house.

Nobody home. Not for some time.

His forced enthusiasm leaked out, leaving a blue cloud over his mood that rivaled the blue cloud of propane before the warehouse explosion less than two days before. He held his emotions in check. There was no reason to be angry. His family didn't know he was coming home this morning. And, even if they did, they didn't know he wanted them to be there, that he had resolved to make this mandatory down-time between missions a turning point in his declining familial relationships.

He headed for the master bedroom upstairs. A shower and a shave would do him good, would perk him right back up. Maybe he could look into some possible family vacation itineraries before Melanie and Seth got back from their respective outings.

He saw the envelope on his pillow, the lavender rectangle standing out from the forest green print of the comforter and pillow covers. In Melanie's hand, it simply said "Richard" on the outside.

Richard. That couldn't be good.

As his weariness seized him again and a tightness gripped his throat, he opened the envelope and pulled out the note.

"Dick," it read, "I can't just keep waiting around, waiting for happiness to return to my life, especially since it no longer returns when you do. We used to have fun, we used to be a team, at least when you were home. Lately, it just feels empty. I deserve more. I need to find my own happiness, my own life. I told Seth I was visiting my mother in Montpelier, but I'm not. I'll call every evening until you're back and we decide together what to tell him. Please let him enjoy the end of his summer break and don't burden him by talking to him about us before we connect and make some decisions. Your frequent absences are burden enough already. Be safe. Melanie."

Crap. He sat down hard on the bed, letting the lavender notepaper flutter downward, sinking like his mood, until it hit the floor. His mind was numb and blank. He had no tactical or strategic response to the assault he had just suffered. After ten minutes, he got up, shuffled to the stairs and down, pushed around bottles in the liquor cabinet until he found the bottle of Glenfiddich the guys on the police force had given him at his going away party. He grabbed it up, using two fingers to snag a tumbler with the same hand, and made his way back up to the bedroom. The single malt had a smoky flavor that reminded him of the lumber yard as he escaped the warehouse fire in Dunedin. He began his mandatory rest period by downing enough of the scotch his memories were wrested from him and he passed out.

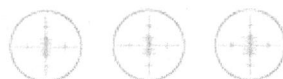

Dick woke to see Seth standing over him, the teen's softly-stubbled face set and hard beneath his tousled, sandy hair. He wore a green T-shirt Dick knew to be Seth's favorite, depicting a vaguely Oriental scene overlaid with the words "Free Tibet Now!"

"Mom's not in Montpelier at Grandma's, is she?"

The taste of stale liquor coated Dick's tongue. He was still groggy from his binge, but a pounding headache was cutting through the haze. "What? Huh? Yeah, I mean, no, sure she is. Your mom's visiting Grandma." He struggled to push himself up to a sitting position with his elbows.

Then Dick saw it, a lavender blur in Seth's hand. The lavender fluttered to the rumpled bedspread. "I know you're lying. I always know when you're lying. Why do you always have to lie? Why can't you just trust me with the truth?" Seth spun toward the door and stalked away, the sudden motion across Dick's foggy field of vision making Dick lightheaded and nauseous. At the door, Seth hesitated for just a moment, then turned back. "I take that back," he said, and for a brief moment relief cleared Dick's lightheadedness. "You don't always lie. Most of the time you're not here to lie. You can't even be bothered to lie. You just leave without saying anything." Seth left the room before Dick could respond, before he could even get his mind in gear. A moment later, Dick heard the boy thumping down the stairs.

Net Impact

Dick stifled the urge to vomit and bolted up, ignoring the sharp pain that shot down his spine as it throbbed in his right temple. He flung himself toward the stairs, yelling after Seth, before he could get to the front door and leave Dick truly alone. "Wait, Seth, wait! Your mother and I, we just have to talk, that's all. It'll be all right, I promise." He got to the staircase just in time to see Seth reach for the knob and open it, the summer sun backlighting Seth into a dark blur in Dick's eyes.

As Dick squinted to make out any detail, the dark blob turned toward him. "You make lots of promises. The only ones you keep are to your job. I don't put stock in any of 'em anymore."

Dick didn't know what to say. How could he explain Melanie's note, her actions, when he didn't fully understand them himself? The bright light behind Seth's head could only mean one thing; Dick had slept through much of the day and it was already afternoon. "It'll be suppertime in a few hours," Dick shouted in the best imitation of his parental authority voice he could muster in his condition. "Where are you going?"

The dark blob shook its head. "You don't care what I'm doing when you're gone. Why do you care when you're here?"

Dick had no immediate answer ready to offer. The darkness turned to move out the door. "Your mother will want to know when she calls," Dick croaked feebly.

Seth's voice softened as he replied. "I'm going over to Brian's. We're tubing all weekend. I'm staying over at his place."

Dick panicked. Part of his addled brain seized upon the notion that if Seth walked out that door into the light, Dick would lose him forever. He tried desperately not to sound desperate. "Hey, tubing, huh?" he bantered with faux nonchalance. "I used to go tubing back in my college days, down in Missouri mostly. Really cool ... or rad, I guess they say now."

Seth turned again to go.

"Why don't I take you and your friend, Brian, camping up in the Adirondacks or someplace this weekend?" he continued, his voice tightening, cracking to a plea. "We could hit the river, tube a bit ... er ... you know, hang out. I'm between jobs for a couple weeks."

The shadow began to move once more into the light.

"We could call your mom. Maybe she would join us. You know, a family thing ... and Brian, any of your buddies who want to come along and tube. My treat."

Seth sighed, a world weary sigh that to Dick's ears belied his son's young years. "That might have been *'rad'* when I was twelve, Dad, but I'm not twelve anymore. Besides, we don't do the same kind of tubing you used to do, believe me."

Dick gave up pleading, switching back to false bonhomie. "Sure. Surf skis, that kind of thing, no doubt, now. Well, have fun. Be safe." He waved feebly, as his nausea reasserted itself. "I'll let your mother know what you're up to. Er ... say 'hi' to Brian for me."

And then Seth was gone. Dick lurched for the bathroom.

His embrace of the porcelain in the master bath meant he didn't get to the phone until the sixth ring, right before it would've kicked over to voicemail.

It was HQ. He had to come in for a meeting. So much for his two week mandatory rest period.

An hour later, Dick was showered, shaved, and heavily caffeinated. He sped down the New Jersey Turnpike to the one place where he was still needed, still wanted: the Subsidiary.

Sometimes when he was in transit or on a stake-out, waiting endlessly for the brief, critical flurry of action to come, Dick tried to imagine telling Melanie what he really did for his life's work.

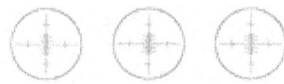

"I'm really sorry, honey, but I won't be back in time for the parent/teacher conference. Duty calls."

"So," Melanie would respond with an edge to her voice, "you're telling me once again that you're choosing a shit-clogged sewer pipe over your own son."

"No, not at all. Look, I'm not really in Puerto Rico advising on improved flow rates in wastewater treatment facilities, I'm ... I'm in Nigeria ..."

"Nigeria? Do they even have wastewater treatment facilities there?"

"I'm not working on treatment facilities. I'm a spy. I'm gathering intelligence on tribal warlords ..."

"Dick, listen to me," Melanie would say, concern warming her voice, "don't go all Walter Mitty on me. Your days gathering intelligence for the Army or the police department, those days are over. You work for a consulting firm."

"No. No, that's just a cover. I really work for this agency called the Subsidiary."

"Whose subsidiary? Are you trying to tell me you work for the CIA?"

"No, not the Company's Subsidiary, just the 'Subsidiary.'" It's not an American espionage and counterterrorist agency, it's an international one, but even more important, an autonomous one, created in the aftermath of 9/11. That way it can identify and assess threats on its own, independent of the biases and turf battles that screw things up in all the government agencies the world around."

"Look, if you're shacked up in Schenectady with a hooker, just tell me, Dick. I won't be happy, but it's better than this Nigerian bullshit about secret agencies founded by God knows who ..."

"No, really, just listen, honey. I can tell you who. The founders, the overseers, of the agency are ... well, they're like an expanded list of the same countries as on the United Nations Security Council, but without any of the *pissant minor players like Cameroon and Finland that circulate in and out of the U.N. circle for reasons of politics and prestige. The countries in charge, they're, you know, the superpowers and wannabe superpowers who are most concerned with global stability, security, and economic prosperity."*

"So you work for a cartel of rich people who want to maintain the status quo and they tell you what to do? Is that supposed to make me stand up and salute?"

"Look, we do good however we see it, by whatever means necessary. The national representatives, sure, they can submit a problem for us to resolve and, true, they don't shake things up for no reason. But we can submit an action of our own for approval, too, without worrying about jurisdiction or budgetary limitations. And once the Subsidiary takes up a case, there's no turning back. No namby-pamby bureaucrat or diplomat can pull the plug on an operation. Consequences of our actions may not always predictable, but the Subsidiary always pursues a problem to the very end: win, lose, or draw. I'm making a difference in the world, Melanie—a positive net impact. I'm making the world better for you, for Seth, for everyone."

"You've lost it, Dick. I'm calling the VA Hospital to get an appointment for you to see them about PTSD, just as soon as I call the credit card company and freeze our account before you spend our mortgage money on gambling or hookers or fighting Nigerian warlords." Click.

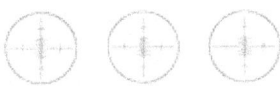

He'd imagined the conversation a hundred times, but it always ended the same way, with Melanie hurt and confused. He couldn't tell Melanie the truth. The Subsidiary wouldn't let him and she would never understand. He had to live with his life of lies, instead.

Besides, there was really no reason to practice a conversation with Melanie in his mind.

Net Impact

Once again, he wouldn't be home when Melanie called.

CHAPTER 8

Luke Calloway searched through the drawers in the computer tech workroom of the Subsidiary's Philadelphia Headquarters until he found a set of jeweler's tools. He laid the tools out on the workbench and set to work on the laptop which had been dropped into his hands by one of the field operatives and Glenn Swynton almost the moment Luke had arrived for his shift.

The assignment surprised Luke. He was really more of a software guy than a hardware guy and, strictly speaking, Glenn Swynton wasn't his boss, Deirdre Tammany was. And even though she was a handsome woman on those rare occasions when she smiled and even though she was friendly enough to tell everyone to call her "Dee," a boss is a boss. Glenn was liaison for the operatives, but Luke wasn't an operative—just a tech plucked straight out of university in Melbourne, Australia less than three years ago. On the other hand, Glenn Swynton was a senior staff member who could be a real ball buster if you got on the wrong side of him.

He didn't want to do that. He liked this gig. Interesting work, gonzo cash, and cutting edge stuff. Besides, the project was a good change of pace compared to the run-of-the-mill research, hacking, and communications tasks his team of computer geeks usually tackled. Reconstructing the laptop's databases would likely require a combination of both hardware and software skills.

Luke felt he was up to the task. How hard could it be? After all, the buggered piece of electronics was just a simple laptop, not a hardened, ultra-secure, hyper-encrypted and booby-trapped portable device like the nuclear "football" dutifully toted around by a Navy attaché everywhere the President went. Something like that he would leave to the hardware and demolitions professionals, while he sought cover at a distance. This was something he could handle.

Net Impact

Of course, the laptop had been in a bit of a bingle ... a smashup he thought they called them here ... and had incurred quite a lot of damage. The bullet that had pierced the laptop had gone clear through, ripping whatever components it touched to shreds. (Jesus, did the field agent think the polished aluminum case was a titanium shield or something?) The flat screen was toast. The keyboard wasn't much better; enough input sensors had been severed to make it impractical to use. The combination CD/DVD drive was perforated and the lithium-ion battery pack had been nicked, causing it to short and discharge in a burst, singeing some nearby circuitry.

None of that really mattered, though. Those were all peripheral; none of those things were the computer. The chip and the hard drive were the keys. Both were intact, although a bit dirty. Luke cleaned them, thinking his assigned task would be a cinch once he had dropped the salvaged components into a comparable device and booted up.

That's where things got a bit tricky. The files were encrypted with a 128 bit algorithmic lock keying off a password requiring manual entry. A password that long buggered up chances for access to be sure. That was the bad news. The good news was that passwords that long were nearly impossible to remember unless they were based off of real world phrases or sentences, which significantly increased the odds of cracking it. He checked the operative's report on the recovery of the laptop. There was no indication the tech had consulted a Personal Data Assistant or piece of paper before entering information into the laptop, so the user had to know the password by heart.

Luke set up a brute force codebreaker which utilized a database of English language phrases 128 bits long and started it running. It was a long shot—if the tech was any good at all, he would avoid the lines of movie dialogue, boasts of sexual prowess, and pop cultural catchphrases an amateur would probably use for such a lengthy input—but it wouldn't hurt to let it run while he tried to get at the problem a few other ways.

Accessing from the Subsidiary's resources the code for the actual Kestrel 84 plans which had been hacked and stolen, Luke set up packet searches that looked for encrypted information in sizes mirroring the unique combination of substantive information packets of the purloined data. It wouldn't allow Luke to access the information on the laptop, but it would tip him off it was there. Several hours passed before he gave up the approach as fruitless. Either the information wasn't there or it had been sufficiently manipulated or altered that it wasn't distinguishable in that fashion.

Luke broke for a quick lunch in the break room—no food or drink allowed in the computer tech workroom for obvious reasons—loading up on caffeine and sugar to sustain him for the duration. The combo had always worked when he was on a coding marathon at university. Luke was having a dessert of fruit-flavored, sugar-loaded Skittles when he caught a disdainful gaze from Glenn Swynton through the window of the break room door. He immediately bolted for the workroom to resume his task.

Back at it, he spent the afternoon going at the problem utilizing a variety of techniques which the Subsidiary had "obtained" from the National Security Agency by means he preferred not to delve into. Knowing how tightly the NSA held onto their techniques, and having read the American's Patriot Act, the whole process made him feel a bit twitchy. It hardly mattered, since the approaches were a full-scale bust in any event. Besides, even though the Maori tech supposedly had the plans to the Kestrel 84, it didn't mean the kid was super-sophisticated about his encryption. He just used a commercially available encryption device with a god-awful long password.

Numeric? He turned off the brute force English phrase attempt and started up a similar routine based on numeric progressions. Simple stuff at first: pi to one hundred twenty-six decimal places, lists of prime numbers, Fibonacci sequences, star dates set forth in the order they appeared in the original run of Star Trek, that kind of crap. He let it run for a bit while he thought. The kid was probably just a hacker geek like any hacker geek anywhere in the world—well, except the guys in the Philippines, who seemed to have a hard-on for viruses and not much else. This hacker geek was just from New Zealand, so he had a few pop cultural peculiarities.

Luke spent several minutes on the Internet and tried entering a few Kiwi references as passwords, like the names of New Zealand cities in order of population, increasing then decreasing, and by latitude, north to south, then south to north. Nothing. He even tried jersey numbers of the team members in the All Blacks, the New Zealand national football team, to no avail. It was a fool's errand in most cases to manually try to guess a password. Hell, the kid was a Maori. He had no idea, for instance, if the Maoris were even big football ... soccer fans.

Suddenly it hit him. The kid was a Maori.

He re-accessed the NSA materials, searching through their brute force phrase tracking protocols. Damn it if they didn't have it. Nobody, but nobody but the NSA would have something like this.

He had hooked up a brute force English phrase password cracker. After a short download and the addition of a few additional symbols to his accessible fonts, Luke started up what he had just downloaded from the NSA databases: a brute force Maori phrase code cracker.

Seven minutes and seventeen seconds later, the encrypted files were unlocked. He had just become Glenn Swynton's best friend for the week, maybe for the whole bloody month. He let out a whoop and began to review the unencrypted files.

Two hours later, he had scoured the cache, the RAM, the file storage, the history of visited websites, even the computer identification numbers. He put together an executive summary and emailed it to Glenn, with a cc to Deirdre Tammany.

Three minutes later he received a return email scheduling a presentation early that evening via the virtual ops center with the Subsidiary's Headquarters staff, Dick Thornby (the agent who had secured the laptop in Dunedin), and the various national representatives overseeing the Subsidiary's mission. He confirmed he would attend—like he had a choice—and began fine-tuning his presentation.

Dee sat in her office as the sun reddened the western sky, going over her notes in preparation for the upcoming meeting of the Subsidiary's overseers.

As always, the meeting of the national representative oversight body for the Subsidiary would take place via virtual conference room. There was no mechanical reason for Dee to actually be at HQ to initiate or attend the conference, nor any essential reason for physical attendance by the personnel who would be making reports: Dick Thornby, the operative who had secured the laptop in question as directed (well, except for the fire still smoldering at the Dunedin harbor); and Luke Calloway, the computer tech who had reconstructed the laptop's data after breaking its encryption. Still, like most bosses everywhere, Dee was a Type A personality with control issues. She liked to direct things in person, if possible, where all the cues (visual, verbal, body language, odor, etc.) could not only be accessed, but also focused upon for real-time assessment. Too much of her interaction with Glenn Swynton, for example, was by audio or video and that relationship wasn't exactly optimal.

Net Impact

All of the HQ attendees (Dee, Glenn, Luke, and Dick) gathered together in Dee's conference room for the larger, virtual meeting. The large room had what looked like a typical corporate audio/visual hook-up, with a wide-angle, zoom-capable camera pointed at the four of them at one end of the table. The Subsidiary's computers used the live feed to generate a signal which depicted the group's virtual reality avatars. Similarly, instead of a screen showing the other participants' physical images to HQ personnel, the screen showed avatars representing each of the overseers of the governing countries as designated by an accompanying flag. No one knew the persons representing the various countries; no one could ever know their names or their faces. That way, the information could not be obtained by the enemies of the Subsidiary (whether evil or anarchist opponents, do-gooder regulatory agencies, or misguided and naive members of the press) by torture, investigation, or inadvertence.

The group waited without chatter while the avatars flickered to life and the flags popped up to indicate virtual presence. Everyone was prompt; it would be the height of arrogance to keep a group of individuals this powerful waiting. Besides, despite their other duties, whatever they might be, Dee believed in her heart of hearts not one had anything more important to do than to guide the Subsidiary down the right path.

There were ten national representatives: Australia, Brazil, China, France, Germany, India, Japan, Russia, the United Kingdom, and the United States. Voices were, of course, electronically modulated and altered by a sophisticated real-time audio synthesizer to prevent identification. Recently, the system had even been upgraded so that instead of producing a flat, electronic voice or the generic Midwestern drawl favored by most broadcasters, the electronics overlaid a recognizable—if somewhat cliché—accent matching the appropriate nation to the random tone and pitch assigned to the speaker for the particular session. Dee Tammany wasn't sure she liked the effect; it was distracting, sometimes bordering on cartoony. Just to ensure there was no confusion about who was speaking even with the accent guidance, however, the flag of any individual speaking glowed to identify him or her as the speaker.

The Russian avatar's flag glowed. "This meeting is convened, all members being present. Director, please state your business."

Dee gave a curt nod. "This meeting concerns the theft of plans for the Kestrel 84, Unmanned Aerial Vehicle, and the potential for increased effectiveness of terrorist, anarchist, and criminal organizations should the technology for such device proliferate." She paused for a breath before continuing, but was immediately interrupted.

"Such mission has already been authorized," said the Japanese representative. Although the inflection was smooth, the abruptness of the statement clearly conveyed irritation. "Our process is quite clear that once a mission has been authorized, the mission goes forward at the Subsidiary's direction, despite any subsequent events or misgivings as to where the investigation may lead or what it may uncover."

"You are correct, representative," replied Dee, moving quickly to continue before she lost control of the agenda. "Each mission authorized by you for the Subsidiary continues to conclusion or abandonment. The purpose of this meeting is to report that the mission has concluded without success and is being abandoned."

A light show of colors flicked across the screen as the national representatives murmured and grumbled in consternation and surprise. The stars and stripes glowed with patriotic fervor as the American representative spoke up in a randomly assigned Texas twang that was just a bit disconcerting, bordering on humorous. "This theft of U.S. technology is a potentially devastating threat to national security. Even aside from our national interest, the technology is inherently destabilizing and, thus, a legitimate concern of this organization."

Dee hit a control button, forwarding an executive summary of Thornby's report to the group. "As you can see, this mission was initially predicated on communication intercepts involving Pao Fen Smythe, a well-known arms merchant operating principally out of Hong Kong. The communication suggested Smythe was arranging to purchase the technical specifications and plans for the Kestrel 84 from certain New Zealand nationals ..."

"Maori boys," interjected the Australian representative.

"Yes, oddly enough, a radical element of native Maoris within the Pan-Pacific Indigenous People's Front who seek to end New Zealand's tourist industry." She nodded toward Thornby. "Agent Thornby 'attended' the meeting set up between Pao Fen Smythe and the local Maori to exchange the plans, along with other armaments." She flipped to the last page of the executive summary. "As you can see from the report ... and news reports from New Zealand ... the Subsidiary disrupted the planned exchange."

France spoke up. "Pardon me, but it would seem these operational matters are within your purview, as the Director of the Subsidiary, and the purview of Monsieur Swynton, as operational liaison between our agents and the intelligence community at large. While I think it is fair to say I speak for all of us when I say the destruction of the Dunedin port seems to have been unnecessary as well as unfortunate, these operational issues and excesses are your problem, not ours, at least at this time."

Glenn Swynton interrupted. "I assure you, representatives, we will deal with any and all operational excesses."

Dee reasserted control. "But you are correct, representative, that this meeting should not be ... and is not ... about operational issues." She pressed a couple buttons on her console. "As you know from

Agent Thornby's report, the laptop which presumably contained the Kestrel 84 plans was recovered and, although damaged, returned to our facilities. Our chief computer tech, Luke Calloway, was, as you can also see from the report I just transmitted, able to thwart the laptop's impressive security features and access all of its files and databases."

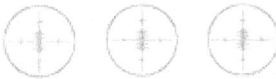

Luke fidgeted while the representatives perused his report. This was his first report to the national representatives and he wasn't sure what to expect.

After a couple minutes, Dee spoke again: "As you can see, there was no evidence the Kestrel 84 plans were ever on the laptop."

"And what was?" inquired the Indian representative.

Luke spoke up, doing his best to tamp down his Aussie accent, not so much because he was trying hard to assimilate to America, but because he had learned from experience that the Australian tendency to make a long "a" sound like a long "i" confused people. (Half the people he introduced himself to in Philadelphia thought his name was "Callowhy"—the other half said almost nothing to him but "G'day" and "Crikey!") He cleared his throat. "The laptop had the kind of things you would expect to find on a young computer geek's laptop, for the most part. Terrorist Threat, that's a first-person shoot-'em up video game, scores of emails regarding pop culture, girls, and plans for the weekend, a shitload ... pardon my French ... I mean, pardon my language ... of porn, and software accessing several M-M-P-O-R-P-Gs ..."

"Several what?" interrupted the Brazilian representative.

"Is that a technical computer term or yet another American military acronym?" queried the Russian representative.

Luke felt a warm flush of embarrassment cross his face. "Er, no. Uh, the acronym stands for 'massively multi-player online role-playing games.' The computer contains downloaded software which allows it to connect to virtual worlds like Reality 2 Be. More relevant to our investigation, the laptop contained a listing of small arms and the surface-to-air missiles we know were an actual part of the exchange, plus online banking software for a dummy entity no doubt used by the Maori to fund their efforts, and a database of airline flights to and from New Zealand by passenger carriers."

France spoke up again. "This still all seems pretty operational to me, but I will nevertheless ask some questions. Couldn't the Kestrel 84 plans be almost anywhere? Another laptop, a CD, a flash drive? Couldn't they be multiple places?"

Dee nodded. "They could. The thing is ... we have no indication they were ever in the hands of the Maori."

"What about emails or other communications with Pao Fen Smythe concerning the Kestrel 84?"

Dee started to answer again, but this time Luke beat her to it. "Nothing."

Glenn chimed in, too. "As you know, the original communications intercept triggering the mission was a phone communication."

Dee didn't like how the meeting was going. The national representatives were inquisitive, Luke's presentation was less than polished, and Glenn kept interrupting. She took back control of the conversation by speaking in a firm, authoritative tone. "I'm sure the

94

representatives know what they know and I do not wish this to be an operational review. The point is, my analysis of the operational information we do have suggests the Kestrel 84 plans were never accessed by the Maori, and are not in imminent danger of being sold to terrorist organizations. Everything suggests the Maori were intent on obtaining surface-to-air missiles for their own political cause, but nothing suggests they had the kind of cash to obtain those devices from someone like Pao Fen Smythe. Hence, a subterfuge. By offering him something even more valuable, but both costless from their perspective and intangible, they lured Smythe into importing what they wanted. Their scam also had the possibility of getting them a sizeable cash kicker."

"Wouldn't Pao Fen Smythe have been a formidable man to stiff?" asked the U.S. representative, sounding like a good ol' boy.

"Yes, he would," replied Dee, "if he had survived the encounter."

"But he did survive," interrupted France yet again.

"That doesn't mean that was the plan," said Dee. "The Maori may have had other assets at the scene. The plan may have been to eliminate Smythe after delivery of the missiles."

"But," came the Texas twang again, "there wasn't any gunplay before ...uh ... we crashed the party, right?"

"No, there wasn't," Dee confirmed, "but they would have waited to confirm funds receipt before taking any action. Based on Agent Thornby's account, the laptop may have been being used to confirm receipt of wired funds."

"Any evidence of such a wire transfer, Mr. Swynton?" asked China. Dee felt her blood pressure rise a bit in irritation. Some of the more culturally traditional representatives from male-dominated cultures tended to bypass her position by dealing directly with her subordinates. She let it slide, but she didn't have to like it.

"No," replied Glenn.

"No," replied Dee a bit louder, hard on the heels of Glenn's answer.

Thornby chimed in, "It was clear to me from their conversation that funds were not being exchanged in person. Pao Fen seemed pretty pissed to be doing anything in person. The Maori tech kid, though, he did some stuff on the computer and then said they were ready for the exchange and Pao Fen, he said that as soon as they had the plans, they'd send the ... Ma ... Maples ... or something. I didn't hear it clearly. That's when things ... sorta started happening. I assumed he was sending the funds in Canadian dollars."

Glenn's faced colored in apparent anger. "You didn't include that in your report. Canadian dollars aren't called Maples. They're called dollars ... or loonies."

"Gold coins from Canada are referred to as Maple Leafs, but they're not generally exchanged via normal banking account wire transfers," volunteered the representative from the United Kingdom.

Luke looked up with a start and turned toward Thornby. "You sure he didn't say 'maypoles?'"

Thornby looked confused. "Maples, maypoles ... who knows?"

"What's a maypole?" twanged Texas.

Dee stared at Glenn, who raised both eyebrows, and then they both turned to look at Luke. "Yes," said Dee, her fingers tapping the table in a light staccato. "What's a maypole?"

Luke flushed red. "Maypoles are the currency of Reality 2 Be, it's a virtual world on the Internet. There's dozens of virtual reality worlds: Home, Lively, Entropia Universe, Second Life, The Sims, Gaia Online, There.com, Spore, Habbo Hotel. The Chinese have one called HiPiHi." He gestured at the avatars and flags in the virtual conference room. "You guys use all this hi-tech virtual stuff every day. Didn't you ever think of what the average bloke would do with it?"

No one responded and Luke continued. "Well, regular people use virtual reality, too. Some virtual worlds, like World of Warcraft or City

96

of Heroes, focus on gaming and battles—weapons, explosives, Kung Fu, magic, and anything else you can think of. Other worlds focus more on social intercourse. People go there and chat and hang out with friends and stuff, but not necessarily as themselves. They create avatars. They role-play, pretending to be cooler, tougher, sexier, funnier, better-looking, and more dramatic than they are in real life. It's like a hyper-reality. Everything is bigger, better, and flashier—all of the subtle nuances and filters of the real world are turned off. That has a lot of appeal for a lot of people. Consequently, massive amounts of money and effort go into building virtual worlds and massive amounts of money are made there, and not just on games. You can shop, both for virtual goods and for real goods. Some require real money, some virtual money. Theodore Maypole—he's the CEO of Reality 2 Be—he named the currency of his virtual world after himself."

Thornby shook his head as if to clear it. "The Maori were being paid in Monopoly money?"

"Oh, not at all," responded Luke. "Maypoles are exchangeable for United States currency at a fixed exchange rate of one hundred maypoles per dollar. You can convert cash from the real world into the game, make maypoles by building things or selling things or whatever online, and exchange the funds back into real money whenever you want."

France interrupted yet again. "What do you mean, building things?

"Buildings, games, puzzles, designer clothes, whatever an avatar might want to have or use in a virtual world," explained Luke.

"You can get real money for building fake things?"

"Sure," continued Luke. He obviously had an easy familiarity with Reality 2 Be. "Let's say you want a T-shirt with a logo on it for your avatar to wear. You design one on your computer using a photography or art program or whatever and download the data to your avatar, who either wears it or carries it around or puts it up for display in a shop. You can then sell the object by transferring the code which creates the object by simply handing it to another avatar. Your avatar can get maypoles from other avatars or give maypoles to other avatars simply by meeting them and handing items back and forth. The folks at Reality 2 Be are even coming out with an ATM card which will let you access your converted maypoles at any cash machine."

The United Kingdom representative spoke up. "That means any sum of money could be exchanged by anyone, anywhere, outside of all banking regulations and oversight."

"That means someone could exchange or disseminate any type of information whatsoever, without any government oversight," added the Chinese representative. Not a happy thought, Dee knew, for the representative of a country as tightly controlling as China.

There was a whistle from the U.S. representative. "Bad guys gotta love that."

Dee frowned. The Subsidiary had a tough time enough catching bad guys in the real world. Adding extra virtual worlds they could do business in wasn't going to make her life any easier.

Glenn stated what they were all now thinking. "So they could have been exchanging the plans for cash in a virtual world."

"Jesus, Luke," said Thornby, "how do you know all this stuff?"

Luke's eyes flicked downward. "Well, I spend some time there ..."

Dee interrupted. "I apologize, representatives. While I had thought the investigation had come to an unsuccessful conclusion, I was wrong. I shall not trouble you further with ... operational matters. This meeting is adjourned."

As the flags began to flick off, she turned to Luke. "You spend time there?"

Luke's eyes hardened. "It's a game. I spend my free time how I want to."

"Ever exchanged items surreptitiously?"

"Some friends, we help fund Chinese dissidents and smuggle out information about government atrocities ..."

"I demand this man be arrested!" thundered the large-screen panel, which still showed one active avatar, the red of the Chinese flag pulsing bright.

Damn it, thought Dee, as her hands flew to the control panel. "This meeting is over," she barked as her button killed the feed.

The meeting was over, but she knew the mission and the battle with the Chinese delegate had just begun.

CHAPTER 9

Sitting in a swivel chair with lumbar support in an air-conditioned conference room, Dick Thornby was considerably more uncomfortable than he had been squatting high up in the shelving in the stifling warehouse at Port Chalmers in New Zealand. He was about to see someone cashiered, he was sure, and that was always awkward and unpleasant. To top it off, Dee Tammany was not particularly pretty when she was angry. Her grey-green eyes darkened with her mood; he wasn't sure they wouldn't darken all the way to black.

"How long?" she demanded, her nicely-shaped right ankle bouncing up and down at the end of her crossed leg.

Luke looked flushed, perspiring despite the cool comfort of conditioned breezes flowing from the air vents. He stared back at her, no doubt doing his best to look hard and collected, but his eyes flicked around the room, giving his nervousness away. "How long, what? How long have I been keeping in touch with my friends back home? How long have I been gaming and chatting with people on the Internet on my own time?"

Glenn took over. He looked just as unhappy as Dee, but he seemed somehow more professionally detached. As operational liaison with the agents, he had probably been through this drill more times than he could count. "How long have you been an agent for a foreign organization working to overthrow a world power?"

"I'm not a foreign agent ... I don't smuggle secret weapons plans or arrange hits or anything like that. I just believe in liberty and freedom of information and democracy and human rights and ... isn't that what we're supposed to care about here?" Luke was defiant, but his voice cracked a bit when he spoke.

Glenn was all business. "Freedom is good. Democracy, too, if you have a literate middle class who can support it. Survival is kind of nice, too. Of course, that means a certain modicum of stability and economic prosperity, with trade and reasonable diplomatic relations and political dialogue, not the chaos and killing and anarchy and disease and disruption which comes from civil wars and insurrections and terrorist vendettas."

"The groups of Chinese students I was in contact with aren't terrorists. They're non-violent ..."

"That's not your call," barked the Director. "That's a political decision. Not part of your function, your job description here. Instead, you've undercut the Subsidiary's position vis-à-vis a national sponsor and compromised my credibility, not to mention this agency's credibility."

Glenn gave Luke a stern look. "That'd better be all you compromised, Mr. Calloway."

Jesus, Dick thought, he can't have been stupid enough to have used agency equipment, can he?

"I'm s-s-sure I don't know what you m-m-mean," replied Luke with a gulp.

Thornby felt like one of those thugs at a Mafia meeting, sitting calmly when he knew the guy the Don was screaming at was about to get gacked right at the table. He looked down at his shoes.

"You said you did this on your own time. That still compromises the Subsidiary. What I want to know is whether you did this entirely utilizing your own personal equipment?"

"The equipment here is better, more secure ..." Luke blurted out.

Dick suddenly felt a vibration in his shirt pocket. He slipped out the phone to check the caller I.D. It was Melanie. Not a pleasant conversation, but perhaps better than the one he was sitting through. "Excuse me, Director Tammany, Mr. Swynton, I have an urgent family call, if you won't be needing me further."

Dee looked as if she had forgotten he was even in the room. "Take it in the hall," she snapped, "but don't go far."

Net Impact

Dick stood and began to leave the room as he flipped open his cell phone. He held it up to his mouth for just a moment. "Just a second, please." He lowered the phone and continued on to the exit without waiting for a response.

Once in the hall, with the conference door firmly closed behind him, he walked a few more paces and held the phone back up to his mouth. "Hello, Melanie."

"You know I hate it when you do that. Answer or don't answer."

"I wanted to take your call, but I was with people. Now, I'm not. Now I can talk."

"I hate to just be kept waiting while you finish your meetings. I don't know why you think your consulting is so damn important it can't wait, instead."

"Clients aren't more important than family. I just kind of hoped that family was more understanding than clients. Besides, I'm talking to you now, right now. I'm not making you wait."

There was a bitter laugh on the other end of the line. "I'm still waiting. I'm waiting until you get home from your latest project. I'm waiting for you to take some responsibility for your son growing up. I'm waiting for you to pay some attention."

"But I am home, I mean I'm back. Two weeks off. Didn't Seth tell you? I thought maybe we would take a family vacation together."

"You didn't answer when I called the house."

"I ... I'm back in Philly, for a meeting. Shouldn't be long."

"I've heard that before."

"Look, I'll call you, just as soon as I finish up here, and we can sit down and talk. Everything will be okay. Where are you at?"

"Just hit re-dial. I'll have my cell with me."

She hung up and Dick was alone with his thoughts. He paced the hall, anxious to tell Melanie he was on his way, to fix things. That's what guys do, they fix things. It's in their genetic make-up. They don't empathize or console. They problem-solve. Accordingly, his mind was awhirl with possible fixes. Maybe not a family trip, but a trip for just him and Melanie. Someplace romantic. Paris or Casablanca or the Greek Isles. Yeah, someplace slow and quiet and sunny. He and Melanie could reconnect. It would all work out.

He looked at his watch. Had Dee and Glenn forgotten he was here? He smiled ruefully to himself. Maybe they were just taking their time disposing of the body ...

Finally, Glenn opened the conference room and motioned for him. "Please come back in, Mr. Thornby. We are ready to proceed with our briefing."

Briefing?

He walked back into the conference room. Everything was the same, except Dee Tammany was standing by the big screen now. Luke Calloway looked a bit pale and haggard, but there was no blood on the carpet.

Dee acknowledged Dick's return with a brief nod. "Mr. Calloway has agreed to accompany you in the completion of our mission."

His head swiveled from Dee to Luke, at the opposite end of the table, and then back. "I don't understand. My mission is complete. I'm on mandatory break, with ... some family issues that ... need attention. You have the laptop. The Maoris are all dead or in hiding, as far as we know. And we have no idea where Pao Fen Smythe is, not that we think he ever got the plans for the Kestrel 84 anyway, if they were ever even stolen. What's left to do? And how would dragging along a computer jockey help?"

Glenn sat back down next to Luke. "Your mission was to recover the plans. You haven't finished the job. Mr. Calloway is going to assist you in doing so."

"You mean he's not fired?" Dick shot a glance at Calloway. "No offence, Luke. But it sure sounded to me like you should be."

"Mr. Calloway's status is not your immediate concern, Mr. Thornby," replied Glenn as Luke pursed his lips and hung his head. "He has been quite valuable in certain aspects of this and other missions. While he has engaged in unsanctioned behavior, our and his immediate concern is to further the mission of the Subsidiary, not our own personal feelings."

Dee spoke again. "Mr. Calloway believes he knows where the plans are for the Kestrel 84 and time is of the essence if they are to be recovered before they are duplicated or exchanged with Mr. Smythe or someone else. Your break and family plans will have to wait."

So much for fixing things up with Melanie on Santorini. "No offense again, but does he have any field experience? I don't need an amateur giving me away. How many hours on the ground does Luke, here, have?"

Dee gave a wan smile. "He has specific expertise in the realm you need to navigate." She nodded at Glenn, who hit a few buttons on the control panel. "Here's your next destination," continued Dee as she nodded toward the screen.

The bright colors of the plasma flat-screen quickly coalesced into focus, showing a panoramic landscape of vivid colors beneath a stylized logo and the words: "Welcome to Reality 2 Be."

What the hell? "No disrespect, Director," said Thornby, "but I don't know squat about fake worlds and stuff. I've got enough problems dealing with this one."

Luke's fingers skittered over the keyboard. Menus and information flashed onto the plasma screen in rapid succession. "We're not going inside Reality 2 Be," he said without any slowdown in his manipulation of the screen images, "Well, not inside the world." A screen popped up showing a sprawling corporate office tucked into a swath of green grass amidst rolling hills in a heavily forested area. "We're going to Reality 2 Be's corporate offices."

"We are?" blurted Dick. "What makes you think Maypole and his guys are behind any of this? Just 'cause they created an environment where crooks can deal with each other in anonymity without government oversight doesn't mean they're directing the effort. By that logic, we'd have nuked Switzerland years ago."

Luke answered. "The most logical way to locate the Kestrel 84 plans, if they are disguised as an item in Reality 2 Be, is to search the world for artifacts of the appropriate file-size and characteristics."

Dick understood. "Or to search for persons ... or avatars, I guess it would be ... exchanging or carrying large enough sums of maypoles to pay for that sort of merchandise."

Luke nodded. "And while you can use a simple search routine to locate specific places or locations of a specified type—you know, dance clubs, concert venues, brothels ..."

"Brothels?" said Dick and Dee in unison.

Luke blushed and flexed his fingers, interlacing them for just a moment and then wiggling them as if working out a cramp. "Er ... yeah. There's some kinky places in virtual worlds. Brothels are on the tame end of the scale." Luke pointed at the keyboard. "You can't do an in-world search for complex items or large sums of maypoles. If you could, people would run the searches, then come kill your avatar, loot the body, and steal your stuff. It's kind of like the third-world that way—you don't flash your cash unless you're with friends or in a safe place."

"You can get killed in virtual reality?" Dick shook his head.

"Not in some worlds, but Reality 2 Be is both a virtual world and a gaming world, so, yeah, your avatar can get caught in a cross-fire or whatever and then, boom, you lose anything he was carrying. That's why they have virtual banks and stuff, although one of those failed a while back and the depositors, they torched the place in protest."

"Don't they have, I dunno, virtual cops or something?" asked Dick.

"Some, but most things are policed by the members themselves. You can complain to the people at the company about something another avatar did, but by the time they look into it, the goods and the maypoles may have been transferred hundreds of times, maybe to innocent third parties. Some people have actually brought lawsuits ..."

Dee frowned. "Real or virtual?"

Luke shrugged. "Both, but courts in the virtual world don't really have much power and courts in the real world, well they don't really understand this stuff much more than Dick, here. No offence."

"No defense," replied Dick with a wry grin. "You learn what you need for your own life; there's plenty out there I don't understand, like what makes our magic sunglasses work or how they know nobody's fixing the vote on American Idol or in the Electoral College."

"So," continued Luke, "like I said, players can't search for that kind of thing, but the powers that be at Reality 2 Be, they can. They should be able to search for and track avatars by category of goods carried or amount of maypoles exchanged. They would need to do so to make sure no one is running a Ponzi scheme or counterfeiting maypoles, for example.

"There's counterfeiting in cyberspace?" asked Dee. The Subsidiary had enough on its plate keeping the real world safe from economic collapse due to large-scale counterfeiting and wire fraud. It looked like they were going to have to expand their horizons.

"Oh yeah, plenty of fraud in virtual reality. And, since maypoles are exchangeable into real dollars at a fixed rate, if someone counterfeits the cyber-cash, they're effectively counterfeiting the real thing, except it all comes out of the pockets of Reality 2 Be."

Dick sighed. "So can't you, you know, hack in and do the searches? I mean, isn't that what you guys do, hack things?"

Luke smiled. "Yeah, that's what we do. The thing about gaming and virtual worlds, though, is that they are mostly populated by geeks who know their way around a security algorithm. Not only are they the targets of the usual anarchists—Filipino virus coders, point of access bombers, and identity theft crooks—they're the target of compu-nerds who just want to get an edge on the game or make a better life for themselves in the virtual world than they have in their parents' basement. The sites are literally besieged with hacks." He gestured broadly with his hands. "Look, I could try to hack remotely. I can put the whole tech group on it if you want." He bobbed his head in Dee's direction. "But if we're in a hurry—and we are—we need to gain access to the servers controlling Reality 2 Be and run the searches directly."

Dee gestured at Dick. "That's where you come in. You need to take Luke and gain access to the necessary equipment at Reality 2 Be's corporate offices. You leave immediately ..." She glanced at the screen. "... for upstate New Hampshire."

While Luke was grabbing some equipment from the tech room, Dick tried to reach Seth at the house and then at his cell phone, without any luck. Finally, he made a call to Melanie. She didn't even say "hello."

"Let me guess."

Dick bit his lip. This wasn't going to be pleasant. "Uh, yeah, change in plans. I gotta go see a ... client. Bit of a delay before I'm back home."

He could feel the frost in the silence before she even replied. "I'm not there, remember? And at this point, I'm not sure I care. Tell Seth, though I doubt he cares either."

"Seth's not at home."

"He's not?   Where is he?"

"I don't know, he went camping or tubing or something with Brian, maybe some other guys. He doesn't pick up on his cell—maybe they're in a dead spot."

"You don't know where your son is," came the response, accusatory despite the monotone delivery. "He might be in a dead spot. Of course, he might be dead. You don't know."

"Look, I left a voicemail. I'm sure he's fine. He can take care of himself. He's a smart kid. Besides, I did teach him a few things when he was growing up about protecting himself."

"Yeah," came the bitter reply, "he'll be perfectly safe if someone comes after him with a paintball gun or a Lazer Tag toy. You were just playing soldier."

"That's what I am."

"Were. Now you're just another shitty absentee father ... with no patriotic excuse."

If she only knew, if he could only tell her. Instead, after a few moments of awkward silence, he fell back to a familiar refrain. "I've gotta make a living. Seth will be fine."

"You don't even care where he is or what he's doing."

"I do care," Dick huffed, becoming more and more exasperated with this conversation, with his life. His voice grew louder, firmer. "You're the one who left him at home while I was out of town ..."

The thing about cell phones is, you don't even hear a click when the other person disconnects.

As he listened to the silence transmitted at the speed of light to his cell phone, Dick was as disconnected with Melanie as he could possibly be.

CHAPTER 10

Dick was unhappy as they headed out of the city, inching through traffic to get to an open road leading to their New Hampshire destination. This wasn't where he was supposed to be. This wasn't what he was supposed to be doing.

Besides, he hated having to drag this Luke kid around with him. The tech was a definite operational impediment. Luke was lanky and fit, but not really muscled, so Dick had no real idea how fast the kid— what was he, twenty, maybe twenty-two?—could move, how much endurance he might have, or how he would handle himself in a fight. At six foot three, with shaggy blond hair that made him look like a surfer dude, and an in-your-face Aussie accent, the kid didn't even blend in well, visually or aurally. To top it all off, it was obvious the tech whiz was nervous about the assignment. The kid kept checking his watch.

"Forget to set your DVR or something?" Dick asked in order to stop the irritating practice before it became a truly annoying habit, but without purposely pissing his protégé off.

Luke started at the question. "Uh ... I was supposed to be someplace."

Dick snorted. "So was I." He glanced over at Luke's furrowed brow. "Don't worry, kid. If she's a keeper, she'll forgive you." An image of Melanie walking out the door to their suburban house flitted into his mind, unbidden. "At least the first hundred times or so."

Luke wrinkled his nose momentarily and gave Dick a tight, lop-sided smile. "You're the seasoned veteran. I guess I'll have to trust you."

Respect. The kid was okay. They rode is silence for a few minutes. Finally, Dick decided they should get down to business. "How long?"

Luke looked over at him from the passenger seat of the car with a blank stare for a few moments, apparently working to get the gears starting to mesh in his mind. "Six or seven hours or so, depending on how fast you drive. It's over four hundred miles."

Dick sighed. Even if the kid wasn't a jerk, working with an amateur was not going to be fun or easy. "No. I already know that. I looked at the map before we left. How long do you need to access the servers or whatever it is you have to do once we get inside the place? Five minutes? Five hours? It makes a difference as to how we approach the infiltration."

Luke grimaced. "I don't know. Ten minutes minimum, just to hook in and get through basic firewall protection." He threw up his hands. "But if we don't have a password and things are encrypted the way I expect them to be, it could be hours. Hell, it could be forever."

Dick thought it over while they inched their way out of the city traffic, heading for I-95 North. "Then we should get a password."

"Oh, okay," said Luke with a sarcastic sneer. "Can I get an order of fries with that?"

"Sarcasm is not an efficient means of communication when you're on an op. You got something to say, say it."

"All right. Passwords don't grow on trees." Luke paused, then continued. "Sorry, metaphors aren't probably efficient communications either. Passwords aren't generally written on index cards pasted to the side of the computer, not in a place as security phobic as Reality 2 Be. And they won't use 'sex,' or 'password,' or '3point14159,' or any of the fallback passwords amateurs use."

"What's that?"

"What's what?" asked Luke. "Ambiguous antecedents don't seem very efficient either."

Dick wanted to backhand the kid, just to get him in line, but it really wasn't Luke's fault. He wasn't a field operative. So he just let it slide and continued his conversation. "3point14159. What's that?"

Luke smirked. "Pi to five decimal places. Didn't you go to college?"

"Fighting Illini. Football scholarship. Plenty of physical education credits; no math courses required. Then Army. Then Chicago Police Department. I never took calculus or any of that stuff, but I do know seventeen ways to kill you that will look like natural causes on an autopsy."

Luke's smirk disappeared. "I'll keep that in mind."

"You do that. And I'll keep in mind you're out of your element and not shorthand things. You need a password; we need a hostage."

"That's kidnapping," squeaked Luke. "That's life without parole. Hell, in New Hampshire, they might still have the death penalty."

"Supreme court has outlawed the death penalty where there are no deaths involved, so maybe not." He smiled. "Besides, that's only if you get caught ... and they take you alive."

Luke was quiet for the next several hundred miles as Dick put together his plan.

Hawk tapped his foot impatiently, sitting in a straight-backed chair shoved into a corner of the seedy hotel room that was the squad's pre-arranged rendezvous point. He had arrived a few minutes before the designated time to sweep the locale for unfriendlies, but only found the usual riff-raff that frequented dumps like this: pervs, under-aged hookers in garish attire, roving wannabe gangs of vandals and petty miscreants who would tag you with their initials in stylized scifi green letters if you stood still too long, and the occasional lost newcomer who would leave the neighborhood without his meager possessions, if at all.

Net Impact

Pigeon and Peregrine popped in at the appropriate time. It was clear from their appearance both had dumped gear to hasten their flight speed and avoid the mysterious orange death ray which had ambushed the meet. Peregrine had dumped his backpack, but still held onto his weapons with fierce determination. Pigeon's backpack, of course, was the most vital thing he carried and he still had it, but he had dumped his weapon, his binoculars, his canteen, and his climbing gear to make it out of that godforsaken wilderness deathtrap and back here in one piece.

Hawk said nothing to the pair, who arrived within seconds of one another. Instead they all waited for Shrike to show up. No sense saying everything twice, especially if you couldn't be sure someone wasn't trying to listen in, even here, even now, in this tawdry dump.

Minutes ticked by.

Pigeon began to fidget. "If he isn't coming, we shouldn't just be sitting around. He might have been killed; he might have been compromised." Pigeon looked up to the water-stained ceiling, with its inert ceiling fan, as if he feared an orange ray of death would blast through it and obliterate him, then looked back at Hawk and Peregrine. "They might be tracking us. You didn't bring back anything from the meet, did you? They might have bugged us."

Hawk could tell Pigeon was losing it; the guy's imagination was running wide open and picking up speed. "Go ahead," Hawk said, his voice more of a request than a command. "Say it. Say out loud what you know we're all thinking. It's the only way we'll move past it."

Pigeon's eyes narrowed. "You say it."

Hawk shrugged. "You're thinking, we're all thinking that Shrike, maybe he got obliterated by one of them death rays, but we don't really believe that. What sticks in our heads is maybe, just maybe, Shrike set us up. Maybe he sabotaged the meet. Maybe our contacts all got fried or, worse, captured and interrogated. Maybe they're all dead now. Maybe they just wish they were. Maybe we're the leftover mess the bad guys have to clean up. And while we're running for our lives, maybe, just maybe, Shrike's counting his pay-off on a beach in the Caymans or some other island tax-dodge."

Peregrine chimed in. "Yeah, I've thought it, but I don't believe it."

Hawk wrinkled his nose. "Me neither, not yet. Maybe Shrike just got delayed. Secondary pre-set rendezvous is twelve hours away. You know the location. We'll just have to wait to see if he shows." Hawk stood and began heading for the door.

Pigeon moved to block his path. "That's easy for you to say. I'm the one carrying around millions of maypoles. I'm the one who is the most likely target if Shrike was a mole ... or if they have some way to track the funds."

Hawk shook his head. The group would never be the same, would never work together and trust the way it had before. Not after this. "Fine." He tossed Pigeon his MAC 10. "You take my weapon to defend yourself if the bad guys start chasing you. I'll carry the cash."

Pigeon didn't say a word in response, but he took the weapon and shouldered off his pack. Hawk grasped it by one strap and headed out of the room into a hallway littered with cigarette butts, empty liquor bottles, and a few dead rats. Pigeon skittered down the stairs and away as quick as possible, but Peregrine covered Hawk's rear until they split up at the subway station.

Pigeon was paranoid. Peregrine was careful. There was a difference, a big difference.

Beverly Lange checked to make sure her DVR was recording all her favorite shows, then put down food for her kitten, Mr. Scruffies, grabbed her keys and lab coat, and headed for the door. The sun was just setting over the White Mountains as she drove south from Conway toward her job in Freedom, New Hampshire. As the sky darkened, so did her mood. That was happening more often lately, as her thoughts would turn to her dreary routine. Here she was, in her mid-twenties, single, with a good job and a nice apartment, and her life was boring. She had her cat, she had her books and her movies and her television shows to keep her entertained, but she was all alone.

Working night shift as a computer geek didn't help her social life, of course, but her employer's computers were the lifeblood of their business. They had to be monitored night and day. Someone had to do it and she had been the one assigned nights instead of one of her counterparts. After all, each of her counterparts on day shift had a family or a spouse or a life that would be interrupted by having to work night shift. She had a kitten, already litter box trained, thankfully, and, let's face it, they sleep most of the time anyway.

Oh well, at least she wasn't as pathetic as some of the geeks who abandoned the real world to live in her employer's virtual realm, Reality 2 Be. She saw the reports. Sure, there was all sorts of activity: meetings, games, building and selling things, relieving people of their maypoles by legitimate and some illegitimate means (the latter of which had to be monitored and stopped before they got out of hand), gossiping, even engaging in virtual sex. It's easy to see how the virtual world could draw you in. But she never understood the fringe groups that were online eight, ten, sometimes sixteen or seventeen hours a day. Didn't these people have a job, a life?

Maybe she would go to the Renaissance Faire down by Manchester this weekend. She'd met a couple of the folk-singers at Barb's summer party last year. She could actually interact with some people in the real world, maybe go out to a bar after the Faire closed down for the evening.

A little excitement. That's what she needed.

CHAPTER 11

Even using bypasses for most of the major coastal towns, it was quite late when Dick exited the interstate and started making his way to their target destination on increasingly less-traveled roads : NH 16 North, then east on NH 25, also known as Ossipee Trail Road. On his left, Ossipee Lake reflected the starlight on its smooth surface as Dick scanned both sides of the road, looking for an indicator of the company campus for Reality 2 Be. Finally, he saw it—a tastefully lit sign with the logo and the words "Reality 2 Be" above and "Corporate Offices" below.

It seemed like a pretty backwater place for a corporate headquarters, snugged up in a small town in New Hampshire close to the Maine border, but he guessed real estate prices were low. More likely, management figured some of the techie types they were constantly recruiting would be attracted to the whole back-to-nature setting close to hiking and skiing and all that crap. Even more likely, Maypole, the CEO of Reality 2 Be, had a rambling, rustic mansion with a dramatic view of the mountains on a couple hundred acres nearby and headquarters was located for his sole convenience.

Dick nudged Luke awake and nodded toward the sign before accelerating lightly and driving past the entrance. He traveled on to the next intersection to the right, turning onto Green Mountain Road to circle back behind the corporate offices of the virtual reality company. It was easy to "hide" the car by backing it into a small patch where a culvert had been tossed into the ditch and covered over with gravel to allow farm implements access to a field. The make-shift parking spot was near the intersection with High Watch Road, where the computerized mapping in the heads-up display of his micro-enhanced "magic" sunglasses showed he would have multiple paths to escape the area if need be.

He grabbed a pack from the trunk, dialed his sunglasses for night vision, and gestured for Luke to follow him with his computer handbag of equipment. As they walked away from the car, he tossed Luke a soft-cover book. "Page one hundred seventy-four," he said in a low voice as they headed back up the dark road toward Reality 2 Be. "Long-Eared Owl. Likes woods near open country. Long wings, long ears, but more narrow ears than the triangular ears on a Great Horned Owl. Makes a whole bunch of different low hoots and whistles, so it's pretty easy to say that whatever we heard, we thought was it."

"Huh?" was Luke's inarticulate reply. It was obvious the kid was still waking up.

"Always good to have an excuse for walking through the fields and woods in the middle of the night. Pretend you're a new birder and I'm teaching you how to find 'em for your life list. You should be able to convey clueless but willing to learn without too much effort. Just like it was natural for you."

Dick kept up a quick and quiet, but not stealthy, pace as they made their way to the back of the grounds for Reality 2 Be's offices. The night was wasting away and he didn't know how much time Luke would need.

Finally, they came to a clearing. Across fifty feet of perfectly groomed lawn was the loading dock for the office building. They were lucky. A lone figure in khaki pants and a loose fitting shirt leaned against the building near the doorway, the glow of a cigarette in his right hand. The guy took a long drag and the red tip brightened.

Dick tilted his head toward the figure, then spoke to Luke in a soft whisper. "The whole non-smoking office thing has been great for those of us who enter buildings without permission on a regular basis. Security goes to the crapper 'cause everyone is sneaking out for seven minutes of nicotine every hour. Since they don't want to record how much time they spend outside smoking on break, the nicotine fiends

117

usually disable the security alarm and leave the door propped open. That way they don't have to keycard in or out.

Luke's mouth was set in a thin line, but Dick got a tiny smile out of him as acknowledgment. "Is he our hostage?"

Dick shook his head and frowned. "Nah, he'd see us coming over the lawn and freak for sure. We'll wait 'til he goes in, then try the door or wait just outside it for the next smoker." A scent caught Dick's attention and he flared his nostrils, taking the smell in by means of a long deep breath. He smiled. "Too bad. Weed. He could have been a good target if we'd arrived earlier. Might've been able to convince him it was all a hallucination by the time we were done." He looked at the smoker wistfully. "Or maybe that we were drug enforcement." He gave Luke a wink. "Stoners are crappy security risks. They're either stupid or scared or don't give a crap. Any of those can work for me."

Luke said nothing in response and they waited in silence until the smoker headed back inside. Then, Dick motioned and they scurried across the open lawn to the loading dock door. Dick reached for the handle, but Luke stopped him. "Shouldn't we have masks or something?"

Dick smiled. "Cover still holds. We're just looking for a restroom instead of taking a dump in the dark. Always look and act as innocent as possible until you need to actually be the bad guy. It can get you out of a jam."

Dick pulled open the door and looked around the hall casually, as if he really might be scouting for a john. Luke followed in, doing a little "gotta pee" dance as he came in the door. Dick gave him a hard look. "Don't oversell it."

They started down the hall and Dick pointed to signs with arrows indicating the various departments. "What do we want?"

Luke pointed to a sign. "Tech Support."

They navigated their way through several sections of high-walled gray cubicles until they came to a door with a small glass window in it. Dick peeked in to find a row of computer equipment and a young woman in a white lab coat hunched over a keyboard, her back to the door. He motioned for Luke to take a look, then nodded toward the door with raised eyebrows and a thumbs-up. Luke gave him a thumbs-up in response.

Dick tried the knob with slow quiet pressure, but it was locked. Automatic lock, no doubt. He shrugged and gave a rap on the door.

Before the young woman could even make it to the door and possibly stand on her tiptoes to look out the window, he called out, putting his hand to the side of his mouth so it wouldn't carry throughout the building: "Got some pizza leftover from the new project meeting. Want some?" He ducked down as he saw her get up and turn toward the door.

Beverly was surprised. Locked away in the computer room, she was almost never invited to partake in late night pizza, half-melted ice cream cake when someone had a birthday, or impromptu hallway soccer matches using a ball of wadded up story-board paper. She told herself it wasn't that she was disliked, just that security procedures mandated the computer room be locked at all times and she was therefore out of sight and out of mind of her late night co-workers. She was just happy to be included this time. She headed to the door and turned the handle without bothering to look through the small window to see who it was—at 5'2", looking up to see out the window only allowed her to glimpse the top of the person's head anyway, except for the gangly new kid, Bruce, in accounting.

Net Impact

As soon as the latch clicked, the door exploded toward her, pushing her back and to the right, throwing her against the desk she had been working on. She hit with enough force she knew she would have a bruise in the morning. This wasn't funny. She twisted back toward her prankster colleagues to give them a piece of her mind, but when she did she saw two men she didn't recognize. The first, a stocky, middle-aged guy, rushed in, pulling a second, taller and younger, surfer-type. This was more than not funny—this was assault. She took in a deep breath to scream her lungs out, but before she could make a sound, the older guy slapped a beefy hand over her mouth. She struggled, not so much to get away—there was no hope in that, the guy's arms were like steel beams—but to make sure her nose was clear of the guy's hand. She still had to breathe.

Her attacker seemed to sense her difficulty and shifted his hand, loosening his grip from crushing to merely painful. He jerked his head toward a nearby laser printer and barked at the surfer guy. "Grab a sheet of paper and write 'Working—Do Not Disturb' so the words show through the window when you tack it up. Move." Then her captor reached into his pack and pulled out a couple pairs of latex gloves, tossing one set toward the younger guy and wriggling his free hand into one of the others. He shifted hands holding her and repeated the gloving process with his other hand. Their attack had frightened Beverly, but the significance of their precautions truly terrified her. She began to shake uncontrollably.

The guy holding her felt her tremors and gave her a surprised look, loosening his grip a bit further. He held up his free hand in a calming gesture, then put a finger to his lips. "Just stay quiet and I can let you go." He slowly let go and took a tentative half-step back as the surfer worked on putting the sign up over the door, isolating her from the view of even Bruce from accounting, not that he would be likely to come by anyway. As soon as she was free from her assailant, she leaned away from him, instinctively drawing her arms protectively across her chest, pulling her lab coat closed.

The older guy took in her movement and seemed to understand her fear. He shook his head and raised his hands for just a moment. "Don't worry. It's nothing like that. I didn't mean to frighten you." He waved his right hand at the computer gear stuffed into the climate and humidity controlled room. "Our only interest is in the computers. Keep quiet and cooperate and we could be gone within a half-hour."

Beverly pushed herself upright from the table and did her best to stop trembling and compose herself. She started to look up, to look them in the eye to show her strength and defiance, but then thought better of advertising the fact she could identify both of them. She turned her gaze downward instead and focused on calming her ragged breathing. Her mind was awhirl. Part of her wanted to believe him, wanted to believe she wasn't going to be raped and killed, that these ... these idiots were actually committing a felony ... multiple felonies, including kidnapping for God's sake ... in order to gain some advantage in a virtual world. She knew some of Reality 2 Be's customers were compulsive, but this was unbelievable. It was the unbelievability of their crime that kept the other part of her terrified it was just a story, that unimaginable things were about to occur she would never be able to forget. She slowed her breathing and fixed her gaze on the floor.

"That's it," cooed her attacker. "Good idea. Let's keep the eyes on the floor. That makes it simpler for everyone." He stepped toward her again, but in a calm, slow movement. "Now, I'm going to bind your hands with a little zip tie, here, not too tight, just so you don't reach for a phone or an alarm." He did so, then looked back at the younger fellow, who had finished tacking up the sign and donning his own gloves.

Net Impact

The older guy looked at the security badge pinned to her white lab jacket, at least that's what she prayed he was looking at. "That's very good, Beverly. Can I call you Bev?" She nodded without looking up and he continued. "Now, as long as you're quiet, there won't be any reason to gag you. Is that okay with you?" She began to speak, but stopped herself and just nodded. "Great. My friend here, he just needs to access your system for awhile." The fellow talking moved her to the side, next to a tall bank of servers. "Let's just give him some room and let him work." The older guy nodded for the other one to sit down where she had been working.

The younger guy was trembling almost as much as she was as she shifted to her right. He sat down quickly in her chair and adjusted its height. Then his fingers started punching keys. "She's already logged in, so that helps," the typist said as he continued. Beverly didn't look at her assailants directly, but she did shift her gaze up to look at the screen, to try to figure out what they were looking for. The older guy started pacing in the brief confines of the computer room as the minutes ticked by and the surfer's feverish hacking continued, screens flashing by. After a half-hour though, the pace seemed to lag and the hacker's under-the-breath epithets began to increase in intensity and frequency. Finally, he stopped altogether.

"I can't access a world search function here, at least not anything more useful than an enhanced version of what you can access in the game itself. There's not a parameter for file size, amount of maypoles carried or exchanged, nothing."

Thieves? These guys were trying to steal maypoles?

"I thought you said you could do it from here. The company has to be able to do enhanced searches to monitor things, don't they?"

The young guy growled. "I know what I said, but I can't find anything on the server menus."

The older guy stopped pacing and started clenching and unclenching his fists. Finally, he pointed at Beverly, who was standing, still quietly quivering, with her face pressed against the side of the server, doing her best not to aggravate her captors or even look at them. "Ask her," he said.

The young guy turned to her. She didn't look at his face, but he clearly had an accent. English? Welsh? He sounded like a cross between Russell Crowe and Pierce Brosnan or maybe Errol Flynn. "Beverly ... Bev, honey, I need to search the Reality 2 Be virtual world for certain objects, certain files and coding that are located there or are in the possession of certain avatars."

She cleared her throat; she had no saliva. "I ... I don't know how to do that."

The hacker flicked a gloved hand dismissively. "I didn't ask you to do it. I can do it, if I can access the oversight menu hosting the main world grid. But I can't find that. Where do I go to gain access to the main world grid menu? Will I need an access code?"

She looked down at the floor even more, if that was possible. "You can't do that from here." She wasn't being heroic. It was the truth. But she knew they wouldn't believe her.

The older guy interrupted. "Where? Another office, another room? Can you show us?"

She shook her head as tears began to fall. "Please, I can't ... You can only oversee the servers hosting the main world grid from the location of the servers themselves."

The young guy jerked in astonishment. "You mean to tell me you're using off-site servers for your main world grid? That seems unlikely."

The older guy grabbed her arm and squeezed. She knew they wouldn't believe her and the old guy, he seemed to have a temper. "Don't lie to us, Bev."

"It's true," she whispered.

The young guy shook his head; she could see the shadow on the floor of his unkempt blond hair flinging from side to side. "That can't possibly be true ..."

"Why not?" barked the other one as Beverly continued to watch the shadows which had crept into her simple life.

The surfer threw up his hands in frustration. "Companies like this, they're manic about secrecy and access to the servers. That's their whole business in a box of silicon chips. Offsite you've got no real security, no control over who might be accessing the servers."

The older guy squeezed her arm just a bit harder. What a dick! "What about it, Bev? Is he right? Is the company manic over security for the host servers?"

She wasn't about to volunteer anything, but she wasn't risking her life, such as it was, for her employer. She wasn't going to risk anything in reality to save some stupid virtual reality. So she answered. "Yes."

"Crap," muttered the older guy as he loosened his grip somewhat again. There were a few moments of silence. Everyone was obviously thinking. Finally, the older guy grunted and made an expansive gesture with his free hand. "Manic about security? We practically walked in here." He nodded his head toward the equipment. "They got enough machines in here to do the job?"

The hacker glanced around. "Not even close."

The older guy scowled. "Most of the building is cubicles. Unless they have a hell of a basement, there's no interior room big enough to host much more equipment than this." He retightened his grip on Beverly. "There's another facility with the servers, isn't there? This is all customer support, accounting, that kind of crap, isn't it?"

She hadn't volunteered, but they had guessed. They were smarter than she first thought. "Yes."

"Where? Tell us where."

"I can't." Once again she was telling the truth.

"You mean you won't."

Tears started flowing again and she cursed them in her mind. She cursed the tears and she cursed these strangely odd attackers and she cursed her dreary little life. "I mean, I can't. I don't know. It's all very hush-hush. I've never been there. Only the senior programmers go and they're gone for days when they go. But I don't know where."

She cringed as the older guy's fists clenched and unclenched repeatedly. It looked for a moment like he was going to slap her around.

Suddenly, the younger guy sat up straight from his slumped position at the keyboard. "Do they turn in expense reports?"

"What?" said Beverly.

"Huh?" said the older guy.

"Expense reports. You said they're always gone for days. That means they have to stay someplace, travel someplace, or something. You said this site handles accounting and stuff. Can you access the expense reports?"

Her eyes flicked up to meet the hacker's for just a moment. Maybe, just maybe he had saved her from his partner. Words began to tumble out of her mouth, unbidden. "I ... yes, all of the accounting data can be accessed here. We have general ledger coding, inventory, payroll, accounts payable, accounts receivable, financial and internal accounting control programs ..." She took a breath, before continuing without thinking. "But ... I would lose my job. Those reports have personal data. Social security numbers, bank account numbers for wire transfer of reimbursements."

"No one will ever know," promised the hacker. "We're not identification thieves."

"Yeah," added the older guy, "we're ... gaming enthusiasts who just wanna get an edge." It sounded lame to her, like even he didn't believe it was true, but she knew that people ... most especially guys ...

125

do stupid, pointless things all the time, like running with the bulls in Pamplona or lighting farts. The older guy's voice firmed as he continued. "Besides, you really don't have a choice. Trust me on that."

Even though she recognized the back and forth as a classic good cop/bad cop routine, intentional or unintentional, it did the trick. She relented. She even relaxed a bit as she and the hacker spent the next forty minutes speaking computerese to one another, entering passwords, skimming menus, and searching accounting databases. The older guy started pacing again, looking at his watch at increasingly short intervals in obvious frustration. "Jesus, it's an expense report," he finally blurted. "How long can it take to look up an expense report?"

The young guy waved his partner off. "We've already looked at more than a score. The one thing we know for sure is that the server complex is in the greater Denver metropolitan area, but there's something odd about all the reports."

"Stop right there," commanded the older guy—he obviously thought he was in charge. "Bev here, she doesn't need to know more about what we think is odd or what we've figured out. Right, Bev?" He gave a stern look at his cohort. "If you have found out all you're going to find out, then let's get the hell out of Dodge. I'd like to be out of this place before dawn. So would you."

The hacker nodded. A wave of relief washed over Beverly.

The older guy tossed a packet of alcohol towelettes to his companion. "Wipe off the keyboard, the door knob, and anything else you touched or sweated on—gloves on or no. I'll take care of Bev, here, and be with you in a minute."

Her relief drained away. A gripping horror squeezed her heart. She could see the hacker's face go pale and a look of revulsion flutter over his countenance before he spoke up. "Take care of ... What do you mean, 'Take care of'?"

126

"It's real simple," said the older guy as he started opening up desk drawers at the table where she had been sitting. When he found her purse, he took it out and opened up the wallet.

"You're robbing her?"

"Shut up," growled her tormentor, as he rifled through the wallet, sorting through it and pulling out three items. He held them up before her once-again tear-filled eyes. "This," he said in a professorial tone, "is your driver's license, with your home address and, by the way, your social security number." He held up a second item. "This is your address book and, judging by the lack of a wedding ring on your finger and your last name, my guess is this entry here is your mother, maybe your sister, but a blood relative who you probably love and all that." He held up a third item. "This is your kitty cat, a young Persian by the looks of it."

He leaned down to her, his face nose to nose with her own runny nose. "I'm taking these three items with me. I know where you live. If you move, I'll still know how to find you. I know where your mother lives. I know how to find your adorable little kitten. If anyone, I mean anyone, finds out we were here tonight, if any alarm is raised, if any report is filed, there will be consequences ... life and death consequences ... to one or two or maybe even all three of these loved ones." She flicked her gaze over to the hacker, his face red and contorted as his partner threatened her life. "Just because my friend here is a nice guy, don't think for a minute I am. I won't even tell him. I'll just do it. I'll just do your mother, your sweet little cat, you."

She began to sob hysterically. She wished she had never wished for more excitement in her life.

The old guy moved toward the door. "We're done here."

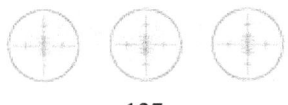

They were back in the car before Dick let Luke speak ... or, more accurately, yell.

"What the hell was that?" Luke exploded as Dick started up the car.

Dick gave his partner an even, emotionless look as he answered with seeming nonchalance. "What the hell was what?" Truth told, he hated this part of his job. Bev was just some bright techie girl who, no doubt, worked night shift 'cause she didn't have much of a life outside of work. And here he had made her narrow little world darker and scarier. Still, he had to do what he had to do.

"You didn't have to threaten to kill her," Luke stormed as Dick jinked the car into gear and started pulling onto the back roads, headlights still off. "She was scared enough, for God's sake. You didn't have to say you'd kill her mother."

Dick turned the car to the east as they came to a more major road, flipping on the headlights. "You're right," he answered as his hands worked the steering wheel, crossing hand over hand for the sharp turn. "If this was Cambodia or Albania or Kazakhstan, I would have just offed her. It's simpler, it's safer for me, for you, for the Subsidiary. But I don't get my jollies that way and leaving her alive probably maintains a lower profile. There is a good chance the brass at Reality 2 Be will never know we visited their offices—a better than even chance."

Luke stewed, squirming and fussing with the shoulder restraint on his seatbelt. "You didn't have to traumatize her."

"I do what I have to. The mission comes first." He accelerated the car into the night. "She needed to be traumatized and, frankly," he continued, catching Luke's eye and staring straight at him for a few beats, "so did you. This is not a game. This is not Reality 2 Be. This is reality. And if you can't handle what we do in reality to make it just a little safer for everyone, then you should leave and go play grab-ass in some software shop in Seattle or San Jose or back downunder and leave saving the real world to professionals."

Luke was silent for a full five minutes before he spoke again. "One more question?"

Dick rolled his eyes. "Sure."

"Where the hell are we going? This isn't the way we came."

Dick smiled. "We were, what, ten miles from the Maine border at that place?" He looked over at Luke. Maybe the kid could learn. "When you're on the run, always cross a jurisdictional border as soon as possible. It won't stop a hot pursuit, but it tends to bollix up law enforcement just enough to give you an edge. Always take the edge."

Dick drove into the night, his mind racing.

CHAPTER 12

Dee Tammany loved her commute.

Her life was her job, no doubt about it. Recruited straight out of college by the CIA, the hard and dangerous world of intelligence gathering and covert ops consumed her waking hours and frequently interrupted her sleeping hours. She loved the challenge of it, the intellectual and psychological puzzles it brought to her, and the chance it provided her to make a real difference in the world, whether the world ever knew of it or not. Oh sure, there were times she cursed the job. Certainly the demands and geography of her CIA stint had been a significant factor in her divorce from Brody. And the politics, first at the CIA and now at the Subsidiary, could be petty and annoying. Worse, the responsibility for the agency, for her operatives, for the fate of unknowing, innocent people around the globe, at times pressed down on her with a weight she did not think she could bear.

That's why she loved the drive to work. It was her only respite, a brief interlude between office and townhouse that left her with time to process her thoughts and retreat into more pleasant reveries.

The office was a constant whir of decisions and reports and keyhole satellite imagery. Every mission, every budget allocation, every meeting with the representatives of the nation states which had created the Subsidiary was, she knew, even if it was not obvious at the time, a life or death determination for someone, somewhere. Maybe it would be the agent she sent out on an operation with misgivings as to whether his or her skills measured up to the task or maybe it would be a frightened young girl in a tent in some third-world backwater as thugs the Subsidiary had failed to stop—or even chosen not to stop for some greater geopolitical reason—came with guns and an animalistic thirst for power and control.

Her townhouse was supposed to be her sanctuary, a place where she could feel safe and relax, guarded by Marco, her live-in protector, trainer, and chauffeur, and coddled by Mitzi, her college-aged housekeeper and connection to the pop culture that most people take for granted: television, music, movies, games, food, and clothes. But despite the safety of her abode and Mitzi's enthusiasm and affection, too often work would still intrude. Dee was easy to reach there and she had had more than one pajama talk with Mitzi interrupted by pompous diplomats insisting on a virtual meeting or by urgent communiqués concerning ongoing operations.

In the car, almost no one bothered Dee. Even in traffic, the time interval between Catalyst Crisis Consulting's—and, hence, the Subsidiary's—headquarters overlooking the "clothespin" sculpture on Centre Square in downtown Philly and her townhouse on the western border of the Rittenhouse Square neighborhood was not long. The two locations were two miles apart at the most. She'd walk it if time and Marco would ever allow it, but most days Marco drove her to and from work in Catalyst Crisis Consulting's discreetly armored limousine. It was certainly more secure, especially since she often carried sensitive documents or equipment, but, with traffic, it wasn't a lot faster than walking.

On most days, however, the commute was a brief respite from the madness of her work life. Things that arose in that short travel interval could wait for just a bit, until she had arrived at one place or the other, depending on the time of day. Since Marco took care of the driving and keeping a weather eye out for security threats, she had no responsibilities in the car. Sometimes she read—reports from work when she was swamped, and lighter, recreational fare, often paperbacks recommended by Mitzi, when she wanted to unwind. Although Dee had convinced Mitzi to stop putting paranormal romances in her book bag, there was still an occasional bodice-ripper mixed in with the epic fantasies, humorous travelogues, and biographies that were always available when she was in the mood to relax.

This morning, she was chuckling at a passage in one of Mitzi's pop culture recommendations, the surprisingly amusing biography of a former *Jeopardy* champion, when Marco interrupted. After lowering the bullet-proof security/privacy panel separating the passenger compartment from the driver's area in the modestly-sized limousine, he caught her eye in the rear view mirror.

"It's Glenn. He needs to talk."

Dee's brow furrowed and she gave a slight growl. "Glenn needs to get a life. Tell him I'll be at the office in ... what, six or eight minutes?"

Marco shook his head as he eased the car left one lane. "Already tried that. Can't wait ... blah, blah, blah ... Chinese representative ... blah, blah ... curses and threats ... blah, blah ..." Marco's hardened expression faltered and his nose twitched. "... er, from the Chinese representative, not Glenn."

Dee half-smiled. "The Chinese representative only talks to me instead of Glenn when he wants to curse and threaten. Besides, just because Glenn, being a proper English gentleman, doesn't verbalize his curses and threats, doesn't mean they're not there between the lines, believe me. This whole call is one big 'get your ass to work and do your job' from Glenn." She dog-eared the page she had been reading and dropped her book back onto the cushy leather seat next to her. "There's a reason Glenn works at headquarters. In the field he would've been fragged by friendly fire long ago."

Marco smiled, his white teeth gleaming beneath his gunslinger moustache. "Just say the word, boss. I could use some live target practice."

She smiled back. "If you killed him, I'd have to get a sock puppet or mannequin or something to stand in, so at least three of the national representatives wouldn't have to dishonor themselves by talking to a

132

woman as an equal, Besides, I'd have to do his job 'til we got a replacement. So, no thanks. Just give me the call."

"Line three," Marco responded as the security panel slid back into place.

Dee punched a button and picked up the receiver on the secure phone. "What?"

"The Chinese representative has been trying to reach you for a half-hour."

Dee's eyes flicked to her watch. "He calls early. He stays on the line late. The guy has no phone manners whatsoever." She sighed. "What's the crisis?"

"He called to see what we had done about Luke Calloway. When I wouldn't tell him, he went apoplectic. Even with the electronic voice replacement software, you could tell the guy was hopping mad. He used swear words even I hadn't heard of."

"That is impressive." She paused for just a moment in preparation. "Conference him in."

There was a click and the line picked up an almost subsonic hum as the second line was added.

"Greetings, esteemed representative ..." began Dee, before she was interrupted.

"I demand to know what has been done about the traitor spy, Calloway."

She refused to be riled. "As I am sure Mr. Swynton has told you, that is an operational matter which is our concern at the Subsidiary and not within the purview of the national representatives."

The electronics were not able to modulate out the venom in the Chinese representative's rant. "It is most certainly within the purview of the national representatives when an operative of the Subsidiary is running independent clandestine operations aimed at the overthrow of the legitimate nation state of one of those representatives. It is not proper conduct for the Subsidiary's resources to be used to spy upon one another!"

"Isn't that what you were doing when you stayed on the line to listen to my conversation with Calloway?" she thought, but was too well-trained to verbalize. Instead, she replied in a smooth, business-like tone: "I am fully aware of the protocols for use of agency resources."

She could almost see an Oriental face flashing red like the Chinese flag would brighten during an exchange in one of the virtual meetings. "Calloway must be interrogated concerning his activities. Given our interest and our knowledge concerning other spies and anarchists he may have contacted, we insist he be turned over to our government for such interrogation."

Dee's voice grew colder. "Even if that were not also an operational matter outside of your purview, the answer would be 'no,' but since you put it so impolitely the answer is 'hell, no.'"

Glenn threw himself in front of the impending verbal explosion from half a world away. "The Subsidiary is fully aware of the inappropriateness of Mr. Calloway's behavior and I promise you, man-to-man, we will conduct a thorough investigation of his activities."

Dee took the cue. "In the event our investigation reveals anything it would be appropriate to share with China in the furtherance of the Subsidiary's purposes, we will share such information. In short, this is our problem, not yours, but rest assured we will deal with it."

The line was silent for several seconds before the response came from the representative of China. The modulated voice was calmer and slower. "Rest assured that if you do not deal with this problem, then we will."

There was a click and the low hum on the line ceased. "Are we sure we're alone on the line?" asked Dee.

There was a pause, then Glenn responded. "We are alone and secure."

Dee stared out the window at the carefree world as she talked, focusing on everything and nothing at the same time. "Backchannel through your contacts in China that we're taking this very seriously and that things are not going to end well for Mr. Calloway. We need to keep them off our backs and off his until we finish this mission."

"Can do," was Glenn's terse response. "What are we going to do with Luke Calloway at the end of the day?"

Dee looked at her discarded paperback. Like *Jeopardy*, the answers at the Subsidiary came only in the form of more questions.

On an intellectual level, Pigeon didn't question the approach. Hawk had explained the spycraft of it explicitly. Dropping off the grid, disappearing from their usual haunts and routines, would make it that much easier for anyone trying to track them to notice an anomaly and finger them as possible suspects. To avoid that, Pigeon and the others needed to do their best to behave normally, interacting with others as if nothing had happened, was happening. It made sense.

But at an emotional level, the approach was driving him to absolute distraction. He kept looking over his shoulder to see who might be about, watching him, spying on him, reporting on his every move. He felt a constant need to be alert, on guard. He craved the feel of a weapon in his hands, but you couldn't just saunter around with an automatic weapon, your finger on the trigger. So, instead of wearing his pack on his back as it was designed, he slung it over one shoulder, only partly zipped. That way his right hand could snake inside and rest, coiled around the trigger of Hawk's MAC 10, the safety off, the weapon set for full auto.

He stepped off of a wide street in a busy, developing section of town, into the neon-bedazzled entrance of a dance club. The club itself was dimly lit, throbbing with a heavy techno beat, and packed with throngs of pulsating, happy patrons dressed in everything from slinky, sequined gowns to almost nothing at all. The crowd was in a fine mood, dancing and drinking and groping each other to the beat of the music. Guys pressed into girls, shouting above the din of the music lame, but somehow still incredibly effective, pick-up lines, then scampering off to one of the even darker side rooms for some casual sex.

He wasn't interested in music or sex, not today, but this was one of his usual haunts. He thought he would feel better in the middle of a crowd, especially a friendly—sometimes very friendly—crowd. But he had been wrong. The dark shadows were somehow sinister, every stranger somehow suspicious.

"Hey, good looking! Wanna dance?"

She was a leggy redhead in a slinky green gown that showed plenty of décolletage. He thought maybe he'd seen her here before, but he wasn't sure. He wasn't sure of anything anymore.

"Strong and silent type, huh? Why don't you take your arm out of your pack and put it around me?" She winked. "I'm sure you can find something to hold on to back there."

His eyes darted about. Was he being set up? "Maybe in a minute," he stalled. "You been here before?"

She giggled. "Lots of times. Seen you before, too. You look a little tense this time, though. Maybe I can help you relax, you know, relieve some tension."

Pigeon remembered why he came to this club. The women were incredibly forward. He felt his concerns lift away. He sidled up to her. "Sure ... uh ..."

"Brandy," she cooed, "but everybody calls me 'Red.' What's your name?"

"Uh ... Pigeon," he replied, his hand loosening its grip on the MAC 10.

She stood on tiptoes and leaned into him, her breasts brushing his chest and her hair caressing his face as she put her lips to his left ear and gave it a nibble. "That's nice, I guess, but I want it to be really good for you. What's your real name?"

Pigeon froze, the fear welling back into his body in a rush. He pushed back from her with his left arm as his right hand once more sought the reassuring comfort of the smooth, cool metal of the MAC 10. "Why ... What do you mean 'my real name'? Why would you need to know that?"

She tried to keep leaning in, wriggling seductively, as she gave a suggestive smile. "Don't you want me to call out your real name, big boy? It's so much more fun than make-believe when you're ... you know ... intimate."

On any other day, it would have enticed him. It was ... she was ... alluring, exciting, seductive. But not now. His emotions convulsed. He backed away. "No. No names. No real names."

She looked disappointed, her mouth in a pout, but did not give up. "Whatever you want, honey," she purred.

He turned and ran for the door. Shouts rang out from jostled patrons whose drinks were spilled or whose whispered conversations were interrupted by his mad dash for freedom, but their angry voices just spurred him onward.

He burst out of the dark club onto the bright expanse of the broad street, blinded momentarily by the contrast. He ran to his left with reckless abandon to gain distance from the club and the oddly inquisitive femme fatale. He didn't really care where he was going. He just wanted to get away. He picked up speed, unmindful of whether he bumped into anyone on his headlong flight. For a moment, a glorious brief moment, he saw nothing but sunlight and bright blue sky and felt that freedom was in his grasp.

That's when he heard the helicopters. Sleek, black, and angular, three WZ-10 attack copters whumped toward him, noses down, gaining speed. He could see the 30 caliber cannon on the nose of each one and the two stub winglets holding HJ-10 anti-tank weapons. The Chinese had found him. He could run, but he would only die tired.

Suddenly, he knew this is what must have happened to Shrike— why none of them would ever see Shrike again. He also knew what had ultimately happened to Shrike was most assuredly going to happen to him. Hawk and Peregrine, they would have put up a coordinated fight—just maybe they could get out of a situation like this. But not him. He dove for the ground, spinning to face upward as he fell.

His world seemed to decelerate into slow motion—every detail crisp and clear. Without removing his right arm from his unzipped backpack, he squeezed the trigger on the MAC-10 as he fell, bullets spitting in rapid fire succession through the cloth and into the air in an uncontrolled arc he prayed would somehow hit something vital on the sleek, five-rotored, Chinese manufactured craft. He longed to see a showy explosion rip one of the copters to shreds, sending fire and shrapnel to envelop the others and bring down the full complement of his pursuers, but he couldn't bet on that and wouldn't wait to see if it happened.

With his left hand, he reached for the button that would end his existence in this world forever. He could never come back, he could never see the results of his last action, but there was no way he was going to risk Hawk and Peregrine and his mission and everything else by being captured and analyzed. He didn't know exactly what these guys could do to him, but he didn't want to find out.

There. There was the button. Still falling, as he faced the sky, he pressed it.

Pigeon was a fine red mist before he could hit the ground.

The speed of light beats gravity every single time.

CHAPTER 13

At first, Luke had just pretended to sleep on the ride back. He wanted to avoid talking to Dick anymore about spycraft or why terrorizing innocent young women was the right thing to do in his world ... their world. But soon the stress and physical and mental exertion of their all night escapade got to him and real sleep came. He woke up in heavy traffic mid-day as they approached Philadelphia once again. He shook away the cobwebs and massaged his face with his hands, before looking over at Dick. The older man looked haggard, but alert, at the wheel, muttering expletives at other drivers as they powered their vehicles from lane to lane haphazardly trying to gain headway in the traffic.

"You want me to drive?" asked Luke, stifling a yawn.

Dick gave him a glance and a harrumph. "Might have appreciated the offer, oh, four or five hours ago. Wouldn't have let you, mind you, but would have appreciated the offer. Now it's just window dressing to ask."

Luke refused to let the guy get another rise out of him. He let the remark slide. "Why wouldn't you have let me?"

That question drew a chuckle from Dick. "Kid, you don't understand operatives at all, do you?" He drove on a bit, his head tilted as if in thought. "Let's just say the short answer is that all spies are control freaks. We control everything we can about a situation. We only trust people we know we can trust."

Luke was taken aback. "You don't know if you can trust me to drive a car down an interstate expressway?"

The lingering smile disappeared from Dick's face. "You were conducting clandestine activities utilizing the Subsidiary's equipment in an effort to undermine a sovereign state that helps fund your paycheck. I don't trust you to aim for the bowl when you piss."

"And the long of it?"

Dick glanced over at him. "Huh?"

"You said the short answer was 'all spies are control freaks.' What's the long answer?"

Dick motioned with his right hand toward the instrument panel of the car. "You probably noticed this isn't the latest model of sedan. Any guesses why?"

Luke shrugged. "Blends in better. Less likely to be identified by a witness."

Dick gave a half-smile. "Not bad for an amateur. Those things are true and good, but they're not the real reason."

Luke looked at the dash for a moment. "I give up."

Dick nodded his head at the steering wheel. "No airbags, not for me ..." he nodded toward Luke, "... and not for you. No ABS brakes either."

Luke thought, but nothing came. "You don't trust me to not hit something if I don't have ABS brakes?"

"No ABS brakes because it's damn hard to do a one-eighty spin at speed if you can't lock the wheels long enough to get into a skid. You can ... well, at least I can ... use the emergency brake on some models in a pinch, but it doesn't have the same feel or finesse as a foot pedal."

Luke simply nodded. Dick continued. "No airbags because you don't want them going off when you have to bump a car off the road in front of you; it also keeps the bad guys from disabling your vehicle by backing into you and causing the bags to deploy. Those things can break an arm if you're in the wrong position and you have to cut them out of the way just to be able to steer."

"Oh."

"Pretty good clearance on this bucket, too. Means that if I have to cross a median strip or drive through a wall or across a field or something, I'm less likely to rip out the transmission or leave a traceable piece of evidence behind."

Luke thought for a moment about what he had gotten himself into. "You drive through a lot of walls?"

"Only when I'm followed by assassins in low-slung, sporty cars, especially convertibles."

Luke turned around and studied the traffic. Was that a BMW convertible three cars back? "Is somebody following us?"

Dick sighed. "That was a subtle way to check, that's for sure. But, no. Nobody's on our tail. That's why it's taken us longer to get back than to get there. I made a few unexpected route changes along the way, just to be sure."

"Oh," Luke said again. "I didn't notice."

"Yeah," replied Dick, "you were asleep. But don't worry. Sleeping when you can is operationally very smart. Besides, you need to be in top form for the next step."

"Reporting in?"

"No."

"You've already done that using the virtual reality feature of your sunglasses?"

Dick gave him a severe look, then turned his eyes back to the road. "I was driving, remember? Hard not to run into things if my glasses are glazed over with screen displays of Glenn Swynton and Dee Tammany chewing my ass out. Besides, there was no reason to wake anyone to tell them I failed yet again to locate the plans for the Kestrel 84 and, oh yeah, by the way, I threatened an innocent little kitten and somebody's mother in the process." He sighed and glanced over at Luke. "It's not pleasant, but it's best to man up to bad news in person."

Luke pondered for a few moments. "So, if reporting in isn't the next step, what is?"

The older man shook his head. "Figuring out where we go next."

Maybe he still hadn't woken up fully, but Luke was confused. "You're lost?"

At the next stop in the stop-and-go traffic, Dick turned to face fully sideways and gave Luke a long stare. "No, you moron. You're lost if you don't figure out where Reality 2 Be's server farm is. As long as you're useful, you're still hanging on, even if it is by a slim thread of bloody razor wire. If you aren't helping on the mission, there's no reason not to feed you to the goons from China."

"Oh," replied Luke. He was certainly awake now.

"And don't think Australia being on the oversight board will save you. The Aussie rep won't even try."

Luke had not imagined anything worse than getting fired. Now he started imagining a lot of things worse than getting fired. None of them were good.

Pao Fen Smythe leaned forward in his desk chair, his elbows on the deep rich grain of the mahogany desktop. "You know that is not the way I do business," he snapped, holding the old-fashioned receiver away from his ear while his prospective client vented. Pao Fen disdained the newfangled headsets so many others favored. Not only did he regard them devices suitable only for salesmen and clerks, he shivered at the thought of someone yelling in his ear and having to fumble about for a volume control to do anything about it. A lot of people in his line of business yelled. Gang leaders, revolutionaries, heads of state, they all liked to bark orders and yell at anyone who didn't kowtow to their every whim. Pao Fen didn't like their attitudes, but he loved their cash, so whenever anyone screamed at him or treated him like dirt, he just increased the price twenty percent and delayed delivery a few days. The smart ones got the message after a few transactions. The rest just paid more for the privilege of abusing him with their self-importance.

"This is not information you can find on Wikipedia or Jane's Defence Weekly. It is not something you can get by having a call girl set up a drunk Second Lieutenant so you can blackmail him with pictures if he doesn't cooperate. My reputation is on the line here and I will take whatever amount of time is necessary to confirm the completeness of the information and its value to my customers."

The client clamored on. Finally, Pao Fen was able to get a word in. "I understand your offer, but you must understand that our expenses have increased, as have our risks. The minimum bid has increased by one million."

He held the phone away from his ear, interrupting the tirade only to say "of course, Euros—nobody deals in dollars anymore," when he saw a light flash on his phone. "Thank you for your understanding. Bids are due at the end of the week. I must take another call."

He pressed the flashing button on his phone without waiting for a reply.

"Report," he said, then did nothing but listen for several minutes. "I told you New Zealand was a dead end, Mr. Lee. Where do you plan to look next?"

Again he listened. "You know, even subscribers are not encouraged to go there." He nodded as he took in the reply. "I will make arrangements. Pace yourself. They say there is 25% less oxygen there due to the altitude, although with the pollution here, you may find the air quite pleasant. Be mindful of your visibility, however. The Americans are increasingly vigilant and arbitrary in their dealings with foreigners of late."

He hung up the phone. It had been unwise to contact potential buyers before he had the Kestrel 84 plans in hand. Now things were delayed and the fiasco at the Dunedin warehouse district had made it abundantly clear someone—some competitor or agency or law enforcement authority—had gotten wind of the theft of the plans and possibly his involvement. What had once been a lucrative transaction on the side had now become a bet-the-company transaction. He didn't mind gambling, but he liked a fixed game better.

Luke was alone again in the tech room at the Subsidiary's Philadelphia Headquarters. Dick had dropped him at the tech lab and, thankfully, gone off without him to report on their activities in New Hampshire to Dee Tammany and Glenn Swynton. Luke felt dirty about the whole business. It was bad enough to have done what he did, what he helped do, to that poor girl. It would be worse yet to recite the details about it like he was giving a staff report or justifying a line item during a budget review meeting. It would be even worse if the bosses here started criticizing them for leaving a live witness behind—that would be more than he could handle.

Luke knew violence was part of the arsenal of methods the Subsidiary used to keep the world safe. He had even been involved before in reports or live communications in which gunplay and death had been component parts. But, before it had somehow seemed apart from what he did here at the Subsidiary. The violence was always at a distance, involving people he never met or saw. That made it somehow artificial, like the violence in his games.

The only acts of violence that had ever touched him emotionally were the reports of the atrocities committed by Chinese authorities on dissidents and democratic freedom fighters in the horrendous Chinese prison system. Those shocking reports had gotten him involved in funding Chinese dissident activities, including spiriting out activist diaries and reports over the anonymous gaming network of Reality 2 Be.

Welcome to real reality.

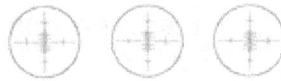

Seth tossed the controller down and rubbed his eyes, leaning back in the big, comfy recliner. Brian set his controller down with more care, then belched and toddled toward the bathroom. They had been playing on their computers all night and their marathon session had been more exhausting than non-gamers ... mundanes ... generally thought. Not only were Seth's thumbs dented with the imprint of the toggles from the controller, but the knuckles on his thumbs and the lining in the carpal tunnel of each of his wrists screamed with repetitive motion stress. His eyes were dry and gluey and his brain was weary, fried by the constant decision-making and puzzle-solving of their computer quest.

He heard the toilet flush and saw Brian stumble back into the room, his slack face, disarrayed hair, and jerky gait giving him the appearance of one of the walking dead—the George Romero kind, back when zombies were slow and not too bright.

Seth started to smile, but decided it took too much energy. "You look wasted, dude."

Brian's lip curled in a snarl. "You should talk. Not only do you look like fried crap, you stink like it, too. How do you work up so much B.O. sitting in an easy chair?"

Seth turned his head and sniffed, jerking his head back as the stench assaulted his nostrils like smelling salts somehow gone rancid. He felt woozy. "It's the adrenaline working its way out, probably. Besides the Naugahyde on this chair doesn't breathe, so the sweat just sticks ..."

Brian held out a hand, palm forward, as he plopped back down on the couch. "T-M-I, dude. Way too much information. I don't wanna know where you've got sweat sticking to you because of the chair, man. Just use the couch next time."

Seth rolled his shoulders to work out some kinks. "Point taken. We got any leftover pizza or something for brunch?"

Brian got up with a groan and made his way over to the dry bar off the basement family room of his parent's house. He poked at a cardboard box, lifting the lid and peering inside. "Some. It's been sitting out quite a while ..."

Seth shrugged. "Just nuke it for ninety seconds. That should kill off anything really harmful."

Brian reached into the box and grabbed the remainder of the pizza. Congealed cheese kept the pieces glued together as he slid them into the microwave without bothering to use a plate. He set the timer and pressed "start," then looked at his watch. "You gotta check in with the 'rents or anything?"

Seth's mood darkened. He shook his head. "Nah. I'll call Mom later. She tends to sleep in on the weekends, even when she's not sitting around some hotel room 'cause she's walked out on my dad. Besides, cell phone reception sucks down here."

Brian nodded, but said nothing.

"And Dad, who the hell knows where Dad is?" Seth continued. "Working, probably. That's my dad's life: work, work, work. Once he figured out I was old enough to take care of myself, he stopped even trying to keep track of where I was or what I was doing, which can be a boost when you wanna go to a party or a concert or ..." he waved his hand around at the room, "... when you wanna hang with a friend all weekend, but it kinda sucks when you wanna learn how to drive a stick or something."

Brian scrunched up his nose for a moment. "I always thought your dad was pretty okay, you know, as far as 'rents go."

"Yeah, he's okay. Taught me some stuff about his job a couple times—stealth tricks-of-the-trade when we were teamed up playing Lazer Tag. You know, security stuff he learned in the Army or when he was a cop. Other cool stuff, too, like how to make sure you're not being tailed and how to hold a gun. Safety stuff, too, like how to get out of a locked room when there's a fire."

The microwave dinged and Brian popped the door and used his fingers to slide the steaming pizza onto a reasonably clean plate he picked up from the counter, swearing every time his fingers touched the tomato sauce. "Ow, damn it. How do you do that?"

Seth continued to work out the kinks in his muscles. "If you can't go through the door, you go through an interior wall. Most modern houses are just plasterboard over studs sixteen inches apart. You tap a couple times to find the studs and just crash through the wall in between."

Brian carried over the pizza, sucking cheese and grease off his burnt fingers. "You mean I could just crash through the wall here?" He pointed at the side wall.

Seth shook his head. "No, numb-nuts. We're in a basement." He waved his hand at the wall. "That's just cheap paneling over concrete. You'd crack your head open if you tried to crash through, not that that would do any real damage."

"I knew that," replied Brian. "Your dad teach you anything else interesting? Cause, I mean, you seem to know a lot of stuff."

A staccato flash of memories warmed Seth's weary mind, but he didn't relate any of them to Brian. "If I told you anything else, dude, I'd have to kill you."

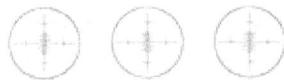

Dee Tammany and Glenn Swynton listened to Dick's entire report without interrupting for questions, although Dee's left eyebrow arched a bit when Dick reported the steps he had taken to assure the silence of the young woman at Reality 2 Be's corporate offices.

There were a few moments of silence after he finished before Dee spoke up.

"Not exactly a rousing success, was it?"

Glenn interrupted before Dick could answer. "At least he didn't blow the place up this time. Good show there, sport."

Dick burned to say something in response, but he just kept his teeth clenched.

Dee responded, looking at Glenn through hard, unblinking eyes. "I wouldn't mind that, if it had accomplished the mission, but there was apparently nothing in New Hampshire worth destroying." She turned to Dick. "I concur with your decision not to kill the girl. There's no need to kill innocents and it might have tipped off the powers at Reality 2 Be someone was looking at their activities. But I wish you had managed to fulfill your mission parameters without involving her. I'm not thrilled about you terrorizing her and I wonder whether even that will be effective at keeping her quiet."

Dick's response was even and low-key. "We needed her to gain access. The threats are usually effective, at least in the short term."

Glenn bristled. "Usually?"

Dick tilted his head to one side. "I got a good motivation spread here. Fear for herself. Fear for her mother or her sis, whoever was in her address book. Fear for her cute little kitty, for God's sake. In my experience, threatening pets is better than threatening random relatives. You never know when someone secretly hates their mom or thinks their brother can take care of himself or whatever, but pets are almost always innocent and beloved in the eyes of the owner and they can't be effectively warned to be on guard."

Glenn's eyes bored into him. "But ..."

Dick ran his tongue over his teeth while he thought for a second. "Look, I don't want to get the kid in more trouble than he already is, but ..."

Glenn seemed almost ready to pounce. "But he undermined your threat?"

"Not on purpose. He just gave a shocked look at me. It might make Bev, the girl, less inclined to believe we'll follow through."

"I'll take care of it," said Glenn simply.

"We don't need her killed," warned Dee, her eyes narrowing to slits with concern.

"Nothing like that," replied Glenn. "I'll just see to it Bev and her pet and her mom or whoever get a few Hallmark cards in the mail in the next day or two. 'Thinking of You,' that kind of bollocks. All anonymous. All untraceable. But from destinations near and far, so she understands the scope of who she's dealing with."

"That'd work," Dick agreed.

"I'll also make some discreet checks with my contacts at the New Hampshire State Police," Glenn continued, "just to be sure no alarm has been raised."

"That still leaves several concerns about the mission." Dee wasn't the hard-ass Glenn was, at least in Dick's mind, but she was still all-business. "Where do we go from here?"

"The kid, Luke, he's working on that. We have a lead indicating the servers are in Denver. He's narrowing down the search based on some of the stuff we downloaded in New Hampshire."

"So he's still useful?"

"Yeah, oh yeah," replied Dick. He knew where this was going, but Glenn went ahead and said it out loud anyway.

"Sooner or later his utility on this mission will end, though, and there's no way the Subsidiary can trust him on future endeavors. You know what that means."

Dick knew. Another part of the job he didn't like.

Dee spoke up. "Even if we were inclined to ... be lenient ..., the Chinese wouldn't tolerate it. They'd take unilateral action. That would be unfortunate for the Subsidiary's relationship with its sponsoring states."

Dick gave an unbusinesslike grunt. "It would be more than unfortunate for Luke. They'd want to extract things, probably not just stuff about Reality 2 Be and this mission either. Things would end slow and painful."

"When the time comes, quick and painless is fine," murmured Dee.

Glenn proved once again to Dick that he had less of a soul than anyone else he dealt with at HQ. "The important part is the ending, though, however you need or want to get there."

The ends justify the means. Since it wasn't a corporation or a governmental bureaucracy, the Subsidiary didn't go in for all that "mission statement" and "corporate creed" bullshit, but if you had to pick five words that summed up everything about the agency, that would be it: The ends justify the means.

Dick simply nodded. He knew his job. He'd better get on with doing it.

CHAPTER 14

Luke's fingers skittered like impromptu jazz over the keyboard, making a matrix out of the expense report information for Reality 2 Be's senior programmers. Bev was right; they did go on trips for several days at a time on a fairly regular basis. Almost all of those trips were to Denver. Maybe if he mapped out the locations of the hotels used and checked the mileage utilized on the rental car receipts he could get a rough idea of the location of the server farm. Then, cross-referencing with power consumption information hacked out of the utility company or repair reports from air conditioning servicemen, he could narrow down things a bit more.

It was a good approach, an excellent approach, even if he had to say so himself because, of course, no one else knew what he was doing. The only problem with the approach was it was completely useless when he tried it; there was no information in the expense reports on hotels or rental cars. He checked for taxi receipts as a surrogate for the latter, but came up empty, completely empty. His eyes scanned with rapid efficiency through the data. All the other usual information was there. Entries for tips, drinks, food, and ground transportation on the New Hampshire side of the trip, as well as for airline flights (all first class) into the Denver area. All of the Colorado flights were into the relatively new Denver International Airport, as opposed to Colorado Springs, an alternate Luke knew was preferred by some computer types who had business at the Denver Tech Center, a corporate park on the far southeast side of Denver favored by cutting edge electronics and tech companies.

Dick expanded the search to pick up the highest levels of company management. There were a few trips to Denver by the company brass, but they showed the same pattern of receipts—no hotels, no rental cars, and no taxis. Of course, the CEO and the Chief Information Officer, they both used Reality 2 Be's corporate jet, a Gulfstream IV, instead of commercial carriers. First Class apparently wasn't good enough for the big boys. It probably wasn't that the Gulfstream was so much more comfortable than First Class, although he would bet his paycheck the flight attendants were younger, prettier, and more attentive than their unionized commercial counterparts, but you almost never had to wait with a corporate jet. The smaller airports that catered to the executive jet crowd weren't nearly as busy as the commercial airports, which meant you could come and go pretty much on a moment's notice.

Luke Googled a bit until he found a listing of general aviation airports in the Denver metro area, then pushed down into the general ledger codes of the expense reports to find out which one they might be using for the corporate jet. It was one more data point—executives didn't like long car rides to their destination, even though they, like the programmers, were apparently being picked up by a limo or some sort of transport owned by the company's Denver operations. No way they were being ferried around in the backseat of somebody's Honda Civic.

He sifted through the information looking for charges for the corporate jet. Not only are jets damn pricey to buy, they have expenses most people never even think about. Not just pilot salaries and the cost of the jet and the fuel, but hangar costs, maintenance fees, inspection fees, licenses, catering fees, ongoing pilot training costs, satellite weather advisory fees, refueling services charges, and landing fees. When he found the landing fee information, it was more than interesting. It was damn unusual and expensive, to boot. He just stared at it for several minutes trying to think of an explanation.

The corporate jet was landing at Denver International Airport, too. Everyone was going to DIA and there was nothing in the expense reports to suggest they ever left.

Suddenly, it all made sense.

Net Impact

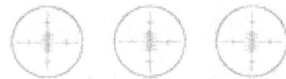

The jagged, snow-pocked peaks of the Rocky Mountains ended with surprising suddenness. The view out the window of First Class in the United Boeing 767-300, shifted from the dazzling whites and greens of the mountains to the mottled brown-green of the dry, baked earth of the Denver metro area. Barren, gullied plains spread north and east as far as Matt Lee could see. Passengers on the opposite side of the plane oohed and ahhed and pointed at the skyscrapers of downtown Denver as the plane descended below broken cloud cover and bounced through the always turbulent winds roiling over the precipices of the Front Range. Straining to get an angle, he caught a brief glimpse of the gleaming white peaks of the tent-like architecture at the Jeppesen Terminal at DIA, Denver International Airport, before the plane shifted to line up its landing.

He would take some time, both to gather supplies he could not bring with him on the plane and to acclimatize to the altitude and the surroundings, but he couldn't dally too long. He had a simple, straightforward mission to accomplish. He was going to leave this pleasant-looking, sunny place with what he came to retrieve or die trying.

An attractive stewardess, Peggy according to her name tag, came by with his sports coat, laying it across the empty seat next to his so it would be handy once the flight had landed. "Are you coming to Denver for business or pleasure?" she asked, her perfect, straight, white teeth gleaming as she smiled. He'd heard once that beauty contestants and others who had to smile constantly for their jobs sometimes put petroleum jelly, Vaseline, on their teeth to make their lips slide more readily over the teeth and produce a glossy smile. He wondered if Peggy did that. He wondered what other things Peggy might do. He wondered how long her layover lasted. He needed to acclimatize and a little exercise would aid that effort. With an athletic build and a classically angular Oriental face dominated by his own bright, flashing smile, finding company when he traveled on business was never difficult.

"Pleasure, I hope, as well as business," he replied with an easy nonchalance. "I was hoping I could find someone nice to show me some sights."

Peggy laughed and winked. "What sights did you want to see?"

Matt leaned forward, allowing him to whisper in her ear and to get a nice view of Peggy's cleavage as she leaned down to talk with him. "Any sights you'd like to show me."

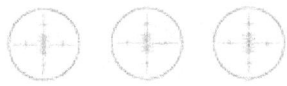

"I give up," said Dick as columns of numbers rolled up the computer screen in the Subsidiary's tech lab. "What exactly am I looking at?"

The information was as dry as a high-end martini, but it left Dick neither shaken, nor stirred. Luke, on the other hand, was all aquiver. The Australian-born tech whiz was apparently too excited to sit, so instead paced rapidly to-and-fro in the limited space behind Dick's chair, stepping and spinning and turning and stepping in fast succession. The nerve-wracking caged beast imitation was broken only by jabs of Luke's pointed finger thrusting past Dick's ear, first on the left, then right, then right-left-right as the invoices underlying the data in the matrix flashed onto the screen. Each one elicited the same unhelpful commentary from the computer geek. "Look, there! See? And look there. See?" Dick was getting a little "see" sick, if truth be told.

Net Impact

Dick furrowed his brow, focused his concentration on the invoices he was being shown, and tried to discern a pattern. Finally, he made the only observation he could think of. "Seems like these guys spend a hell of a lot of money just to land a plane, but what does that prove? That they're egocentric, narcissistic, Type A personalities who care more about their personal convenience than the bottom line? Welcome to corporate America."

Luke stopped pacing and his hands wriggled as if wanting to grab something and strangle it. "It's not just that it's expensive to land, especially compared to other airports not so far away. It's where they're landing. They're landing at DIA."

"So?"

Luke brushed by Dick to manipulate the mouse for the computer, pointing and clicking faster than Dick could follow. "And look, there. See?"

Dick's hands wriggled as if wanting to grab something and strangle it—Luke's throat. He stifled the urge and simply raised his hands in surrender. "I give up. What am I supposed to see?"

A jabbing finger flew by the side of his face once again. "They disembarked at a gate. At a terminal gate! There's the charge."

Dick didn't bother to look at the screen, turning his head instead to look at his agitated companion. "Don't most people get out at a gate?"

"Commercial passengers, sure," exclaimed Luke with obvious exasperation, "but not general aviation. They go to a hanger or one of the general aviation tarmacs."

Dick rubbed his temples. "So, these guys are spendthrifts. Sue me. Better yet, sue them."

Step, turn, step, spin, step. The pacing began anew while Luke continued to rant.

"Don't you get it? These guys are never leaving the terminal. There's no cab, no limo, no rental car, because they never leave.

There's no hotel expense, because they never leave. They fly into DIA instead of Jefferson County Airport or somesuch, because DIA is where they're going."

"You mean ..."

"Yes," exploded Luke, "I mean that Reality 2 Be's missing computer server farm is located in a secret underground facility beneath Denver International Airport!"

For a moment, Dick had thought he understood. But Luke's last statement caught him completely flat-footed once again. "What? How do you get from 'they're staying at DIA' to 'secret underground facility'? Are you a whack job?"

Luke gave Dick a stern look. "Well, there's no place for that kind of server farm in the above-ground facilities. It's all concourses and lounges and ticket counters and overpriced fast-food restaurants. It's gotta be underground."

Dick stopped rubbing his temples and massaged his face with his open palms. He hated working with amateurs. They saw too many spy movies and developed a warped sense of reality concerning espionage.

"Look, Luke, you seem like a level-headed fellow ... or bloke, as you would put it. But what you're suggesting is impossible. Not unlikely. Not surprising. Impossible. Evil villains seeking to dominate the world don't just build vast underground fortresses in dormant volcanoes or underneath Cuban lakes or major international airports. Who would do the work who wouldn't talk? Deaf mutes? How would the neighbors not happen to notice? Mass amnesia? Where would they get their power? Dilithium crystals? Who would provide site security? Deaf mute commandos? You couldn't in a million years keep something like that hidden. People would talk. Evidence would exist. The truth would leak out."

Net Impact

Luke had calmed down considerably during the course of Dick's diatribe. He gave Dick a wry smile. "You're absolutely right. Nothing like this could be completely hidden. Something would leak. The word would spread." He leaned forward to manipulate the mouse again, this time with a slow and deliberate movement. "It already has."

Hawk was on time. He was always on time. It was his responsibility as a soldier and his duty as a leader. Still, he didn't have high hopes for the upcoming encounter.

He moved with a purposeful stride, not rushing, but not loitering either. Except for the scheduled encounter, there was very little at this place that held any interest for him. Ignoring the distractions to either side, he peered well-ahead of his position and saw exactly what he had expected to see. Peregrine was sauntering toward him at a casual pace, his head turning from side to side to assess the passersby.

Hawk and his teammate were moving in from opposite sides of the mall and walking toward the fountain and benches at center court. The mall, itself, was a huge, grandiose temple to commercialism in all its tacky glory. It drew customers from near and far to buy and shop and buy and talk and buy some more. All around him, the usual stores catering to middle-America, as well as a few specialty shops, were arrayed with gaudy window displays beckoning to the throngs of teenaged girls that strolled through the place in packs of three and four. The girls giggled at private jokes and pointed at merchandise and sometimes pointed at him, winking and giggling and mouthing "Oh my god!" to one another when he gave them a stern look. He wasn't quite sure if the jail bait found his chiseled muscles and air of authority attractive or whether he intimidated the shit out of them. He didn't really care. He wasn't here for flirtation or small talk or ... oh my god, a dalliance with the underage shopaholic groupies. He certainly wasn't here to shop for things he didn't really need or want or sometimes even understand. He was here on business, serious business, life and death business.

He sauntered into the central court and sat down at a bench at the edge of the jetting center fountain. It was a good spot to meet and talk. The fountain made it difficult to hear any conversation from nearby benches or walkways, foiling any electronic bugs if the site of the meet or any of the expected participants had been compromised. He wasn't being overly-dramatic. Shrike had disappeared and Pigeon's mood at their last meeting had given him a bad feeling about the boy.

Peregrine sauntered up, looked at the empty seats on either side of Hawk, and sat down, a tight frown set on his face. Hawk had known Peregrine would be at the meet. The question was, were they the only two left in the squad? If so, things were even more serious and dangerous than he had ever expected them to be on the mission. It was a simple operation, nothing but an exchange. Information coming to him—really his taskmasters. Cash going to the rebels. He had done plenty of similar jobs before without these kinds of problems.

Hawk nodded at Peregrine.

Peregrine nodded back. "I've got two grand local that says Pigeon never shows."

Hawk started. It wasn't like Peregrine to throw around that kind of cash, not even in local currency. Truth be told, the guy was cheap. Hawk shook his head. "No bet. How can you think I would ever encourage a bet against the squad, even by taking the other side? It's ..."

"Bad karma?"

That almost made Hawk smile. "It's poor leadership. It's disrespectful."

They sat in silence for a few minutes. Peregrine seemed to be ogling some of the feminine flesh on display, but Hawk's focus never wavered from practiced security protocol. He kept up a lookout, his eyes moving at regular intervals from spot to spot, first the way he had come in, then down the snaking arm of the mall to his left, then to his right, searching for Pigeon or some threat in lieu of Pigeon.

Despite his security training, he didn't take any special note of what looked to be an eight-year old boy until the youngster ran up and grabbed his elbow. Crap! Didn't the Viet Cong use kids to carry improvised explosive devices into the midst of unsuspecting personnel? His instincts screamed for him to snatch the kid up and over his head into the fountain, then beat feet out of the perimeter of the blast and take cover. But he didn't do any of that. He was in a shopping mall, dammit, not Tikrit.

The kid wore a brightly colored shirt with horizontal stripes, blue jeans, and trendy, high-end athletic shoes. He had black hair and green eyes and was cute as could possibly be. Peregrine looked at the kid with terror on his face. "Hey, mister," said the kid and Peregrine flinched, sliding to the far end of the bench.

Hawk smiled. "What, kid?"

The kid scrunched up his nose. "This guy, he gave me these new shoes just 'cause I said I would give you a message." He held out a grubby fist with a folded piece of paper in it.

Hawk scanned in all directions looking for Pigeon or for someone else showing too much interest in his conversation with the young boy. Nothing.

"You know," Hawk said in a calm, soothing voice as he took the proffered slip of paper, "you shouldn't talk to strangers. Not to him, not to me. And you probably shouldn't let them buy you presents or ... agree to do the things they might ask you to do. It's not safe."

The boy laughed. "You're funny!" he cried out as he scampered away, running and jumping high with his bright new shoes flashing as he moved into the crowd of shoppers.

Hawk looked over at Peregrine, who seemed to have relaxed somewhat, although his frown was still present.

He held up the note. "I told you not to bet against the squad."

"Pigeon's still a chicken-shit or he wouldn't have asked a kid to go someplace he was afraid to go himself." Peregrine leaned forward to look as Hawk opened up the message. "What did he say? Is he okay?"

Hawk flinched when he saw the words. "It's not from Pigeon. It's from Shrike."

"Huh?"

CHAPTER 15

"Huh?" Dick shook his head in confusion, as if shaking things about his brain would make the oddly-shaped pieces of information he had received fall into some logical order. "Whaddya mean word's already leaked out about a secret facility hidden at Denver International Airport?" He spread his hands and looked around the room, as if seeking support from someone, but, of course, there was no one in the room but him and Luke. "Nobody sent me the memo. It doesn't show up on my free gas station map."

Luke looked confused. "They give away free maps at petrol stations?"

Dick scowled at the youngster. "Just explain to me how people could know about a secret facility at DIA, but not know about a secret facility at DIA."

Luke rubbed his stubble with his right hand. Finally, he looked at Dick and spoke in almost professorial tones. "Look, let's say you want to build a huge computing facility, but you want it to be secret and secure, what do you need?"

Dick shrugged. "Bunches of computers, a lot of space to house the computers, power for the equipment, and people to run the facility."

Luke nodded. "The computers and servers and routers—that's the easy part. You can buy those lots of places and it's pretty easy to hide your trail if you don't want someone to know who's buying them or how many the single facility is actually buying. Let's skip that. No sport in it."

"Fine."

"Let's take a look at the facility needs first. You need a very large warehouse or similar facility and good hookups to the power grid, as well as optic fiber and cable facilities. Are you with me so far?"

"No need to be patronizing, kid."

Luke flushed. "Sorry. So let's say I wanted to build an extremely large facility and I wanted it to be hidden and easy to protect. Where would I put it?"

Dick scrunched up his face. "Underground. Easy to control access. No one sees it's there. Hell, temperature is probably easier to maintain at a constant level, too, and you don't have to worry about wind or tornadoes or snow causing problems. Tough to push that much dirt, though, without being pretty obvious—unless you're strip-mining nearby."

"Or," Luke said, "building a really large building or facility above the secret one. People don't understand construction. They know there are foundations and pylons and drainage and utility issues, stuff like that. But most people looking at the initial stages of constructing a high-rise, for example, have no idea why things are being driven into the ground one place, while dirt is being removed in another." The kid consulted some notes. "A hundred and ten million cubic yards of dirt was moved to build DIA, according to their own public estimates— that's more than thirty percent of the amount of dirt moved to build the Panama Canal—and the airport's built on flat ground. Think about what a big project that is. And the bigger a construction project, the easier it is to build something pretty massive in the midst of it—even right underneath it—without it really being noticeable. Stick an elephant in your living room, everyone notices. Paint one bright pink, but drop it on the Serengeti Plain and people might not even notice. And if someone did notice, others might not even believe him."

Dick leaned back in his chair. "That makes sense." He wriggled a bit to get comfortable. He could tell Luke was just warming up.

He was right. "How much do you think it cost to build DIA?"

Dick scratched an itch on his nose while he thought. He knew the project had been tens of millions of dollars over budget. "I dunno. Couple billion, I guess. It's pretty big and kinda fancy looking."

"It is that," Luke agreed. "Try five billion dollars. Five. The new airport facility the Chinese built more recently for the Olympics was only three and a half billion."

Dick laughed. "Yeah, but we have union labor here. They've got slave labor there."

Luke didn't even smile. "Let's keep moving," he said quickly with a grimace of distaste, as if Dick had just farted during a business meeting. "Airports have great hook-ups for electricity, cable, optic networks, satellite arrays, and on and on and on. DIA has five hundred thirty *miles* of optic cable, along with more than eleven thousand *miles* of copper cable. You need that stuff to make sure you've got dependable access to air traffic control, communication with aircraft, hook-ins to airline reservation systems, and a massive number of people popping open their cell phones every time another jumbo jet lands—and that's every couple minutes. So you've got no problems connecting into the mother-lode of electronic and communications grids."

"Given," murmured Dick. The kid could be a bit uptight, even twitchy at times, but he was clearly in his element here. Dick was kind of enjoying Luke's enthusiastic explanation.

"We've already covered security, with the underground location. But, as a bonus, airports are reasonably secure plots of land. They were even before 9/11, but more so now, so nobody is going to be sneaking up on you."

Dick merely waved his hand for Luke to continue.

"At the same time, you need to have employees, supervisors, evil overlords, and what-not come to visit. That's a lot of people coming and going and it would get noticed if you were someplace remote. The roads would be too busy. It would be hard to hide the employee parking lot." Luke paused, letting Dick ponder the issue for a moment, before continuing to the answer Dick knew was coming. The kid would have been a pretty good teacher if he hadn't gotten sucked into the spy game. "Airports have huge parking structures. They're served by public transportation and shuttle buses. People are coming and going all the time. No one notices a few dozen or even a few hundred extra people coming and going, when more than a hundred thousand people are doing it by air or land every day. The employees don't even have to hide where they work. There are probably computers for the airlines and the control tower and all that crap all over the place at DIA. The workers can just say they are computer geeks for the airport."

Dick wrinkled his nose. "But the computer skills needed for airline reservations aren't necessarily the same ones needed for running Reality 2 Be or whatever an evil overlord needs, are they? Won't somebody notice?"

Luke laughed out loud. "Trust me. Nobody who doesn't work in computers has the slightest idea what people who work with computers actually do. My friends all think I design computerized investment algorithms for a hedge fund. It's not a hard cover to pull off—not like yours, with trips to odd places and no ability to stay in contact with your friends and family."

Dick winced, but Luke just continued on.

"All I have to do is mumble a few arcane programming language names and a bit of jargon and all my friends just nod politely as their eyes glaze over. They just grab another can of Four X from the igloo while I'm cooking up steaks on the barbie and make sure never to ask me about work again."

Dick thought of all the times he had tossed off phrases like "effluent parameters" and "treatment co-efficient" when people, even Melanie, had asked him about his cover job as a wastewater treatment consultant. Nobody really wanted to have a conversation about that kind of shit at a social gathering. The cover Luke was talking about could work. Still, it wasn't foolproof.

Dick leaned forward in his chair. "Everything you've said makes sense. But it's not tight. It's harder to notice the construction, but someone would—maybe some grunt pushing dirt in ways that don't make sense to him. All those employees, they have to go down corridors and get into elevators that people who work at the airport would begin to wonder about. You admitted it yourself. You said word of the facility had leaked, but people don't know about it. That doesn't make sense to me. Either people know there's something secret there or they don't. You can't have it both ways."

Luke turned the screen of his computer to face Dick. "Spend much time surfing the Web?"

Dick gave a dismissive wave. "Seems like a big waste of time to me. I do what I need to do for the job, but that's it. My leisure time is the old-fashioned kind. Watching sports on the big screen with a beer in my hand. Used to play football."

Luke beamed. "Me, too!"

Dick chuckled. "The other kind, kid." Luke looked positively crestfallen that their moment of male bonding had been ruined. "My kid, Seth, he seems to spend a lot of time on the computer. At least that's what his mother says." Dick's mood suddenly darkened. "I'm away a lot. Too much."

"Then you've probably been through DIA quite a few times. It's a major hub airport."

"Sure. So what?"

"Ever notice anything peculiar about the airport?"

"You mean aside from the fact they delayed opening it for a year and a half 'cause they couldn't get the automated baggage system to work?"

Luke's eyebrows hopped up. "Great way to explain cost overruns and why the place was filled with computer techs and electricians for months after all the construction workers had gone away, isn't it?"

Dick had to admit it. "True."

"But that wasn't what I was getting at. I mean the facility itself. What about it?"

"Out in the middle of nowhere. Flat for miles around. The architecture for the main terminal is fancy, like I said before. The roof is a huge white tarp of some kind, fixed to poles that jut way up into the sky. It's supposed to make the roofline look like snow-covered mountains or something like that. Your tax dollars at work."

A picture popped up on the screen of Luke's computer. The sharp white peaks of the passenger terminal stood in sharp relief to the blue sky above. "The Jeppesen Terminal's got a nice look to it. Unique. Peculiar. Maybe even avant-garde. Probably makes the average bloke think nothing of it when the artwork inside is similarly ... unique. Ever notice any of the artistic details inside?"

Dick thought back. "The place is kind of weird. They have these bright blue paper airplane shaped metal things hanging from the ceiling where you get off the underground tramway." He started. The *underground* tramway. "And there's, like, propellers in the tramway shaft that twirl in the wind when the train goes by and sculptures of, like, hands holding a pick axe coming out of the wall down there, too."

Luke's hands flew over the keyboard. Pictures of the art Dick had mentioned pulsed onto the screen. "What else?"

The images came flooding into Dick's memory. Odd stuff. Not odd enough to cause any worry or problem. Just stuff that made you go "Huh?" He began to gesticulate as he recited what he had seen to Luke. "There's weird stuff imbedded in the floor at what appear to be random places. Swirls of metal or what look like dinosaur footprints or fossils or something. Random words or letters."

167

Words etched into fancy-looking stone appeared on the screen. "Dzit Dit Gaii," read one. The grain of the marble was almost too strong to read the next one, but it seemed to say "Cochetopa." "Yeah, that stuff," mumbled Dick with a wave of his hand. "I always kinda assumed they were Indian ... you know, Native American, blessing the place or explaining where the stone came from."

"Some are native languages, some just nonsense according to the websites. Nothing to do with the source of the marble, some of which was shipped in at pretty hefty expense from locations all over the world, even Australia, not that you would know that from just walking about the concourse."

"Yeah, that always sort of bothered me, come to think of it" mused Dick. "Here there are, weird symbols all over the place, but no brass plate explaining what they're supposed to be. It's like a bizarre museum where there's no information on what the displays are."

More rapid keystrokes. Picture after picture after picture. Just as Dick remembered it. "What about the art?" asked Luke.

"Not my taste, that's for sure," replied Dick. "Big murals. Kind of a Mexican style, I think. One had dead babies and coffins in it, which I found distasteful and, well, disturbing for, you know, public art. But Mexicans have that whole 'Day of the Dead' thing, so maybe it means something I'm just too uncultured to understand."

The picture appeared on the screen. A few more keystrokes and various portions of it were enlarged. Luke clicked on to other pictures and did the same thing as he identified the images. "Here's a six-pointed star on a child's outfit. Here's a kid wielding a sledge hammer. A flaming city in the background. A hallucinogenic plant. A civil defense symbol on a badge a child is wearing." He let the screen linger on the next image. "This guy looks like a Sasquatch skeleton in a Nazi uniform, if you ask me."

The pictures flashed on and on as Luke continued at an ever-increasing pace.

"If you went outside for a smoke, you might have noticed that the stone over the time capsule they buried when the airport opened has a Masonic symbol on it. The ceremony was organized by 'The New World Airport Commission.' An offshoot of the New World Order? You know, the secret organization actually running the world in collaboration with Skull & Bones." Another picture appeared. "If you look at an overhead shot, you can see the runways make a swastika pattern."

"That's not a swastika," Dick blurted out. "They ... they have runways going different directions so they can land planes safely no matter what the wind patterns are." Dick wriggled in his chair. This was getting ridiculous.

But still, Luke continued. "There are websites claiming witnesses to the construction of the airport have been silenced or have simply disappeared. Reports of strange odors coming from below. Even local newspapers have done stories on the different conspiracy theories."

"Theories? Plural?"

"Oh, yeah," responded Luke. "Some say alien lizard creatures are using small children as slave labor to hollow out a huge cavern where the citizenry will be herded to serve their evil masters when the end of the world comes. Secret societies are mentioned in password-protected online whispers. Other sites claim the Prince of Wales is buying up land in the area for sinister reasons." The pitch of Luke's voice had been rising as the images and explanations got more and more outrageous, reaching the cracking point.

Dick leapt out of his chair, gesticulating in agitation. "You're not telling me you believe any of this crap? It's bizarre. It's fantastical. It couldn't possibly be true." He gave Luke a hard look. "Please reassure me you are not going to tell Dee Tammany and Glenn

Net Impact

Swynton you've uncovered a plot whereby alien lizardmen have conspired with the Prince of Wales to kidnap missing children so they can build a hellish holding pen for the unholy two miles beneath Denver International Airport while the righteous fight the Antichrist using stolen Kestrel 84 technology." He glanced to either side before continuing. "My job may suck—my family certainly thinks so—but I still wanna keep it. Suggesting any ... any of this ... will get both of us blacklisted as mental cases faster than you can spit. You can't possibly believe any of this is true!"

Luke leaned back from his keyboard and interlaced his fingers behind his head. When he spoke, his voice was once again deep and calm and professorial. "I don't believe a word of it, mate."

Dick tried to shake the confusion from his mind. Then what was the kid's point? He wanted to ask, but the words just wouldn't form properly. Instead he simply blurted: "But, then ... What? ... Huh?"

This time the kid chuckled. "I don't believe it. I didn't think you'd believe it. The average Joe on the street, as you would put it, wouldn't believe it for a minute, either, even if by some bizarre twist of all we know and understand any of it was true." He held up his hand, index finger raised, in triumph. "That's the point."

Dick sat back down with a weary plop. "It is?"

"Let me explain. If I were an evil overlord who had built a secret underground facility underneath a massive public works project, I would definitely try to get some input into the art and architectural committees. Donate some work. Pay for certain artists. Suggest certain avant-garde design features. Then, when people began to wonder about some things, like why so much dirt had to be moved to construct a facility on a flat plain, or how come they dug six stories down beneath where a runway was scheduled to be, or why certain corridors or elevators are off-limits to even the airport security personnel, I would post an anonymous comment here, a wacky website there, drop a few speculations into an overly-loud conversation at an airport bar, and so on. Suddenly, it's *The DaVinci Code* mixed with Area 51, *Men In Black*, and *The National Enquirer*."

"You mean these sites are fake?"

Luke shrugged. "Probably not, at least not most of them. It's even better if those spreading the unbelievable rumors are, in fact, true believers. Scarily fanatical in some cases." He paused for a moment as if in thought. "Paranoia can be your friend when you are trying to create a situation like this and you can induce even rampant paranoia with minimum effort. Move around a few paintings for unexplained reasons. Release a noxious odor when someone is sneaking where they don't belong. Refuse to answer inquiries about the art or the words or the construction. It doesn't take much and, voila, a few conspiracy theories are born. A few late night calls where no one's on the line and those spreading the stories become convinced they're being watched and threatened because they're on the right track. The theories become more complex, more sinister. Many are strange, even creepy. Some of those spreading the story try to fit it into their pet theories about other conspiracies."

"Couldn't this get out of hand? It sounds like this could bring unwanted attention to the site." Dick was suddenly glad he had never been assigned to spend time with the PsyOps guys when he was in the Army. Screwing with people's perceptions, ultimately with their minds, was scary stuff.

Luke didn't seem put-off at all by the question, or the subject. "That's why outlandish conspiracy theories are great and multiple conspiracy theories are helpful. It doesn't matter if some of the theories are reasonable, the fringe elements taint the entire field. That means the serious conspiracy enthusiasts and the full-bore whack-jobs will tend to cancel each other out, especially in terms of credibility. If you're lucky, some conspiracy buffs will get even the most obvious, easily verifiable facts wrong. Then, if and when responsible people research the various theories, the true things you don't really want the public to know get lumped in with a bunch of inaccuracies and bizarre ruminations. Consequently, the truth is ignored as coming from a non-credible source or simply lost in a blizzard of bullshit." He smiled. "Once you get a conspiracy going, people find 'facts' that fit it and ignore those that don't."

Dick perked back up. "Like the whole 'Paul is Dead' thing."

"Huh?"

"Paul McCartney. The Beatles. Please tell me you've heard of The Beatles."

Luke sighed. "Like the baby-boomers would ever let anyone go through life without knowing about The Beatles. Criminy. It was more than forty years ago. Give it a rest."

"Let's avoid the music criticism class, shall we? I tried that with my kid once and it didn't make for a winning father/son memory." Dick motioned with his hands as if setting the subject physically aside. "Back when The Beatles were hot ... well before you were born, okay? ... some kids at Michigan State or someplace got this rumor started that Paul was really dead and had been replaced by a look-alike. But the other band members, they couldn't say on pain of death or something, so they placed clues on all the album covers and in the songs. There was even stuff back-masked onto the records."

"Back-masked?"

"Stuff recorded backwards in the background, so you could hear it when you played the record backwards."

"Sounds unlikely." Luke's brow was furrowed and his mouth was pursed in distaste. "I mean, how would anyone ever find that? Do people actually spend their time listening to backwards music in America?"

Dick tilted his head down and gave the kid a stare. "You find it because you are looking for clues to support a theory you've already heard someplace and found credible for some reason. Once the rumor started, people looked for support all over the place. In the music, in the album cover art, in the lyrics. And the back-masking crap was the bonanza of the whole idiotic quest." Dick wrinkled his nose before he made his confession. "I'll admit it, I did it. Even though this was really before my time, when I heard about it, I had to check it out. I wound the turntable backwards by hand to hear the back-masking. Some of it was pretty creepy."

Luke tilted his head down and furrowed his brow yet further, his half-squinted eyes lasering in on Dick. "So you think Paul McCartney is dead. Then who do you think paid Heather Mills millions of pounds in their divorce case?"

"No, I don't believe Paul is dead," spat Dick. "The back-masking crap was probably just John having a laugh. The point is ..." Dick pointed his hand, index finger extended in mimicry of Luke's earlier motion, "... once the snowball got rolling, people found clues all over the place, more than could have ever been planted as a lark or a publicity stunt. You were right before. People get compulsive ... they get crazy ... about conspiracy stuff."

Luke nodded. "Exactly. There is a facility underground at Denver International Airport. One that has nothing to do with alien lizards, Prince Charles, or the end of the world, as we know it. One that has everything to do with Reality 2 Be's server farm for their virtual reality game."

Dick thought for a few moments. "One problem."

"Yeah?"

"Wasn't all this construction done well before Reality 2 Be ever existed as a game?"

Luke nodded. "Yeah. I'm still working that one out."

CHAPTER 16

"Holy crap!" muttered Peregrine. "I thought Shrike was, you know, dead. Gone. Never to be heard of again." He leaned in even closer. "What does he say?"

Hawk read the words on the paper the young boy had given him, then handed the note to his twitchy companion. The words, written in block letters on plain white stock, were clear enough: "Compromised. Can't meet. Can't ever meet. Not here. Not by other means. Not anywhere. Run. Hide. Disappear. Now. Forever. Sorry. Shrike."

It was all so odd. Shrike's fear seemed orders of magnitude greater than Peregrine's or even Pigeon's paranoia. Could the danger really be so great? Was this message even really from Shrike?

Perhaps it was his intense focus on Shrike's message that made him dismiss as unimportant the marked ramp-up in volume of the general background hubbub emanating from the distant reaches of the four different wings of the mall. But then a booming whoomph and explosion rattled both the foundations of the mall and his composure. Even as Hawk dropped to the floor beside the bench, his combat instincts took over—not just seeking safety and cover, but analyzing and categorizing the sounds he heard. Ear-splitting explosions reverberated through the canyons of the shopping mall, followed closely by a clanking noise and the echoing chatter of what could only be machine gun fire. He'd heard that combination before, but only on a battlefield.

He looked over to Peregrine, cowering beneath the next bench over. "What the ..." But then there was another blast from a different arm of the mall and then another and another, drowning out all thought, all action. Soon, though, the anguished screams of the crowd rose above even the sustained chatter of the machine guns as everyone in the mall seemed to rush toward the fountain. Everywhere Hawk looked matronly shoppers and teenaged girls still clutching bagsful of expensive purchases were running at him in full panic, shrieking and OMGing and trampling over anyone who fell during their headlong rush to the center. It was as if Godzilla was attacking the four far-flung entrances to the mall simultaneously and the fountain was the city center of Tokyo. He heard more and more booming crashes echoing in an eerie cacophony of destruction from all directions. Smoke and construction dust billowed toward him, overtaking the fleeing throngs, causing them to scream even louder.

The entire scene was unreal. How could this be possible? Who could orchestrate such a thing? The property damage alone would be billions and the citizenry wasn't about to stand for this kind of chaos. Who could possibly be so powerful as to be able to launch such an attack and so stupid to actually do it? And for what, the money he carried in his pack, the information he carried in his head? This was too big to remain a localized incident. This would have repercussions ... real repercussions.

Peregrine bolted, flying towards the nearest store that had an outside exit.

Hawk crouched beside his bench watching the universe's biggest shopping mall be blasted into smithereens, whatever the hell a smithereen was.

Who?

How?

That's when he saw the tanks. Chinese Type 99 main battle tanks, each with a 125mm smoothbore main gun blasting away at the mall fixtures as two machine guns mowed down the crowds to their fore. Even the rapid fire of the machine guns was not sufficient, however, to clear a path. The tanks just bore on, though, slowed not only by the debris and confines of the mall, but by loss of traction to their treads as the armored vehicles plowed heedlessly through the crowd.

Net Impact

Hawk saw one brave soul turn to face the enemy as those about him fled in a mad rush to clear a path for the relentless tanks. For just a moment, the foolhardy hero stood alone in the tanks' path like that anonymous individual in Tiananmen Square had years ago during China's first and last mass demonstration for democracy.

The tanks never hesitated. Hawk turned away at the last second so he would not see the impact, but he heard the "thud" and the mangled cry that ended abruptly as the tanks continued their onslaught. Another nameless hero ground down by the Chinese Army.

The message had been from Shrike. And it had been true, truer than Hawk could ever have imagined. What had he gotten himself into? Had Shrike's cover been blown? Had his? Were the Chinese after him? If so, it was a game he could not lose.

He did his best to follow Shrike's advice: to run, to hide, to disappear forever. But he doubted he could leave this place of devastation without leaving a piece of himself behind.

And that, he now knew, could be the death of him.

Luke might not have it all figured out yet, but Dick knew the two of them were headed for Denver, one way or the other. That meant a few awkward conversations were in Dick's future. Since he preferred those conversations be in his past, he decided he might as well get them over with. He always did what he had to do.

He left the computer tech room and headed to an empty conference room, flipping open his cell phone and opening the screen that showed recent missed calls.

None.

That was depressing.

He punched in the speed dial for Melanie's cell phone and mentally prepared the message he would leave when the voicemail triggered. There was no way she would pick up his call and, at this point, he didn't really blame her.

The voicemail switched on after the fourth ring: "This is Melanie. I really want to talk with you, but I won't use this thing while I'm driving, walking, eating at a restaurant, watching a movie, or meditating. I'm not sure why I have it at all. But if you leave a message with your name and number, I'll eventually get back to you and then we can talk, really talk." It was the same cutesy message Melanie had used for years, but he was somehow depressed by it now, just the same.

"Hi, Melanie. It's Dick. I hope things are going better for you and I do want to talk. Really talk. But I have to go to Denver on an emergency for work. Same old shit. Won't bother you with the technical details. Shouldn't be more than a couple days." He finished his canned lie and began to flip the phone closed, then suddenly stopped, opening it back up before it disconnected and holding it back up to his face. "Love you, Melanie. Miss you, too." He flipped the phone closed and sat alone in the dark conference room for almost a half-hour.

By the time he left, he was sure no one would be able to tell he had been crying.

"Damn! Did you see that? Did you see that equipment?" Seth had leapt up from his computer and was pacing about the basement rec room at a furious rate. "Did you see what they did? The community will never stand for it. They'll go bonkers, absolutely ape-shit. You can't allow stuff like that. It trashes the whole economic underpinnings."

Finally he slowed his diatribe and his pacing enough to focus on his friend, Brian, who was simply staring at his own computer screen, his eyes wide, his hands shaking as they rested atop the controller he had so furiously been toggling and manipulating only a few moments before.

Seth continued his rant. "I'm shocked, too, dude. The property damage has gotta be enormous. I mean, yeah sure, it's all virtual, but it still costs real bucks in the real world to buy the virtual land and build the virtual stores and code the virtual inventory so people can shop in-world. The retailers will be freakin' apoplectic. I can't believe there won't be repercussions."

Brian finally spoke in a hoarse whisper. "There'll be repercussions, Seth. That's the problem. I think there will actually be … actually be … repercussions. To me, to us."

Seth stopped pacing and stared at his friend. "What are you talking about? That wasn't our fault. No one can blame us. Why would someone come after us for what happened at the mall?"

Brian looked down at his controller. His hands were still shaking, but with obvious deliberate effort he managed to press the sequence of buttons which replayed the last five minutes of screen shots from their computer game.

Seth witnessed the gory spectacle of destruction again, this time from a slightly different perspective, until the screen went blank.

"I'm dead, dude," murmured Brian. "I'm dead." He looked over at Seth. "So are you. It's just a matter of time."

Seth plopped down on the sofa and began to think hard. "I'm not dead, not yet," he told his friend, his voice firming as he spoke. "And I don't intend to go out without a fight."

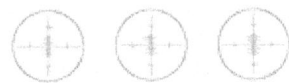

A few minutes after he left the conference room, Dick was in the office of Dee Tammany ... for the second time in one day. He didn't really like all this "reporting-in" crap. He liked to work alone. Still, he'd gone through the process enough times in the Army and the Chicago Police Department to know the drill. It was like the pretend lawyers on television always told their pretend clients before pretend depositions: Answer the question with a "yes" or "no," if possible. Don't volunteer anything. Finish as soon as possible.

His last conversation in here had not been pleasant. At least Glenn wasn't here this go around. Dick grunted for attention, then waited quietly while Dee finished reading a piece of paperwork. He didn't wait for pleasantries when she looked up.

"Luke's pretty sure he knows where the facility is. I'll be requisitioning some equipment."

"You didn't need to see me to requisition equipment," replied Dee.

"There will be some weapons and ... we'll need to bring them from here, rather than pick them up on the other end. Charter jet from a private airfield—it's the best way to get the equipment into the secure area at the airport itself." Dick waited for her to react, to ask for him to explain, but Dee said nothing. "The secret facility is underground at the airport."

"I know."

"You know?" Anger flared inside, but he kept it at bay. "When were you going to tell us?"

Dee spoke in a flat, matter-of-fact tone. "I know because I was monitoring your conversation with Luke in the tech room."

"You're spying on your spies in spy headquarters?"

"Luke's a proven security risk. I do what I have to do. Given the situation, you can bet Internal Audit is listening. All the rooms here, except my office, Glenn's office, and the main conference room, are surveillance-enabled."

Dick gave her a hard stare, before turning and heading for the door. "Then you already know everything I was going to report," he said with just a touch of a snarl as he exited the room. Had she "monitored" him crying in the conference room, too?

Sometimes he hated his job.

CHAPTER 17

"Are you ready to go?" asked Dick by way of greeting when he returned to the tech room where Luke was still fussing with his computer.

"To Denver?" asked Luke without looking up.

"Yeah, to Denver. That's where you decided the servers are that you need to access directly. Did you have another destination in mind?"

Luke finally looked up, his expression placid. "Reality 2 Be."

Dick was getting irritated. His conversation with Dee had been unpleasant and unsettling and his phone call to Melanie had been plain depressing. He didn't really need mysterious puzzles from the conspiracy-meister. "An hour ago you told me Reality 2 Be's server farm was underneath Denver International Airport. Have there been developments I don't know about?"

"Yes and no."

Dick's fingers twitched. "Which is it? 'Yes?' Or 'no?'"

Luke's wide eyes conveyed puzzlement and innocence. "There have been no developments countermanding our supposition that the server farm for Reality 2 Be is located beneath DIA. The additional development which has occurred is that I have come to the conclusion we must infiltrate Reality 2 Be at two locations."

"You mean somebody has to go back to New Hampshire?"

"No," replied the young tech with a shake of his head. "Somebody has to go into Reality 2 Be, the virtual universe, at the same time we're infiltrating the server farm."

"Don't look at me," protested Dick. "I already told you before I don't know nuthin' 'bout virtual reality." He waved toward the bullpen, where the rest of Luke's geek companions were still busy handling communications, setting up computer covers, and hacking into information databases for the Subsidiary. "You got a bevy of geekaholic gamers right next store. Can't you get one of your tech guys to infiltrate Reality 2 Be? They'd certainly be better at it than I would."

He had expected Luke to smile at his characterization of the Subsidiary's tech squad, even if his tone had been a bit gruff, but Luke didn't smile at all. His face was set, motionless, serious. Deadly serious. "I think we both know it would be best not to get anyone else involved in our trip, don't we?"

Damn it. The kid had figured out he probably wasn't coming back. And he was worried that anyone else involved, any of the gang of technology nerds he had worked and laughed with for several years, would be put at risk of elimination if they knew too much or, worse yet, witnessed what was inevitably going to happen. Not only was Luke doing what he had to do for the mission anyway, despite that knowledge, he was protecting his friends at the same time. That would make things that much harder for Dick when the time came.

Dick pretended to ignore the question. "Why does someone need to be in the Reality 2 Be universe? And why can't it be you?"

"Just because we can use the server farm to find where the data on the Kestrel 84 is located in-world doesn't mean we can grab it easily. But if we can go in-world to meet the avatar carrying the data, maybe we can take it away or at least find out information about the avatar that facilitates retrieving the information off the servers."

"And why can't you ..."

"I might be busy. Besides, you taught me how to infiltrate a secure office building. The least I can do is show you how to navigate in-world at Reality 2 Be. Who knows, maybe when we're ... you're ... done with the mission, you can online game with your kid or something."

Seth liked computer games, Dick knew. That's why he spent so much time in his friend Brian's basement ... at least, according to

Melanie. God, he hoped the kid wasn't getting too immersed in that first-person shooter crap. From all he heard, those games were getting more violent and more graphic all the time—not quite the same as playing cops and robbers in the back yard with SuperSoakers.

Damn. He needed to call Seth, too.

He pulled himself back into the moment. "Sure," he replied. "Do I get a joystick?"

Luke gave a wan smile. "They're called 'controllers' now. But, yeah, you can get a joystick, too."

What exactly did that mean?

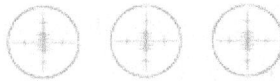

Seth picked up his controller and sat back down in the genuine Naugahyde recliner. "We have to go back into Reality 2 Be again. You understand that don't you?"

Brian made no move to pick up his controller. "My avatar's dead. Yours has obviously been *made* by someone with more power in-game and probably out of it than I ever want to know about." His head twitched from side to side. "No way, man. Game over."

"We were in the midst of doing something kind of important when things started going bad," replied Seth, leaning forward in the chair. "Or did you forget that?"

Brian's brow wrinkled. "Let's just give the money back to the people who gave it to us. Let 'em get someone else to finish the mission.

Seth shook his head. "They contacted me. I don't know how to get in touch with the people who sent us. I don't even have a drop for what we're picking up—I'm just supposed to send the activist diaries to *The New York Times.* I can't ask for a replacement team. It's us or nobody."

Brian folded his arms across his chest tight. He looked to the side, staring into the corner of the basement near the dartboard, as if he was afraid to look his best friend in the face. "Look, dude. I'm all for the cause and everything, but our mission, our exchange of maypoles and information, that's all a lost effort. Our rebel contacts are gone, man. Toast, if you don't remember. We'll never see any of them in-game again. Never."

Brian wouldn't look at Seth, but Seth continued to stare at his friend, his tone even and forceful as he responded. "People are depending on us, Brian. Not just avatars. There are people controlling those avatars that need the maypoles we have to give them to fight and survive. And we need the information they're supposed to be giving us. It's not a game; it's life or death."

Brian snorted. "Death seems more likely. Your avatar would be resting in pieces inside of five minutes if you reactivated him and he's the one with the shitload of maypoles." Brian paused, unable or unwilling to continue for a moment. He trembled and seemed to hug himself even tighter to make the trembling stop. "And that might be the least of our worries."

Seth scrunched up his face. "So we'll make new avatars."

Brian finally turned toward Seth, his face pale. "Dude, they've obviously got our computers' identification numbers. The bad guys are connected into the system in some way. Even with new avatars, they'll know it's us and it won't take long to figure out." Brian shook his head and turned away again. "And our new avatars wouldn't have the maypoles, anyhow."

"So, we'll use different computers. Someone's gotta do what needs to be done." Seth paused and thought. "Your mom and dad both have laptops, right?"

Brian turned sharply back toward Seth. "Jesus, Seth, my dad would have a conniption if I used his work computer."

"So, we won't tell him."

"But it's got, like, confidential work information and stuff on it. What if it gets screwed up or someone, you know, with scary awesome hacking abilities accesses his business information?"

Seth's brow furrowed as he gave his friend a sidelong glance. "No offence, Bri, but your dad works as a regional manager for Target. What could he possibly have on his computer anyone would want to see?"

Brian seemed to relax a bit. "I dunno. Pictures of next season's clothing line?"

Seth laughed out loud. He was relieved when his good friend, his best friend, joined in. "Yeah, I'm sure some thugs working for Wal-Mart are busily beating that vital information out of some mook from Target as we speak."

Brian unfolded his arms. "Yeah, okay." He got up from his chair and headed toward the staircase. "I'll get my folk's laptops."

"Lock the basement door when you come back down. At least we'll be able to shove the laptops under the cushions before they catch us using 'em."

Brian halted halfway up the stairs. "We still gotta get the maypoles from your avatar, dude. Or this is just a big waste of time."

"Already working on that." He tilted his head to one side. "It'll take a bit of time. We have to create and equip new avatars, even play them for a while to establish a credible in-game cover. Then we'll get the maypoles."

"We can't just trade for them," Brian mused. "That would be too obvious. We'd just put the bad guys on our tail."

Seth shrugged. "So, we'll just steal them. A mugging would be believable."

Net Impact

Brian's eyebrows turned down. "And you think the powers that be in the game will buy that kind of random violence and theft?"

Seth leaned back in the chair once more, already playing the scene out in his mind. "Oh yeah," he responded. "People do stupid, violent things for money all the time."

CHAPTER 18

Matt Lee was amorously occupied when the phone call came, but he didn't let it break his cadence. He always answered his phone by the fourth ring and he always finished his tasks, whether they be lethal or carnal in nature. He continued boffing Peggy as he took the call. After all, the President of the United States had discussed Bosnian troop deployments while being serviced—talented people were good at multi-tasking. He clicked on the call and the voice of General Tsao Cho of the People's Liberation Army came static-free through the Blue-Tooth earpiece he always wore.

"Please proceed immediately to New Jersey for an assignment."

"I'm occupied at the moment," Matt responded, causing Peggy to gasp and open her eyes, which had been closed in the throes of their lusty lovemaking. She obviously had not seen the flashing blue light indicating an incoming call. He winked at her without breaking rhythm. "I can be there in two days."

Peggy smiled and melted back into her sexual ecstasy with a languid shudder and a contented moan.

Right, thought Matt, as if I am going to spend two days with you. Another two hours and he would be back to the terminal to start on his assignment for Pao Fen Smythe.

"Perhaps you did not hear my statement," responded Tsao Cho without emotion. "There appears to be some noise on the line. I said 'immediately.'"

Matt managed to make Peggy moan again, this time louder, just to tweak the placid General. "I have another assignment I need to finish first."

Still the General did not raise his voice. "Your freelance activities for Pao Fen Smythe are tolerated because they—or details regarding them—are occasionally useful to the state. Certainly, Comrade Smythe also provides you with levels of remuneration which allow you to maintain your current, decadent, lifestyle, which, in turn, allows you to be available to us as an asset without any obvious connection to The People's Republic. No matter the assignment, if discovered, our counterparts in espionage will presume a connection to the Smythe organization and not state-sponsored activity."

Blah, blah, blah. There was more about the tolerance for his lifestyle, the hostilities and prejudices his country still faced, and the needs of his government in dealing with a dangerous world. By the time the General finished droning on, Peggy had finished with a quivering climax and rolled over to fall asleep smiling. Matt slid over to the side of the bed and sat up. "That cover falls apart if I start skipping off in the middle of something important."

"You seem to find time when you need it," replied the General without irony.

"What's the job?"

"Two murders in New Jersey." The General never shied off of describing Matt's duties by using euphemisms. Matt liked that about the guy. There were no "hits," "eliminations," "terminations with extreme prejudice," or "erasures." There were just murders. And the occasional murder by arson or terrorist bombing. Matt knew what he was, what he did. He didn't mind the honesty one bit.

"Can't you get someone else?"

"We already did. The complete job is twice as big as we're giving to you. Four targets. A cell working to overthrow the government. But our first assassin is bogged down. He took out one of his targets, but is having trouble locating the second. We can't let too much time go by or the rest of the cell could get wind of the first victim's demise and take precautions."

"So I'm cleaning up somebody else's screw-up." Matt knew that failing to complete a project for the General was not conducive to a positive career trajectory. The first assassin would be in a yurt in the

outer provinces overseeing radio intercepts within the week if he
didn't off the second target soon.

"That's not your problem," replied the General without emotion.
"Focus on the job."

"High profile? Hard targets?" Matt was already thinking about
how much time the task would take and how he would put off Pao Fen
in the meantime.

"Low profile. Extremely soft targets."

Matt smiled. A flight out to Newark. Pick up a sniper rifle from
one of his New York stashes or contacts, then duck into New Jersey.
Locate targets. Sight. Bang. Shift sighting to second target. Bang.
Walk away. Less than eight hours on the ground if he was lucky.
Then a flight back to Denver. He could sell that kind of delay to Pao
Fen.

The General continued as he was making his calculations. "It needs
to look like an accidental death."

"Accidental? Or just non-professional?" Non-professional would
eliminate the use of a sniper rifle, but a nine millimeter round at close
range in the gut, angled upward, could look like a mugging gone bad if
done right and still wouldn't take too long to set up.

"Accidental. Do I not always mean what I say?"

"Of course, General. You are very specific and precise, as always."
Matt frowned and tilted his head from one side to the other, then rolled
his shoulders to work the tension out of his muscles. No guns or
knives at all. No car accidents either. Too many variables and the
damn crumple zones and airbags were just getting too good to be sure
the accident would inflict lethal injuries, especially with the speed and
quality of medical care in the U.S. He stood up and headed to the
bathroom.

Murder by arson, then.

"Details will be forwarded by the usual secure means."

Net Impact

Matt doubted China's encrypted emails were quite as secure as the General thought. The NSA did some pretty good work from everything he read, but he knew they were inundated with more and more electronic data every day. They could find something if they were looking for it, but he doubted they were looking for him. He said nothing about the NSA to the General, though. "Fine," was all he said as he lifted the seat to the toilet.

"Fine," the General replied.

The connection was cut off before the sound of splashing liquid could further demonstrate Matt's ability to multi-task to his superiors.

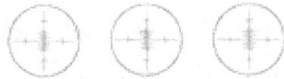

When Dick had built his avatar for the Subsidiary's virtual meeting room system, it had been a fairly simple process. Hair color, height, weight, eye color, clothes (business suit or casual), and facial features. Being a field operative, Dick had avoided creating an avatar which matched his own features as bad spycraft—his looked a lot more like Pierce Brosnan than could be explained by coincidence. But Reality 2 Be had a lot more choices.

"Human or non-human?" asked Luke as they got underway.

"Huh? What are the other choices besides human?"

Luke called up a chart on-screen. "Giants, orcs, trolls, gnomes, elves, dwarves ... all the Tolkien and Dungeons & Dragons type stuff ... elementals, ghosts, goblins, witches, poltergeists ... all the late-night horror movie stuff ... comic superheroes, animate vegetables, insects, animals, and furries."

"Furries?"

Luke blushed. "Like man-sized plush toys or stuffed animals. Beanie Babies on steroids. Some people find them ... er ... erotic."

Dick had seen plenty of things in his life, but erotic stuffed animals were not among them. He glanced at the screen. "They must come better equipped than human avatars. This prototype looks like a Ken doll."

Luke blushed even redder. "Don't worry about that for now. Human, then?"

"Sure."

"That's probably good. You'll be more comfortable with it and humans don't stand out in most situations."

"Most?"

"Well, if we sneak into a virtual castle populated by alien lizardmen, a human is going to stand out."

Dick clicked a few menu choices. "What's your avatar look like?"

Luke tilted his head to one side. "What do you mean? I'll generate one as soon as you're done."

"But you've been in-world before, so you must have an avatar. What's he, she, or it look like?"

Luke looked away, as if he couldn't meet Dick's gaze. "Uh ... human male, a bit brawnier than me. But I can't use him."

Dick stopped clicking on menus for a moment. "Why not? We're on a mission. It wouldn't be unsanctioned ... like before."

"He was ... might have been ... compromised. It's possible he's being traced and tracked. It wouldn't be safe to use him if someone in-world is out to get him."

"It's just an avatar. So what if he gets gacked?" Dick regretted both the topic and his choice of words as soon as he said them, but it would only get more awkward if he backed off now. "You're not, like, emotionally attached to your avatar, are you?"

A short burst of hollow laughter escaped from Luke's mouth. "No, not really. Nothing like that."

"Cause I've heard that happens in role-playing games."

Net Impact

Luke sighed and shook his head. "Don't believe everything you hear about RPGs or the Internet. There are a whole lot more young males emotionally attached to their cars than to their avatars, and the reasons for the attachment are pretty much the same in both cases. Both represent significant investments of time and/or money. Both project the image you want to project to the world—or at least those portions of the world you care about, primarily other young males. Both take skill to operate and can be upgraded with fancy, shiny accessories. The only big difference is that in a role-playing game, whether Internet or old-fashioned table-top, acting in character—acting as if you are the character in the make-believe world—is part of the game. Part of the fun is acting as if the game is real. People get so used to behaving like their character in-world that sometimes they do it instinctively—they talk and act in-world in ways that are appropriate to their character, rather than ways that make sense from a real world point-of-view."

Luke's explanation made a certain amount of sense to Dick. Although he wasn't one of them, he knew plenty of guys who named their cars. Hell, some guys named their privates. And lots of people did stupid or risky or just plain oddball things to impress their friends or move up the pecking order in their own little world. He nodded at Luke. "I get what you're saying, but you know better than that, so there's got to be some other reason you're still queasy about using your old avatar. Right?"

Luke gave a curt nod in response. "I'm more security conscious than you—or Dee—give me credit for, I guess. I don't want to get 'made' in game."

"How would that happen?"

"The way the software works, your avatar is the thing which identifies you to the universe, to the servers that run the game, but the information is embedded in your avatar's coding, like DNA in the real world. If someone 'gacks' you, as you so tactfully put it, then there is some possibility they can trace to your computer's individual protocol address, access the information used to create your payment account, and identify you in the real world."

"But the Chinese, they already know you did stuff in the game world that they don't like."

"Sure," replied Luke, "but I'm still holding out some faint hope that they don't know what avatar did those things. If they already do, or if my avatar gets gacked and traced back to me, they might be able to identify my contacts or my fellow travelers."

Dick rubbed his face. "I noticed my sign-in screen had me identified as a fourteen year old Filipino, but that I have an American Express card."

"I used a stolen credit card to set up the game fee payments. It seemed the most credible choice."

"It does seem like it would be pretty dangerous to go wandering around Reality 2 Be if someone could off you for your credit card information."

Luke laughed softly again, but this time the laughter sounded genuine. "It's not that much like the Wild West in there. Your ... or in this case ... Margaret Swenson's ... credit card information is encrypted. While getting a piece of your avatar would let another player with sophisticated computer skills track down your personal data—in this instance the fake info about the Filipino kid, it wouldn't get the stolen credit card info, not unless they could break the encryption or had access to the server farm and could obtain the base encryption algorithm."

"Like the folks at Reality 2 Be."

"Sure," replied Luke, "but it would be pretty obvious if they were ripping off their own customers. Word would get around. Gamers talk to each other."

Dick tilted his head to one side and nodded briskly, then stopped, lost in thought. "Or the folks running the secret facility under DIA," he mused aloud.

Luke whistled. "This could be not only older than Reality 2 Be, but a lot bigger."

"Yeah," replied Dick. He looked at the computer screen. "Buy some clothes and crap for my avatar, will you? I've gotta add something to my equipment request for our trip."

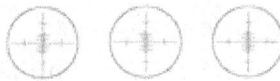

Matt Lee looked over the electronic dossiers. They were thin. Two civilians from New Jersey. What could they possibly have done to piss off the Chinese government so much it was sending a professional assassin to murder them? It must be something serious. The Chinese, they didn't play games.

CHAPTER 19

When Dick got back to the computer tech room, Luke had two computers set up next to one another on one of the high tables. Controllers lay to the side and there were stools drawn up to the table for them to game side by side.

"Did you get me fully dressed?" asked Dick as he sauntered toward the two screens. He swung a leg over one of the stools and plopped down, eyeing the avatar rotating slowly in the middle of the screen. "Logoed spandex? I look like a superhero sponsored by Nike, for god's sake."

Luke smiled. "That's why I named you 'The Swuush.'"

Dick saw the name at the bottom of his screen. "Shouldn't that be spelled differently, you know, with two o's instead of two u's?"

"Trademark infringement," laughed Luke. "There's a protective program for sponsoring organizations to prevent trademark infringement."

Dick wrinkled his nose and slitted his eyes, looking askance at the logos prominently displayed on each and every piece of clothing The Swuush was wearing, including a neon green headband with the words "Do the Dew" splashed across it. "This isn't going to make me conspicuous?"

"You can take off the headband if we go sneaking around anyplace. In the meantime, you look relatively normal. Advertisers supply all sorts of gear and clothing in the virtual worlds—most you can buy with points you get from soft-drink bottle caps and fast-food promotions. Your cover would wear that kind of thing—it's cheap and commonplace."

Dick arched one eyebrow. "Sounds like my cover has low self-esteem."

"Not at all." Luke slid onto the other stool. "This wouldn't be your cover's main avatar. That would probably be a giant troll stacked out

195

with more magic, loot, and firepower than you can imagine. This avatar, he would just be used to steal stuff—maypoles, gear, whatever—that could be cashed in or swapped in order to gear up his main guy."

"Why doesn't he just max out the stolen credit card, exchange the cash for maypoles, and buy whatever he wants?"

"Good question," said Luke with a nod, "but that would most likely trip the parameters marking the card as stolen. A small, monthly game charge could, on the other hand, go quite some time before getting noticed by the owner and reversed. Besides, some players create their own unique equipment. There's plenty of cool stuff you can't buy. You have to make it, steal it, or trade for it. That's how we tumbled into this whole mess, remember?"

"Yeah," replied Dick with a sigh. "I remember."

Luke showed Dick the sequence to call up and enter the Reality 2 Be game world. Soon they were on a flat, featureless plain.

"Kinda dull place, isn't it?"

"They leave the entry portal desolate so as to not aggravate any parental units who may be supervising their kid's entry into the game world and, of course, to allow people room to learn how to walk."

"Huh? Learn how to walk?"

Luke held up his controller. "It's not as easy as you think. It's not instinctive. You have to press this controller button and push up on this toggle to put your right foot forward, then ease it back while your other hand mimics the same movement for your other leg." Luke demonstrated with his own spandex clad avatar, named The Dewdster, walking in a circle around The Swuush.

Dick gave it a try and The Swuush jerked and twitched its away across the screen. It was hard work, damn hard work to get his pudgy fingers to manipulate the toggles of the controller with sufficient finesse for the scene not to look like a cheap zombie movie. Worse yet, he could tell Luke was working hard not to laugh out loud.

"Why do they make it so hard just to play the game?" growled Dick as he continued to manhandle the controller, before finally giving up and letting it lay lax in his beefy hands.

"It's a lot easier if you spent a lot of time playing computer games as a kid. You know where the buttons are and how sensitive they are to various movements by instinct." Luke shrugged. "It probably also discourages the parents from hanging around while you learn how to play."

When Dick looked back from Luke to the screen, his avatar was floating away. "What the hell?" he shouted as he grabbed the controller, stabbing at the controls and causing The Swuush's legs to spasm in random jerks without gaining purchase.

Luke laughed again. "Newbies have that problem all the time. They tend to rest their thumbs a bit too heavily on the toggles or fail to neutralize all inertial momentum when they intend to be stationary. It makes them float a bit."

"You can float? Isn't there gravity in this world?"

"Not so much. It's factored into certain things, like liquids. Blood, rain, drinks—they all fall when not contained. You also fall when you leap or trip. But gravity's not incorporated into everything. Targeting trajectories, for example. Most weapons just shoot straight as a laser here. It takes more computational power to factor in a weak force like gravity, when inertia works for most purposes. It also makes it easier to hit what you're aiming for with a ranged weapon, which keeps the customers happy."

"So, if I don't toggle with precision, I'll just keep going?"

"Only in the air. Friction counteracts inertia pretty effectively on the ground. That's why if you're going to travel a considerable distance ...

and Reality 2 Be is one massive universe ... most people tend to fly. It's just faster and easier."

Dick stared at him. "You can fly?"

"Why not?" replied Luke. "It's a pretend world. Why shouldn't you be able to fly?" Luke leaned over and showed him the sequence of controls that operated the flight characteristics. They weren't instinctive, either, but were much easier to learn than how to walk.

The two companions flew together, one a bit more unsteady than the other, for a few moments. "Why in the world did you start me out with walking?" asked Dick. "This is much better."

"You might have to walk where we're going. Ceiling might be too low. There might be impediments or even traps. C'mon, mate. Back to the ground and practice walking, then running."

Dick marveled at the weird stuff one needed to learn to be a spy. And to think, kids did this crap for fun.

It took a while, but he finally got the hang of it. He could walk, run, turn, jump, duck, and fly. He might not look good doing it, but he was functional.

"Great," said Luke—the guy really would have made a great teacher—, "now we can walk around a bit and look at the sights. I'll take you to a few places I used to visit."

As they walked away from the entry point, buildings began to appear on the horizon, along with signs and advertisements for places and things both in the real world and the game world. Soon they were surrounded by billboards that flashed and popped up all sorts of advertising, complete with spinning graphics, fireworks, and grating sound effects.

Dick looked at the vista with distaste. "Kind of a cheesy place, isn't it?"

"It's like the real world. Parts are really nice, spectacular even. The entrance is ... well ... sort of like Anaheim before you get to Disneyland."

Dick looked up at a giant sign featuring the type of images that would occasionally pop up in spam porn come-ons advertising Barry's House of Babes. "This doesn't look like Anaheim to me."

Buildings appeared on the somehow-too-near-horizon. Seedy-looking hotels flanked dance clubs, bars, and assorted storefronts, including one offering residential and commercial real estate, even ongoing businesses, all located in Reality 2 Be. As they got farther from the entrance, he could see more and more other avatars walking and flying about. Most were human or at least humanoid, but he could also see dragons and pixies and dwarves. As they got to the outskirts of the virtual city, a dwarf walked up to the two of them.

"Want to buy a johnson?" the dwarf asked. "Best quality. All sizes available."

"What the hell?" blurted out Dick.

Luke pointed at the keyboard. "You have to type to talk in-world."

"Who was talking in-world?" grumbled Dick as he typed: "Huh?"

The dwarf tapped his foot, as if impatient, folding and unfolding his arms. "Hey, buddy! Wanna buy a johnson or not?"

Dick simply looked at Luke. "Okay, let's try it in the real world. Huh?"

"He's trying to sell you a penis."

"He's ... what?"

"He's trying to sell you a penis. You noticed yourself the avatar prototypes aren't anatomically correct. It saves a lot of trouble with parents who may help their kids create an avatar when they sign up for the game. But, just like other ... er ... equipment, they can be acquired in the ... aftermarket."

"Hello?" The tinny, gruff voice of the dwarf avatar erupted from the speakers to Dick's computer. "Anybody playing this avatar? Or is this one of the new robotics from North Korea?"

Dick typed. "Yeah. They call me 'The Swuush.'"

"Gr8. No names. You wanna buy or what?"

"Sure," Dick keyed. "Show me what you got." As the unnamed dwarf opened his jacket to reveal a variety of johnsons, Dick turned to Luke. "North Korea? G-R-8?"

"A lotta people in third world countries without much in the way of employment prospects play games for a living. They create zillions of avatars and pre-program most of their activities, trying to make enough money doing virtual manual labor or mugging newbies or somesuch that they can funnel some maypoles to the programmer. In the fighting arenas, they battle each other for prize money or to loot the loser's body for stuff or just to increase their skill levels so they can sell the avatar on eBay for real cash."

Dick made his avatar lean down to look at the dwarf's wares as Luke continued. "G-R-8, as you so parentally put it, is text for 'great'. I thought you said you had a teenage kid who was computer literate."

"We don't text much," grumbled Dick. "So, should I buy a dick from this guy, or what?"

Luke glanced over at his screen. "Decent quality, but a bit overpriced. Yeah, go ahead. It's what a fourteen year old Filipino kid would do."

"But I thought you said this wasn't his main avatar. If it's just a throw-away, why would he spend money to make it ... fully equipped?"

Luke's eyebrows jumped up as he gave Dick a hard stare. "He's a teenage boy. There's no way he's going to spend a significant amount of time in-world without a johnson. He might miss out on a chance to get laid."

"He's fourteen," Dick sputtered. "That can happen here?"

"Welcome to the Internet," Luke intoned. "Anything can happen, including—no, especially—sex. Of course, it's more likely a perv pedophile from Denmark is manipulating the controls, than a real, live girl, but kids on the Net don't think of that."

"Hello?" grumbled the dwarf over the speakers. "You buying? Or do you just like perusing penises?"

"Sorry," typed Dick. He manipulated the controls to make his avatar point. "That one."

"Excellent choice," intoned the dwarf as it held out the purchase. A chime sounded and an option appeared on Dick's screen indicating the price, with an on-screen button to push if he wanted to purchase. He pressed the button and watched as his maypole account was debited. Another button popped onto the screen: "Press here to add professional installation for only one hundred maypoles." He looked over at Luke.

"I'm not installing it. So if you want it functional, rather than carrying it around in your pocket, I'd get it installed."

Dick growled. "My outfit's spandex. I don't think I even have a pocket." He grimaced and pressed the option to have his dick installed. He didn't watch what the dwarf was doing during the thankfully brief installation process.

Luke also made a purchase.

When the dwarf had departed, Luke turned to Dick, "C'mon, I'll show ..."

Dick interrupted. "If you say 'I'll show you mine, if you show me yours,' this training exercise is over."

"No worries, mate. And, no, I wasn't going to show you how to use it." On-screen, The Dewdster gave a vigorous hip thrust. "Let's just say it's more intuitive than walking."

Dick felt queasy, but said nothing.

"What I was just going to say," continued Luke, "is that I'll show you the main mall in town, where avatars come to socialize and buy stuff. Stuff for their avatars and stuff that is shipped to them in the real world. After that, we can head off for Denver."

Dick grunted assent and The Dewdster took off, flying in a low circle until The Swuush joined him. The sky grew more and more crowded with other avatars as the cityscape whizzed by below them. Most seemed to be flying to or from the point toward which they were headed.

Suddenly, a large, low building came into view. It looked like what Dick imagined the Mall of America would look like from an aerial view, except much larger. That and the fact it was partially collapsed and belching smoke. A large crowd of avatars surrounded the scene of destruction. The majority were working to douse the flames and dig out survivors. Many others, most of them in non-humanoid form, were diving in, scooping loot out of the destroyed stores and rocketing away at high speed.

In the near entrance, Dick could see what looked to be a virtual representation of a Chinese Type 99 main battle tank. A mob of avatars had apparently tipped it over. A few were standing on its side, arms outstretched in victory. Amidst the destruction farther away, Dick could see another similar tank, still maneuvering as gangs of avatars tossed Molotov cocktails and magic fireballs at it.

Luke swore out loud. When Dick looked over, the kid was staring in shock at his own screen, which showed only a slightly different view of the same scene. Suddenly, the kid began to shout. "Pull up! Pull up!"

On Luke's screen, The Dewdster went from a streaking Superman flying position to standing straight up at a full stop, somehow hovering in the air, a trick Dick knew he would not be able to duplicate. Dick half-expected to hear a screeching sound as his teacher's avatar skidded to a stop. The Dewdster turned in the air and rocketed away, back toward the entrance to Reality 2 Be. Luke turned to Dick. "Get your avatar out of there now!"

Dick did his best to comply, but had barely gotten underway when Luke finished his own escape and grabbed his controller away from him, manipulating the controls in a mad frenzy until both of their avatars had left the game.

The kid was panting and sweating by the time the computers were both shut down.

"You wanna explain that?" asked Dick.

"No," replied the kid.

"Not good enough. Try again."

Luke's breathing was returning to normal, but the kid was still shaking. "My previous avatar was clearly traced. My team was compromised. Let's just say that if ... this mission ... doesn't kill me, I think the Chinese will." He took a deep breath. "And not just in-world."

CHAPTER 20

Dee Tammany sorted through her routine paperwork as she was chauffeured from Philadelphia to an in-the-flesh meeting off-site in New York City. The Subsidiary wasn't foolish enough to locate its central headquarters in a city that was a terrorist's wet dream, but being close to the centers of power in New York and Washington was handy. Drives like this also gave her a chance to catch-up on her more routine administrative responsibilities.

Truth be told, a decent executive assistant could handle much of the drudge work she was doing, but Dee was a bit of a control freak. Besides, it was one of the few relatively relaxing tasks she had at the Subsidiary and a good way to keep in touch with everything going on in the office. Sometimes she even learned an interesting tidbit or two from even the most mundane emails and paperwork.

Her eyes skimmed over Dick Thornby's request for support for the Denver leg of his current assignment. The charter flight was expensive, but she completely understood the necessity. Security at any airport was only as good as the security at the airports sending flights there. If you wanted to get a gun or even something more into the secure area of a facility where the Transportation Safety Administration and Homeland Security were doing a bang-up job, all you had to do was to get it onto a private jet landing there that had taken off from a facility where security sucked, or was compromised.

The Subsidiary, like the CIA and any decent national espionage agency, had a number of corporate subsidiaries which helped out with tasks like these. In this case, Nine-To-Five Business Charters operated charter jet services from a variety of private airports around the country and around the world, including from an airfield in central New Jersey. They could get anything the Subsidiary had access to on a plane and to anyplace it needed to go. It was expensive, but it was worth it. She initialed the request—it was over the agent's discretionary limit, so needed approval—and flipped the page to see if there were any other non-routine items requiring her assent.

"Holy ..." The Subsidiary worked hard to prevent sovereign nations from getting and using this kind of device and now Dick Thornby wanted one? She picked up her phone.

Dick picked up his cell phone. He had been dreading this conversation, but he had put it off for too long. He scrolled to the speed dial marked "ICE" and pressed. In the acronym obsessed world of espionage, ICE usually meant United States Immigration and Customs Enforcement, but post 9/11 the acronym meant only one thing on a cell phone: "In Case of Emergency," a handy way for anyone finding a dead or injured person with a cell phone to get hold of their emergency contacts or loved ones for medical information or notification.

The phone rang at home, but no one picked up. He didn't leave a message.

Dick thumbed the button to scroll through and clicked on Seth's cell phone number. He was going to have to tell his kid, yet again, he was going out of town on business, despite his promises, despite the fact Seth's mom had left and there were plenty of things to work out, things that needed to be worked out now, before it was too late. He didn't know exactly what he was going to say, how he was going to explain how his cover job as a wastewater treatment consultant was more important in the grand scheme of things than keeping his own family from disintegrating.

Stopping an epidemic break-out of dysentery in India? Could he sell that? Would Seth get suspicious that there was nothing about it on the news? Did Seth even watch the news or read about world events? Did he get all of his information from website blurbs and The Daily Show on Comedy Central?

He heard the phone attempt to connect, then an annoying beep before a bored voice informed him the "cellular customer was not in service."

Seth and Brian could be tubing, river rafting someplace remote, out of cell phone range. Or they could simply be in Brian's basement, playing computer games. At least, that's what Seth usually claimed was the case when he didn't pick up on his calls. Cell phone reception was crappy underground.

Of course, the kid could just be screening his calls and turning off his phone when he saw dear old Dad calling. Dick didn't like that idea, but he knew he deserved it.

He flipped his cell phone shut. Then re-opened it and called home again. This time he let the machine pick up.

"It's Dad. Uh ... look ... I gotta go out of town for work for just a couple days. Big emergency. I'll call soon to talk. Hope you're just tubing with Brian and not getting into any trouble while your mom and I are both out of the house. Take care, Seth."

He'd try again from Denver, before he went underground and lost reception.

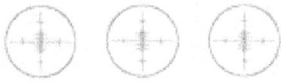

The trip to Denver was quiet. After a bit of compulsive verifying of equipment—Luke checking the two laptops and associated cables, batteries, and other paraphernalia that went with him, even though he had checked it all just before they left the computer lab, and Dick checking the duffel bag waiting at the plane to confirm it contained everything on his list—there didn't seem to be much to do. Dick mulled over potential approaches to their goal at DIA for a while, then decided to catch some shut-eye during the flight. Luke, he was sure, had bigger, more personal issues, to think about. Still, he hoped the kid would get some sleep, too.

Four hours and twelve minutes later, the corporate jet was circling northwesterly around Denver International Airport so as to be able to land on runway 16R into the moderate southerly winds blowing across the edge of the Front Range. Coming in from the east, north of the airport, the flight path gave the two passengers a good view out the port windows of the dazzling white peaks of the main terminal on the desolate plain east of the suddenly rising peaks of the Rocky Mountains. To the southwest and ahead, to the west, the mountains were spectacular: white-capped at the top, with purple and gray down to the tree-line, below which swaths of dark-hued green predominated. As the plane made a steep bank to turn south toward the landing strip, the airport proper was lost to view and the mountain vistas shifted to the starboard windows. The "Please Fasten Seatbelts" light pinged on.

Luke, lawful good little soldier that he was, immediately moved to buckle his belt, his neck craning in what looked to be uncomfortable ways to still try to catch a glimpse of the mountain vistas. Dick never gave a thought to buckling in. Instead, he reached across his companion's lap and flipped up the buckle of the belt.

"Hell, kid. We're going to be in a whole lot more danger than this every single minute after we land. Might as well enjoy the ride ... and the view in the meantime."

Luke hesitated just a moment, then gave an uncertain smile and stood up, leaning down to the starboard window to watch the mountains as they glided in, descending in a steep, but controlled, path to touchdown.

Once down, Luke stood upright again and looked at Dick. "Where are we disembarking?"

Dick ran his tongue across his teeth. "We're pulling up to a gate, just like the Reality 2 Be boys do. In this case, Concourse C. A gate for Delta that's not in use at the moment."

Luke's face darkened. "Isn't that a bit ... I don't know ... noticeable? Wouldn't it be stealthier to alight at the corporate jet annex?"

Dick sucked at a piece of food his tongue had found between two teeth. "Maybe. But we can't take a chance of having to carry our "equipment" through security. That's the whole point of the charter, to get this crap into the secure areas of the airport."

"That's expensive, isn't it?"

"Saving the world always is, kid. Besides, it ain't our money. It's not even our tax money at work, at least not directly."

The two men walked up the jetway into Concourse C. Once they entered, Dick couldn't help but glance down as he walked past the other gates, looking for odd things embedded in the floor.

Luke apparently noticed the direction of Dick's gaze. "Carpet by the gates, so you won't find anything here. Besides, the weird stuff in the floor is pretty much all in Concourse B. And most of the art is in the main terminal, on the other side of security."

"What do you think that means?"

"Just another data-point for the conspiracy freaks to obsess over," replied Luke. "So where do we go from here? Do we sneak into the tramway tunnels and try to find the staircase down?"

"Not a chance."

"Why not?"

Dick shook his head. "Think about it, kid. There might be access from there, but who knows for sure? The one thing we do know is that people enter this secret facility every day. Employees, overseers, executives from Reality 2 Be ... whatever. What I am pretty sure of is that all those people aren't crawling around tramway tunnels opening secret doorways while thousands of passengers zip by on trams heading out to their gates."

"Luggage handling area?" offered Luke. The kid was clearly guessing.

"Again, perhaps, but not likely. Too many laborers around—they can't all be in on the secret. Besides, it's grimy and the access is clearly controlled by the TSA boys and girls. I don't see a parade of corporate suits wandering in there on a regular basis without being noticed by a lot of people."

Luke's hands twitched up in a gesture of defeat. "Where then?"

"First off, I would put the entrance on the level above the main passenger paths and gates."

Luke looked up, as Dick continued. "Yep. I would have people go up to go down. It's counterintuitive and there are less people on that level to notice you. Besides, where can someone go dressed in normal business attire, that has controlled access, but not secure access, and where no one will give it a second thought if they don't come back out the door for an extended length of time?"

Luke opened his mouth, but said nothing.

"That's right," said Dick, clapping his companion on the back. "Airline lounges. Restricted to frequent fliers and first class passengers, but accessible to even the lowly upon payment of an exorbitant daily fee. They're mostly on the upper levels at DIA. Access is restricted, but not secure, and passengers sometimes go in for hours and hours at a time and no one gives it a second thought."

Luke closed his mouth. "That actually makes sense."

Dick smiled. "A whole lot more sense than alien lizardmen lurking in the tramway tunnels." He headed toward the nearest lounge. "And, it comes with free drinks and a buffet of fruits and cheeses. We can grab a snack and a soft drink while we reconnoiter." He turned back to motion Luke to come along. "Trust me, that never happened during reconnaissance missions when I was a Ranger."

CHAPTER 21

Luke had always thought field agents were all rough and tumble mates. You certainly got that impression, at least in comparison to your own life, when you sat in the communications center at the Subsidiary monitoring live feed of infiltrations and fire fights or watching footage of a once busy port facility in New Zealand going up in flames. Certainly, Dick Thornby's talk about car chase evasive maneuvers and his knock-about, impromptu invasion of Reality 2 Be's corporate offices in New Hampshire did nothing to disabuse Luke of such notion. On the other hand, the willingness of the guy to listen to Luke's ideas, to discuss what he was doing and why, and to put himself into the mind-set of the bad guys showed more intellectual analysis, introspection, and, frankly, patience than Luke expected from a field operative who had a reputation for blowing things up.

"Do your best to look bored and travel-weary," whispered Dick to him as Luke pressed the button to call the handicap access elevator to go to the upper level of Concourse C to check out their first airline club lounge. "We can't just go in and poke about, then move on to the next place. It could attract suspicion. We're going to have to hang about each place for at least an hour, seeing who comes and goes, 'accidentally' trying locked doors in an effort to find the 'men's room,' and the like." Luke could see Dick checking out the elevator mechanism through a small window in the doorway as the box descended to pick them up.

"Hydraulic," grunted Dick. "Slow and dependable. The kind of elevator that can't really fall and so doesn't frighten people with disabilities. Not a design that is useful for more than a couple floors, so not relevant to our investigation."

The door slid open at a ponderously slow pace as a deep voice intoned. "Door opening. Access to club lounges, first aid station, and lost and found." Dick hefted in his duffel and pressed the button for the floor above.

"What about checking out the first aid station and lost and found?" asked Luke. He wanted to be thorough.

"Nah. Can't imagine dozens of people wandering into those places every single day without the janitors or somebody getting suspicious. If there's a chapel in one of the concourses, though, that could be worth checking out. Some people are very regular about their religious devotions, so recurrent entry wouldn't be suspicious, but then again, neither would an irregular volume of strangers—some staying for considerable lengths of time." The elevator continued its agonizingly slow climb. "Not a top candidate though. Most public chapels are just one big room, so if you go in and someone follows and doesn't see you, that's pretty obvious. Not like an airline lounge, where they have phone booths and Internet cubicles and conference rooms which would quickly put you legitimately out-of-sight to someone following."

The doors slid open and Dick picked up his bag to exit the elevator. "But I like the fact you're thinking, kid."

They approached the lounge and Dick reached into a pocket, pulling out a wallet and plucking a premium-level airline frequent flier card out of it. Dick grinned. "One of the perks of the job."

"Lots of frequent flier miles from your mission travels?" whispered Luke, confused. With all the different aliases and airlines these guys used, he didn't see how they could rack up significant miles in anybody's program. Consolidating multiple accounts would be a definite security breach.

Dick snorted. "Nah. The guys down in 'Identification and Documentation' can whip up a forged one of these, complete with a magnetic code strip, in a matter of minutes." He moved toward the entrance.

Luke halted. "Wait a minute," he hissed after his currently jovial companion. "I don't have one."

Dick looked over his shoulder and motioned Luke forward, waiting until he caught up to speak in a low voice. "You're my traveling companion. I get you a day pass. It'll explain why you're so clueless and awestruck by everything in the lounge and why I have to show you around and whisper and point at things." The middle-aged spy gave Luke a once over. "Clueless and bewildered you can do. Always use a cover that plays to your strengths."

And then they were in the door and standing at the entrance desk, where Dick's elite status quickly got Luke a complimentary day pass, not to mention a flute of champagne even before he had gotten to one of the comfy seats in the lounge. Dick wandered about the place a bit, pretending to show off its features to Luke, but Luke could see his mentor studying the wear patterns on the carpet, listening for the sound of elevator equipment behind locked maintenance doors, and the like. Luke did his best to play along.

Dick was right. Luke could do clueless without even trying.

They stayed just over an hour. They snacked, watched the other passengers, used the restroom facilities, and pretended to read the newspaper. Luke even checked his personal email, while Dick made one of his frequent, unsuccessful attempts to get his son on the phone. Whether it was aggravation with himself, his son, or the cell phone industry, Dick seemed to Luke to be increasingly on edge as time passed. Luke humored his partner by pretending not to notice. Finally, the old guy just stood up and motioned to Luke. "Time to go."

They departed and repeated the routine at another, smaller lounge. After striking out at all the Concourse C frequent flier lounges, they used the staircase back to the main level and then took the tram to Concourse B.

Net Impact

The largest and busiest of the gate hubs, Concourse B housed almost nothing but facilities for United Airlines. Dick seemed to be taking a pretty relaxed approach to surveillance here, although they did take a few moments to ogle some of the items embedded in the floor on the main gate level. Brass dinosaurs. Marble wings. Weird words— sometimes difficult to see, much less read, as the thundering masses rushed for their connecting flights.

Their stay in the frequent flier lounge was shorter than the stay on Concourse C.

"Not a good candidate location," explained Dick after they left. "Too busy. The staffing is too homogenous, too."

"Too homogenous?"

"Everybody in the concourse works for the same airline. Strangers would be noticed more. Employees would talk to each other more about anything that struck them as odd." They headed for the tram to Concourse A. "Look sharp for the next concourse, though," advised Dick. "That's a likely scenario."

"Not homogenous?"

"Now you got it," replied Dick with a wry smile. "Eight, ten different airlines, including several international carriers, so nobody knows everybody else and nobody raises any suspicion, even if they don't speak much English. A good mix of big companies with big planes and small companies with small planes, where the pilots carry your luggage and take your ticket, too. Easily accessible to the main terminal by causeway without too much walking. Right near the Airport Office Building, so office types won't look out of place—they could simply be buying incredibly over-priced fast food for lunch."

"So why did we start with Concourse C, if Concourse A is a more likely location?"

"Because we're thorough." Dick grunted and readjusted his bag from one hand to the other. "And 'cause we got off the plane there and

I don't want to schlep this bag back and forth any farther than I have to."

Luke felt suddenly guilty. He only had a backpack with a couple laptops. Who knew how much hardware Dick had in his bag? "Sorry. I should have offered to carry it."

Dick looked up at him, his held tilted down. "Nah. Control freak. Remember?"

Luke shrugged. "We probably could have gotten a gate at Concourse A. A couple of the carriers here have been cutting back their flights lately."

Dick shook his head. "More obvious. Anyone looking for trouble coming will be looking at the gates here, or more likely the walkway over from the main terminal. We're sneaking in the back door."

Luke was impressed. Dick always was thinking more steps ahead than Luke could ever imagine. He wanted to try to catch up to his partner's preparations.

"How deep?" Luke asked.

"Huh?"

"How deep do you think the secret facility is? A mile down, maybe?"

Dick gave him a queer look and motioned him to follow over to a bench, where the two of them could sit as people passed by. He dropped his bag with a thud and plopped down onto the bench, turning to Luke as the kid shouldered off his backpack and sat down next to him.

"Think about it, kid. Think about how you said the construction was hidden. A shaft a mile deep takes a real long time to tunnel out and it can't be disguised as an optic fiber gangway. Getting people in and out of a tunnel that deep would take forever. You couldn't for a minute fool visiting outsiders into thinking they were just in a reservations computer center or something like that. Not to mention the ventilation problems. You know how hot the ambient bedrock is a mile underground?"

Luke had no idea. There was lots of mining in Australia and some of his school chums had gone to work for BHP or Rio Tinto, both big mining concerns with interests in the outback, but those were mostly gigantic surface mining operations—strip mines they called them in the States. He shrugged. "I don't know. Caves are generally cooler than surface temperatures aren't they?"

Dick rolled his eyes. "Caves, at least caves people visit, are generally relatively near the surface and wet—evaporation cools. The pressure a mile down is enormous and pressure creates heat. The rock that far underground has gotta be a hundred, maybe a hundred twenty degrees, Fahrenheit."

"Oh."

"You're the tech guy," continued Dick. "Tell me how deep you would need to go to protect electronic and computer equipment from EMP."

"Electromagnetic pulse?" blurted out Luke, a bit louder than he intended. A passing mother pushing a stroller with a sleeping baby gave him a severe look. He lowered his voice to a whisper. "EMP hardened facilities, that's something you Yanks and the Russkies and the other superpowers worry about in protecting nuclear weapons and command and control facilities. You know, missile silos in Kansas and secure undisclosed locations for the Vice President to scurry off to in the event of a crisis." Luke lowered his voice even farther. "You only worry about EMP if somebody's nuking somebody."

Dick rocked his head to one side. "Humor me. You know the science, the math. How deep do you have to go to protect a server farm? Assuming you can toss in a shitload of concrete and even steel or lead shielding during construction."

Luke ran some calculations in his head. "I don't know. Sixty, maybe a hundred feet. You'd have to make sure the pulse didn't propagate straight down through your access shafts."

"So you'd go six, ten stories down, say from a terminal concourse, then lateral out to a location buried under tons of concrete and reinforced steel, say under a runway. Sound like a construction project you've heard of?"

Luke whistled. "Very impressive."

"Don't look at me, kid. You figured it out. You just didn't think through what it meant, at least not all of what it meant."

"So there's more going on here than plans for the Kestrel 84 and the secret server farm for Reality 2 Be?"

Dick touched his nose with his index finger and then pointed at Luke. "Bingo." The older man stood and picked up his bag to continue on to the escalator down to the tram.

Luke hurried to follow him. "But what?" he whispered urgently. "What's going on?"

"I have a few ideas," answered Dick, "but I'd like to see what conclusions you come to when you've thought about it and ... when we've seen the facility. Ponder on it in the meantime." He winked. "That's what you're good at, kid."

Just before they went down to the tram, Dick pulled out his cell phone, obviously trying yet again to reach his son, apparently to no avail. The worried father shook his head as he folded the phone shut and dropped it back into a pocket.

"I wonder what that kid is up to."

Net Impact

One moment, Hawk was just getting his bearings. The next moment, they were upon him, knives flashing, scoring a few superficial slashes on his upper arms and shoulders before he could even respond. He put up his arms in a standard defensive posture, protecting his face and chest, his vital areas, from the onslaught. At the same time, a hidden switchblade in his sleeve snicked out, ready for use to go on the offensive.

Passersby gaped at the brazen assault in the middle of a crowded street, but no one immediately stepped forward to help, although Hawk caught the brief flash of at least one state-of-the-art cell phone being brought up abruptly to an onlooker's face. He prayed they were dialing 9-1-1 and not just recording the event for You-Tube.

That's when Hawk realized his combat stance was completely ineffective. There were no slashing blows to parry, no inside thrusts to draw a counterattack. The assailants weren't out to kill. Their knife slashes were all directed to his back, to the straps holding on to his pack—the pack carrying their package for the exchange.

Thieves!

He tried to turn in place, to present his front, his own knife, to the assailants, but with a last, forceful tug, the pack was pulled free and they fled into the sky.

Hawk dropped his knife and unslung his weapon. It would be like shooting ducks from a blind. Blast away and then go recover what fell. If only he had a Labrador Retriever.

The thieves were making good time, flying higher into the air as they made distance laterally, but they were fools. They flew in a straight line.

He sighted the heavy assault weapon and pulled the trigger on full auto, but somehow his body betrayed him. His shoulder refused to tense against the recoil and the first shot threw off his aim. Each new bullet in the rapidly expending clip added to the margin of error, until he was firing a random, uncontrolled spray into the sky as the thieves escaped.

What had happened to him? What had they done to him? Was there something on the blades of the knives?

He had barely formed the thought when blackness came for him and the world disappeared.

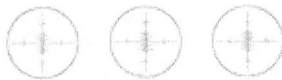

Three computer screens glowed in the gloom of Brian's basement. Seth had barely begun to lean back into the soft cushions of the basement couch, setting down the controller in each of his hands, when Brian smacked him on the shoulder with the back of one hand as he set down his own controller with the other.

"What the hell were you doing, dude? That took forever in game time! We might have gotten made. We barely got the pack away."

Seth smiled. "It had to look credible and it did."

"But he was shooting, on full auto. He might have hit us."

"Not much chance of that."

"I saw him, man," barked Brian. "He was aiming right for us."

Seth leaned forward and turned the screen of his computer so it faced Brian. "I set him on auto-defense mode, so he'd fight back. But there was no chance he would stop us. Dude, I transferred almost all of his strength and endurance points to charisma before he was even re-activated in-world. He could barely hold up the gun, much less control the recoil once he pulled the trigger. I had to make it look good or it would have been suspicious."

Brian frowned. "But the first shot, it could have gotten me."

Seth turned the computer back toward himself and powered it down. "But it didn't, did it? Now we can complete our mission and we are totally in the clear."

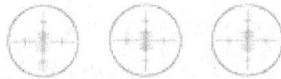

Matt Lee searched the house in New Jersey where his first target lived. He'd already determined no one was home, so he took his time, sauntering about the house, poking at Sierra Club calendar and notes on the refrigerator to see if he could find any clue about his target's whereabouts.

If not, he'd have to take care of his second target and return here to wait. He frowned. This job was already interfering with his schedule on his project for Pao Fen Smythe. He hoped he wouldn't have to hang around too long waiting for his target to show up.

He was searching the kitchen when he noticed a light blinking on the phone. There was a message. It took only a few moments to access it.

"It's Dad. Uh ... look ... I gotta go out of town for work for just a couple days. Big emergency. I'll call soon to talk. Hope you're just tubing with Brian and not getting into any trouble while your mom and I are both out of the house. Take care, Seth."

Matt smiled as he headed for the door. His targets were together, probably at Brian's. Excellent. One accident killing two close friends was a whole lot more credible than two accidents killing two close friends on the same day.

Thanks, Dad.

Maybe this wouldn't take so much time after all.

CHAPTER 22

Game time.

Dick and Luke made their way to the second level of Concourse A, where it linked to a walking bridge to the main terminal for those who didn't want to take the tram to the nearest concourse. Once there, Dick walked past the entrance to the Rocky Mountain USO facility without even a second glance. When Luke started to ask about it, the old spy hand merely waved him off: "Not only would a parade of civilians going in and out stick out like a DayGlo Orange vest over camouflage, nobody in their right mind—and the bad guys, they're usually not stupid crazy—would put an entrance into a secret facility in a room filled with guys who have been trained in infiltration and observation techniques and can kill whether or not they're carrying weapons."

Instead, Dick approached the door to one of the frequent flier lounges with Luke trailing close behind. Here, Dick was the expert and the kid was the novice. All of the opening moves were up to Dick.

He flashed an airline card in front of the comely attendant at the desk, then nodded back toward Luke. "The new hire's with me ..." He squinted at the attendant's chest, ostensibly to discern her name, but he lingered on her bosom longer than necessary. "... Taylor." He knew his behavior was crude and that he was married, but there is nothing that says boorish middle manager more than ogling the female help when you're out of the office and won't be slapped with a harassment suit. He played the part well. Finally, he tore his eyes away and refocused on Taylor's pleasant face, sighed and rolled his eyes. "You got a peanut free zone in there? The kid says he's allergic."

"Certainly, Mr. Ferguson," answered Taylor. "Right this way." She got up and headed down a short corridor, away from the buffet table laden with fruit, cookies, and other snacks for waiting passengers. She swung her hips as she walked and he paid close attention to where she was going, his eyes flicking from her hip motion to the surrounding layout of rooms to her hips to the carpet wear patterns and back to her hips again, taking everything in and filing it away for future use.

Taylor didn't appear to notice. She was probably used to, or maybe even liked, the attention of the frequent fliers to her physical appearance. When she arrived at the door to a well-appointed conference room, she stopped in the doorway, motioning them inside. The smile she dialed up seemed genuine enough to Dick's wandering eyes, but maybe she was good at her job, too. "We save this room for our more sensitive passengers. Please, enjoy your stay."

He resisted the temptation to squeeze past her into the room, instead standing aside until she understood he was waiting for her to head back to her post. He didn't want to overplay his part. He used Taylor's long walk down the corridor as an opportunity to stare in that direction, confirming his earlier observations. Then he went into the conference room and motioned for Luke to follow.

He dropped his duffel onto the floor and plopped down into one of the fancy conference chairs, leaning back and swiveling the ergonomic delight until he could put his feet up onto the conference table.

Luke still stood near the door, a look of bewilderment on his face. "What makes you think I'm allergic to peanuts? I actually do have an allergy ... but it's to cilantro. It makes my face swell up like a puffer and I spend the next day and a half in the WC hurling like ..."

Dick held up a hand, palm forward. "Stop, already. I have no interest in your hurling technique. I made the allergy up so we could score a private conference room in a less public area of the lounge. Peanut allergies are so bad in some kids these days, they can't even be in the same room with peanut dust—that's why the airlines don't hand out packets of peanuts on planes anymore. But the effect varies by individual; this way we can make you as sensitive as serves our purpose." Dick winked at his colleague. "You're not the only one who can role-play."

"Oh."

"You betcha. And it paid off."

"It did?" replied Luke, looking around wide-eyed.

"Sure," declared Dick. "You saw it, too. Just think it through. What did you see?"

Luke unshouldered his backpack and took a seat. "That you're almost thirty years older than her and a dirty old man."

Dick smiled. "Glad I was convincing, but don't worry about it. It's part of the cover. Besides, most professionals in the biz don't screw around on the job. It's distracting, potentially compromising, and involves leaving DNA evidence behind, which is never a good idea for someone involved in clandestine operations. Besides, you don't want to have to deal with her boyfriend or her husband or her boss or ... quite frankly ... her once the deed is done." He paused for a moment, but Luke said nothing. "I meant, did you see anything relating to our reasons for traveling to this fine, mile-high city?"

Luke scrunched up his nose. "Two other conferences rooms right near the entrance to the hallway and a short spur off to the left leading to what was labeled a storeroom—probably for the food and drink— and a service elevator beyond." He paused for a moment. "They probably bring the food and drink in from the service elevator straight to the store room. It's conveniently located and leaves all of the deliveries out of sight of most of the travelers hanging around in the main area of the lounge."

"Undoubtedly, that's exactly what they do. But did you notice the traffic patterns on the carpet?

Luke scrunched up his face again. "Showing some wear all the way down the spur, but with a bit of a curve into the storeroom from this end, but not from the elevator end."

"And what does that tell you?"

Luke frowned. "Not much. I mean, that pattern makes sense, since they go into the storeroom to re-supply the food and drink a lot more often than they run supplies from the elevator to the storeroom."

"All true," replied Dick, waiting for just a moment to see if his partner would put together the pieces. When Luke simply sat there, staring at him, he continued. "That same logic says there should be less wear along the straightaway after the storeroom, than before it, but there's not. A lot of traffic goes all the way down the spur from one direction or the other."

"So that's the secret entrance? A service elevator? It's not even disguised as anything."

He nodded. "That's the entrance and, no, they don't disguise it. That way they can tell the occasional visitor who's not aware of the real function of the facility that they're using a service elevator because of maintenance on the main entrance. Hell, they can tell the regular employees the entrance to their workplace is where it is as a simple security measure or, who knows, maybe they have another entrance in the Airport Office Building they run the low level employees through."

"So what do we do now?"

He could tell the kid was getting nervous, both from his voice and his unnaturally straight posture in the comfy chair. Dick leaned back and looked at his watch before interlacing his fingers behind his head. "We wait. It's late afternoon. If I'm right, there should be some traffic down the spur hallway in the next hour or two as the day shift ends. Not huge herds of people, mind you, but clumps of two and three every ten or twelve minutes. They probably tell the employees they allow flexible hours as a perk, but they really just don't want everyone coming and going over the same ten minute span." He closed his eyes. "Once the shift has changed, we'll go down and do our thing. In the meantime, relax and keep your ears open."

"I don't understand. How are we supposed to find our contact?"

Seth looked over at his friend, Brian. Despite his confusion and misgivings, Brian worked his controller feverishly, causing his new avatar to follow close behind Seth's own new avatar as it streaked across the heavens of Reality 2 Be like a ballistic missile. "We'll go back to the circle of stones and just wait. It's our only known contact point. If I were them, I'd go back there and hope to re-initiate the transaction."

Brian shook his head as he continued to supply thrust to his jet-propelled avatar. "But if I was the bad guys, that's a place I would watch. That's a place where I'd even maybe try to trap guys like us by pretending to be the rebels we were supposed to be meeting."

"Maybe," Seth admitted. "But bureaucrats don't always think like gamers. Besides, they don't need to trap us, remember? They already know who the avatars were that were involved in the first attempted exchange. That's why they've sent tanks and helicopters and the friggin' clone army to waste our asses. They don't need to resort to subterfuge to find out which avatars were involved in the first place."

"Maybe," Brian admitted back. "But we still don't have a code phrase to identify the rebels. We can't just use the old one. It's been compromised."

Seth paused for a moment. "So we'll do like they always do in the World War II movies to identify a German spy. You know, baseball teams, sports trivia, and stuff. We'll ask them questions they won't know the answers to if they're bad guys."

Brian's eyebrows tilted in. "I don't know any baseball trivia. That game is just too boring for words." He worked the controls for a minute, before continuing. "NASCAR. We can ask them about NASCAR trivia. Like, Dale Earnhardt, Jr.'s number or something ..."

"I didn't mean sports trivia literally. They're Chinese dissidents, not NASCAR fans. But we could ask them about Buddhist philosophy or quotes from the Dalai Lama ... the Red Army guys wouldn't know that stuff."

"Yeah, that would work. We've got a plan. It's always good to have a plan."

Luke finally couldn't stand it any longer, so he just blurted it out: "So, is there a plan or are we just showing up, guns blazing? A plan would be good. A plan I know about would be even better."

Dick looked up. "The plan was to go in after the day shift left. I assume you've been listening. Groups of people have been going down the hall over the last few hours, just like I predicted."

"That's it?"

"We'll just act like we're supposed to be there. It usually works." Dick closed his eyes again.

"Wouldn't it work better if we were actually supposed to be there?" Luke didn't know what irked him more, that he was so keyed up about this infiltration of a secret fortress or that Dick was so nonchalant about doing it without a plan.

Dick opened one eye. "You gotta way to do that?"

Luke stood and headed for the conference door. "I'm at least going to try."

Dick closed his eye again. "Stay away from the nuts or you'll blow our cover for using the back conference room."

Luke walked quietly down the hallway, pausing for a moment to look down the spur to the service elevator. Damn, if Dick wasn't right about the wear patterns on the carpet. He headed on toward the main lobby and reception area, snagging a chilled can of brand name cola as he entered. Taylor still sat at the reception desk near the door. He headed toward her, his heart pounding, unsure of what he would say.

She looked up at him, her smile quickly turning to a look of concern. "Are you alright? You look a mite flushed. You didn't go by the buffet table with the peanuts did you?"

"Er ... uh ... no." His mind raced. He had to think of something. He had to do something. Now. It was just like the role-playing games he played in university—to dither was to die. "It's my boss ..."

"Mr. Ferguson?"

"Yeah, yes, Mr. Ferguson. He wanted to know if our companion from the ... uh ... Honolulu office had arrived to meet us and asked me to check, but ... I've ... well, I've forgotten his name and didn't want to tell Mr. Ferguson that, but I don't know how to check without revealing my ... ignorance."

"Now, honey, you just let me help you out. I imagine your boss can be a bit of a problem at times."

"He's a dick sometimes, alright."

Taylor consulted a screen, then typed in an entry and looked at the new screen that appeared. "Well, the mid-afternoon flight from Honolulu's been in a while. And the next one isn't due for almost two hours."

Luke craned his neck as if to look at the screen, but dropped his gaze instead to the open day-planner on her desk. Names were listed next to times. All of the names for times already in the past were neatly crossed off with a single line, except one: A Post-It Note next to the unlined entry read "Delayed."

Luke straightened up and coughed lightly. "Well, I'll just say there's no word." He started to leave, then coughed again. He turned back to Taylor. "If it wouldn't be too much bother, could you get me a glass and some ice for my soda? They're too near the buffet table for me not to worry."

"Sure, honey," said Taylor as she rose and sashayed toward the table.

Luke reached over and snagged the Post-It Note, wadding it up and dropping it in his pocket in one swift move.

Taylor quickly returned with a glass filled with ice.

"Thanks," said Luke as he moved back toward the hallway to the conference room. "See you later."

Taylor glanced at her watch. "Diane will be taking care of you this evening. I'm off in just a bit."

"Well, enjoy your evening. I bet it will be better than mine," Luke replied in a cheery tone, before heading back.

When Luke got back to the conference room, Dick opened one eye again.

Luke sat down and poured his soda into the glass of ice. He took a long pull of cool, sparkling caffeine, then looked at his mentor. "Go take a walk for a half-hour. When you come back, tell Diane your name is Matt Lee. L-E-E. You were delayed, but scheduled to be here. I'll meet you at the service elevator with our stuff."

Dick sat up in his chair and opened both eyes. "Not bad, kid."

CHAPTER 23

A half-hour later, Dick walked back into the airport lounge without luggage. He barely glanced at Diane as he announced: "Matt Lee. I'm expected."

He looked about the lounge reception area with faux disinterest as Diane checked her day book. "Yes, sir." She stood up. "Let me show you the way."

Dick waved her off as he headed for the corridor back to the conference room and the service elevator. "No need. I know the drill."

The receptionist hesitated for a moment, then sat back down. She punched in an extension and he heard her say. "Mr. Lee has arrived." Then Dick turned the corner. Luke was waiting in the spur corridor with Dick's duffel and Luke's own equipment. A few moments later, the elevator door opened and they stepped inside.

A quick scan of the elevator revealed no obvious cameras, but Dick took no chances. He dropped his duffel on the floor right up against the elevator door, the least likely place for any clandestine surveillance to focus, and bent over it, shielding it from any view from the upper rear of the slowly descending elevator with his body and Luke's. Dick grumbled, as if to himself, for cover as he opened the bag and picked a few items out. "Damn phone. I gotta get a new phone or a new plan. Every time I leave it on when I fly, the battery wears down while it searches for signal at thirty-five thousand feet and then when I get where I'm going, I have to put in the spare battery and find a place to plug-in and charge the old one."

It only took Dick a few moments to secure the items he needed to have on his person when the door opened. Sure, he could have loaded up and carried them around the airport while he killed time, strolling the corridors and musing on alternatives for the upcoming penetration. But there was a chance Matt Lee or anyone else "expected" to use the lounge for an entry into the secret realms below would be searched, by hand or otherwise, as he entered the lounge. It was a small worry on a long list of worries about what could happen. Plenty of things could go wrong on their infiltration of the facility beneath Denver International Airport, but a good agent crossed off as many of those worries as possible.

There were other, bigger, worries he could do nothing about. The worst was that he and Luke were going in blind, knowing nothing about the facility, those running it, or what security features it might have other than a fog of protective, but bizarre, conspiracy theories and a secure location with limited access.

He also wasn't overly fond of the fact he was going in impersonating someone who he knew nothing about. Had this Matt Lee been here before? Who did he represent? What was his business? Would he, should he, recognize anyone here by sight? By name? Luke had shown some moxie by coming up with the infiltration approach. Diane's call ahead suggested that his and Luke's next best option, an unheralded trip down the elevator, would have generated a red-flag for security.

Still, he couldn't help but be a bit keyed up about what might happen next, as the elevator slowed and began to settle into place at the bottom of the shaft. He could handle himself, but having a computer geek with next to no operational experience outside of virtual reality as his back-up was worse than no back-up at all. He couldn't trust the kid's instincts, couldn't trust the kid with his life, but he still had to protect him. It was like a federal marshal charged with protecting a mob accountant in the witness protection program dragging the witness along during an off-the-cuff assault on a meeting of Mafia Dons. It could work, but you sure wouldn't do it that way unless you had no choice.

The elevator doors opened into a small anteroom. There was a greeting committee waiting: a junior executive type in a suit flanked by two thugs wearing gray security personnel uniforms and loosely cradling MAC 10s pointed in the general direction of the elevator door. Dick strode purposely forward toward the executive. Not only was it the correct thing to do for his cover, it also immediately compromised the field of fire for the goons. They couldn't fire without risking hitting their boss.

The opening gambit of their infiltration might have been more effective if Luke was a better actor. Instead, Dick heard a muttered "Er ... uh ..." as the kid balked at exiting the elevator. To his credit, however, the kid manned up after a couple seconds and finally followed his lead. Dick rolled his eyes at his underling for the benefit of the junior executive as he extended his hand.

"Matt Lee," he said giving his counterpart a quick, strong, shake. "Don't mind my associate. He's from Australia, a society with a surprising lack of security consciousness for having sprung from a population of thugs and criminals."

The junior executive glanced over at Luke before returning his attention to Dick. "Frank Egbert," responded the executive. "I was not told you were bringing an associate. I shall have to reprimand Diane for her communications oversight." His eyes narrowed.

"Not her fault," responded Dick. "My associate, Luke, arrived hours ago and was just sitting around the lounge waiting for me. Didn't know enough to check in, but then he wouldn't have been on your list anyway. So he just waited. He does what he's told. Don't you, Luke?"

"Er ... y-y-yes sir, Mr. Lee," stammered Luke while Dick rolled his eyes yet again.

"See?" said Dick. "He's harmless." He gave the two thugs a once over. "Not a threat, not like your companions here." He shrugged. "Search him if you like."

Egbert smiled. "It is clear he is not accompanying you for security and I have no desire to offend you or anyone from Mr. Smythe's organization."

Smythe? Had Pao Fen Smythe sent Matt Lee here for the same reason he and Luke had arrived? To track down the location in Reality 2 Be of the plans for the Kestrel 84? Sometimes it was better to be lucky than good.

The executive paused, giving Dick a long, hard stare. "It's just that ..."

Dick exploded in laughter and clapped the executive hard on the back. "It's just that given the location and make-up of Mr. Smythe's organization, you were expecting a Chinaman! Go ahead, Frank, you can say it." He looked around exaggeratedly, as he continued to chortle. "There's no chinks around to offend." He grabbed Egbert by both arms and looked him straight in his reddened face. "Those dickheads down in communications who set this up didn't spell my last name with an 'i' again, did they? I get that all the time. Their little joke." He dropped his arms, but still looked Egbert straight in the face. "But it's Lee, L-E-E, not L-I. Makes me easier to find in the phone book, or it would if I had a listed number and the phone book was in god-damn English."

Egbert joined in the laughter. "No, no. Your name was spelled correctly. I assumed ..." He stopped. "I was just caught off-guard by you being accompanied by an associate and ..."

"And you got suspicious. That's okay," responded Dick, looking back at Luke, who was still looking awkward. "Luke, here. He's my computer jockey." Dick waved his hand toward the long, long corridor outside of the elevator anteroom, from which a faint electronic hum emanated. "You don't think I understand all that electronic, cyber mumbo-jumbo you guys do here, do you? Gotta have my own geek to, you know, interface with the equipment and your geeks."

Egbert seemed to have regained his composure. "Certainly. Of course." He started to move toward the exit into the corridor. "Let me take you to a workstation where you ... where Luke ... can access the information you require." He smiled, clearly reverting into tour guide mode. "I think you'll find our facilities here quite impressive."

Crikey!

Luke's head swam and not just because of the guys with guns who had met the elevator or Dick's manic improvising as Matt Lee. He was short of breath and not just because of the altitude or the eight minute walk down a long corridor broken only by several right angle turns, the kind of layout used by Iraqis in construction of safe rooms and underground bunkers to prevent shock-wave propagation. It was their destination and its contents which really impressed him.

The room was huge and open. Concrete pillars at regular intervals supported the massive, concrete ceiling cluttered with exposed ventilation ducts, electrical conduit, and regularly-spaced sprinkler heads—not for water, but for a Halon 1301 inert gas fire suppression system. It was the type of extinguishment system used in many corporate computer rooms to put out fires without using water, which would damage and short-out expensive and intricate electronic and computer systems. There was certainly plenty of equipment to protect. The huge room was filled to capacity with top of the line, sophisticated computer gear. There were rows upon rows of blade server configurations, modems, routers, and mainframe storage and back-up units. The footfalls of the group echoed on the hollow flooring system that held the equipment above the true, undoubtedly concrete, floor and allowed power cords, optic fibers, cabling, and more ventilation shafts to service all the equipment without being an impediment to walking down the narrow alleys between the rows of electronics.

While there were a few techs present, monitoring machines or servicing equipment, computer gear outnumbered the humans by a factor of at least a hundred to one. The minute whines and hums of the various pieces of electronics joined to provide a deep, harmonious thrum throughout the room. Not only could you hear it, but you could feel the vibration with every portion of your body and see it on every surface that wasn't reinforced concrete. This was a massive amount of cyberware, a binary bonanza, a cornucopia of computer electronics sufficient to make every gamer geek in the world climax in orgiastic delight if it were laid out in a centerfold of Consumer Electronics. It was clearly more than needed to power the computing needs of a small country.

It was also clearly much, much more than needed to power the virtual world of Reality 2 Be. Dick was right. More was going on underneath DIA than a clandestine site for Reality 2 Be's server complex. He didn't know what, but his eyes roved over the equipment, assessing it, inventorying it, analyzing its possible uses.

After another tremendously long walk, Egbert finally showed them to a work station along what Luke figured was the westernmost wall of the gigantic server complex. A series of low, modular, cubicle walls blocked off the view of the main, open area. Along with several personal computer towers familiar from any office setting, with corresponding flat-screen monitors and keyboards, there was a horizontal bar with a variety of outlets, jacks, ports, and hook-ups for pretty much any kind of cable or equipment Luke could think of. Several black-mesh, ergonomically-designed chairs with adjustable lumbar support completed the set-up.

It was all Luke could ever wish for.

"Will this be satisfactory?" asked Egbert. He looked at Matt ... Dick.

Dick looked at Luke.

Luke played it cool. "It should be. I need to find ..."

Egbert cut him off. "I don't need to know. I don't want to know what you need to find. I just need to know if you have the tools to do what you need to do."

"I need to have access to the main menu for the Reality 2 Be servers. I need to be able to do a bounded parameter search in-world. Can I do that from there?"

"Yes," responded Egbert. "But you will need a password."

Luke had memorized the passwords which Beverly had used in accessing the accounting records back in New Hampshire. "I have the Tech Support codes. Do I need more?"

Egbert hesitated.

"I could call Pao Fen and see if he has more," volunteered Dick.

Egbert stiffened. "No. Guests are not permitted to make outside calls. Besides, contacting Mr. Smythe will not be necessary. My instructions were to accommodate you in every way, Mr. Lee." He handed a stiff plastic card to Luke. The card was plain and white, without markings.

"RFID?" asked Luke.

Egbert nodded.

Luke turned to Dick, who had a quizzical look on his face. "It's got a proximity chip, just like your passport. With the right hook-up, security doors will just unlock and open when you approach, just like in Star Trek."

"Cute," replied Dick.

Luke turned to Egbert. "I might need this for awhile."

Egbert shrugged. "I'm not leaving 'til you leave," he said, then sighed.

"What's the matter?" asked Dick. "Hot date tonight?"

Egbert's eyes looked heavenward, as if he was imagining a mental picture of a hot date, but he quickly looked back at Dick. "I wish. But, no. It's just that I'm going into the mountains early in the morning for a little diving. Not to worry, though. I brought my gear along, just in case I got stuck late and had to leave straight from here."

Mountains? Diving? "You're going sky diving in mountainous terrain? That's pretty dicey, isn't it?" asked Dick.

Egbert grimaced. "No, that would be insane. No way you want to land a chute in a forest, much less in a remote location with few trails and even fewer roads." His face brightened. "No, I'm going scuba diving, cave diving—well, scuba diving in an old, abandoned mine that's flooded. You wouldn't believe how clear the water is. Cold as all get out, but crystal clear."

"Oh," interupted Luke, "of course. That makes more sense." He said it, but he didn't mean it. Luke had scuba training, of course—he'd worked the Great Barrier Reef a couple summers to lay up cash for school—and he could see the appeal of looking at coral, tropical fish, and the occasional bikini-clad bimbo in warm, clear water off some island paradise on vacation. But the notion of taking a limited air supply into a dark, frigid fissure of water deep underground with nowhere to surface in case something went wrong just struck him as adrenaline-junkie stupid.

Dick just smiled. "We'll try not to make you late."

Egbert shrugged, then seemed to remember something and grabbed a piece of notepaper from the nearby desktop and scribbled a four digit number.

"PIN?" asked Luke.

Egbert harrumphed. "Extension. Call me when you're done and I'll retrieve my card and give you an escort out." He motioned at the security guards. "Take up stations at either end of the row. Make sure no one bothers Mr. Lee ... or his associate."

The two thugs did as ordered and Egbert left with them, leaving Luke alone with Dick. Luke gave his buddy a big grin, as he grabbed one of the comfy chairs. "This'll be easy."

"Unless Mr. Lee arrives for real. You said he was delayed, not dead."

"Oh."

"Yeah. 'Oh.' Let's move it along. I don't want to be delayed or dead."

Pao Fen was pacing, yet again, in his office. Arms dealing had, of course, always been a stressful occupation. You dealt with unsavory individuals who you knew had access to weapons and a willingness to use them. Trust was always an issue, with buyers, with sellers, and even inside your own organization. In addition, the logistics of transport, the risks of getting caught, and the potentially violent penalties if you failed to perform as expected, all added to the stress. But the higher he had moved up in the organization, the more he had to depend on others to perform as expected. He could live or die with the stress of his own failure to deliver, but to be at risk because of the failures of others was a management attribute that was giving him ulcers.

He could stand it no longer. He picked up his phone and pounded in the numbers for an international call. He practically barked into the phone as soon as his target picked up. "You've been in Denver for some time. Why have you not reported you have secured the files you were sent to retrieve?"

There was a long pause. The cell phone connection on the far end popped and hissed so much, at first Pao Fen thought the call might have been dropped, but finally he heard Matt Lee's voice.

"I've been delayed."

Pao Fen gripped the handset so tightly it shook. "How long?" He had a schedule to keep with impatient people.

There was another pause. "I'll be at the facility in the morning, local."

Pao Fen's blood pressure rose. "You're not there? Where the hell are you?"

"That's not important," replied Lee, his voice flat and dispassionate even under stress, in the way of all of the best contract killers. "I was delayed. It couldn't be helped. I'll be at the facility in the morning."

Pao Fen was fuming, but there was nothing he could do. He couldn't get anyone to Denver any faster than morning. If Lee was efficient once he arrived there, Pao Fen's organization would still make his deadlines. Barely. Of course, there was no way Pao Fen was going to tell this underling that.

"See that you are," he replied tersely. "People are waiting for you."

"I called the facility. They know I'm delayed."

"Those weren't the people I was referring to."

"Oh."

"One last thing, Mr. Lee."

"Yeah?"

"I'd better not find out this delay has tits."

CHAPTER 24

Dick felt as useful as tits on a bull. As Luke worked his magic on the keyboard, Dick just sat in a spare chair at the work station, idly twirling back and forth. He'd already given this place a good hard look, identifying the locations of the few doors leading away from the massive room and checking out where the few individuals or clumps of people working the night shift were located, in case the information should prove useful later. Now he had nothing to do for minutes or hours until Luke was able to find the Kestrel 84 plans on Reality 2 Be's servers.

On missions past, he would often spend such time reminiscing about good times with Melanie: trips to the Caribbean back when Seth was just a baby; snuggling in front of the fireplace when the power went out one winter when he was still on the police force in Chicago; laughing while watching Seth play with the new puppy sixteen years ago this Christmas; making love in his dorm the first time. It was a pleasant way to spend the hours of waiting that unfortunately filled the life of any covert operative.

But he couldn't do that anymore. Not since Melanie left. The pain was too great. Thinking about it, about her, would be torture—hours of torture. He had to avoid that pain, that distraction. Even thinking about thinking about her left him numb and confused.

Dick glanced at Luke, his fingers dancing, his countenance infused with concentration and energy, yet somehow simultaneously serene. It was the look of someone in love with their work, someone alive and enjoying life, even though it would soon be over. Luke was no dummy. Dick knew Luke understood on an intellectual level, even if not on an emotional level yet, that he was doomed, that the end of this mission meant the end of his life. He had probably even guessed by this point his demise would be at Dick's hand.

Jesus, these minutes or hours until Luke located the missing file were going to be damn depressing.

Fortunately for the mission and Dick's mental health, it only took minutes.

"Got it!" exclaimed Luke.

"Already?" blurted Dick, infected by Luke's excitement. "Are you sure?"

Luke swiveled one of the flat screens to face him. "Once you have access to the oversight menu hosting the main world grid, all you have to do is a parameter delineated file search and it identifies all avatars possessing any file of the appropriate characteristics. See?" Luke pointed to an entry on the screen.

The coded gobbledy-gook on that particular line of the screen looked no different to Dick's middle-aged, non-tech-savvy eyes than any other line of gobbledy-gook on the page. "Of course," he intoned in a flat, dry monotone, "it's right there in black and glowing sci-fi green. A child could see it." His tone warmed. "Great job, Luke."

Always support your partner, even when you're minutes away from killing him.

Luke flushed. "It's a rigorous, cohesive, well-constructed piece of programming for something so complex. A lot of game systems are cobbled together out of pieces from different software shops or teams, so they can get the game out quickly. Someone spent a lot of time on this one ... a lot."

"And the Kestrel 84 plans, they haven't been copied? They show up in just one place in-world?"

Luke frowned. "It's impossible to tell for sure they haven't been copied, before or after they were put into the hands of this avatar, but they definitely only show up one place in-world and ..."

Dick interrupted. "So, you've deleted the files and our primary mission is accomplished." Luke did not respond immediately. "Right?"

Luke shook his head. "It doesn't work like that. I know this specific avatar has the Kestrel 84 file. We have the exact specs of what was stolen and the file size parameters meet those specs exactly." His hands worked the keyboard for a moment and another screen popped up. "And we know the avatar carrying the files was created by a New Zealand user. It would take some time, but I could probably track it to the IP number for the Maori kid's laptop."

"So delete the file."

"I can't do that. When your avatar picks something up, it comes under the protection of your avatar's own algorithmic security coding. I can't take away the file from the avatar remotely without knowing that code."

"But you broke the kid's password, remember?"

"It's not the same thing. This is a level of encoding which is not only algorithmically based, it's assigned randomly when you acquire an object that is non-standard in the game world. It helps protect stuff from being stolen by ... you know, hackers, like us."

"Wait a minute. You said people steal stuff in the game all the time."

Luke sighed. "Avatars steal stuff from other avatars in-world. That's different."

Dick was getting perturbed. The kid had probably figured out his fate. Was he just stalling now? "Then what was the point of this trip?"

Luke looked taken aback. "To locate the item in-world. We now know which avatar has the file and where that avatar is. Now all we have to do is go get it."

"Where? There's another facility?"

"No," replied Luke. "In-world. That's why I created avatars for us. Remember? We have to recover the item in-world."

"That can be done from places a lot safer than here, can't it?"

"No, not really," said Luke, pointing again at a screen of incomprehensible coordinates and other arcane symbols. "I know where the avatar with the file is, but not necessarily where it will be." He pointed at some digits on the screen. They were changing. "The guy is on the move—pretty slowly at the moment, but that could change. I need to monitor his location from here while we're both in-world, robbing him."

"Great." Dick swiveled his chair so he could access one of the laptops Luke had gotten out from his pack. Luke plugged in the controllers and ramped up the game on both of the laptops he had brought along. When The Swuush appeared on screen, he looked different to Dick—a mishmash of equipment was strapped to the avatar's torso.

"What the ..." he exclaimed, looking over at Luke.

"I hooked up and logged on during that last half-hour upstairs while you were walking around the terminal waiting for Diane to come on shift."

His eyebrows shot up in surprise. "Needed to relax?"

Luke gave a wry smile. "Needed to mug a few newbies for their cash and weapons. We might not be the only ones looking for this avatar, so I figured some firepower would be useful."

That made sense. "Whaddya get me?"

"Not much. A knife, a couple grenades, and a loaded AK-47."

"The weapon from hell ..."

Luke looked up. "What?"

"Nothing, kid. Army Ranger thing. All these third world warlords, that's their bread and butter. Weapon of choice for lowlifes with low budgets and low-intelligence. Any idiot can use an AK-47. And too many of them do."

"Well, Rambo up, old man. It's time to go search and destroy."

They took off flying almost the second they were in-world. The Dewdster kept increasing speed and Dick had to make every effort just to keep up. He paid no attention to where they were headed— supposedly Luke had that all in hand. Besides, they were rapidly so high above the virtual landscape of Reality 2 Be that identifiable landmarks were difficult to discern. Yet they kept going higher.

Dick looked over at Luke. "Are we going to have trouble breathing?"

"Huh?"

"The altitude. Trouble breathing?"

Luke wrinkled his nose. "Hey, I'm from Melbourne and Brisbane by way of Philadelphia. Port towns, every one. I've been out of breath since we got to Denver. Mile High City and all that, but I thought they meant in the mountains. We're in the plains and I'm out of breath."

"The plains are a mile high. Gradual slope up all the way west from the Mississippi River. The snow-capped peaks you saw when we were coming in for a landing are two, almost three miles above sea level. But I wasn't talking about that. I meant in the game. Are our avatars going to suffer from oxygen deprivation without special equipment?"

"Nah. Graduated air pressure is not necessary for the operation of a virtual world. Constant pressure works fine. Just another place gravity is ignored. In fact, constant air pressure makes the coefficients for wind vectors easier to apply "

Dick looked back at his screen. The two avatars were still jetting upward at increasing speed. "Doesn't look like friction is figured in either or we would be glowing by now."

"It's a world. It's not the real world."

"So we could fly to the moon?"

That caused Luke to chuckle. "Probably not. There's undoubtedly a cap on altitude. No sense wasting computer power on a bunch of empty space."

"Now you sound like that guy from *Contact*."

Luke shrugged. "There's a guy from Oxford. He supposedly calculated there's a twenty percent chance the 'real' world is just one big computer simulation."

Dick laughed. "That's me, kid. Protecting the world from all enemies ...," he nodded toward the screen, "... real or imagined."

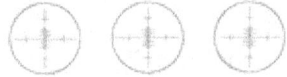

It didn't take Matt Lee long to find Brian's house. It was relatively close by and the late evening hour meant there was little traffic. Even in the dark, with the twisty-turny streets that so bedeviled American subdivisions, the place was easy to find. Matt could access the Internet on his cell phone and Google Earth was amazingly useful to a would-be stalker. Not only could he find his prey, he could scope out surveillance locations, exit routes, and hiding spots by clicking on the aerial views before he ever even went near the place.

He pulled over to the curb a few doors down from his target and grabbed a random map, pretending to be looking at it for directions. With the broad expanse of the unfolded map blocking the street-side window and part of the windshield, he took out his thermal imaging scope and scanned the house through the passenger-side windshield.

The usual hot spots from appliances glowed dull orange, but he could not see anyone inside. He drove to the end of the block and turned, pulling over again and repeating the map routine. This time, he scanned the house from side and back.

The results were no different. He watched for a bit, but there was no change. He would have to wait for someone to arrive or check out the place after it was late enough he was sure not to be interrupted.

Brian and Seth sat in the basement, staring at their laptop screens, which showed nothing but slightly different views of the same circle of huge stones surrounding the grassy, oval field Hawk and Peregrine had visited before. Except now the grassy field was littered with abandoned weapons and camping gear, but strangely, no avatar bodies.

Nothing moved. Not on the grassy field, not in the protective rocks, not in the mountains far on the horizon. The air was clear and blue and empty.

Still they waited.

"It could be hours, days even," muttered Brian.

"It could be forever," replied Seth. "We don't know what happened to the avatars we were supposed to meet."

"We don't know what happened to the Chinese dissidents controlling those avatars."

"Bad things," admitted Seth. "That's why it's important we get the maypoles to the dissidents, if any remain, and get the information from them about what the authorities are really doing in China far away from the big cities where tourists and reporters usually stay. It's an important mission."

Brian sighed and leaned back, putting his feet up on the coffee table next to his laptop. "It's a boring mission."

Seth looked at his friend. "You asked me what else my dad taught me. Well, here it is. Always finish what you start. Whatever it takes."

Brian sat up suddenly, pointing to the screen. "What's that?"

Seth looked down at his own screen. A tiny point was streaking through the sky in the distance. He squinted, but couldn't make out any more. "I dunno. Maybe it's a bird."

Brian grinned. "Or a plane ..."

Seth caught the reference. "Well, we sure know it's not Superman."

"Trademark infringement," they both said aloud.

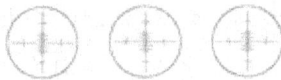

Dick could see that Luke kept The Dewdster's focus fixed straight ahead, upward to infinity. Luke's screen was a uniform ice blue.

Dick, on the other hand, kept twisting the controls so The Swuush would look around. Maybe it was his Army Ranger training asserting itself. Maybe it was paranoia generated from back when he was on an elite team in the Chicago police force that took on the toughest bad asses in town by any means necessary, then ended up getting pilloried in the press, investigated, and disbanded for their harsh tactics in protecting the good citizens of Chicago. Whatever it was, he couldn't help it. He had to have The Swuush cover their six. So despite the fact it made his avatar wobble a bit and lose a little distance in following The Dewdster, he swiveled The Swuush's gaze to look down at the still receding ground and back along their flight path.

The ground was a distant conglomeration of geographic features, like a topographic map, but without the natural curves and flow of a map of the real world. There were mountains and valleys and broad expanses of plain, but the edges were straighter, more angular, than in the real world, like the whole place had been laid out on graph paper before it was built up out of papier-mâché and colored in. Sure, there were curves, even a small oval of boulders in the distance, far, far below, and the buildings and the city borders near the horizon were a disorganized mish-mash of shapes of all sorts and sizes, but it was still unreal. The foreign vista gave Dick an uneasy feeling. Fortunately, when he checked the rear there were no missiles, fighter jets, or johnson-hawking dwarf avatars in close pursuit. As far as he could tell, The Dewdster and The Swuush owned the ionosphere of Reality 2 Be.

Dick turned the Swuush's attention back to where he was going, then glanced over at his companion and his two screens. Luke's attention alternated between the screen showing the clear blue sky of Reality 2 Be and the screen of the computer with an ever-changing array of incomprehensible coordinates and other arcane symbols.

"We're getting close," announced Luke. He squinted at the laptop screen showing the upper atmosphere of Reality 2 Be, then pointed. "See the dots? There's stuff up ahead."

Dick started to lean over to look at Luke's screen, then clapped his palm to his own forehead, before instead staring into his own screen, now showing the same dots in the distance, growing larger by the second. He had expected to only find one object up here, the avatar with the Kestrel 84 plans. Instead, there was a scattering of dots dispersed randomly across his screen. Ambush? It didn't look like the dots were organized in any way. A few were stationary, but most were moving slowly. He might have attributed the movement to the prevailing winds, except there was no uniformity to the movements. Dots—he could see now most of them seemed to be avatars—were moving in different, even opposite directions from one another, changing trajectories only when they collided with each other.

247

"What the ..." he exclaimed, not for the first time in this realm.

"Slow down," urged Luke, a bit more loudly than their normal verbal exchanges. "We don't want to overshoot." His eyes flicked to the other computer screen. "Our target is moving at almost a right angle to our flight vector."

Dick pressed down on the controller hard, cutting speed drastically as they approached the area of randomly floating avatars and other objects and bits of debris. "This looks like the Ninth Ward after Katrina. What the hell is going on here?"

Luke looked over at him. "We've obviously reached the altitude limit of Reality 2 Be's game world. You can't go any higher than this."

"Duh," growled Dick. "I meant what are all these avatars doing here?"

Luke thought a moment, then his countenance brightened. "This is where the zombies go!"

"Huh?" Dick looked at the inventory list at the bottom of his screen. What would kill a zombie in-world?

"Avatars that are no longer being played, but were never actually logged out of the game." He pointed at an avatar floating by on-screen. "Remember how your avatar would float away if you weren't careful when you were first learning how to move it? Well, if you just stop playing an avatar, odds are it had some slight inertia when you stopped playing it, or it will eventually get bumped by somebody. If any of the motion is ever upward, even the slightest little bit, you'll eventually float to the altitude limit for the world and just bump along the ceiling going in the same direction unless you collide with someone else."

Dick nodded. "Like an astronaut on a spacewalk untethered to his capsule. If he gets shoved, he just floats indefinitely wherever he was pushed."

Luke's eyes glanced over at the screen of sci-fi green digits on the other computer. "Until he falls into a gravity-well. But you're basically right. That's obviously what happened to the avatar with the Kestrel 84 plans. His player got killed and no one was operating the avatar, so he just floated off to the limit of space up here."

"Easy pickings, then," replied Dick with a touch of glee. "Just point me to the right guy and I'll loot the body."

Luke's head swiveled back and forth between the two screens. "There," he finally declared, pointing at a nearby avatar wearing a large back-pack and still gripping a large, Army-green weapon in his hands. "I should have guessed. This guy has equipment, weapons. Most of the rest of these avatars are obvious newbies. Flashy clothes, minimal gear, not much in the way of weapons. Newbies are much more likely to simply quit without logging off, thinking their avatar will still be there when and if they ever come back to it."

"Great," said Dick as he began to move toward the avatar. "This is just like a lowlife mugging an el-train full of drunks at three in the morning on March eighteenth. Everybody's so drunk from St. Patty's Day, they don't even notice you're stealing everything, including their shoes, until they wake up the next morning barefoot."

Suddenly, a deep voice boomed from the tinny speakers of both of their laptops. "Avast there, me hearties. I wouldn't be doin' that, if'n I were you. That there salvage, like all in this heavenly realm, is the property of Cap'n Drake Keelhaul Cutter and his band of misbegotten, misbehavin', misfit cutthroats."

"Shit," moaned Luke with despair in his voice.

"What?" shouted Dick as he jabbed at his controller to shift his avatar's point-of-view.

"Pirates. We've got pirates."

CHAPTER 25

"Why? Why in God's name do we have pirates?" growled Dick.

"Cause clowns would be too scary?" replied Luke with a weak grin.

Dick gave him a stern look. Pirates weren't funny—not in the real world and not here. Even though they were in a game, they didn't have time for games. "I'm serious. Who are these jokers and why are they here?"

"Think about it," Luke responded, his words growing more rapid as he continued. "Someone else had to figure out in the course of Reality 2 Be that there were hundreds or thousands of avatars floating around at the altitude limit. Most may not have much equipment, but they have some. A few maypoles, too, probably. And every so often an inactive avatar will have more—lots more."

"Like top secret weapons plans."

"I doubt they figured on that. Someone just put together a crew to harvest the loot. They simply costumed and accessorized thematically to match their activities. Role-playing, remember?"

The crackly speakers were shaken once again. "Leave now, ye rancid scallywags, or we'll be blowin' you from the sky, we will."

Dick cursed, then barked at Luke. "Get the backpack with the plans and get the hell out of here. I'll hold 'em off."

Luke hesitated.

"Do it!" Dick hissed. "Those plans are the only real thing here. It's not like I'm actually risking anything to cover you." Dick worked his controller, twisting his avatar's body to bring the AK-47 to bear and let off a burst toward the ship to distract their scurvy opponents. Minimal recoil. That was helpful. "Now!"

The floating pirate ship dominated Dick's laptop screen, but he could see on Luke's screen that The Dewdster had used his knife to slice the straps on the target avatar's pack and was rocketing straight down, out of range, before the pirates could recover their swagger.

Luke's attention moved back to the screenful of locational coordinates, no doubt to confirm their information was in the purloined backpack. After a few moments of searching, he turned and gave Dick a big thumbs-up.

There was a "boom" from the laptop speaker, followed by a burst of static. Dick looked back at his screen. The floating pirate ship had slewed sideways to come broadside to his position and was firing its cannons. The Swuush was buffeted and thrown back by the shockwave of the blast and pushed into the Maori kid's avatar, but the cannon ball missed. Dick wondered idly whether the ball would ever fall to the terrain below, or just bounce along the ceiling for eternity in this world.

He tried to fire The Swuush's AK-47 again, but he had expended the limited ammo. It didn't really matter—all he had to do was to hold off the pirates from chasing after The Dewdster for a few more moments. That's when he noticed the undercarriage grenade launcher on the large weapon the Maori kid's avatar still clasped.

This could be fun.

Dick's limited gaming skill meant that The Swuush was not nearly as quick or proficient as Dick would have been at wresting away the grenade launcher, arming it with an incendiary grenade, and taking aim at the pirate ship. He muttered under his breath at his clumsy slowness.

On the other hand, his enemy had to take the time to prime and load friggin' cannons. He liked his odds.

He aimed at amidships, slightly above the row of cannons, and fired. The grenade shot forward, puncturing the wood about two feet below the main deck and then exploded with a crack that overloaded the computer's crappy sound-system, but was vividly shown in crisp, LCD display as red-streaked, orange flames shot from every cannon station, porthole, crack, and knothole of the pirate ship. The wooden ship bulged outward incongruously before the speaker kicked back in and he could both hear and see the wood begin to splinter. Then a gigantic secondary explosion obliterated the ship and whited- out The Swuush's view, the speaker failing once again as the blast overwhelmed it.

The Swuush's view screen went from white to black and Dick could see from the statistical data at the bottom of the screen The Swuush had made the ultimate sacrifice for the cause. Now he knew what it felt like to be collateral damage.

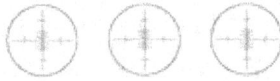

"Dude," yelled Brian, sitting up and pointing at the screen of his laptop. "Look at that!"

Seth looked at his own screen. A bright ball of light had blossomed high in the sky, well north of their position in-world. "What is it?"

"I dunno," replied Brian. "The Death Star exploding in space?"

Seth raised an eyebrow. "Maybe. Maybe it's just a shooting star. Do they have those in-world?"

Brian shrugged. "I dunno. If it was, we should each make a wish."

The two boys were silent for a moment.

"What did you wish for?" asked Brian.

Seth felt his face redden slightly. He looked down at the floor, not willing to look his friend in the eye. "I wished that my dad could help us get out of this mess with the exchange. I think the Chinese government—the real Chinese government—is on to what we were doing. We could be in danger. Maybe we should even call somebody." He looked up at Brian. "What did you wish for?"

Brian gave him a sheepish half smile. "A naked lapdance from The PussyCat Dolls."

Seth couldn't help but laugh. "Awesome, dude. Awesome."

"Dude, that was awesome," said Luke with a grin as he looked up from the screen.

Dick grinned in response, then quickly reverted back to reality. "Do you have the data? Is it confirmed?"

Luke nodded. "In possession. Confirmed to be the Kestrel 84 plans."

"How do we destroy, delete—whatever—get rid of them for good?"

Luke was all business now, too. "I logged off from the game. The plans aren't in-world anymore." He pointed at his laptop. "That's the only place they exist now, except for, you know, the computers at the Subsidiary, the Pentagon, and the new defense contractor."

"Good. Delete 'em. Wipe the hard-drive, whatever it takes to make sure they don't leave this room."

Luke hands darted over the keyboard. Dick did his best to wait patiently through the multiple maneuvers. Finally, Luke looked up. "Deleted, fragged, reformatted, wiped, and cleaned in every way I can think of."

Dick nodded. Give me the memory chip or whatever used to have the info on it."

Luke rolled his eyes, but did as he was told. While Luke opened up the laptop to retrieve the components, Dick opened up his duffel and retrieved a geologist's hammer and a well-cushioned Thermos of liquid.

When Luke handed Dick the vital innards of the computer, Dick dropped down to the floor and located a stout, metal brace for the subflooring. Using his body and the duffel bag to surround the cyberware and keep the pieces from scattering, he methodically smashed the components to bits, gathered up the debris and dropped the residue into the jar of liquid.

The jar hissed and gave off a nose-wrinkling odor.

"Sulfuric acid," murmured Dick to Luke, who was looking on with a bemused look of incredulity. "We like to be sure."

"Nuke it from orbit, then," replied Luke.

"Huh?" replied Dick, obviously missing yet again some pop culture reference.

"It's the only way to be sure."

Now Dick remembered. *Aliens.* But he didn't smile. Luke didn't know how right he was.

"What about back-ups when the avatar was in-world?"

Luke turned back to the cubicle's computer and typed furiously for a few minutes. "I can't find any indication the system's been backed-up offsite since before the file date."

Luke's answer didn't track, not in Dick's mind. "Isn't that unusual? Don't most businesses back-up their files everyday?"

Luke didn't look concerned. "Business data, sure. The quantities are limited and the need for recreating data environments in case of disaster is high. But this is a game world. Most players back-up their avatar on their own computer if they're that hyper about losing items or levels or whatever—though our Maori kid hadn't bothered, at least not on the laptop. But backing up the whole world everyday would be expensive and bothersome." He consulted a screen. "They only drop the system to back-up once a month according to their automatic task scheduling system."

Luke stopped typing and waved his right hand at the massive room of equipment just beyond their oversized cubicle. "Besides, would you back-up if you had a set-up like this? It's perfect. Concrete walls, ceiling, and supports. Arid climate, so no risk of flooding. A complex-wide Halon 1301 bromotrifluoromethane fire-suppressant system—which is odd, but extremely effective at protecting your data ..."

"What's odd about the Halon system?" Dick hated anomalies. All spies did. They usually meant something, something important.

"Well, it's an inert gas. It suppresses the fire by basically displacing all of the oxygen in the room, which is great for putting out an electrical fire in a big hurry, but you gotta get your personnel out of the way, too, cause it displaces the oxygen people need to breathe to live. You usually see this kind of thing in smaller spaces, with a big red panic button near the door. In case of fire, the personnel head for the exit and the last one out hits the button to shut the exit and release the gas."

Dick scanned the parts of the room he could see from the cubicle once more. There were no large red buttons near the few doors from the room. Hell, there weren't any glowing "Exit" signs. He guessed that the Occupational Safety and Health Administration never inspected this place. They probably didn't have minimum wage and EEOC posters tacked up in the lunch room either, assuming they allowed their employees to eat lunch.

Dick looked back at Luke. "Maybe there's a control room or a large exit we can't see from here."

Luke scrunched up his nose. "Nah." He pointed up at the sprinkler head that would release the Halon 1301 in the event needed. "Heat activated sprinkler heads. They'll go off on their own if the need arises. If you hear an alarm, I'd run like hell for the elevator."

Dick let the information soak in. It could be useful.

Luke waited patiently while Dick thought. The kid's composure impressed him. Luke knew, he had to know, what came next. Luke wasn't leaving this room alive, once their mission was complete. He had compromised the Subsidiary with his clandestine activities on agency equipment to aid Chinese dissidents and neither the Chinese

Net Impact

nor the Subsidiary could tolerate that. Neither espionage organization, for its own reasons, would let a loose-end like Luke live.

They had to be sure.

CHAPTER 26

Finally, it was sufficiently late for Matt to proceed. He took one last scan, then drove away. Two right turns later, Matt pulled into the next block over, parked opposite the back of the house, and grabbed a small gym bag with essential supplies. It didn't take much gear to kill two teenaged kids, even if he did have to make it look like an accident.

A quick walk around the block and he approached the recently re-sodded, two-story colonial from the front. He strode up to the door, waving as he approached as if to someone inside, and opened the screen door. The lock was simple enough and his lock picking skills good enough, that a passerby would have merely thought he was shifting the gym bag from one hand to the next before turning the knob and breezing in through the door as if he belonged there.

He shut the door quickly, but quietly, then simply stood for a moment, letting his eyes adjust to the dim gloom inside as he listened. He heard muffled noise from a television or something, coming from below. He reached into his bag and pulled out his thermal imaging equipment once more, doing a quick three-sixty before focusing it on the floor below him. Two individuals glowed yellow/orange/red down in the basement, next to two red spots that were undoubtedly computers. His targets, no doubt.

Not one to leave anything to chance, not when the Chinese government was calling the shots, he quickly returned the thermal imaging device to his gym bag, and groped at the other items in the bag. A few seconds later he pulled out a piece of heavy, flexible cable with optics fitted on both ends. Moving with feline grace toward the kitchen at the back of the house, he quickly located a door underneath the stairs up to the second level. Basement access, he was sure. Tract houses were all about functionality and ease of construction—he expected no imagination whatsoever in the layout.

Net Impact

After creeping to the door, he listened for a moment to the now-somewhat-more distinct sounds of two guys talking while tinny computer-game music cycled endlessly in the background. No surprises so far. He flexed the cable, then snaked it under the door, angling the optics of the far end down and to the left, so it would look down the stairs which tracked beneath the house's other stairway.

Sure enough, two young men were chatting while their computers sat ignored in front of them. Matt caught a few of the words. They seemed to be discussing whether they should call someone ... maybe the authorities ... and whether they were going to get into trouble.

The answer to the first question was "too late" and the answer to the second was "more than they could possibly believe."

Matt left his perch near the door for a few moments and moved over to the wall phone in the kitchen. Donning a pair of leather gloves, he lifted the receiver and quickly tapped out the number for time and temperature. Once he heard the mechanized voice beginning its spiel, he switch-hooked and got a dial-tone on the second line used for call waiting and conferencing functions, then called time and temperature again. In a few seconds, he heard the familiar information begin on the second line, too. Then, he simply set the receiver down on a stack of clean kitchen towels, muffling the polite and repetitive sound as the requested information was updated and announced on both lines every ten seconds.

A phone line in use can't be used to call the authorities or anyone else. And the great thing was, time and temperature would never hang up on you and free the line. He would never have thought of the technique, but he had cashiered an executive once who called time and temperature late every afternoon and just let it run, so he would make sure to leave in time to catch the express train home. Matt had made sure the guy missed the train and caught an express ride to hell, instead. But through it all, the garroting, the brief clean-up, and the lengthier search of the guy's office for the purloined goods Matt's client had sought to recover, Matt had left the phone service running. The constant reminder of passing time was really quite a productivity motivator.

He wasn't worried about the boys' cell phones. No matter what the television commercials say, American cell phones are notoriously useless in a concrete-construction basement that doesn't walk-out to a sloping backyard. If his victims had any final thoughts about "more bars in more places," he hoped they were pleasant memories of drinking at a wide variety of beachfront dives during spring break, because cursing out your cellular provider was an awful waste of your last few moments of life.

Having eliminated the ability of his targets to call for help, Matt set about the task of eliminating their ability to physically escape while he "accidentally" killed them. Scooping a few pennies off the laminate counter-top in the kitchen, he went back to the basement door and inspected it. The house was old enough that the door was not the flimsy particleboard crap one would usually get nowadays as an interior door. It was solid wood, with a deadbolt so it could be locked from the downstairs side.

He gently tested the door. Yep, the boys had locked it—no doubt to prevent any interruption when they progressed from gaming to soft-core porn DVDs later on. This would do nicely.

Gauging the gap between the door and the frame near the dead-bolt, he slid two pennies into the gap, then held them in place with his left hand while he used his right hand to push one more penny between the other two, forcing it all the way in until the three pennies were wedged hard between the door and the jamb. The force of the pennies would press the dead-bolt firm against its metal housing, making it nigh impossible to unbolt the lock. The guys were now trapped in the basement. As he left, he would drop a log from the living room fireplace into each of the two narrow window wells, thereby negating the alternate escape route mandated by state building code.

Below the boys still argued, clearly clueless he was above, dooming them to a short life and a hellish death.

An amateur would probably douse the pilot for the stove, turn on the gas, and leave, figuring the boys would die in the inevitable resulting explosion. The problem with gas explosions, however, was that they were good at killing people in the kitchen or in a nearby room on the same level from concussive force, but the explosion was so forceful that it didn't necessarily start a fire. Worse yet, it was so noticeable that the fire department would be on the scene fast.

No, Matt preferred a good, old-fashioned conflagration.

The trick here was that he needed it to look accidental, but expand quickly, and with white hot intensity, especially downstairs. He poked around the pantry and the kitchen sink, even the garage, gathering up all of the flammable household chemicals he could find: paint, pesticides, performance boosters for the car, whatever. Accelerants were usually a tip-off of arson, especially when they were poured all over the place. But you could make even accelerants look accidental.

Grabbing a cardboard box with a flimsy, folded bottom, he block-printed "HAZARDOUS RECLYCLING" on the side, and placed it near one of the hot air registers on the floor along the side of the stairway halfway between the kitchen and the front door. Then he reached for a glass vial of acid from his gym bag and dripped a few drops near the bottom edge of each can.

In about five minutes the acid would work its way through the metal at the sealed edges of the cans, allowing the flammable liquid to escape, drain out through the partially open bottom of the cardboard box and seep down the hot air duct and into the floorboards around it, sending accelerants where he needed them most in a credibly accidental way. He doubted any of the cardboard would survive the flames, but if it did, the lettering on the box would be convincing to the arson squad.

All he needed now was a credible point of ignition. He found a candle on the dinette in an alcove in the kitchen and slid it close to the gaily-colored curtains on the alcove's windows. Then he lit the candle and the drapes. The fire would spread quickly—these ersatz colonials built during the explosion of the Jersey suburbs in the seventies and eighties were all wood-frame construction. The accelerants would leak and the fumes would help move the fire quickly in that direction. The fire would surge down, into the basement stairs. And even if his targets braved the flames to get to the door, they would find it impossible to open. The fire would burn the door eventually and the pennies which had prevented it from being unlocked would simply fall to the ground, one more piece of detritus in a devastating house fire scene.

He grabbed two stout logs from the fireplace and went out the back door into the darkness of the quiet night. His shoes got wet as he crossed the soggy new sod to the window well, but he wasn't worried about footprints. The firefighters would trash the landscape in their futile attempt to fight his fire. He gently positioned the logs to block the window well exits and crept between houses to retrieve his vehicle. He left the peaceful neighborhood and took up a position on a nearby hill to confirm his kills before leaving. Nothing useful could be seen in the dark from his perch at first, so he grabbed the thermal imaging scope.

Maybe this wasn't a game, but he didn't want to miss the fun.

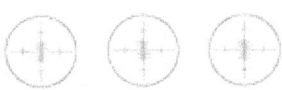

Net Impact

Luke watched with growing dread as Dick returned equipment to his duffel bag. This next part wasn't going to be fun. Luke knew what was coming and while he didn't really want to make it any easier, there was no reason to make it harder on Dick. It wasn't the old guy's fault. It was Luke's fault. He never should have gotten involved with the illicit virtual reality exchanges between Chinese dissidents and the organization that had contacted him to help out with the cause after he had signed a few petitions supporting a free Tibet. He wasn't even a leader in the effort—just another worker bee, just like in the office.

Well, he might not have the guts to be a leader, but he did have the guts to face the consequences of his actions. Best to take it like a man. Best to take it from Dick, rather than from the Chinese assassins who were no doubt looking to eliminate the threat to governmental stability posed by him and the others from the cyber-squad in Reality 2 Be.

"What now?" he asked, as Dick fumbled through his duffel bag.

Dick stopped looking through the duffel and looked up at Luke. The old man tilted his head to one side. "Whaddya mean?"

"What next? What happens next?"

Dick stood up. "We eliminate the facility."

Luke looked at Dick, dumbfounded. "We got the plans. I guarantee it. There's no need to 'eliminate the facility,' whatever the hell that means, to make sure the Kestrel 84 plans are secure."

Dick simply stood there for a moment. "You can't guarantee there hasn't been an on-site back-up that includes the plans. Besides, you've seen the facility now. You know there's more going on here. Remember what we were talking about before? Why was this facility built, back before Reality 2 Be was even a gleam in some programmer's eye? Why is it this size? Why is it shielded and protected the way it is?"

Shielded? Dick had asked him before about how deep you would have to construct a facility for it to be shielded from EMP. "This was put here to protect it from electromagnetic pulse in the event of a nuclear war? You guys have been watching *Dr. Strangelove* too much. This is part of some effort to overcome the 'mineshaft gap?'"

Dick gestured expansively at the complex. "This look military to you?" He looked Luke straight in the eye. "Trust me, this is not a government facility. Not our government. Not anybody else's. That kind of thing, the Subsidiary is very, very good at knowing. Somebody, somebody with a shitload of money, built this and built it secretly, and has kept it secret with all the rumor mongering and misdirection, and operates it at great expense and with great difficulty. Why would they do that?"

Luke's mind was a fog. "Why do bad guys do anything? Money and power."

Dick nodded. "Power, that's the key. But money, that's always good in the meantime. And you're right about bad guys being behind it. So put it all together. You've seen the scope of this place. If you were a bad guy with unlimited access to computer power and server farms and routing hook-ups, what could you do with it?"

The mist persisted.

Dick gave him another prompt. "What's the fastest growing area of law enforcement at all levels?"

"Drugs?" offered Luke.

"Old news," grumbled Dick.

A lightbulb came on. "Cybercrime, computer fraud." He looked around again, this time his eyes truly seeing to scope of what was before him. "Porn, digital music and video downloads, Nigerian bank scams, phishing, identity theft, credit card schemes—the local cops don't have jurisdiction to stop most of it and the feds are constantly subpoenaing Internet providers for customer info that all seems to originate in Russia or the Philippines or someplace impossible to track down or squelch."

"Someplace like here," volunteered Dick.

"Here?"

"You're the computer geek. What's the Internet made out of? Who owns it?"

"Nobody owns it. It's ... it's just connections of computers, really. I send a message or ask to access a site and the command goes from my computer into my Internet server provider's routers and servers, which connect up with other routers and servers 'til I get to the one hosting whatever I was trying to access or send a message to."

"And all that routing, that goes through what?"

"All the ISPs and the commercial and university and governmental systems, they're connected to one another through hubs and optic fibers and satellite networks."

"How many?"

"How many what?"

"How many hubs?" asked Dick.

Luke gestured futilely with his hands. "I don't know, at least anymore. A bunch. In the early days of the Internet, they used to say there were seven primary switching hubs. There was one in Atlanta and one in Virginia, near Washington, D.C., and some others. The word was some of the switching hubs were at undisclosed locations, you know for security reasons, so you couldn't knock out the Internet with just a few targeted attacks."

"Voila," replied Dick, with yet another expansive gesture.

"This is one of the secret hubs of the Internet?" Luke couldn't believe it. Then he gave it just a moment's thought. Yes, he could. "This is one of the secret hubs of the Internet."

"Not quite, I think," said Dick. "This isn't a hub. It's a secret way-station on the Internet—a tumor on the backbone of the World Wide Web. It hijacks the flow of packets of information on the Internet. Monitors them, changes them, whatever, then passes them along.

Think about it. They can capture clandestine information on the digital bits that flow through here more easily than the NSA. They get access to every credit card number, social security number, and password that passes their way."

Luke swallowed hard. "That's more information than Facebook! But with no privacy settings or opt outs. And no government control or social outrage to limit what they use it for."

Dick nodded. "They probably also provide servers and hosting for every terrorist organization or group of mafia thugs that needs or wants those to go about their business of crime and terror. Reality 2 Be is most likely just a front for criminal groups to exchange data and money unregulated and unseen by governmental authorities. The gaming and social aspects are just cover for the real reason the virtual world was created. This operation gathers information and makes money now and it sets the bad guys up for a power move in the future."

"In case of nuclear war?" Most of what Dick had said made sense to Luke. This was a great way for bad guys to use the Internet for moneymaking opportunities, even espionage. But he couldn't really buy that the thugs of the world thought there was going to be a nuclear war, even if all the crime bosses had been kids during the Cuban missile crisis.

Dick seemed to understand what Luke was thinking, even if he hadn't said it out loud. "First strike, three-hundred and fifty million dead, that kind of thing, no. But a high altitude burst over the Midwest fries most of the country's electronics with EMP. Suddenly, all the nation's Internet capacity dies, all the info is lost—except for this shielded facility. Now who has power?"

It made sense. This was big, much bigger than the plans for the Kestrel 84. "So, we're going to take out the facility?"

"Yep."

Luke was dubious. "I think you're going to need a bigger hammer and a larger volume of acid, not to mention a lot more time, if you're planning to do that."

Dick ran his tongue over his teeth. "I was just making sure the smaller, initial mission was complete in case the bigger mission goes bad."

"So you have the capacity to take out this entire facility in your duffel bag?"

"Yep."

"Without my help?" Luke scanned the massive complex. "Because I have no clue how to do that."

"Yep."

Luke thought for a moment, but nothing came to mind. They weren't near a body of water, so there was no way to flood the place. The damn sprinklers didn't even use water and the gas they did use was inert. He shook his head in defeat. "I give up. How are you going to be sure you wipe out this entire facility?"

"You said it yourself."

"I did?"

"Yep. Nuke it from orbit. That's what you said. It's the only way to be sure. That's what we're going to do." He began fumbling about in the duffel yet again.

Luke's head swam in a daze of confusion. "You're going to nuke the facility from orbit?" He looked around at the concrete-reinforced facility deep beneath the runways of Denver International Airport. "We talked about this. This place is more shielded than Sadaam Hussein's bunker. I'm not sure a nuke would take it out, even if you didn't care about the northeastern quarter of the Denver metro area. Are you crazy?"

Dick looked around the facility, too, including at the guards at either end of their row. "Keep your voice down," he cautioned. "And, yeah, you're right about the facility and, whatever you think of the ruthlessness of the Subsidiary, they do give a shit about civilian casualties. That's why we're not going to do it from orbit." He pulled out a bulky case which had taken up a good portion of one end of the duffel bag. "We're going to do it from here."

Luke took a half step back from the bulky device, as if that would help. "You brought a nuke? They gave you a nuke? Are you crazy? Are they crazy?"

Dick gave a broad smile. "Yeah, that part took a little persuasion."

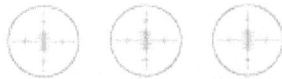

"Are you crazy?"

Dick had expected his equipment request would trigger a call from on high and he knew Dee Tammany would lead with an insult. He had expected her to be pissed and the conversation to be peppered with accusatory questions. He let the first one just hang there for a moment, so she would continue and get them all out of her system. She obliged with a more detailed follow-up: "Are you just a pyromaniac on payroll or are you really stupid enough to think you could get away with requesting a device like this—after the Dunedin debacle, for God's sake—on a simple cyber-crime mission?"

"I see you've gotten my equipment request," he replied with cool nonchalance.

"You can't be serious. There is no way in hell you're getting a nuclear weapon. The fire in Dunedin not big enough for you?"

"I don't know. I didn't stay to watch it and it provided damn little light when I was jet skiing across the bay to the Otago Peninsula in the dark."

"Risks of the trade," snarled Dee. Dick knew Dee was a no-nonsense boss, one who didn't like insolence or surprises. Either one could make her almost as unpleasant as Glenn.

"I only ask for the tools I need to get the mission accomplished," responded Dick, trying to get the emotional upper-hand by refusing to reply in kind.

"You need a nuke to retrieve the plans for a UAV?"

"No, I need a small nuclear device to create an electromagnetic pulse to save the world from a much greater threat ..."

"And what would that be?" asked Dee. No matter her personal emotions, Dick knew Dee always was willing to listen to a threat assessment. And so he spelled it out—not only what Dee already knew Luke had figured out about the facility, how and where it was constructed, and how it might be kept hidden, but what Dick had extrapolated about what that might mean the bad guys were up to, both now, and in preparation for the future.

His vision of the present and the future calmed her down considerably.

"That's very convincing, Dick, but I can't risk blowing up Denver International Airport. Not only would the civilian casualties and the property damage be completely unacceptable, there is no way the Subsidiary would survive. It would either be exposed to the public or shut down by its sponsors. Even if by some miracle that didn't happen, Internal Audit would go ballistic. I do my best to avoid conversations with Pyotr Nerevsky. He may be polite, but he is unrelenting."

"Fuck Nerevsky," replied Dick. "He's not in the field." Like all cops, Dick had no tolerance for the organization's Internal Affairs division, even if the Subsidiary dressed it up with the corporate-sounding Internal Audit moniker and ran it though Catalyst Crisis

Consulting's accounting department. The fact Nerevsky was ex-KGB didn't help Dick's opinion of IA either.

"Besides, look carefully at the request. It's for an NE 417. It's not a conventional nuclear weapon, it's a neutron device—reduced blast and fireball effect and enhanced EMP and radiation pulse."

"Leaving the airport buildings standing doesn't really matter if the radiation kills everyone in the airport and for miles around. Why not just call in a Lightning Team?"

The Lightning Teams were the Subsidiary's heavy-duty firepower squads. At a moment's notice, they could swoop down and lay waste to everything in sight if needed. They were only used in desperate situations when agents were in trouble or more subtle approaches to solving a really big crisis had failed. They cleaned-up problems with a thundering rate of automatic weapons fire, leaving no witnesses behind. Often, the resultant carnage was later attributed to a failed coup attempt or gang warfare. Dick liked the Lightning Team guys, but they weren't right for the job. He couldn't be assured he could get them in and he couldn't be sure their means would accomplish what needed to be done.

"Hell, Dee, the Lightning boys would be more conspicuous than the nuke," Dick replied with a chuckle. "You're caught up in semantics of this thing being a nuclear weapon, rather than thinking about the technical specs of the device, itself. The NE 417's not even a conventional neutron bomb. Even though it blows up, you shouldn't really think of it as a bomb at all. It's a device the Americans developed that generates a concentrated electromagnetic pulse by using a small amount of fissile material. It blows itself apart before it can reach the kinds of blast and temperature you would see in even a small-yield, regular nuclear weapon. The shockwave is strong enough to kill people and destroy delicate equipment in the immediate vicinity, but it's insufficient to cause more than a tremor to reinforced concrete. It's the perfect device for what we need to accomplish here if I'm right. The spherical blast will be constrained by the walls of the reinforced facility, causing the shockwave to propagate laterally where unconstrained. It'll do some damage on the level of the blast, but probably not even enough to destroy all the equipment. It depends on how big the facility is. The EMP will range farther, within the shielded confines."

Dee paused. That was a good sign. "If all you need is EMP, why not use an explosively pumped flux compression generator? They're small and just as easy to carry as an NE 417. And they create EMP and nothing but EMP."

"Their radius is pretty limited and I do want more than just pulse—I need the radiation and limited shockwave, too. I don't want these guys to be able to return to the scene of the crime, repair some equipment, and be back in operation again in a week or a month or even a year. The point of using the NE 417 is that between blast, EMP, and radiation, the entire facility will be rendered ineffective, short-term and long-term, but the device won't hurt things up above. You know we won't get a second chance at this—it'll be much better protected the next time around. The EMP will wipe out the bits and bytes of clandestine information and criminal Internet activity throughout. I don't mind a small shock wave destroying some or all of the equipment, but I really need to leave a residual radioactive charge which will make the place unuseable going forward."

He heard Dee swear under her breath. "Shockwave? Radiation? Any way you cut it, this device is nuclear. This is different from blowing up a warehouse—seriously different—and I wasn't happy about that. What about the people in the airport? The planes in the midst of landing?"

"The shielding should work as well to hold in EMP as it will to hold it out. It should also shield for radiation. I already told you the blast won't be big enough to collapse a hardened facility, just take out some of the equipment and bad guys inside. Even if the place is smaller than I'm guessing and the shock wave bounces between the concrete walls until everything inside is practically vaporized, the space itself should maintain integrity. A little puff of dust through the ventilation ducts to the outside. That's all. Minimal risk."

Dee paused again. He knew he had her. "Late night, just to be careful."

"Of course, Dee. Just what I had in mind. You know I'm always careful."

CHAPTER 27

Luke shook his head. "You go tubing and you wind up setting off a nuke beneath Denver International Airport. Who would have thought?"

"What?"

Luke waved him off. "Yeah, I know, an EMP generator, not a real nuke. Still who would have thought?"

"Not that." Dick narrowed his focus on Luke with an intensity at least an order of magnitude greater than Luke had ever experienced from the guy before and, let's face it, they had already been through a lot. "Tubing ... What did you mean by that?"

Luke relaxed. "Tubing, that's what they call playing in Reality 2 Be. If you're in-world in Reality 2 Be, you're '2 being,' so the kids, they all call it 'tubing.'"

Dick gave him an ashen stare.

Luke couldn't help but comment. "Dude, if you could see yourself you would be totally R-O-F-L-M-A-O." Luke didn't usually use, and certainly didn't spell out, IM abbreviations in verbal conversation, but he couldn't help himself from tweaking Dick just a bit more about the old guy's lack of knowledge about the Internet.

"What?"

"Rolling on floor laughing my ass off. OMG—that's 'Oh My God' in the real world—if you're going to tube, dude, you've got to learn some IM lingo."

"That's what Seth, my kid, said he was going to do with his friend, before I left Jersey. Tubing." Dick's face hardened. "Seth is involved in Reality 2 Be—the virtual world of choice for spies, thieves, and evil overlords."

"It's a game world. That's its cover. I'm sure there're lots of people playing it who have absolutely no idea what else it's being used for."

"But why didn't I ever notice?"

"POTS," replied Luke with a shrug.

Dick's brow wrinkled. "What's drugs got to do with this?" His face grew hard. "My kid isn't on drugs."

"Parents are always the last to know." Luke tilted his head to one side and raised his eyebrows. "How can you be sure?"

Dick's expression softened and he looked at the floor. "I ... well, I tested his hair. The test claims to be able to show residual signs of drug use for months, back even further if the kid's hair is long."

"Very trusting. But I wasn't talking about drugs. Reality 2 Be has a P-O-T-S button." When Dick looked back up and just stared at him, he continued. "It stands for 'Parents-Over-the-Shoulder.' Sometimes people call them 'panic buttons.' If you wander by when Seth doesn't want you to see what he is doing on-screen, he pushes the POTS button and the screen flips over to something benign and vaguely educational, like a random Wikipedia listing or a breaking news feed."

"Great," Dick moaned. "Just G-R-8."

"Kids spend more time online than their parents realize. It sucks up all their concentration and they don't realize how long they stay on. It's a tremendous time-sink."

"Maybe that's why I haven't been able to contact him. Could I do that in-world?"

"Even if you know his avatar's name, it would be a task," replied Luke. Suddenly he had a thought. "Although we could use the oversight search feature, just like we did for the Kestrel 84 Plans. Do you know his avatar's name?"

Dick frowned. "No, but I know his real name and his credit card number—he's on one of my accounts. Can that get through?"

Luke shrugged. "Probably. But are you sure you want to stop in the middle of all this to, like, phone home?"

Net Impact

"It'll take me a few minutes to set the NE 417—you know, the EMP device—so why not? Besides, I've been a bit twitchy about not being able to reach the kid for some time."

Luke sat down at the cubicle terminal once more. "Might as well. I've got nowhere to go."

"There's nowhere to go," wailed Brian as he tried to force open the second, narrow, window in his basement. "There's something blocking the way in this window well, too."

"Can you break the glass?" yelled Seth in response. This was bad. This was very, very bad. Seth needed his friend to hold it together long enough for them to get out of the situation. But, unlike the game world, it only took seconds for panic to arise in the real world. Less than a minute had passed since he had leaped up as fire flowed down the wall on one side of the basement stairs. "The opening may be a bit smaller, but we can still crawl out through the hole left by the broken window," directed Seth, trying desperately to keep his own voice calm as acrid smoke billowed across the basement ceiling.

"The pane's made out of Plexiglas," cried Brian. "After those burglaries last year, Dad had 'em installed. Said the neighborhood was going to hell."

Seth knew they would both be going to hell and getting pre-heated on the way there if they didn't get out of here soon. "Try to break it anyway," he instructed. "Find a hammer or something heavy. If you can make a hole, you might be able to move whatever's blocking the window." He coughed in the increasingly smoky air. "We might be able to call for help. We might be able to get some air." He knew the influx of fresh air might accelerate the fire, but he also remembered

274

that more people died of smoke inhalation than actually burned to death in house fires.

During the whole frantic conversation with Brian, Seth had been hitting redial on 9-1-1 on his cell phone, but still had no signal. The landline down in the basement was blocked, blathering on about time and temperature and he couldn't seem to do anything to disconnect it and get a dial tone. If the fire wasn't enough, he had a really bad feeling about the recording on the phone line, not to mention the blocked window well.

This was arson. This was murder.

And he couldn't help but think that it was all a result of their escapades in Reality 2 Be—that the Chinese government had caught up with the squad and that somewhere Shrike and Pigeon were in similarly desperate straits. Or already dead. Seth had led his squad of virtual commandos into a real-world ambush that would kill them all.

Brian continued to flail at the window well, coughing and screaming incoherently. It was up to Seth to save them. What should he do? What would his dad do? He couldn't crash through the walls, not in a basement, so his dad's fatherly wisdom was to no avail. But he knew his dad had more knowledge up his sleeve than he had ever overtly revealed—not just because he used to be an Army Ranger or a cop, but because Seth knew his dad was a spy.

Seth had stumbled across the information quite by accident several years ago when his dad had left some briefing materials out, thinking Seth was not home yet. Ever since then, Seth had paid careful attention to what his dad was really doing and saying when he said he was working. Seth listened in, glass to the wall, from his own bedroom when his dad was on the phone—really on the computer—in private. Seth also tucked a webcam in his dad's study to pick up the screen shot from his laptop when he received his missions. He knew, for example, that most recently his dad had been sent to New Zealand to foil a Hong

Kong arms dealer selling weapons to terrorists. It sickened him; the residents of Hong Kong had more freedom than the billion residents of the rest of China and they used their limited freedom to engage in crime and profiteering.

Of course, Seth had never said anything, would never say anything, to compromise his dad's position. But the knowledge of his dad's secret life had given Seth a new appreciation for his dad's abilities. It explained why his dad was so kick-ass at Lazer Tag, for one thing. It also explained much better than sewerage catastrophes ever could why his dad took off all the time on so-called business emergencies. It was no wonder his dad was stressed, not that his dad's absences didn't still piss Seth off.

Of course, living up to his dad's cloak and dagger example was why Seth would soon be dead, even though what he was doing was so much more noble and innocent than trafficking in arms or assassinating dictators or any of that other serious shit that real spies did. Seth and Brian and the rest of their virtual squad, they didn't do any of that. Yet here he was, about to be burned alive for the crime of helping people tell the truth about their oppressors.

Of course, his dad's cloak and dagger example was also why Seth would do anything it took ... anything ... to get Brian and him out of their dire situation. That's what his dad had always said when accepting a new assignment. He would do whatever needed to be done to accomplish the mission.

All this flashed through Seth's mind in an instant while he looked at the staircase, the far wall already engulfed in flames, the carpeting on the treads starting to flare up, emitting who knows what kind of noxious gases. "I'm going out the stairs," he shouted back to Brian. "I'll let you know if we can get out that way." Then he gulped in a deep breath of hot, smoky air and held it burning in his lungs as he lunged for the hellish firestorm blocking their only exit.

Seth's left side was seared with heat as he bolted up the stairs, three at a time. Flames surged and boiled on the left wall, but the right wall was still cool and relatively unaffected by the fire. That the fire had not yet spread there was the only thing that gave Seth hope they could escape out the basement door. He grabbed at the door handle at the top of the stairs without thinking and scorched his left hand severely as he grabbed the red-hot metal. His concentration overwhelmed his instinct, however, and he did not flinch back. He took the pain and twisted the knob. It turned, but the door held firm.

The deadbolt. Seth slid his burned hand up the wood until he found the latch and twisted it. It held firm, neither unlocking, nor turning, no matter how hard he tried. Still holding his breath, Seth pushed on the door, but again nothing happened. He put some weight into it, shoving his right shoulder into the door he could no longer see because of the black smoke gathered at the top of the stairs. It wouldn't budge. This exit had been blocked, too.

Seth was at the limit of his endurance. Severe pain surged up his legs. Tongues of flame grilled his body. He pinched his eyes shut from the acrid smoke and heat and desperately tried to keep his equilibrium despite the disorientation of the conflagration and the wooziness brought by severe oxygen deprivation. If he collapsed here, he would never get up again.

He had to retreat. He could hold his breath no longer. Stale air exploded out of his mouth as Seth turned and dove back down the stairway in a desperate attempt to reach relatively clear, fresh air before his lungs involuntarily expanded to take in a deep breath of hot, poisonous gases. He hit the bottom of the stairs in a controlled tumble and rolled instinctively away from the flames, toward the back of the couch.

Almost immediately, Brian was at his side, patting out the flames that had sprung up on the left shoulder of his "Free Tibet" t-shirt and covering Seth's face and mouth with a cool, wet towel. Adrenaline speeded his recovery.

"Diet Dr. Pepper?" Seth said as he pulled the brown-liquid soaked towel off his eyes and across his nose.

Brian's eyes flicked to the empty two liter jug on the floor. "It was the handiest liquid available," he said with a grim smile. Gallows humor.

As Brian helped Seth stand, Seth caught the glow of the laptop screens on the other side of the couch. They were still showing the same vistas from Reality 2 Be they had shown for the last several hours.

"Dude," he shouted, pointing at the screen. "Call for help on the computer. The WiFi is still operating."

Brian looked over at the screens. "I don't think the local cops or firemen even have a website," he responded as he began to dash around the couch toward his laptop.

Seth attempted to vault the couch to get at his own computer, but fell. He was still dizzy, dazed by the lack of clear air. "IM and email ... message anyone ... everyone you know and tell them to call 9-1-1," he instructed. He shook his head to clear the cobwebs and began to hobble unsteadily around his end of the couch, bouncing off the edge of the Naugahyde recliner. He glanced at his watch as he plopped down onto the cushions. It was late, but not that late for a gamer. "Someone's got to still be online."

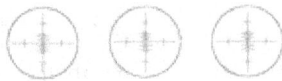

"I think I found him," reported Luke, as Dick finished arming the nuclear EMP device. "But it's weird."

Dick kept his eyes on his work. The timing component was a bitch to set with his pudgy fingers. "What's weird?"

"The only avatar he has in-world at the moment is a newbie." He typed in a few additional keystrokes. "And it's just sitting in one place, not moving. I thought you said he played all the time."

Dick glanced up. "Maybe his old one died. Maybe he's on a bathroom break. Who the hell cares? Can I talk to him or what?"

Luke gave Dick a hard look, but Dick just broke contact and turned back to his task. "You know," said Luke with an edge to his voice, "you're pretty crabby when you're on a mission."

Dick didn't respond. Luke's statement rung true, but what of it? Arming nuclear weapons and being instructed to gack your partner at the end of the mission tended to make a guy tense. "Just type in what I tell you to say," he finally said as he continued to dial in the timing data.

Luke sighed. "You've got to be where he is to talk. You can't shout across the entire Reality 2 Be universe."

Dick grunted without looking up. "So get me there or ... you there, I guess. Whatever. Where's he at?"

A glance showed that Luke was booting up The Dewdster to insert him back in-world. In a matter of moments, the avatar was streaking through the sky in a ballistic arc. Dick finished with the timing mechanism and, after a quick glance down the aisle for the row of cubicles to make sure their guards were still standing their posts, disinterested in their activities, he turned his attention back to the screen of Luke's laptop.

The avatar had reached the apogee of its flight and was descending in a smooth, flat arc toward a point in an area of mountainous wilderness in the Reality 2 Be universe.

Suddenly, Luke's movements became jerky and agitated. All the color drained from his face. "Shit!" he exclaimed, more loudly than Dick really liked. "Shit. Shit. Shit."

"What?" replied Dick. "And keep your voice down."

"Your kid's avatar is just sitting and waiting in that ring of boulders. There's another avatar there, too." His fingers typed madly on the keyboard for the cubicle computer. "Another newbie." The circle of boulders grew more prominent on the laptop screen as The Swuush approached. "Damn. Damn. Damn." The oversight menu popped onto the cubicle screen.

"So," whispered Dick, with growing irritation. "What's the problem with that?"

Luke stopped muttering at the screen and turned to look at Dick. "That's where the team I was on made its last contact with the Chinese dissidents."

"Coincidence?" asked Dick, knowing it wasn't true. A vision of Seth in his green "Free Tibet" t-shirt flashed into his mind.

"No," replied Luke in a flat voice. He pointed to the screen for the cubicle's computer, scifi green letters glowing steadily. "He's got the same amount of maypoles we were carrying for the exchange. I think your kid was my squad leader."

Dick felt like he had taken a 9mm round in the center of his chest body armor. The shock was massive and it was hard to breathe. "He didn't ... he isn't involved in anything seriously bad, is he?" In his mind's eye, he saw that old Christmas tree teetering as Seth tugged on it, wavering toward the tipping point and the inevitable crash and mess that would follow because Dick hadn't been paying attention. He blinked away the memory and looked over at his companion. His voice caught, but he choked out the words. "Tell me I didn't raise a terrorist."

Luke gave a wry smile. "Your kid's not a terrorist. He didn't do anything I didn't do. He wasn't involved in anything evil—not like the shit Pao Fen Smythe and the Maori guys were doing. He was just being naively idealistic, like me, helping oppressed people. At least, that's what we thought. But that doesn't mean that the Chinese and ..." Luke swallowed hard, "and ... others don't want me and him dead."

The pieces of the puzzle slammed into place in Dick's mind. He knew now why Luke's face had gone deathly pale. "He's just a kid," Dick blurted out. "The Subsidiary wouldn't ... couldn't ..." Even though he had been tasked to eliminate Luke for compromising the agency with his extra-curricular espionage and it was clear Luke had figured it out, he somehow couldn't bring himself to say the words out loud. He couldn't say "The Subsidiary won't kill him like they're having me kill you." Instead, he simply said: "He's got nothing to do with the agency."

Still, he saw from Luke's face that the computer geek got his meaning. "Fuck the agency," spat Luke with bitterness. "The squad's been compromised by the Chinese government. They could be after him right now."

Dick lunged at the keyboard for the laptop. He had to warn Seth. He had to save his son from the fate that faced Luke if he ever left the complex beneath DIA alive. He toggled on the IM switch for in-world communications and began punching at the keys with his pudgy fingers. The same pudgy fingers that moments before had been setting the NE 417 to wipe-out a virtual world in an attempt to save the real world, were now jabbing at the keyboard, trying desperately to save his son, his family—the only world Dick cared about at this moment.

Luke had scrambled out of Dick's way as he had lunged for the keyboard, but a lanky hand snaked its way to the corner of the keyboard as Dick began typing. "All caps means shouting in-world," he said simply and pressed the button down as Dick continued to type.

Brian was already typing out a plea to call 9-1-1 to every group email list he had, when Seth leaned forward to do the same. As he did, he saw an unfamiliar avatar come jetting into the circle of stones in Reality 2 Be. He was about to ignore it—contact or no, he had no time for Chinese dissidents right now—when the IM function came on.

seth itS DAD YOURE IN DANGER

What the hell? Dad? Could it really be his dad? Or was it a trick to distract him while the fire blazed away?

Prove it

The screen cursor flashed a few moments while Seth waited, Brian typing furiously at his side.

YOUR MOM LEFT YOURE TUBEING WTH BRIAAN

Holy crap, it was his dad. His hands flew over the keyboard.

Trapped in brian's house by fire. CALL 911 helpo us!!! Doorr blockd

GO THRU WALLL

Cant Dont type, call

FREND CALLING NOT OUTSID WALL, INTEREOR BTWN STUDS

Basemnt. Stairway door wont break

WALL AT TOP OF STAIRS NOW

Why hadn't he thought of it? The wall, the cool right wall at the top of the stairway. It was nothing but drywall. He glanced over at Brian, who was sending yet another bevy of messages. Seth grabbed the Diet Dr. Pepper soaked towel, as he headed to the ever more-fiery stairway.

"Soak a shirt or something and follow me. We're going through the right-hand wall at the top of the stairs." Seth saw Brian grab another open bottle of soda pop and empty it over his head. Then Seth saw nothing but smoke and flame as he rushed toward the stairway inferno that was now their only hope.

Gulping in a huge breath of foul air, Seth leapt into the flaming staircase, leaping up as many steps as he could at a time, his eyes shut tight against the flames and the smoke and the heat, until he sensed he was high enough. Then, without slowing down, he crashed hard to his right into the wall near the top of the stairs.

He felt the drywall crack and give. Seth braced his left foot on the flaming, carpeted tread of the stairs and thrust into the wall again, ramming his right knee painfully up into the crack at the same time. He broke through, but the ragged edge of the drywall against his throbbing knee revealed the hole was much too small. He gritted his teeth against the horrific, fiery pain now licking its way up his legs from his melting, blazing shoes. He knew he only had one more chance to succeed.

Seth expelled the air burning to escape his lungs with a guttural roar as he rammed his body against the weakened wall with all of his remaining strength. The plasterboard gave with a sharp crack and he fell forward into the smoke-filled, but cooler, dining room on the first floor of Brian's house. He could see and feel the fire consuming the kitchen through the walk-through pantry to his left. He could also sense his friend coming up from behind.

"Go, to the right, over me!" he croaked and felt Brian's athletic shoes scramble over his thighs and butt, then leap for the relative safety of the dining room. "Don't stop. Window!" he yelled hoarsely as he tried desperately to bring his legs—his jeans now fully ablaze he knew—underneath him to join his friend.

"C'mon!" he heard Brian yell. Then he heard a crash of glass as Brian took his advice and leapt through the bay window of the dining room. As Seth looked to see if his friend had been hurt by the breaking glass as he escaped, he caught view of the automatic sprinkling system giving the fresh sod a refreshing overnight watering.

So close.

Seth longed for the cool wetness of the grass as he continued to struggle to stand, to escape, to survive ... to make his dad proud. Then a wave of night air surged into the house through the open window and the hellfire consuming him roared in approval, rushing forward to devour the fresh source of oxygen and everything else in its path.

A siren in the distance wailed in response.

Then he heard no more.

CHAPTER 28

Luke hung up the phone. "The fire department is on their way."

Dick stared at the laptop screen in an apparent daze. The two avatars on screen were motionless, as if dead. The IM chat box was still, the last entry simply reading: "SON?"

"He's not answering," Dick whispered to the universe. "He's not answering."

Luke had kept one eye on the ongoing dialogue as he had placed the call to 9-1-1. He had been relieved to get an outside line, even more relieved when directory assistance had quickly put him through to the fire department in the Jersey suburb that Dick had told him during his frantic exchanges on IM was home. He put his hands on top of Dick's on the keyboard. "He followed your advice. It was good advice."

"I should have been there. I should have been at home. Then he would be safe at home ... not trapped by a fire because he was staying with a friend."

"He's not online anymore because he took your advice. He left to escape. He might be safe."

Dick's eyes did not move from the screen.

Luke eased the laptop away, called up a new screen and began to type furiously. "I'm letting HQ know about Seth and the fire. Maybe they can help."

He saw Dick's mouth try to form words, but nothing came out.

"Don't worry. It's a dead drop IM account the techies use to ask each other to cover when they take a long lunch. It's secure."

Dick remained unresponsive, motionless.

Luke's eyes caught movement. Egbert was talking to the guard at one end of the aisle. Damn. The outside call. He thought he had heard a click on the line. Egbert clearly knew something was amiss.

Luke grabbed Dick by the shoulders and turned him so they were staring at each other straight in the face.

"We've been made." Luke flicked his eyes to the EMP device. "Is that armed and running?"

Dick nodded dully, but his eyes seemed to be coming back to life.

Luke shook his mentor lightly. "The guards are coming. What do we do? What do we do?"

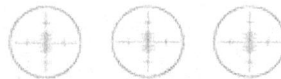

It was like waking up back in the Army Rangers to the sound of a mortar round exploding sixty feet away. The fog lifted quickly, dissipated by adrenaline and gentle shaking. In a matter of seconds, Dick was in full combat mode.

He quickly untangled himself from Luke's well-meaning grasp and checked the guards at either end of their cubicle corridor. There was no time, almost no time at all.

He reached into his belt at the small of his back and came out with a 9mm handgun. As Luke's eyes widened in terror, Dick leaned out of the cubicle and snapped off two shots, dropping the guard to the north and causing Egbert to dive awkwardly for cover nearby. Then Dick spun and did the same thing in the opposite direction. The guard there had already brought his weapon up and managed to squeeze off a poorly-aimed burst before joining his companion in the hereafter. The burst made a thundering racket and scored chips into the concrete wall close by, but caused no damage to Dick or Luke. It did, however, trigger a cacophony of screams and shouts from the scattered personnel that remained in the cavernous computer center during night shift.

This was bad. If Egbert got to a phone, the exits would be secured and reinforcements would flood the area. Sure, the EMP would probably go off before the bad guys could get to it. The explosion would destroy the facility, completing Dick's task to eliminate Luke for him and killing off a bunch of bad guys in the bargain. But Dick hadn't been planning on getting caught in the blast. The plan had been to live through the mission. He prayed he still had something to live for.

His eyes darted about, desperate for anything which might spark an idea how to get out of this particular basement fireball. His situation wasn't so different from Seth's; it was just entirely of his own making.

His gaze fell upon the sprinkler system. He grabbed a piece of paper out of his pocket and shoved it at his still stunned partner. The paper had four digits printed on it.

"What?" muttered Luke.

"It's Egbert's extension. Call it. If it goes to machine, hang up and call it again. Keep doing that 'til I tell you to stop."

Luke looked dumbfounded, but Dick saw him move to obey. Luke was a good kid, despite all the trouble he had caused. Hell, even Dick had been idealistic when he was younger.

Dick reached into the duffel bag and pulled out several flares. He popped the cap on one and used it to strike the end. An intense reddish flame sputtered to life with a hiss, producing a billowing stream of white smoke.

"Flares? You brought flares?" murmured Luke.

"I thought we might have to go somewhere in the dark," growled Dick, as he leapt onto the desktop of the cubicle. He held the lit end of the flare up to the heat sensor near the sprinkler head directly above.

It took only a few seconds for the heat sensor to melt in the red flame. The sprinkler valve released, triggering a chain reaction down the line and across the cavernous room. A heavy, white gas began to pour from the sprinkler heads as an ear-splitting alarm began to sound. While still atop the desk, Dick hurled the sparking flare as far as he could toward an area where he could see no people. He struck another flare and dropped it on the other side of the cubicle wall from where they sat into a pile of paper print-outs. He knew the fire wouldn't cause major damage—the Halon 1301 would see to that—but he had to make sure the gas kept coming. That meant he had to engage in a little pyromania. He lit the last of his flares and looked about at what he had wrought.

Smoke was curling up from the cubicle next door and from the area where he had thrown the first flare. Gas was gushing down from sprinkler heads across the facility. Alarm bells rang and lights flashed near the main exit. Despite the deafening noise of the alarm, he heard urgent shouts of panic.

He scanned the room for enemies. Every person he saw was bolting in apocalyptic abandon for the main exit.

He looked down to see Luke looking up at him, eyes wide with fright and confusion, the handset for the desk phone still in his hand. Luke's finger poised over the redial button on the keyboard of the deskset phone.

"Tell me when it pauses between rings," Dick shouted.

Luke's mouth fell open, but he made no immediate response. Finally, Dick's words seemed to register on his face. Luke put the handset hard against his ear as he pressed the redial button on the deskset. "Pause," he yelled back at Dick. "Pause ... pause ... pause."

Dick strained his ears in every direction between Luke's rhythmic yells of "pause." There! The sound was faint against the clamor of the alarm, but Dick was sure of the cadence, sure of his destination.

He leapt off the desk into the swirl of heavy, fire squelching, gas, now more than knee-deep on the floor. He abandoned his knapsack and the NE 417 EMP mechanism, which was hidden by the dense, swirling Halon 1301. "Follow me!" he yelled and took off at a full run down the corridor, almost tripping on the dead guard at the end, who was hidden by the ever-increasing amounts of bromotrifluoromethane cascading down. Every sprinkler head in the room continued to spew forth white, heavy gas in an effort to extinguish both the minor fires Dick had set and, coincidentally, every oxygen-breathing creature left inside the secret world beneath DIA.

Dick paused for a moment during his flight to finish off his act of arson. Using his last flare, he torched another paper-strewn desktop, along with the fabric covering of the cubicle wall. Both fires were still above the level of the fire squelching Halon, for now. They would keep the flow of gas coming.

He took off again. As he did, he could hear Luke running and stumbling along behind him.

"Where are we going?" his friend shouted. "The exit's the other way."

Dick did not slow down. There was no time. The Halon was accumulating faster than he had guessed it would. "Egbert's office," he tossed back over his shoulder. "I located it by the ringing phone."

The two ran in silence for a few seconds, their fast passage setting off little whorls in the heavy gas to either side as they passed, tiny tornadoes of oxygen-depriving death.

Finally, Dick heard Luke gasp. "Fine. Why?"

Dick arrived at the larger, higher walled, cubicle from which he had heard the phone ringing less than a minute before. "In here."

He immediately began searching, glancing up as Luke turned into the cubicle, gasping from the run and coughing from the swirls of gas which billowed up in front of him as he turned the corner and halted.

"I'm betting our lives Egbert didn't leave his mine diving gear in the trunk of his car." He tore open cabinets and a narrow coat closet in a desperate attempt to find the equipment.

A glance at Luke showed Dick that the kid understood not only what was at stake, but also what he was looking for. As possible hiding places became more and more scarce, the lanky kid dove into the cloying, white gas underneath the desk. Almost fifteen seconds passed before Luke reappeared, dragging a heavy red bag. Dick took it from him as the kid gasped for fresh air, pulling himself up by pushing off the desktop to get at the slightly clearer air above.

Dick grabbed at the bag, ripping the zipper open so fast it gave a high-pitched whine. He reached in and pulled out the scuba gear—a regulator, mask, and two bulky canisters of compressed oxygen. He searched the pockets and zippered pouches of the bag frantically.

Luke, now standing atop the desk and breathing heavily, but without coughing, looked down at him. "What are you looking for? You've got everything you need. Oxygen. Mask. Regulator."

The gas crept over the level of the desktop, tendrils twirling around pencil holders and reaching into the crevices of the desktop keyboard as Dick kept searching the bag. "A spare regulator ..." he replied as his search ended unsuccessfully. He looked up at the lanky Australian computer geek. A smart, good, well-meaning kid, who had gotten in over his head and who, in just a few more minutes, would literally be in over his head, breathing an inert gas that would starve him of life.

Not his son, but somebody's son.

"We'll just have to share ..." Dick offered as his hands worked quickly and efficiently to turn on the oxygen and set up the regulator. "You know, buddy breathing. Not optimal, but it'll do."

Luke gave a gentle, sighing huff. "We both know I'm dead anyway. Here, from the gas or the bad guys ... or you. Outside from the Chinese." The kid looked up and scanned the immense room. "The main exit's shut, but there seems to be a door on the south wall, about a hundred yards down. Trail your hand against the concrete wall and you can't miss it."

Dick filed away the information, but still hesitated. This wasn't how it was supposed to be. This wasn't how saving the world was supposed to feel.

"Go," urged Luke. "Oxygen deprivation isn't a bad way to go, not compared to what my other alternatives might be outside. Save yourself. Save the world again another day. *Go find your son.*"

With that, Dick pulled down the facemask, inserted the mouthpiece of the regulator and dashed for the cubicle entrance. The gas was even deeper in the corridors, where it could disperse without having to seep around corners. In seconds, Dick was immersed in a milky fog, unable to see Luke, unable to see ahead, unable to see what the future might bring.

He trailed his right hand along the concrete wall and stumbled through the haze of frightening emotions and deadly gas engulfing him from all sides. He trusted his partner to get him to safety.

He came to a door, groped blindly for the handle until he found it, then twisted and pushed. He leapt through the opening into the unknown.

"How the hell did he get out of there?"

Matt saw one of his targets crash through the dining room window into the cool spray of the sprinkler watering the front lawn. He knew what that would mean and immediately threw down the thermal imaging scope before the sensors were overloaded and the screen blanked out. He saw the fireball caused by the sudden rush of air into the superheated colonial without any electronic enhancement, but it was still better than the any of the slow-mo, multiple camera angle renditions you always saw in action flicks. A few seconds later he felt, more than heard, the shock wave from the fireball moving through the silence of the wee hours. The unconfined fire was now bright against the night sky, destructive and chaotic against the ordered sameness of the suburban subdivision. Matt loved the look and feel and sound and taste and smell of an inferno; it brought him joy. Even more important, it brought death to the enemies of his people—an act of war that would never be known as such. Instead, it would be investigated by the local fire inspector and catalogued as an unfortunate combination of stupidity and decorative candles.

Made in China, no doubt.

The fierce flames consuming the wooden structure made it clear to Matt that the second target, whichever one that was, was probably not coming out of the inferno alive, but he could see the first one still moving weakly on the grass.

He might survive. Worse yet, he might talk. Neither was acceptable.

Matt started up his vehicle and rushed to help. A passerby—a good Samaritan, they called them here—might check for breathing and give resuscitation, pinching the nose closed to force the air into the victim's lungs, but not actually blowing in the mouth when he covered it with his own. Or he might lean a bit too hard on damaged lungs or break a few ribs when attempting to give CPR. Even with an ambulance and paramedics on the way, this could still look like an accident and he could still fade into the night, mission accomplished, and return to Denver on the first flight out to complete Pao Fen's little cyber-location task.

Matt would complete his task—on the lawn, in the ambulance en route to the emergency room, in the hospital if he had to, although he preferred to avoid those warehouses of disease, decay, and death. From his experience, they were crueler to the victims, even the survivors, than he would ever be, at least without good reason.

He would succeed. The price for failure was too high.

He pitied his counterpart—the assassin assigned to take out the other two members of this anti-Chinese cell. One of his counterpart's targets was missing. Maybe the target would reappear, but there was some chance the target had rabbited, fading into the mists. In that case, the assassin dared not return to the General—to China—until he found and eliminated the target, even though the target might never be found, dead or alive.

CHAPTER 29

Dick slipped through the heavy, steel door and pressed it shut behind him. It wasn't that he feared being followed. With the Halon 1301 filling the enormous facility and the NE 417 within ten minutes of detonation, no one still inside that room would ever be seen by anyone again. He did, however, want to block the Halon 1301 from filling the dimly lit corridor which stretched in front of him and he didn't want to be backlit in case there were guards up ahead. Besides, one more piece of metal between him and the blast and radiation of the NE 417 was a good thing as the seconds counted down. He might get delayed.

Dick didn't know with any precision where the tunnel went, but he could guess: A long flat area underneath the western runway, then a shift to the east and a gradual slope to the terminal and some other hidden entrance or exit to the facility. He didn't pause to consider it further. He took off at a jog, ditching the scuba gear noisily as he went. A small fluorescent fixture every fifty feet or so provided the only illumination. Aside from those fixtures and the conduits supplying them and larger conduits providing electrical, fiber optic, and cable feeds to the facility, there was noting to see in the corridor. The floor, walls, and ceiling were all featureless gray concrete, although the concrete on the floor had been brushed to provide better traction.

Dick used the traction to increase his speed. Not only was a nuclear blast chasing him from behind, but there would undoubtedly be increased security at the exits. An alarm had been sounded. Somewhere Egbert would be reporting in to someone.

And there would be consequences.

Just as he figured, the corridor did make a hard left turn. Dick didn't bother to slow down and peek around the corner. If there was anyone there, they would have heard him coming and would probably be expecting him to do just that. Of course, they didn't know what was about to happen in what was now nine minutes. Being cautious was more likely to get him killed than being reckless—at least at this distance from ground zero.

No one waited around the corner. Instead, the corridor stretched for hundreds of yards ahead before the next turn. The slope angled upward as he had suspected. His escape route was as featureless and regular as the way he had already come, so Dick did his best to increase his speed yet again, despite the slope. There were no hidey-holes or side tunnels to conceal an ambush, so speed was definitely his friend. Besides, not only was he running for his own life, he was desperate, desperate to get to where he could find out what had happened to Seth. Did he even have a son anymore? Did Dick, himself, even have a life worth going back to, worth saving, anymore?

He ran and turned and ran again in heedless flight. Another corner, then another. His legs and his lungs burned by the time he could see the end of the corridor. Fucking altitude. He didn't care about the pain, but it's hard to hear when you're gulping for breath. And hearing is important when you're in the dark and your night vision is screwed up by a bright light every fifty feet.

Despite his handicaps, Dick saw a flash of light past the open exit of the tunnel and heard a rumble each time it appeared.

The underground tramway. The corridor came out somewhere in the tunnels for the underground tramway. For just a moment, Dick could literally see the light at the end of the tunnel. He could see, hear, and taste the future—escape from the bowels of DIA and a life for him back in New Jersey with Seth ... and Melanie if she would have him back.

And then there was a burst of automatic weapons fire—a MAC 10 by the sound of it—from the end of the corridor. He saw the muzzle flash near the corner of the exit, but no silhouette of the shooter. The guy was firing blind, based on the sounds of Dick's footfalls echoing off the concrete.

Net Impact

In same split second he perceived the situation, Dick's training began to implement a response, without Dick ever having to consciously think it through. Dick cried out in a sharp yelp, then dove for the floor, his echoing footfalls ceasing in a jumbled thump and clatter. As soon as he was prone, he brought his weapon to bear, sighting on the edge of the exit where he had seen the muzzle flash.

The mope of a guard fell for it. You just can't get good lackeys these days. Sure enough, the shooter not only looked around the corner to see the consequences of his random burst, he stepped out from behind his cover.

Dick squeezed the trigger of his weapon and the guard's brain matter exploded out the back of his head—not that the guy had made much use of it when it was still intact. Dick was back on his feet and running almost before the guard's limp body hit the concrete floor.

Six minutes to go.

The gunfire would probably attract attention, especially since everybody who knew anything about the underground complex was undoubtedly already on alert. Dick encountered no other guards in his rush for the exit, but there was a strong electronic hum in the air as he got to the end of the corridor.

He didn't slow to investigate, but did notice the edge of the corridor entrance was metal, not concrete, on all four sides. As he rushed through the humming framework, he felt a tug on his weapon and his Micro-Emmisive sunglasses flew out of his pocket and adhered to the frame. When a quick look around what was obviously a maintenance bay for the tramway revealed no immediate targets, he reached back and snagged his sunglasses back from the ceiling edge of the framework.

Cute. A running electromagnet at the corridor entrance to the underground complex would not only spook any casual interlopers, it would also scramble any electrical devices they had brought along to document the existence of the facility their conspiracy theories commanded must exist. Digital cameras, electronic recorders, even communication devices would be wiped or scrambled by the strong field. A field that strong could even induce nausea and disorientation if you stayed in it too long. Dick doubted his sunglasses would ever work properly again.

His glance back also revealed a few other things that would simultaneously discourage entrance to the corridor and fuel the conspiracy buffs. The wall surrounding the corridor was adorned with various symbols. Dick didn't recognize them all, but they ranged from the standardized biohazard and radiation hazard warning symbols to the kinds of things you always saw in bad slasher movies about Satanic cults. Pentagrams, evil eyes, that kind of crap. There were also a few symbols in writing that was alien to Dick and undoubtedly meant to look alien to anybody else.

He started to smile—it was a nice piece of handiwork, even if it was done by bad guys—then he remembered the time. Five minutes, maybe? Four?

He looked down at his watch, but it had been fried by the electromagnet.

Damn.

He quickly scanned the maintenance bay. Aside from the angled tunnel connecting the tracks of the bay with the main tramway run, a small staircase of six concrete steps led to a landing with a metal door. He grabbed the metal piping that served as a railing to the concrete stairway and vaulted up to the landing, twisting the knob and pulling open the door in a fluid movement. A faint, sharp smell greeted him as he looked in to see a workroom lined with spare parts, worktables, power equipment, and tool boxes. Another, linoleum-tread staircase led upward at a right angle from the far end.

Net Impact

Dick scooted between the workbenches and started to turn the corner to take the stairs up when he suddenly saw booted feet at the top end of the stairs coming down. Muffled shouts of "Hurry!" and "Intruder!" convinced him this was not the late night janitorial crew. He gave a thought to blasting his way out, but that could take awhile—certainly longer than four minutes—if there were reinforcements up above. Besides, someone might also come up on him from behind during the firefight. He didn't want to get trapped.

Instead, Dick darted back through the workroom, his eyes flicking over the equipment for any assistance it might give. There were plenty of screwdrivers if he needed a makeshift weapon for hand-to-hand combat, a wheel assembly he could pull off the table to slow the way of someone following him, some brake pads that might have enough asbestos in them to give someone mesothelioma thirty years from now, and a lathe that would undoubted be featured prominently if this was a fight scene in a spy movie, but nothing that was of any real practical assistance in his situation.

Then he saw it, next to the lathe, near the door where he had first entered the room—the source of the sharp scent he had smelled when he first came in and which he had automatically attributed to another attempt to discourage visitors. A rectangular stainless steel container, festooned with warnings of the hazards of skin contact, held benzene, used for cleaning grease and grime off metal parts and workmen's hands—OSHA might require the warning labels, but nobody made the workers read them or obey.

In violation of everything OSHA stood for, Dick dumped the benzene on the floor and, after opening the door to the maintenance bay to make sure he had an exit, reached into his pocket and flicked his lighter, touching it to the near edge of the clear pool of liquid and pocketing it again as he exited the workroom to a whoosh of flame.

Sure, he could have tossed the lighter onto the vaporizing benzene to light the flame, but you never knew when a lighter would come in handy, even if you didn't smoke. This one had already saved his butt today and he wasn't home free yet.

Even though it was late, Dee was still awake. Thornby and Calloway had been out of contact now for hours and hours. Although she knew all of the reasons why that might be necessary, she still couldn't help but worry. It wasn't that she fretted for her agents' lives. She had given the termination order on Calloway herself and Dick knew the risks of his profession. Besides, he was a bit of a jerk—too reckless, too focused, and too fond of heavy weaponry. Useful in certain situations, to be sure, but not someone who would ever advance above his current station at the Subsidiary.

She wasn't worried about Dick's life or his prospects for a career path. But she did worry about the life and prospects of the Subsidiary. She cared about its missions and she worried about the collateral damage those missions might cause. It wasn't that she was squeamish about civilian casualties. If she was, she never would have been put in a position of authority at the Subsidiary. She understood sacrifice for the greater good.

Everybody knows, for instance, that when you build a major bridge or a dam it's more than likely three or four people will get killed in the process. Accidents happen. But the project still goes forward, because the benefit is worth the cost. Global security is worth a much, much higher cost than some damn infrastructure improvement and it is a price she and the Subsidiary were willing to pay.

Net Impact

No, Dee worried about collateral damage only because deaths raised the profile of a mission. That, in turn, risked exposing the Subsidiary. Exposure of the Subsidiary was the only cost she was not willing to pay. The world needed the Subsidiary too much.

Since she was up anyway, she sat at the kitchen table at her apartment, sipping herbal tea and catching up on electronic paperwork via her secure laptop. A chime indicated one of the national representatives was trying to contact her. She quit sorting email and entered the virtual meeting area.

It was the Chinese representative. She wasn't in the mood for this.

"Greetings," she said by way of acknowledgment.

"Traitor Luke Calloway has disappeared," shouted the Chinese representative, the new accent program on the voice modulation kicking in so heavily she could barely make out what the representative was saying—if this program were ever used in the corporate world the ethnic minorities would have a ipso facto case establishing a racist work environment.

"That is an operational matter and none of your concern, representative," she replied sourly. "Besides, I thought you wanted Mr. Calloway to disappear."

"Our need to interrogate Mr. Calloway concerning his traitorous duplicity is our concern. While we do not interfere with the Subsidiary's operations, we have a right to protect our sovereignty."

"If you aren't interfering with the Subsidiary operations, how could you possibly know Mr. Calloway is missing?"

The Chinese representative ignored her question. "I am sending an agent from ... I am sending an agent to interrogate Mr. Calloway. He will be on the next flight, connecting through Denver."

It would be an unlikely coincidence, but she couldn't let it happen. This "agent" could blow the operation if he ran into Calloway at DIA, assuming Thornby didn't blow the place up. "Have your agent take the connecting flight through San Francisco, representative," Dee replied. "While a few hours later, it is a much more pleasant journey and I assure you Mr. Calloway will not be available for interrogation earlier," like, she thought, in my lifetime ... or his.

As soon as she finished, she sent an email to the Computer Services Department at HQ. "Remove the accent subroutine from the voice modulation program immediately. Deirdre Tammany, Director of the Subsidiary."

Dick quickly wiped off his weapon and tossed it back into the angled tunnel to the maintenance bay. His ammo was low and he probably wouldn't need the gun anymore. Getting caught by the TSA or airport security with a weapon was a bigger concern at this point than the possibility of needing to shoot his way out.

Dick ran into the empty tramway tunnel, ignoring the pinwheels and other artistic gewgaws that were among the bizarre artistic clues which brought him to this place. All he had to do was to run to one of the stations and he would escape, at least if his calculations of damage to the airport facility from the underground blast were accurate. As Dick began to race down the relatively well-lit tunnel, though, a nearby pinwheel began to slowly turn. When he turned to look at it, he could feel a brush of wind on his cheek. A tram was headed toward him, the air being pushed by it causing the pinwheel art to perform for the airport patrons.

With two minutes to go, he couldn't wait for the tram to pass. He needed to make a run for it. Despite the oxygen-deprived altitude of the Mile High City, breathing wisps of bromotrifluoromethane, running almost a mile uphill, and engaging in a few fire fights along the way, Dick ran for his life.

Maybe it was his life flashing before his eyes as the moments ticked down to the nuclear blast below. Maybe it was the emotional baggage of Melanie leaving and his last, maybe the last, conversation with his son, Seth. Maybe it was a hallucinogenic combination of the benzene from the workshop mixing with the adrenaline coursing through his veins, but as he ran, Dick pictured a day years ago when he had sat with Seth, back before his first day of kindergarten. He had tried to teach the kid to read, so he would get a head start on school, on life. The words flashed before him.

Look.

See Dick run.

Run, Dick, run.

Then a light fell upon the page he was envisioning and he knew it was the tram behind, catching up to him. A station loomed ahead, but it was blocked by a wall of windows and automatically triggered doors. There was a space beneath the raised concrete walkway on the other side of the tunnel, if he could make it in time, but it would be hard to dive into its narrow concrete confines without leaving part of his body hanging out into the tramway tunnel. If he was lucky, the driver would see him in time to brake just enough so he wouldn't be crushed by the tram—though that also meant he would likely be herded up by airport security or worse. Before he had even finished the thought, Dick angled toward the opposite side of the tunnel and tensed for the awkward dive.

That's when he remembered. After all his trips through DIA, all the rides on the tramway, looking out at the bizarre art in the tunnel, sitting on the ledge at the front or the rear of the car, so you didn't have to stand with the crowd near the doors, all these last moments running for his life in front of the tram, he only now remembered. DIA trams have no drivers and no conductors. They also have a sensing system which slows the tram if anyone is in the passage in front of it. He stopped pushing through the pain and glanced back at the tram, slowing behind him.

He dropped down to a walk. It slowed further.

He stopped, for just a second. It jerked to a halt.

A lone passenger in the front car stared out at him in confusion, but no one was radioing ahead to the authorities.

One minute.

He loped to the station, found an emergency button to open the doors, pushed himself up to the station platform and headed for the escalator, taking the steps two at a time as it moved.

When he arrived at the exit from the tramway into the main terminal of the airport, he noticed the blue and white metal airplane/birds that hung over the exit quiver as the NE 417 detonated beneath the western runway.

Most people in the airport would barely notice, but he knew the control tower would feel the vibration and the EMP would undoubtedly leak through a few conduits, blowing lights or circuits too near the epicenter of the blast.

All flights would be delayed. He headed for the exit and caught a cab to take him to Jefferson County Airport. He bummed a cell phone from the cabby and called in to HQ to request a charter flight and to report mission accomplished, details to follow.

Then he called Seth's cell phone.

No one answered.

Net Impact

The Lightning Team's black, specially modified Bell ARH-70 helicopter lifted off the roof of Catalyst Crisis Consulting's headquarters in Philadelphia less than two minutes after Glenn Swynton issued the emergency scramble call. Jake Martzen knew Swynton loved to press the team's buttons with constant drills, but this was a bizarre one: go to a house fire in suburban New Jersey only a few minute's flight time away and take "appropriate" action. It didn't make sense. They weren't a search and rescue squad; they were an assault and clean-up team. You only called in a Lightning Team when things were massively screwed up and, then, only if you weren't too worried about what the body count would be to make things right.

As the copter tilted far forward to accelerate to its maximum speed of more than 160 knots per hour, three more instructions from Swynton popped up on the heads-up view-screen on Jake's helmet: "This is not a drill. Save occupants. Remain unseen."

What the hell? How was he supposed to do that?

The house fire was an easy-to-find target destination. The copter whispered in on the ultrasonic rotation of its flexible, sound-dampening rotor blades, hovering over the yard next door to the fire for only a few moments while Jake's four-man squad rappelled to the ground in the fierce wash of the rotors and ran in low crouches toward the blaze. Then the copter gained height and banked away in the direction of the agreed rendezvous point—a schoolyard less than two blocks away.

Jake knew the squad didn't have much time. Even with the slower response time the village's volunteer fire department would have compared to a professional company, the hose-jockeys would be on their way soon. He'd heard the long, low wail of the departmental siren calling the volunteers to the station as the squad had flown in. Now that siren call had stopped, which meant the trucks were loading and about to roll. He was also worried about neighbors gathering to watch the blaze. With a late night fire, nearby residents might not notice the blaze until the village's fire trucks were roaring down the street, but you could never tell—their transport was stealthy compared to the average helicopter, but it wasn't completely silent and it did kick up a fair tempest flying just above the treetops.

In accordance with their quickly compiled deployment plan, squad members Peters and Mazerbaum kept their eyes peeled outward, looking for trouble or witnesses. Every thirty seconds, they reported status. "Clear one," whispered Peters over the headset, quickly followed by Mazerbaum's low "Clear two." Jake and his second-in-command, Cortez, moved into the front yard of the target house at speed, assessing the situation as sprinklers frittered away precious water on new sod while the house blazed nearby.

One body, a teenage boy, lay sprawled on the wet sod. Jake squatted and placed his fingers on the boy's neck, turning the boy's head away from himself as he did so, assuring he would not be seen if the boy gained consciousness while Jake checked for signs of life. The kid was not only alive, but his pulse was strong. No doubt the kid had simply passed out due to smoke inhalation.

As Jake scanned toward the house, taking in the broken dining room window through which the teen in the yard had undoubtedly escaped, he saw another figure, this one amidst the flames of the dining room, near some broken plaster board. While the dining room table had protected the body from flaming debris, the body wasn't moving.

"Clear one," cackled his headset. "Clear two."

He heard the sirens of the fire trucks leaving the station.

Damn. There was no time.

Jake slung his weapon and grabbed a large piece of muddy sod with each arm and leapt toward the broken window. "Follow me in with a sprinkler," he yelled as he threw himself through the opening into the hellish conflagration. He flung the dining room table to one side with a hard elbow thrust and threw the two heavy, water-laden strips of Kentucky Bluegrass on top of the motionless body, ignoring the hiss of steam as they landed on the victim' burning jeans.

"Clear one."

"Clear two."

A moment later Cortez was with him. Thankfully, Jake's second had followed instructions, grabbing a functioning sprinkler head and ripping it out of the soft mud. The flexible piping feeding the water to the sprinkler head had enough slack that it followed along for about ten or twelve feet before catching, bringing the cooling spray of municipal water into the dining room proper. Cortez angled the sprinkler head to provide as much coverage as possible for the now sod-strewn victim. Jake didn't know if the kid in the house was alive or dead, but there was no time to do more.

"Clear one."

"Clear two."

With a few brief hand-signals, Jake motioned for Cortez to follow and the two Lightning Team members exited the house. Elsewhere, the fire was blossoming, but in the dining room, the flames were dying down. It was one hell of a half-assed rescue, but all Jake could do, given their parameters.

As the squad hustled toward the rendezvous point, Jake squatted for a second time near the boy outside, gripping the teenager's right hand around the flexible tubing of the sprinkler system and quickly smearing the kid's clothes with mud from another loose piece of sod, which Jake then left in a clump at the boy's feet. If the victim inside made it, the kid would be hailed as a fast-thinking hero, even if he professed not to remember anything.

Jake was okay with that. The world needed heroes. It didn't matter who got the credit.

"Clear forward," reported Peters.

Jake unslung his automatic rifle and faded into the darkness to follow the squad, content for the briefest instant that the team had completed their mission within parameters. But, he heard no confirming rejoinder from Mazerbaum for agonizing seconds.

"Vehicle inbound, rear," hissed Mazerbaum, watching out for Jake even as he and the rest of the squad hurried away down the street.

Jake froze as a car screeched to a halt in front of the flaming residence. Without even thinking, Jake sank into the shadows to watch this interloper as the rest of the squad rushed toward the school yard. Something was not right.

"Orders?" asked Cortez from up the street.

"Keep moving," ordered Jake. He would handle this alone, whatever it was.

Jake's eyes narrowed as he assessed the situation, noting that the car's headlights were out and that it bore car rental agency plates. A fit-looking Chinese man leapt from the car and rushed toward the teenager laying in the soggy, sod-strewn yard. When Jake saw the man quickly glance in either direction, then place his hands over the unconscious teenager's mouth and nose, Jake didn't hesitate.

In a blur of motion, Jake brought his weapon to bear. A split-second and a rifle-crack later, the Chinese interloper was thrown away from the body as a bullet slammed into the side of his head and exited the other side. Jake followed his bullet a heartbeat later, policing his brass with a quick grab and streaking toward the fallen man before the blood spatter of the kill even began to soak into the mud and grass. God, he hoped this guy wasn't just some random passing tourist who didn't know how to check for a pulse.

Expletives his momma would never know flew from Jake's lips as he snatched up the interloper's body, using a fireman's carry to hump it as quickly as he could to the waiting rental car. He opened the passenger door—there was no time to look for the trunk release—and dumped the body unceremoniously inside, head first in a jumbled heap. He shoved a trailing limb in and slammed the door, skidding across the hood to the driver's side, wrenching open the door and clambering in. Fortunately the guy—the assassin?—had left the car running. Jake jinked the car into gear, flicked on the lights, and floored the accelerator, slowing only for a moment as he saw the fire engines turn down the street coming toward him.

"Get the hell out of here," he barked over his headset to the squad. "I've secured my own ride and will meet you back at the barn."

What the hell had just happened? And why?

Porch lights flicked on as Jake continued out of the subdivision with his unexpected, grim cargo. He drove with deliberate precision toward Philadelphia, obeying the speed limits and making sure to use his turn signals. Traffic stops could be a bitch when you're driving a stolen car with a dead body leaking blood onto the center console.

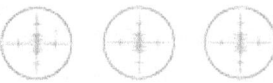

Once at Jeffco Airport, Dick retrieved secure communications equipment from Nine-to-Five Business Charters, the Subsidiary's in-house air charter service. Before reporting on his mission, he insisted Glenn Swynton check on what had happened to Seth. By the time Dick finished briefing Dee Tammany on the details of his DIA incursion, including Luke's sacrifice, Glenn came back with a report. Dick listened intently to Glenn's recitation of details, but the whole thing made no sense to his weary mind.

Somehow a Lightning Team had beaten the fire department to the house, intercepting and killing a Chinese assassin, and dousing the flames long enough for the volunteer fire department to save the day, all apparently without being seen. Seth was alive, with smoke inhalation, as well as third degree burns over forty percent of his body. He was stable and in the midst of being airlifted to a Philadelphia trauma center. Brian had made it out of the house with fewer burns than Seth, but had also suffered severe smoke inhalation.

"A Chinese assassin?" Dick yelled. "You knew a Chinese assassin was after my kid and didn't tell me?" Damn lucky Glenn Swynton was on the other end of an encrypted cross-country phone line, because Dick would've killed him on the spot had he been on the jet, then dumped the body over the North Dakota badlands.

"We had no idea," Dee interjected. "We still have no idea why."

The Subsidiary had apparently not connected Seth and Brian to Luke's surreptitious activity. Had the Chinese? Or was this some kind of payback from some adversary from some unknown prior mission? "Then why'd you send a Lightning Team?" asked Dick, shaking his head to waken any remaining neurons.

"Mr. Calloway informed us your kid was in trouble," replied Glenn with a sniff. "We run training drills all the time. The helicopter was just sitting on top of the roof anyway."

Dee interrupted. "We take care of our own."

For a moment, Dick almost felt a touch of kinship with both Glenn and Dee, but then Glenn reverted to his usual heartless bastard motif by launching into a review of the cover story for the DIA incident. At this point, though, Dick was barely listening. He simply hung up and closed his eyes as the world slid beneath him.

Net Impact

He tried, as usual during long flights, to bring up happy memories of home and family, but once again they would not come. They might never return again. His wife had left him. His son was near dead, scarred for life, and Dick would probably never know for sure if it was because of him, because of what he did for a living.

The unspoken rule among spies is that you don't go after family members. But, of course, some spies—and even more bad guys—don't always play by the rules.

Dick leaned back heavily in the comfy leather seat of the charter plane, completely overwhelmed. He was dead tired—physically, mentally, and emotionally drained. He had hit the wall.

The words floated in front of his eyes, unbidden: *GO THRU WALLL*

He fingered his wedding ring as his eyes filled with tears. He had to call ... no, he had to see ... Melanie to tell her what had happened, to explain everything, to reveal he had lied to her. He knew it might be the last time he would ever see her. Deep in his soul he feared there was no coming back for them, no future after what he had allowed to happen. Still, he clung to the hope that it was not too late, that the horrific events of the day might somehow bring them together, that they could heal as Seth healed, that they could be a team once more, that Melanie would smile her dimpled smile once again ... at him.

He sent her a text message that he had to talk to her face to face ... at the house ... today. As he waited for her reply, he vowed he would never lie to her again, no matter what the Subsidiary wanted. You don't lie to your team. He would tell her everything, then take her to the hospital. Seth needed her ... he needed her. He didn't think she would make him ask for help, but he would ask for her forgiveness, ask for her help ... whatever it took.

When his flight landed, he headed for home one last time.

He always did what had to be done.

He had been forced once too often by his job to go it alone. Things were about to change.

EPILOGUE

If a tree falls in the forest and no one is there to hear it, it still makes a sound. And if a secret underground facility is surreptitiously destroyed by a covert espionage agency using a nuclear-powered EMP device in the dead of night, it still gets noticed.

Seismic graphing equipment at The University of Colorado-Boulder registered a shockwave. Late night airport workers heard a faint rumble as the liquid in their coffee cups vibrated. The sprinklers in the maintenance bay for DIA's tram were triggered by a fire in the shop. Some runway lights blinked out, mostly along the western edge of the airport. Homeland Security's radiation sensors tripped momentarily and then reset. The ancient VCR in the DIA employee lounge started blinking "12:00."

Safety protocols kicked in. Flights were held up during the wee hours—inconveniencing few passengers, but delaying overnight cargo shipping. Pagers were beeped and on-call workers dragged out of bed. Airport authorities made sure everything was safe before flights recommenced the next day.

The Subsidiary was the unseen participant in getting things going again fast at DIA, as well as in explaining the "minor incident." Utilizing its spidery web of contacts in law enforcement, academia, government, and public relations, Glenn Swynton's plausible cover story quickly took hold.

A natural gas explosion in the gangways for electrical and communications conduits had caused the tremor at DIA. The Subsidiary's contacts consistently referred to the minor blast as the "Burp," a catchy, trivializing term that caught on in a jiffy with airport employees and press, alike. While the Burp had caused little damage, it had released a pocket of radon gas, tripping the Homeland Security radiation sensors, but quickly dispersing in the open air.

Radon gas, as the population of western states well knows, is a naturally occurring radioactive gas found in certain geologic formations. The gas seeps into basements in sufficient quantities it can be readily detected by radiation sensors. Detection is important, because the radiation from the odorless, invisible gas can cause the same scary types of medical maladies caused by other, better known, sources of radiation. Out west, even residential housing often contains ventilation systems in underground areas to prevent radon accumulation, along with the cancers and other sickness it can cause over the long-term.

After a few days, the news cycle moved on from DIA to other stories. The Burp disappeared from public view, even in the local press. Soon it was forgotten by most of the world, replaced by similarly fleeting stories concerning the latest celebrity gossip, the bankruptcy of a small gaming company called "Reality 2 Be," and the gruesome details of the riverbank discovery of the bloated body of a thirty-one year old wife and mother most likely murdered when her jackass of a husband spied a younger, prettier woman with low self-esteem to control and belittle.

On the World Wide Web, the stories were somewhat different. Chatrooms were atwitter with technical discussions about minor disruptions and hardware glitches along the myriad pathways of the Internet—events all tracking to the time of the Burp. Spam filters filled with scams attempting to scare recipients into purchasing overpriced and ineffective radon detection and ventilation systems. And a coterie of websites by various fringe conspiracy enthusiasts attempted to reveal the truth about a massive explosion that had taken place in a warren of secret, underground tunnels and facilities beneath Denver International Airport.

Some of the websites revealed how the Gates of Hell were opened to allow demon lizardmen to gather their army for the coming

Net Impact

Armageddon. Others reported on the matter/anti-matter explosion that resulted from the sabotage by slave laborers of alien technology situated in the hollow veins beneath the surface of the earth. And a few whispered about the nuclear destruction by a secret international espionage agency of a massive, EMP-shielded, computer facility run by international criminals and terrorists who were raking in billions through theft and manipulation of data sent over the Internet and setting themselves up for ultimate world domination.

Of course, no one believed any of it.

THE END

Dick Thornby returns in _Wet Work_.

Read the first few pages, below.

Wet Work:
Dick Thornby Thriller #2
by
Donald J. Bingle

Prologue

Jerry hated his wife's car. He loved the hybrid's gas mileage, and he didn't mind saving the planet for future generations, but he was six foot two and husky. Squeezing behind the wheel practically let him steer with his beer belly.

Worse yet, his claustrophobia was heightened by a smoke-belching stream of growling Mack trucks hemming him in as they hauled gravel down the double black diamond sloped street plummeting to the intersection at the entrance to the Joliet bridge. The rusting, Erector Set style span crossed both the shallows of the Des Plaines River and, on the near side, the darker, deeper Sanitary & Ship Canal. With traffic moving, Jerry felt like he was running with the bulls at Pamplona as powerful behemoths thundered about him. When stopped for a red light, like now, he felt like a surfer caught in the break as he paddled out, praying a monstrous wave wouldn't crash down from above and pulverize him.

So Jerry kept his eyes glued to the rear view mirror ... just in case.

Today his watchful paranoia paid off. A fully-loaded dump truck crested the hill with the momentum of a tsunami, threatening to obliterate him like one of the splattered moths littering his windshield.

Damn.

Jerry manhandled the wheel hard left as he checked for oncoming traffic, then punched the accelerator to escape being rear-ended to death.

The subcompact whined like an overstressed golf cart, inching to the left until the gas motor kicked in, then trembled into stuttering acceleration. Jerry stared at the mirror, watching as gravel flew off the looming truck's payload and skittered across the roof of its cab. The unshaven driver inside braked hard, his eyes wide, a lit cigarette falling out of his surprised mouth, as his body lurched forward from the attempted emergency stop.

It was going to be close, closer than Jerry's morning shave with the quadruple blade razor the kids got him for Father's Day.

Jerry wasn't a religious guy, so no prayers whispered forth as he watched his ignominious death approaching, his grim reaper laying black rubber on the pavement and churning out white smoke as worn tires tried to overcome the momentum of tons of loose, shifting rock. Instead, a stream of invectives flowed from Jerry's lips as he imagined the huge tires of the gargantuan machine rolling atop his wife's mouse of a car and stomping it down, greasy, bloody, and flat. He was going to die a stupid, needless, painful death simply because his wife traded days for the neighborhood carpool to school.

He hoped she would feel guilty about it at his funeral.

Closed casket, of course.

But, then ... then the crappy automatic transmission shifted up. Jerry leaned forward instinctively, as if that could possibly save him. As he swerved farther into the open lane on the left, the truck driver jinked right toward the curb and the empty sidewalk, each action incrementally slowing the rate at which the gap between the vehicles was shrinking.

Maybe, just maybe ...

Suddenly, the hybrid farted forward, as if it had just seen what was about to happen via its reverse view camera. Jerry kept his foot on the floor—he didn't want to take any chances. He couldn't do the math to figure the angles and vectors, but his big, fat gut told him he was going to make it. His pursed lips turned up into a tight smile. But when he looked ahead he saw a lumbering garbage truck turning into the oncoming lane from Canal Street, which fronted the dark, murky waters of the commercial canal.

Jerry had snatched his life from the jaws of defeat only to thrust it into the jaws of a Browning-Ferris Industries garbage truck. He kept the steering wheel hard to the left, hoping to jump the opposite curb to the far sidewalk. With any luck he could stop before he reached the corner and t-boned the big, green machine with "BFI" blazoned on its side. He twitched his foot up and to the left, then stomped down on the brake as hard as he had flattened the accelerator only moments, yet an eternity, before.

Nothing happened.

Nothing fucking happened.

Net Impact

His foot ground the pedal against the floor, but the brakes did not engage. He searched frantically for the center-mounted emergency brake with his right hand as he gripped the wheel tight with his left, his eyes wide and forward, scrutinizing this new terror. Jerry's fingers grazed the emergency handle for a millisecond before the bump from bouncing over the curb flung them up and off, grasping at air. He jerked the wheel to the right now, straightening the car to avoid hitting the brick building flanking the sidewalk. At the same time, his foot stabbed repeatedly at the brake pedal. He gritted his teeth, bracing for the BFI, the Big Fucking Impact, to come. But somehow his lizard brain took over and he whipped the steering wheel back left again just at the correct moment, at the very edge of the corner.

The shitty car careened to the side, miraculously clearing the back of the garbage hauler by a whisker, avoiding the BFI.

There was a wondrous moment of sweet, sweet bliss before his still accelerating midget auto-coffin crossed the narrow breadth of Canal Street and rocketed up and off the grassy embankment. The toy car sailed into the air, defying gravity in glorious flight before arcing down and plunging into the stabbing cold, foul black waters of the Sanitary & Ship Canal. The windshield shattered upon impact, water enveloping him in a torrent as he sank deeper and deeper.

Fuck.

The only things he feared more than enclosed spaces were drowning and hypothermia.

Oh boy, a threesome; just not the kind he'd always craved.

The tiny car settled rear down from the weight of the batteries as Jerry—still trapped by the cold shock of the water, the heavy pressure of the deep, and an auto-tightened seatbelt—struggled for freedom. As the last wisps of faded gray-green light abandoned him, he watched in mounting terror as the air in the car rushed past him from behind, bubbling out through the broken windshield, seeking a sunny, warm freedom he would never know.

As his consciousness faded to match the cold black of the muddy bottom of the canal, one last thought flittered through his fading neurons.

He really, really hated his wife's car.

Chapter 1

Dick Thornby stepped off the pathway in Singapore's Jurong Bird Park and eased into the foliage near the hundred foot tall waterfall dominating the spacious confines of the African Aviary. He tugged at his cap, making sure it nestled low against his aviator-style sunglasses, then eased off his backpack, accessing a pocket and slipping on a pair of latex surgical gloves. He was taking a chance by sneaking into a prohibited area to find cover, but he figured waterfall maintenance was generally handled when the park was closed. A pair of scenic overlooks atop the falls normally provided tourists a panoramic view of the four acre aviary, as well as his chosen perch. But he'd dropped a couple of clapboard signs indicating the pathways to those lookouts were closed for maintenance, guaranteeing his privacy.

That the waterfall was one of the most picturesque and most photographed features in the sanctuary didn't help his tactical situation. But between his camouflaged clothing and his "act like you belong wherever you go" movements, he didn't think gawking tourists would raise any issue. A suppressor threaded onto the end of the rifle barrel would minimize any flash when the time came to take his shot, as well as lessening the rifle's normally booming report.

Escaping after the fact would be good, too, and taking up a position in the enormous bird sanctuary literally as far from the park entrance as one could get was tactically suspect. On the other hand, there was

Net Impact

no denying the top of the falls was the best spot to pick off his target during a scheduled meet with a local thug seeking to up the quality and the quantity of his gang's armaments.

He was willing to take some risks to pop Pao Fen Smythe—the Hong Kong arms merchant who had indirectly caused the death of his last partner and been the moving force behind his son's crippling third-degree burns. Yeah, he'd risk a lot to take out Pao Fen Smythe ...

Read the rest of <u>Wet Work</u>, available in print and ebook now.

AFTERWORD / ACKNOWLEDGEMENTS

Just in case you were wondering ... Yes, there are virtual and gaming worlds in which players spend substantial amounts of real money to buy imaginary things. In some such worlds the imaginary currency is exchangeable into U.S. dollars at a fixed exchange rate. Those mechanisms, and the ability of players to chat and exchange information, currency, and items through their avatars, are of real concern to police, financial, military, and security organizations.

Yes, there really are strange, unexplained words and items embedded in the floor of Concourse B at Denver International Airport, as well as some bizarre art elsewhere in and around the terminal. And, yes, there really are a variety of websites filled with a plethora of conspiracy theories associated with the airport, the airport's construction, and the meaning behind various pieces of artwork. I've changed some of the details here and there, but not the overall tone of what's contained on many such sites and their multitude of links, where you can find entire listings of the various underground fortresses in the United States and the sinister aliens, monsters, and fringe groups occupying them. Other sites, even respectable newspapers, have run articles on the DIA conspiracy theories, sometimes debunking them in some detail.

Yes, I know that some of the details about where things are at Denver International Airport are not correct. For one thing, there is a lot less use made of the second floor of all three concourses than is indicated in the book. No doubt, some critics who don't read this far will denounce me for not having bothered to go to the airport or for not bothering to research my novel.

Net Impact

The thing is, though, I am not a true believer of any of the DIA conspiracy theories, even though the art is the art and the statistics that I cited about amount of earth moved and cabling installed are from DIA's own information. The art and the conspiracy theories are useful real-world items to work into a piece of fiction, not pieces of a puzzle on which to base a non-fiction exposé. Accordingly, I do not really want to encourage too much investigation by fans of the book. Noticing the mentioned items next time you are at DIA is fine, but I discourage airport visitors from attempting to follow the trail, like the artistic clues in a Dan Brown novel, snapping pictures and interrupting mundane passengers and airport personnel. Thus, I changed things up a bit in ways that were helpful to my pacing and plot, but which do not conform to reality.

Please keep in mind that Denver International Airport is a secure environment and a working business. It is clear to me that airport personnel are already tired of being asked about the artwork. Do not bother them or anyone else at the airport if you go to look at any of the clues referenced in this novel or on many of the myriad conspiracy websites. Do not venture into secure areas or make yourself a nuisance. If you do, please do not blame me or my novel. Computerized research I've done for this book and my other books (*GREENSWORD* and *Forced Conversion*) and short stories has probably already attracted the attention of the NSA or other authorities—I really don't need the additional visibility with people who carry guns and own black helicopters.

My thanks for the many friends and fellow writers who have supported and encouraged me with this project and/or read all or some of the text and offered suggestions, including: Joni Holderman, John Helfers, Jean Rabe, Beth Vaughan, Feroze Mohammed, Tim Waggoner, Kerrie Hughes, Mike Stackpole, Marc Tassin, Dewey and Cheryl Frech, Steve Saus, Kathleen Tennant, Rick Holinger and the rest of the St.

Charles Writers Group, The GenCon Writers Symposium, Linn Prentis, Bruce Steinberg, Tim White, Stephen D. Sullivan, and my family, including especially my wife, Linda, who puts up with my constant complaints about how bad the spies are in most popular movies and television shows.

Please go to my website at www.donaldjbingle.com to find out more about my writing or follow me on Facebook, Twitter, and Goodreads @donaldjbingle to hear my latest announcements. If you liked this book, please post a review and tell your friends, neighbors, social networking pals, and twitter buddies, as well as random passersby. If you didn't like this book, please just keep it to yourself—after all, you don't know who could be listening.

Donald J. Bingle
Writer on Demand ™
St. Charles, Illinois

P.S. This version of *Net Impact* is a re-release with a spiffy new cover, published in connection with a Kickstarter for *Wet Work*, the second installment in the Dick Thornby Thriller series. My additional thanks go to all of the people who backed that Kickstarter for their support of both books. Also, special thanks to Christine Redford, Jean Rabe, Lori Swan, Mary Konczyk, Joni Holderman, John Helfers, Richard Lee Byers, Kelly Swails, William Pack, Brent Meske, Juan Villar Padron, Marianne Nowicki, Christine Verstraete, Paul Genesse, Richard Bingle, the St. Charles Writing Group, everyone who read and reviewed *Net Impact*, and especially my wife, Linda, who puts up with my constant complaints about my computer, my interminable struggles with formatting software, and my rants on marketing frustrations.

Net Impact

ABOUT THE AUTHOR

Best known as the world's top-ranked player of classic role-playing games for the last fifteen years of the last century, Donald J. Bingle is an oft-published author in the science fiction, fantasy, horror, thriller, steampunk, romance, and comedy genres, with a half dozen published novels (Forced Conversion, GREENSWORD, Net Impact, Frame Shop, The Love-Haight Case Files, and Wet Work) and about fifty stories, many in DAW themed anthologies and tie-in anthologies, including stories in The Crimson Pact, Steampunk'd, Imaginary Friends, Fellowship Fantastic, Zombie Raccoons and Killer Bunnies, Time Twisters, Front Lines, Slipstreams, Gamer Fantastic, Transformers Legends, Search for Magic (Dragonlance), If I Were An Evil Overlord, Blue Kingdoms: Mages & Magic, Civil War Fantastic, Future Americas, All Hell Breaking Loose, The Dimension Next Door, Sol's Children, Historical Hauntings, and Fantasy Gone Wrong. A number of his stories have been collected in his Writer on Demand™ Series, including Tales of Gamers and Gaming, Tales of Humorous Horror, Tales Out of Time, Grim, Fair e-Tales, Tales of an Altered Past Powered by Romance, Horror, and Steam, Not-So-Heroic Fantasy, and Shadow Realities.

Donald J. Bingle is a member of the International Thriller Writers, Science Fiction and Fantasy Writers of America, Horror Writers Association, International Association of Media Tie-In Writers, and Origins Game Fair Library. More on Don and his writing can be found at www.donaldjbingle.com.

Dick Thornby Thrillers by Donald J. Bingle:

Net Impact
Wet Work
Flash Drive (forthcoming)

Novels by Donald J. Bingle:

Forced Conversion
GREENSWORD: A Tale of Extreme Global Warming
Frame Shop: Critiquing Another Writer Can Be Murder
The Love-Haight Case Files (with Jean Rabe)

Stories and Story Collections by Donald J. Bingle

Writer on Demand™ Vol. 1, Tales of Gamers and
Gaming
Writer on Demand™ Vol. 2, Tales of Humorous Horror
Writer on Demand™ Vol. 3, Tales Out of Time
Writer on Demand™ Vol. 4, Grim, Fair e-Tales
Writer on Demand™ Vol. 5, Tales of an Altered Past
Powered by Romance, Horror, and Steam
Writer on Demand™ Vol. 6, Not-So-Heroic Fantasy
Writer on Demand™ Vol. 7, Shadow Realities
Crimson Life/Crimson Death
Season's Critiquings

Merry Mark-Up
Holiday Workshopping
Santa Clauses and Phrases
Gentlemanly Horrors of Mine Alone
Running Free: A Tale Inspired by Patsy Ann
Father's Day Deluxe 3-Pack

Also from 54°40′ Orphyte, Inc.

Familiar Spirits **Edited by Donald J. Bingle**
Ratfish **by Buck Hanno**
Surrounded by Love: A Story of Orphans and Family
by Marjorie L. Bingle

**Semi-Finalist in 2015
Soon-to-be-Famous
Illinois Author Competition**

From its lurid, over-the-top prologue to its quirky addendum, *Frame Shop* mixes violence, humor, and occasional writing advice in a format that will keep mystery lovers, aspiring authors, NaNoWriMo participants, and established writers turning the pages.

Harold J. Ackerman thinks his latest cat mystery proves he is the best writer in the Pleasant Meadows Writers' Guild and Critiquing Society, not that the motley assortment of poets, poseurs, and wannabe writers in the PMWGCS provides much competition. But then Gantry Ellis, the NYT best-selling author of the Danger McAdams mystery thrillers, joins the group and wows everyone. Still, Harold hopes to leverage his connection to the famous author into a big break, but soon his efforts lead to murder ... and then more murder.

Visit donaldjbingle.com for more information.